RECIPE FOR PERSUASION

Also by Sonali Dev

Pride, Prejudice, and Other Flavors
A Distant Heart
A Change of Heart
The Bollywood Bride
A Bollywood Affair

RECIPE
FOR
PERSUASION

A NOVEL

SONALI DEV

𝓌𝓂
WILLIAM MORROW
An Imprint of HarperCollinsPublishers

P.S.™ is a trademark of HarperCollins Publishers.

HarperCollins books may be purchased for educational, business, or sales promotional use. For information, please email the Special Markets Department at SPsales@harpercollins.com.

FIRST EDITION

Designed by Diahann Sturge

Library of Congress Cataloging-in-Publication Data has been applied for.

ISBN 978-0-06-283907-7

20 21 22 23 24 LSC 10 9 8 7 6 5 4 3 2 1

For Aie and Baba for disregarding the "in-law" in daughter-in-law from the very start, but more importantly for doing away with all the patriarchal nonsense that goes with it. Without your unconditional love and support this journey would not be half as joyful.

Acknowledgments

Some books have such a deep impact on you that they shape how you expect to love and be loved. Jane Austen's *Persuasion* laid the foundation for how I felt about love and constancy in the face of society's influence. Ashna, Rico, and Shobi's story is my tribute to that timeless tale and what it taught me about second chances. As in the writing of all my books, I stumbled through this one lost at first, then slowly found my way because so many people held my hand.

Thanks first and foremost to Annika, Mihir, and Manoj, for their endless, albeit amused, support and to my parents, for their unconditional pride. The creation of any story comes second only to our family, even though our vacations might forever be interrupted by deadlines.

Writing a soccer player was exciting (read: terrifying) and I could never have hoped to capture the nuances of the game without the patient sermons from my sports-mad nephew, Sarang Navkal. You are brilliant and I'm sorry for all the times I laughed when you cried for the loss of your team. It was unforgivable of me. Thanks also to Lynne Hartzer, for making sure my soccer cleat did not end up in my mouth. For those of you who take such things seriously, I apologize for taking liberties with the historical accuracy of World Cup and Premier League wins.

My deepest thanks to Patricia Friedrich and Frances de Pontes Peebles for sharing their invaluable cultural expertise and their lovely books. I love Rico deeply and he could not be who he is without your generous input. Any inconsistencies are all my own.

Now to the heart of my writing process, my beta readers and critique partners: Emily Redington Modak, Sally Kilpatrick, Virgina Kantra, Falguni Kothary, Robin Kuss, Katherine Ashe, Nishaad Navkal, and Priscilla Oliveras. Thank you a million times over; without your eagle eyes and insights I couldn't say anything halfway coherent.

A huge thanks to my editor, the endlessly patient, kind, and brilliant Tessa Woodward, who finds the diamonds even when I send them to her in a sack of coal. To my agent, Alexandra Machinist, for letting me bask in her baddass brilliance. To the entire William Morrow and Avon team: Pam Jaffee, Imani Gary, Elle Keck, Kayleigh Webb, and Kaitie Leary, my endless gratitude for your tireless and creative support.

Finally, as always, my greatest thanks to you, dear readers; if not for you I would not enjoy the greatest of all privileges: living my dream.

Chapter One

Ashna Raje couldn't remember the last time her restaurant had thirty occupied tables. The gentle hum of customer conversation drifted into the kitchen from the dining area. It was nowhere near the nightly five-hundred-person din from when her father ran Curried Dreams, but it kindled the tiniest glimmer of hope inside Ashna. She snuffed it out. Hope terrified her. Ashna didn't credit her parents with much humor, but giving someone like her a name that meant "filled with hope" was definitely a cruel joke.

"Angry customer at table twelve, boss." One of the servers ran to her just as Ashna finished plating an order of biryani and slid it onto the counter. "She's demanding the crisp fried okra we served last week. I told her we took it off the menu. But she won't listen."

Ashna released a breath, expelling whatever scraps of hope she had left, and patted the server's arm. "Thanks. I'll take care of it."

She made her way into the tastefully ornate, albeit slightly run-down, dining room, stopping to ask the two tables on her way if they were enjoying their meal. She got one noncommittal shrug and one enthusiastic "Everything is delicious!" from a couple celebrating their engagement. She stayed to hear the story of how he had proposed in a hot-air balloon, then signaled the waitstaff to bring the couple complimentary champagne and the noncommittal table complimentary gulab jamuns.

By the time she reached table twelve, the customer demanding the fried okra—which Ashna had removed from the menu and was never putting back on—looked in no mood to be placated.

"I *have* to have that okra," the woman said as soon as Ashna introduced herself. She didn't seem used to being denied things.

The man sitting next to her patted her hand, earning himself an impressive glare for his effort. "We're pregnant," he declared, ignoring his wife's glare and the fact that he was, obviously, not in the least bit pregnant.

"How lovely," Ashna said pointedly to the woman. "Congratulations."

She was about to add that they were no longer serving the special menu when the woman threw Ashna the most tortured look. "Thank you. It's been a rough two months. I haven't been able to eat anything."

"Anything," the husband echoed, rivaling her desperation.

"James brought me the bhindi last week and it's exactly how my mother made it when I was little. It's literally all I can keep down."

"Literally all she can keep down." Another echo.

The okra recipe was one Ashna's friend DJ had created when he helped her come up with a menu to resurrect her failing restaurant. Why oh why did her friends have to be so good at what they did?

The couple blinked up at her, matching pleading looks widening their eyes.

"Of course." Ashna smiled, even as her heart raced. "We can prepare the okra for you. I'll send out jal jeera. My cousin says the mint and cumin settle her nausea. She's pregnant too."

The woman jumped up and hugged Ashna, then sat back down and dabbed the sweat off her husband's forehead with her napkin.

Any other time, Ashna would have found the man hilarious. But as she hurried back into the kitchen, she could barely breathe. Fortunately, her sous chef hadn't left yet. Ashna had promised Mandy that she could leave early today, but seeing that she was still here filled Ashna with relief.

Mandy paused in the act of putting on her jacket and the attention in the kitchen shifted to them like a spotlight. Two line cooks, the prep staff, the dishwasher, the bussers carrying trays, everyone pretended a little too hard to focus on their tasks.

When Ashna had returned from culinary school in Paris ten years ago and taken over the restaurant, she'd been buzzing with new recipes. But the first time she'd tried to cook something that wasn't Baba's recipe in this kitchen—his kitchen—the panic attack had knocked her off her feet, literally. It had felt like a truck driving onto her chest. Fainting and waking up surrounded by her staff staring down at her on the kitchen floor was an experience she'd sworn she would never risk repeating.

Then a few months ago DJ had helped her revamp her menu and she'd forced herself to try again, only to find that nothing had changed. For a month Ashna had relied on Mandy to prepare DJ's new recipes. Then her sous chef had asked for a day off and Ashna realized that she had to be able to cook her menu herself, without passing out. She had reverted to Baba's original menu.

Now, the panic truck revved close to her chest as she retrieved okra from the pantry and turned to her assistant. "The customer's pregnant. Can you take care of the okra?"

Mandy took off her jacket and tied her smock back around herself just a little more forcefully than necessary. "Sure, boss."

Ashna resisted the urge to fall to her knees in relief. Instead, she put her heart into a simple "Thank you," and got back to the next drop.

Her hands flew over sautéing garlic for the dal makhani. The act of preparing Baba's recipe loosened the panic in her chest, along with the congealed grief lodged deep inside. It had been twelve years since Baba put a bullet through his head. Ashna had heard the shot seconds before she found him facedown on his desk, a month before her eighteenth birthday.

After his death, Ashna had left Curried Dreams in the care of his two most trusted employees and gone to Paris to fulfill Baba's dream of attending culinary school there, and to lick her wounds. It had been an indulgence she'd been paying for ever since she returned to find her father's legacy destroyed and buried in debt. The two men had siphoned five million dollars from Curried Dreams and made off with the money.

Baba's life had ended in a single deafening blast, but his restaurant had continued to bleed out for the past ten years. And Ashna was responsible for both.

With Curried Dreams she was determined to stem the bleed. So, thirty tables was definitely a victory, foreclosure notices notwithstanding.

After the last customers left, including one very grateful pregnant *couple*, Ashna thanked her staff, saving the announcement of the budget cuts for another day.

Mandy, who had stayed on after missing the baby shower she'd been headed to, pursed her lips as Ashna waved goodbye to Khalid and Wilfrieda. Her line chefs grabbed each other's hands as soon as they were out the kitchen door, making Ashna smile. Ah, fresh young love! It was like the smell of cumin roasting in butter: you couldn't hide it for anything.

"Which one of them are you going to fire, then?" The sharpness in Mandy's eyes nipped Ashna's sigh in the bud.

"I have a plan," Ashna lied cheerily.

"Of course you do." Recently Mandy's cynical gruffness had morphed more and more into bitterness, something Ashna refused to allow into her own heart.

Filling the copper kettle with water, she put it on the stove. What Mandy needed was a good tulsi oolong tea to relax her.

Mandy ignored the overture, hung up her smock, and for the second time that evening grabbed her jacket from the closet. Mandy was always the last of the staff to leave. There was something comforting about their nightly routine of taking stock of the day and planning tomorrow together.

Except tonight, Mandy didn't throw Ashna her usual: "Get some rest, how will you catch a man if you look this exhausted?" Instead, she placed a hand on her hip and paused as though she didn't quite know what to do.

Ashna dropped the tea leaves from her jars into a tea ball, and waited.

"You've been promising me a raise all year," Mandy said finally.

Ashna forced herself not to squeeze the tea ball too tight. Fidgeting made her look helpless, and she was anything but helpless. She dropped her arms loosely at her sides and acted as though this didn't feel like being kicked in the gut.

"We had thirty tables today, and we've had twenty-five a few times this week. It's an upward trend." More than anything, she wanted to give Mandy a raise, give her entire staff raises.

"You know the definition of insanity is doing the same thing over and over and expecting different results, right?" Her assistant's hand on her hip was a familiar pose, but Mandy had never taken that tone with her.

Ashna had hired her five years ago, after Mandy's teenage daughter left her month-old baby sleeping in Mandy's house one night and disappeared. When Mandy came in for the interview, her desperation wrapped tight in the cloak of cheery optimism had felt only too familiar to Ashna. She'd let Mandy set up a cradle and playpen for the baby in the room behind the kitchen. As someone whose mother had walked away from her without a backward glance, anyone who did not abandon a child had Ashna's full support.

Then two years ago Mandy's daughter returned for her baby, setting the harried grandma free, but Mandy had stuck with Ashna. The look on her face said that the statute of limitations on that obligation had come to an end.

"You wouldn't be the first person to call me insane for holding on to Curried Dreams," Ashna said gently.

"If you hadn't reverted to the old menu, our thirty-table dinner rush might be a hundred-person rush by now." Mandy was never going to let that go.

Ashna squeezed the bridge of her nose, then pulled her hand away. "I understand that our financial condition is frustrating to you." She sounded imperious, much like her royal ancestors, and tossed in a smile, because she had to stay upbeat. "But Curried Dreams stands for something."

Irritation flooded Mandy's face, freckles darkening against her pale skin. "It stands for decrepitude and dated recipes, Ashna."

Ashna's hands squeezed into fists. "Where I come from, we call it history and tradition." *And respect for the dead.*

That last part stayed unsaid. Nonetheless, it echoed through the spotless (not decrepit, thank you very much) kitchen, and Mandy's eyes softened in response.

She sighed, half remorseful, half giving up the fight. "Where I come from, there's no trust fund to indulge my need to stay stuck in the past."

Ashna's smile slid off her face. She unclenched her fists. "I have to run Curried Dreams the way I want to run it," she said quietly, surprising herself with how calm she sounded.

Mandy buttoned her jacket. "Even if it means running it into the ground?"

Ashna took a step back. Mandy had never spoken to her this way. Something was very wrong.

Ashna's mind started racing. Mandy had taken a day off last week and uncharacteristically not told Ashna why. Suddenly it was obvious what this was. An image of Mandy going to an interview at another restaurant formed in her mind. She imagined the sharp stab of abandonment when Mandy told her she had found a new job. It was inevitable, surprising that it hadn't happened already.

"When were you going to tell me you had an offer?" The words were out before she could stop them.

Embarrassment colored Mandy's cheeks, proving Ashna right.

The familiar discomfort of being left behind ballooned inside Ashna too fast. She swallowed it down. "You should take the job," she said.

Mandy raised her chin, hurt and indignant. "Do you really want me to take it?"

If Mandy had gone looking, it was just a matter of time before she moved on. "You deserve to do what's best for you."

"Fine." Mandy's voice was too soft for what was happening. "Consider this my two weeks." She opened the door. "I'll see you tomorrow."

The door creaked shut behind her. It needed a fresh coat of paint. The gray had peeled, exposing white patches of primer.

Decrepit.

Ashna ran to the door and pushed it open. Cool night air whipped her face. Mandy was halfway across the parking lot to her car. The lampposts painted ominous halos around everything. The idea of two weeks now, with the connection between them damaged—Ashna couldn't imagine it.

"Mandy," she called, making her turn around. "I know you deserved much more than I could pay you. So . . . so why don't you take two weeks. Paid. Take that trip to Sonoma. Take a break before the new job."

Relief suffused Mandy's face. She didn't want two more weeks of awkwardness either.

"Thanks, Ashna," she said.

"Thanks, Mandy."

As simply as that, it was over.

Back inside, the kitchen wrapped around Ashna, unchanged over the years. Bricks, mortar, steel. Solid, dependable, predictable. Not fragile and breakable like the connections between people.

Sure, the appliances needed updating and the exhaust fans had become maddeningly loud—to a point where they sounded like a dead animal was stuck in the vents and screaming for mercy—but the steel countertops gleamed. Not a spot of grime anywhere.

Evidently, Ashna didn't have as hard a time with pride as she had with hope. Plugging in her headphones, she turned on her playlist. To the power blast that was Alicia Keys's voice belting out "Girl on Fire," she made her way to the storage area and pushed out the janitorial cart. Then, snapping on the bright orange rubber gloves, she got to her nightly vacuum, dust, spit-shine routine.

Letting the cleaning service go a year ago had been an easy decision. It's how she had avoided cutting Mandy's salary or hours. Mandy, who thought there was a trust fund to cover all this. Well, that wasn't how royal wealth worked.

The physical exertion of cleaning made Ashna feel alive.

The mosaic floors needed a good buffing, the velvet jacquard on the chairs was frayed in places, and the teakwood tables could use a coat of varnish, but as she wiped and scrubbed, everything got a little brighter and took on the familiar gleam of long-owned artifacts. New things were overrated anyway.

Baba had hand-selected every fitting and fixture to his exacting standards. Every little thing here was a handprint he'd left behind. With Bram Raje at the helm, Curried Dreams had been Palo Alto's hottest spot, the Bay Area's first fine dining Indian restaurant. Reservations had been a coveted prize, favors Ashna's father handed out in his magnanimous Prince Bram way.

Ashna switched the vacuum cleaner off and wrapped up the cord. She refused to turn toward the half flight of stairs that led to Baba's office, where she had found him in a rapidly growing pool of blood. If she let the darkness knock her down, who would keep Curried Dreams alive?

"What are we going to do?" she whispered to the beloved walls. She was all out of options.

A ping sounded in her ear, interrupting Alicia's rapture over New York City.

We're at the door. A text from her cousin Trisha.

In a mad dash Ashna put away the cart, rubbed rose-scented lotion into her hands to cover the chemical smell, and ran to the door.

It was just past midnight, but a visit after closing time from one of her cousins or her best friend, China, was a common occurrence. Everyone Ashna knew worked too hard and too late, and after all the restaurants in the area closed she was everyone's favorite food source. She opened the door and found herself to be right twice over. Both China and Trisha pushed their way into the kitchen.

"We've been knocking for five minutes!" Trisha said accusatorially.

"You're still here, thank God!" China added.

"Where else would I be?" Ashna headed for the fridge. "You hungry?"

They shook their heads. "We ate," they said in unison.

Very strange. A midnight visit without a food agenda.

"We'll take some tea," Trisha said, even as she found Ashna's cup and took a sip. "I can never drink chai anyone else makes. You've ruined me for substandard chai."

Ashna smiled. Most people did murder tea. They didn't understand how spices interacted with leaves and basically just threw stuff together and called it a blend. Some even had the gall to call it "tea" when there was no tea in it.

"Don't drink it cold." Before Ashna could finish the sentence, the cup in Trisha's hands had been drained.

Ashna sighed and refilled the kettle. China and Trisha exchanged a speaking look. Something was definitely up. Trisha might be Ashna's uncle's daughter, but they had grown up together and were more sisters than cousins. Also, Trisha had the world's most transparent face.

"Anyone want to tell me what this is about?"

China extracted a beer from the cooler. "Maybe it's too late for tea."

Trisha noticed the stack of mail Ashna had brought in earlier and started filing through it. The kettle whistled.

China and Trisha jumped.

"Okay, what's going on? What do you two want?"

Instead of answering, Trisha picked out an envelope and waved it like a victorious flag. "I think we finally know how to get rid of these foreclosure notices."

China took a gulp of beer and nodded.

"They're just warnings." Ashna snatched the envelope away. "And I don't need any more of your harebrained ideas."

Last week Trisha had tried to convince DJ, who was her boyfriend and one of the Bay's hottest private chefs, to insist on all his offsite parties being held at Curried Dreams. DJ had been one of Ashna's closest friends since culinary school in Paris. Ashna was, in fact, the one who had introduced DJ and Trisha, a matchmaking win she would always be insufferably proud of. But she was not going to let DJ hold his clients ransom for her restaurant. He had already done enough for her with the Menu She Couldn't Cook.

Trisha made a face. "I've never had a harebrained idea in my life. Neurosurgeons can't have harebrained ideas. It's in the Hippocratic oath."

Trisha was being only half facetious. The woman was abnormally brilliant and Ashna was obnoxiously proud of her cousin, but when it came to ideas for saving Curried Dreams, not so much.

Ashna sighed. "I'm sorry. I appreciate the effort. It's not like I've come up with anything that works either."

China and Trisha high-fived. Were her best friends high-fiving her failure?

Trisha grabbed Ashna's hand, dragged her into the dining area, and pushed her into a chair with the stupid know-it-all smile Ashna was only too familiar with.

Looking at China for answers simply caused her friend to study her beer bottle.

"Now that you have a boyfriend," Ashna said to Trisha, not attempting to hide her irritation, "shouldn't you be home spending time with him instead of worrying about Curried Dreams?"

Trisha dropped into a chair across from Ashna. "First, you should smack me upside the head if I let myself get involved with someone who doesn't understand how much you and Curried Dreams mean to me."

Fair enough. But Ashna kept her eyes stubbornly narrowed.

"Second, this actually has to do with said boyfriend. DJ needs your help." Trisha tried to look pleading, but she was incapable of pulling off helplessness.

Ashna very much doubted DJ needed help, and she could clearly imagine the scene where he had tried to stop Trisha from whatever fanciful errand she was on.

"Right," Ashna said, leaning forward in her chair. "First, if DJ needed my help, he'd ask himself. Second, I know that face." She stuck a finger at Trisha. "And that one." She moved her finger to China's face. "What are you two up to? Spit it out. I need to be at the farmer's market at five A.M."

"There's my girl. We would very much love to spit it out." Finally China spoke, relief clear in her alpha-of-the-pack voice. Her ability to lead crews through crazy schedules had made Food Network steal her away from a local production company earlier this year.

"So, you know how DJ was going to be a pro on my new show?" China was one of the producers on *Cooking with the Stars*—a new competitive show that followed the format of *Dancing with the Stars*, where they teamed up celebrities with professional chefs and the duos duked it out for viewer votes and judges' scores.

Ashna had helped China and Trisha talk (bully?) DJ into it. DJ was handsome, madly talented, charismatic, and had that magic element for American television: a Very British Accent.

"Did you say *was*?" Ashna asked, alarmed.

"Yeah, he's not going to be a pro chef on the show anymore." Trisha sounded far too cheery.

"I thought he was all excited about it. What happened?"

"Well," China said, "Aaron Smith, our host for the show, his wife has cancer. So he had to quit to take care of her."

"Oh no. That's so sad." Ashna pressed a hand to her mouth.

"Yes. But the prognosis is excellent. Catching ovarian cancer at stage one is a win." Trisha sounded every inch the doctor she was. "DJ is taking over as host."

"DJ? Our DJ?" Ashna sat up.

"The very one." Trisha beamed like a smitten fool. "It's the accent. Also, he's actually a better fit to host the show than

Aaron was in the first place. He knows so much more about food. Plus, I was a little worried about him working with a celebrity. He's such a diva about cooking, I can't imagine him teaming up with someone who might not turn out something utterly perfect."

Ashna grabbed China's beer and took a sip. "What does all this have to do with me?" The moment the words left her mouth, she knew she shouldn't have asked.

"Well, the network is set to announce the pro chefs the day after tomorrow on a special episode of *Iron Chef*. We've been promoting it for months." China grabbed the beer back and took a sip. "And we're short a chef."

"Oh no, look at the time." Ashna jumped out of her chair. "If I don't close up I won't be able to get to the farmer's market before all the best produce is gone. Palo Alto chefs are ruthless. You won't believe how fast everything gets swept away. Last week they ran out of bitter melon because I was twelve minutes late."

Using both hands, Ashna tried to yank China out of her chair, but she didn't budge. "This doesn't sound like an emergency." It totally sounded like an emergency. For Ashna, not them. "We can discuss it tomorrow." She tried to move Trisha with similar results. "Don't you have work tomorrow? Surgeries maybe? Saving lives and all that?"

China made her best puppy-dog eyes. "Trisha will have her lives to save. You'll have your restaurant to run." Her sigh took on a desperate quality that didn't sound like she was faking. "But I won't have work to go to. Not if I don't have a new chef to replace DJ by tomorrow."

Boom.

Trisha and China stared at Ashna with all the gleeful expectation of friends who had you perfectly cornered.

"Of course you'll find a chef to replace DJ. Chefs have to be scrambling to get on your show."

"Like who? We start shooting in less than a month. How will I run auditions before the announcement in one day?"

"How about . . ." Ashna racked her brains. Why oh why hadn't she worked harder to network with her peers? She wanted to help. Truly, she did.

"You know how hot DJ is," Trisha said.

"We need someone hot and talented," China said.

"I can't think of anyone—"

"We can," they both said in a perfectly delusional symphony. "You, Ashna."

A giant ball of laughter gathered inside Ashna and came tumbling out like an avalanche. "Very funny. No, really, you guys are hilarious," she said between hiccupping and—bordering on maniacal—laughter. "Hil-fucking-arious." She pressed her hands into her sternum. Her heart felt like it was going to explode. And she couldn't stop laughing.

Identical worried frowns creased Trisha and China's foreheads. Ashna couldn't remember the last time this panic-fueled laughing fit had happened to her.

China brought her water.

"Do you need a paper bag?" Trisha asked.

Ashna shook her head and sucked in several deep breaths. It took a few moments, but she forced the laughter to subside. "What are you going to introduce me as? 'Ashna Raje, owner and executive chef of the soon-to-be-foreclosed Curried Dreams?'"

"But if you do this, there will be no foreclosing. They'll pay you a signing amount, and the prize for winning is a hundred grand. Think about the exposure Curried Dreams will get!" China swept an arm around the room. "You'll be able to make repairs, freshen things up."

It stands for decrepitude and dated recipes.

Another spurt of laughter burst out of Ashna. She pressed her lips together as tightly as she could.

Trisha nudged the glass of water toward her. "Calm down and think about this without freaking out."

Too late. Ashna forced herself to focus on the cold glass in her hand, at the mosaic lamps hanging from the ceiling, the jasmine diffuser scenting the air. She grounded herself one sight, one sound, one smell at a time. The laughter died out, but her heart still galloped in her chest.

"Okay?" Trisha asked, studying Ashna's pupils in her doctorly way.

Ashna pushed her away. "I'm fine, but you're both insane."

"Why is helping your two best friends in the whole world, *and yourself*, insane? Why?" Trisha said, her usual relentless self. "You know what's insane?"

"If you give me the 'definition of insanity' line right now, I will strangle you with my bare hands," Ashna snapped.

"Okay, I won't. But look at you, Ashi, you've been doing the same things for the past ten years and it hasn't helped. Sometimes it's just a matter of changing something. Doing just one thing differently."

Ashna didn't bother to hold back her groan. "I can't."

The idea of cooking in front of a camera made Ashna want to bring up her dinner, bring up all the dinners she'd ever eaten. She wished she could explain why to them. But how could she explain something she didn't understand? How could she explain the ugly panic that choked her when she tried to cook anything but Baba's recipes? All she had was how her loved ones saw her, as strong, in control. A little bull-headed, but capable. Easy Ashna. Dependable Ashna. If that went away, all she'd be was the girl to pity, to tiptoe around.

Been there. Never going back.

"I'm begging," China said, standing up. "At least take the night to think about it."

I can't. But she didn't know how to repeat it. Not with the dogged hope sparkling on their faces.

Chapter Two

As always, routine relaxed Ashna. Her day started at the farmer's market. The night sky had not yet fully transformed into day. She loved when the sun peeked at the edges of the sky while the moon was still not quite hidden away. The carts overflowing with plump and fragrant fruit and vegetables added to the magic of the hour. Vendors and chefs talked in hushed tones in deference to it.

There was plenty of bitter melon today, glossy and lime green with lush scalloped ridges. Ashna let Charlie, her favorite farmer's son, sell her everything he had left, an extra five pounds, so he could go home early. He was taking care of business while his father recovered from colon surgery—which Charlie felt the need to explicate in lurid detail as he helped Ashna carry her bags to her car.

Apparently, the pre-surgery "bowel clean-out" hadn't gone as smoothly as they had hoped.

Ashna patted the poor boy's shoulder and asked him about high school, and they bonded over every Asian child's favorite topic: their family's obsession with grades and college applications. Charlie's parents were Vietnamese, and Ashna much preferred the image of Farmer Dang as an exacting parent to any sort of bowel clean-out association.

"You're a good son," she told him, and he blushed, which was incredibly endearing given that talk of bowels hadn't embarrassed him in the slightest.

Ashna dropped off the produce at Curried Dreams. Extra bitter melon was never an issue. The unpopular vegetable was a favorite with the Rajes, none of whom were daunted by the bitterness that sat atop the other, more complex underlying flavors. She would take some over to her aunt and uncle's house later.

Her grandmother could make magic with bitter melon, stuffing it with fried onions and then frying the entire thing to a buttery, salty crunch. Baba's recipe at the restaurant was derived from Aji's recipe, but he'd made it richer with cashews added to the stuffing and a creamy onion sauce. Decadent, the way all of Baba's versions of traditional recipes were. Ashna could make that version in her sleep, but she preferred the taste of the one her grandmother made.

After washing and sorting the produce at Curried Dreams she headed home to shower. Her restaurant and her home were separated by a cedar fence and a thicket of jacarandas, a distance of barely one hundred feet. Ashna's father had built both buildings—the mansion-style restaurant and the Spanish stucco bungalow—from the ground up just after they moved from Sripore to California when Ashna was ten years old. Before that Ashna had only ever lived in the palace her ancestors had built centuries ago.

With Curried Dreams and the bungalow, she had watched the backhoe break ground as she stood there with her cousins, smelling long-buried earth being dredged up. She'd walked on newly laid tile and touched freshly plastered walls, watched furniture being moved in, tapestries being hung and rehung to Baba's satisfaction.

Until he built Curried Dreams, Bram Raje had been the quintessential spoiled prince, the youngest son of the royal family of Sripore, one of India's oldest princely states. Unlike his older brothers, Bram had lived up to the stereotype of indolent entitlement and fed his antics to the hungry media machine that surrounds royals everywhere. Until one such antic had landed him in trouble with the law and forced him to flee India.

His older brother Shree—HRH, as Ashna and her cousins called him—had rescued Bram (yet again) and brought him to California. Then he proposed (Raje code for *dictated*) that Bram channel his taste for decadent food and his passion for keeping the public entertained into an Indian restaurant that wasn't the usual curry house in a strip mall.

HRH had been right, as he often was. Curried Dreams had finally given Bram the sense of responsibility his family had hoped for as they'd bankrolled business after business to help give him purpose that might save him. They had gotten it right that last time; Curried Dreams *had* given Bram purpose and taught him responsibility, which even having a daughter had not managed to do. But Curried Dreams hadn't saved him.

Ashna stopped to pluck the few dandelions poking up among the roses along the side of the house. She had just enough time to get in a run before returning to the restaurant. Today was her yoga day, but there was no way her mind would stay quiet enough for yoga. Putting her phone on silent all morning had been cowardly, but she didn't care.

The downside of choosing cowardice was that there was only so long you could hide. Problems were patient. They always waited you out. On her way to the front stoop, she finally checked her phone. Surprisingly, there was only one message from China and nothing from Trisha. Thinking about the Herculean effort that must have taken made her smile. She had agreed to take the night to think about the show. Not that there was any way she could do it. Unsurprisingly, there was nothing from Mandy either. So it seemed like that chapter was closed.

China's message was a simple *Call me.*

All night Ashna had tried to think of another chef who might do the show, but she'd come up empty.

Just contemplating cooking off-script made her heart race so hard she had to breathe through it.

Dear judges, I have for you today: a giant meltdown.

Nope, never going to happen.

How tidy her life had felt yesterday. Thirty occupied tables, a sous chef who helped her find solutions for the restaurant, best friends who didn't think she was too selfish to help them. What else could possibly go wrong?

She picked up her phone and was about to call China when the name of the last person she wanted to think about right now flashed on her screen.

Every bit of sense Ashna possessed told her to ignore the

call. Another minute and she would have missed it anyway. But it had been six months since she'd spoken to her mother. A long gap even for them. That last silently destructive fight— a specialty of their mother-daughter bond—had been one of their most spectacular ones. Ashna had even wondered if they'd ever speak again.

She pressed talk.

"Hello, beta. Why does it take you so long to answer the phone?"

Why oh why had she asked what else could go wrong? Obviously she was in no position to tempt fate.

"Hi, Mom," she said with the casualness of a daughter who didn't care that she hadn't heard her mother's voice in half a year. "What's wrong?" Not the smartest question, given that when it came to them that answer could take a while.

"Can your mother not call you without something being wrong?" Her tone was perfectly self-possessed, not a whit of emotion in those words. Shoban Gaikwad Raje probably didn't even remember that it had been six months since she'd spoken to her only child.

The hard blast of anger in Ashna's belly meant she needed to calm the heck down. She breathed in through her nose and out through her mouth, and then did what she did best with Shobi: stayed silent.

Shobi gave a self-deprecating laugh, the one that always came out as a huff-cough. "Well never mind all that. How are you?"

If Shobi had been standing in front of her, Ashna would have checked over her shoulder to see if she was talking to someone else. But Ashna was an adult woman; she could handle this without regressing. She took the phone into the house and removed her shoes. "Everything is peachy with me. How about yourself?"

Her (admittedly overdone) breeziness was met with a long pause.

Shoban Gaikwad Raje, whose most recent TED Talk had tens of millions of views, was not given to pausing.

A short, almost unsure clearing of the throat followed. Another most un-Shobi-like move. Putting her shoes in the closet, Ashna made her way up to her room. If Shobi was giving her a silence to fill, it had to be a trap. Ashna had been raised by her aunt, whose first rule was: read the room before you show your hand.

Finally, Shobi went for self-deprecating laugh, round two. "Actually, I have news." Her voice did a strange wobble. Which had to be Ashna's imagination, because Shobi did not waste her time on displays of emotion. She wasn't called Dragon-Raje by the Indian media for nothing. "I know we didn't leave things in a good place the last time we spoke, but you had to be the first person I told this to." The quiver in Shobi's voice was unmistakable this time. "They're giving me the Padma Shri."

Ashna started to pace, words failing her. The Padma Shri was one of India's highest honors for achievement in a field.

"Ashna, your mother is winning the Padma Shri! All my hard work, all my sacrifices. It's all paying off." The excited quiver raised Shobi's pitch a few levels. She was entirely unaware of the fact that she was saying these words to the sum total of all her sacrifices.

This time Ashna cleared her throat. "That's amazing," she said, because she wasn't a colossal enough bitch to be unkind when someone was excited about winning an award only a handful of people won.

"Thanks, beta," Shobi said, clearly struggling with how her inexplicable daughter could be so underwhelmed by her brilliance.

There was another awkward pause, awkwardness being their default mode. Ashna took herself to the bathroom and turned on the tub faucet. A shower wasn't going to cut it today.

"Listen, Ashna. I know this isn't easy for you to understand, but it hasn't been easy for me either."

Which part? But Ashna knew the answer to that already.

The part where Shobi had to abandon Ashna to achieve what she was born to achieve. You couldn't ask a question like that without being reminded of how dispensable you were, and even worse, how selfish you were for feeling sorry for yourself for being dispensed with for the sake of "changing the world."

Truth was, nothing was ever hard for Shobi. She had been the star of the Indian national women's cricket team. After retiring from that, she had singlehandedly taken sports advocacy for girls to the remote corners of India, a country that determinedly ignored all sports except men's cricket.

As if that weren't enough, she had transformed her sports advocacy into a weapon to change the lives of girls and women across the country by building sports-focused schools for girls. Her network of grassroots female empowerment projects brought together millions of dollars from the world's greatest philanthropists. She made conscienceless politicians tremble, manipulated corrupt media, and managed to employ hundreds of people who truly cared about her cause in an entirely self-focused world. If anything dared stand in her path, she leveled it like the champion she was. In other words, she was the polar opposite of her daughter in every way possible.

Ashna had been struggling to keep one restaurant afloat for ten years. For the entirety of those years, Shobi had been waiting for her to fail.

"I see that you're not going to make this easy for me," Shobi said with the deep regret she used in fund-raising speeches. It was a tone that could guilt people into coughing up every penny they could afford.

"I'm really happy for you," Ashna repeated in the most upbeat of her collection of upbeat tones. The emptiness that overtook her when she spoke to Shobi didn't make it easy.

"May I say something? I know you don't want to hear this."

Dear God, every single time that line came out of Shobi, she followed it up with something that started a fight.

Please don't do this today. That sense of barely holding it together that Ashna kept firmly at the edge of her consciousness closed in. Every time Shobi showed up, it pushed its way to the center of her. What kind of dumbass let someone do that to them over and over?

But of course, no one stopped Shobi from doing exactly as Shobi wanted.

"I think you've forgotten what it means to be happy."

Ashna sank down to her knees next to the tub. A stray hair marred the spotless floor. She picked it up and threw it in the garbage.

"Are you going to say anything at all?"

Ashna wanted to, but her words had a way of hiding away when they sensed Shobi's presence.

"Ashna?" She couldn't tell if Shobi was reprimanding her or if that was concern in her voice. Not that she had any experience with recognizing concern in Shobi's voice.

"You're wrong, *Mom*. You can only forget something you knew."

Her mother gasped and Ashna realized that she had said the words out loud.

In the moment that Shobi said nothing, relief and hope rushed through Ashna. She imagined her admission filling Shobi with regret and understanding.

"That's not fair, Ashna."

How could Ashna not laugh at that? Of course Shobi would make Ashna's admission that she had never learned how to be happy about herself.

Ashna knew exactly what Shobi would say next. "Why is it so hard for you to understand your mother?" Bingo. And then . . . "You always understood your baba no matter what he did. No matter how wrong his choices."

How many times could you have the same fight? Baba had stuck with Ashna, always. Well, until he hadn't, in the end. But Ashna had never known Shobi as anything but a visitor who was either arriving or getting ready to leave.

Shobi had been gone a lot when they lived in Sripore, and then she hadn't moved to America with them. Just visited. At first Ashna had tried hard to believe the visits weren't reluctant, but over time, they grew shorter and farther apart, proving how wrong she'd been.

"Anyway, I didn't call to have that conversation again. I was hoping maybe we could move past all that. Isn't it time to fix things?"

Wasn't this just precious? Now that Shobi had achieved the ultimate validation for her work, it was time to start taking stock of collateral damage.

Yes, well, Ashna wasn't doormat enough for that. Being vulnerable in her mother's presence was a mistake. She got herself up off the floor. The tub was full. She turned off the water. "There's nothing to move past. I'm happy for you. And I'm proud of everything you've achieved." There, she'd said what a dutiful daughter would say. "Good luck."

"Oh, Ashna, maybe someday you'll mean that. I *have* changed the lives of thousands. I've worked hard for it. It would be nice to have the person I gave birth to acknowledge it."

"I'm proud of you," Ashna repeated, trying to reach into that part of her that still remembered how proud she used to be of Shobi. The water was the perfect temperature. She dropped a capful of eucalyptus oil in. The steam rising from it turned intoxicating. She sank down to her knees again and inhaled it.

"I don't mean repeat the lie. I mean, actually mean it. You

have no idea how badly I wish you could see my life. Understand it. *See me.*"

"Across the thousands of miles you've always put between us?"

Instead of another gasp, another pause followed. A potent pause, filled with things Ashna didn't want to hear, places she didn't want to go with the woman who had birthed her.

Ashna skimmed a circle on the water's surface.

"You're right," Shobi said, her voice determined. "Let's fix that."

Ashna's hand jostled the water, disturbing the surface, splashing herself. Why hadn't she just stayed silent? It was the only strategy that worked with Shobi.

"Actually, that's why I was calling, I just didn't know how I was going to ask. So I'm glad you brought it up. Why don't you come to India?"

Ashna took her face close to the water's surface. The tip of her nose touched the liquid warmth. The weight of her heavy bun skewed to one side of her head.

"Ashna?" Shobi pushed into her silence.

"I can't do that." Her whisper reflected off the water, the mint in her breath mixing with the eucalyptus. She picked out the distinct familiar scents and let her mind linger on each.

"Why? This is the perfect time to come home. Share this experience with me. They asked me to choose someone to introduce me at the awards ceremony and, naturally, I want you to be the one to do it. It's been too long, beta. You haven't been to Sripore in thirteen years. Come home!"

Sripore was not her home. "Palo Alto is my home," she said quietly, "and Woodside," she added to make sure her punch hit home. Woodside was where her aunt and uncle lived. The people who had been more parents to her than Shobi ever would.

The punch landed squarely where Ashna had aimed it and Shobi's patience snapped. "You're being deliberately hurtful again," she said. "You aren't a teenager anymore. This anger isn't going to get you anywhere. It's not healthy. You're thirty. It's not—"

"I am the least angry person I know." The irony of her hiss did not escape her. "I have a business to run. I'd love to help you, but I just can't." She forced herself to regain her calm.

At least Shobi had gotten her age right this time. Shoban Gaikwad Raje had the fabulous distinction of having asked her child "So, what grade are you in?" on multiple occasions.

"Getting away from that place is exactly what you need. I can't believe your father saddled you with—"

"Curried Dreams is my life," she hissed again, because the only thing being upbeat would get her was a bath gone cold.

"That's my point exactly. You need to find a life outside Curried Dreams!" said the woman who lectured all and sundry endlessly about how a woman's work should be just as important to her as her family. "It's time for you to break the chains that have been tying you up for years. Reset your priorities."

Dear God, not chains! Chains were Shobi's favorite metaphor. "Women in Chains" was the general theme of all her lectures. Once Shobi started on this topic, she'd never stop.

Ashna straightened up. Curried Dreams wasn't what was tying her up in chains. Shobi was, and she always had with her promises of love that she kept just out of reach. Always. For Ashna's whole life the woman had wielded those chains with ruthlessness.

Finally, in this moment, it hit Ashna why. It had been so Ashna would be here, waiting, when Shobi was finally ready to fix that neglected part of her life. Because Shobi had always set her priorities exactly the way she wanted them.

"You're right," Ashna said. "I do need to break the chains. Which is exactly why I'm not coming to India."

"That makes no sense, Ashna. You're stuck, don't you see? You've been doing the same thing for—"

"I have a new job, Mom."

No! Why on earth had she said that? Ashna wanted to wring Trisha's and China's combined necks for shoving stupid ideas in her head.

"You're moving on from Curried Dreams?" The almost gleeful hope in Shobi's voice strummed every one of Ashna's overstretched nerves.

Baba's been dead for twelve years, she wanted to scream. *You can stop fighting with him now.* "No, I'm not. But I'm going to be on a competitive cooking show as a pro chef." Her voice sounded strong and clear for the first time since she'd heard Shobi's hello. She leaned in and met her own eyes in the mirror.

"Reality TV? You?" The voice on the phone stretched between skepticism and outright disbelief.

Shobi's favorite metaphorical chains stretched at the links

around Ashna. "Yes. If I win I can pay down the debt on Curried Dreams. And no, I'm never giving up on it."

The frustrated sound Shobi made was so delicious that for one lovely second Ashna didn't care about anything else. "You are so Bram's daughter. He was a great expert at cutting off his nose to spite his face."

"Being Baba's daughter is something I'm proud of."

"Don't I know it? But there's no wisdom in ruining your life to stick it to me, child. Being punitive will get you nowhere."

So, the gloves were off now. Their conversation arriving at its inevitable destination.

"Hard as it is to imagine, not every decision I make is motivated by you."

"I know. It's motivated by the guilt your father dumped on your head before leaving."

Leaving. How clean she made death sound. Shobi had *left*. Baba had *died*.

"Thanks for that. I have to go." She disconnected the call, finally doing what she should have done the moment she started to lose control of the conversation, long before letting her bath go cold. Then she pulled the plug and watched the water drain away.

Chapter Three

Rico Silva watched as giant sprinklers dropped down from the absurdly high ceiling and rained water on the mud pit, where bikini-clad women wrestled with a bunch of his mates. There was nothing quite like a bachelor party to strike terror in any sane—or sober—person's heart for the future of humankind. Across the room at the giant bar, Josh—wearing horns of some sort—watched a woman—wearing the most minimalist of sequined pasties and thongs—take a shot from between his knees. Needless to say, Josh was in his underwear, which made how much he was enjoying this evident to all present.

Rico threw a look around the room to make sure no one had their cameras out. This was the Hold, Vegas's most elite and secret club, and the lighting used a special wavelength that made taking photographs impossible. Even so, for every technology invented to protect privacy, there was a counter-technology invented to violate it. It was the world they lived in. You didn't have to be a Premier League football player to know this, but if you were, you knew it well. Not that any of these knobs remembered their names right now, let alone the lessons they had learned. Most were young enough to still believe themselves invincible after enough whiskey recklessly mixed with every other kind of alcohol.

Del was on top of the bar and about to grab a rope dangling from the ceiling to take a Tarzan-style swing across the room. Fortunately, the season was over and they didn't have to get back on the pitch for training for a few more weeks.

Well, not them, exactly. Rico was never getting back on the pitch. The torn iliotibial band and shattered kneecap had made sure his career was good and over. Not that he could complain. At eighteen he'd moved Sunderland from the relegation zone back up to the Premier League, kicking off the kind of career he could never have imagined in his wildest dreams. He'd won the World Cup and the Champions League, and been purchased by Manchester United for a record sum. At thirty, he'd had a run he was more than a little proud of.

The part he wasn't proud of was how badly he was handling the pain. His knee hurt as though the screws and plates substituting for bones and tissue were made of solidified acid. As always, the pain sharpened when he thought about it.

He had read somewhere that human nerves blocked out chronic pain after a while, but the sensation of pain returned when you were reminded of it, like when you heard someone else talk about theirs. It was as though the knowledge of another person's pain reminded the nerves of what they were trying to forget.

Rico was here to tell all skeptics that the theory was indeed accurate. He adjusted his leg on the booth couch. The body-armor-style brace itched like the depths of hell and he couldn't wait to get it off in a few days.

"What's got you all grumpy?" Zia, his best mate and the groom—which made him the man of the hour—slid into the booth Rico was hogging all to himself. Not that the other guys had any interest in leaving the dance floor, or the mud pit, or the bar with the Tarzan vines hanging over it.

"Nothing. Just jealous that I can't join the guys in making such perfect arses of themselves." Much as Rico detested the brace, he was grateful for it today. He was in no mood to get out there and prove how much of a party animal he was. Not that he wasn't perfectly adept at that. As a Carioca born and raised in Rio de Janeiro, knowing how to have a good time— while preserving his dignity—was in his blood.

Zee knew he was joking, but he still looked at Rico in that way good friends looked at you when you were off your game: one part concern, the other part impatient hope that your affliction would pass fast. Zee looked ready to bodily shake off this ridiculous blue mood that had been clinging to Rico recently.

"Thanks for being here." He thumped Rico's shoulder and threw a wince at his leg, which was more than the rest of them dared to do. Their other teammates avoided the topic of the surgeries and the sight of Rico's knee as though torn connective tissue that ended your career were contagious.

Rico shrugged. A brace and crutches wouldn't keep him from his best mate's bachelor party. For a few moments, the two of them took in their teammates acting like this was their very last opportunity to hold on to the stupidity of their youth.

"Tell me again why you let Del plan this?" Zee asked. "Wasn't it your bloody job as my best mate?"

"I was in the hospital, remember? And Del and Josh thought it was the perfect excuse to take over. I don't think any of the guys were stoked about catching *Hamilton* in New York to celebrate you losing your bachelorhood."

Zee laughed. "That actually sounds fecking brilliant. Except Tanya would kill me if I went without her, even though she's seen it four times."

As always, that fuzzy *I just took a hit of something potent* look crossed Zia's eyes when he talked about Tanya. It was well deserved, of course. Tanya was possibly the best woman Rico had ever met. Steady and badass and madly warm and nurturing.

"How the hell did I get so lucky?" Zee said.

"I don't know, mate. How *did* you?"

"I guess we caught each other young and watched each other grow, eh? Luckiest break of my life." Tanya and Zee had been college sweethearts.

"By that definition, it's pretty much too late for the rest of us." Rico took a sip of his club soda, wishing for something stronger, but his meds didn't mix with alcohol.

For all his reputation for being a rule breaker on the pitch, Rico was, in fact, never stupid about which rules he broke. His father hadn't had a chance to teach him much, but the one thing he had taught Rico was that you couldn't win if you got thrown out for committing fouls. Staying in the game was a requirement for winning.

"Does that mean there's no chance of you and Myra getting

back together, then?" Zee asked, running his hand through his blond-highlighted hair, his very obvious worry tell.

"That would be hard given that she just got engaged to her new boyfriend. Apparently, *he* wasn't *emotionally unavailable.*" To her credit, Myra had tried not to break up with Rico before the spate of surgeries started almost a year ago. But he hadn't wanted her nursing him through sickness if she was done with him in health.

Zee gave him the kind of look only a happily-in-love person could give a single friend, especially one they believed had no idea what being in love felt like.

"So, on to the next relationship, then?" Zee said, meeting Rico's gaze over his almost-empty glass. "Frederico Webster Silva and his string of lovely women, each one of whom has gone on to make someone else a lovely wife."

"You sound like you're trying to say something, mate. Blokes like you who have it all always have something to say about things you know nothing about." Rico held up his club soda and clinked glasses with his friend.

"Hey, all I know is that you're my best mate and you have no interest in playing the field. You're an excellent boyfriend—my old woman's words, not mine. I don't understand what it is you're waiting for."

"I'm waiting for someone like Tanya who keeps the ball and chain tight without letting it chafe."

Zee let out the deepest sigh any human should be allowed to sigh. Seriously, if all those rabid female fans saw him moon over Tanya, there would be a serious threat to the poor woman's life.

"I do love my ball and chain." Zee punched his phone screen and a sleepy "Baby? You all right?" came across the phone.

"Never all right without you, love. My mates are knobs. I want to be home, baby. Home with you, not here with these hairy, stinky bastards." Then he dropped his voice. "All I want is to be buried deep inside you right now."

Rico turned away and started scrolling through his phone, blocking out the lovestruck whispering.

"You can stop pretending to check your phone now, I'm done being a sop," Zee said when he was done, and Rico had to smile.

"It's okay. But only because Tanya deserves a sop like you," he said less lightly than he'd intended.

Zee didn't notice, lost as he was in his groom raptures. The general belief was that only brides went into a wedding haze, but men were worse. Where brides tended to get lost in the wedding details, Rico had noticed that men tended to get hit on the head by the idea of getting to hold on to the woman who made them come apart.

"I'm telling you, man. I want this for everyone. This single-minded need for a woman. No other shit in life comes close to this. You know what I mean?"

I know exactly what you mean.

It was a thought Rico hadn't had in years. He didn't allow himself to have it, ever.

Zee was wrong in thinking that no other shit came close. Rico had spent the last decade proving that a lot of shit came close.

It's just that none of it came close enough.

Rico shifted in his seat. The immobility from his propped leg made him restless in a way he couldn't explain. Restless in a way he hadn't been in a very long time.

He reached for Zee's drink. Not drinking had to be messing with his brain.

Zee, being Zee, moved the glass out of his reach. Not that Rico would have actually broken doctor's orders and taken a sip, but it was good to have someone to nudge you back into place when you slipped.

"Bloody hell, I'm being an arse," Zee said. "Here you are with Myra marrying someone else, and I won't stop going on about things. Talk to her. She was really into you. It's not like there was closure. You're still friends. Maybe it's not too late."

Rico had to laugh at that. "This isn't one of your Bollywood films. I'm not going to ride into her wedding on a horse and whisk her away. As a matter of fact, there *was* closure. That's why we're still friends."

"You're really not broken up about her marrying someone else, are you?" Zee looked abjectly disappointed, but Rico wasn't sure if it was at not getting to witness the drama of a filmy reconciliation or at Rico's inability to feel deeply enough.

"Myra's exactly where she wants to be. And I want her to be happy."

This was true. But Zee's other assumption wasn't. Rico would never admit it to Zee, or to anyone else, but Rico did, in fact, know exactly what Zee meant about single-minded need. Or he had once. Maybe pain receptors weren't the only things that worked like jealous mirrors. Maybe pain wasn't the only thing your brain refocused on when it was reminded of it.

Zee and Tanya had always dug up memories of something. Someone, rather. Someone who deserved neither the comparison nor the single-minded devotion Rico had felt.

Unfortunately, he'd been too young to choose how he reacted to her, and by the time she had proven herself unworthy of those feelings, it had been too late. Now here he was, relationship after relationship, unable to be that Rico again. The one who had no idea how to be emotionally unavailable.

She had taken that away from him. The reckless freedom of being emotionally available.

After all these years of doing all he could to wipe away his memories of her, the realization hit him like a body blow.

All he had succeeded in doing was building scabs, and blocking himself off emotionally. He was running around in a hamster wheel of his own making.

Closure.

The word ricocheted in his head, setting off a raging longing for relief.

He touched his knee, where throbbing pain wrapped tight on the outside even as it pushed from the inside, the brace holding everything in place until he was healed and ready to go on as normal. Maybe it was time to cut open another wound and sew that torn muscle together too. Regain the use of other parts he had lost.

Zee chugged what was left of his drink. His gaze bounced from the empty glass to Rico.

"There's plenty more where that came from. Go on. I'm fine," Rico said.

His friend studied him for another second, then opened and

closed his mouth a few times. There was nothing he could say that Rico wanted to hear right now. Zee was smart enough to know this. He thumped Rico's shoulder and headed to the bar.

The guys rushed at Zee and lifted him up above their heads, carrying him to the dance floor, where EDM boomed against the walls and broke into strobes of fluorescent light. They could have done this anywhere in the world. The wedding was in London, where Zee and Tee were from. But they had chosen to come to Vegas for the bachelor party.

Nevada was right next to California.

That could be a coincidence, but what was it they said about coincidences? That there weren't any.

Rico leaned his head back and closed his eyes. The psychedelic lights continued to flash behind his lids. The pain on Myra's face as she told him she was done with him danced there with the lights.

I know you try, but it's not enough. I'm sorry. Her eyes had brimmed with tears and accusation.

Rico's own lack of sadness at those words had felt like a hole inside him. Then there had been the relief. The worst part was that Myra had seen the relief and it had multiplied the accusatory hurt in her eyes.

What you feel for me is fondness, not love. Love hurts. I can't hurt you, no matter what I do.

She had been right. He liked being with her, but losing her hadn't shattered him. He hadn't asked her why it was important for her to be able to hurt him. Truth was, nothing had hurt him in a very long time other than winning and losing matches.

Sitting up, he pulled out his phone. Before he could think it through, he texted Myra. *Did I say Congratulations?*

Maybe he should've cared what her fiancé thought about Rico texting her in the middle of the night, but Myra wasn't a bone to fight over and Rico certainly didn't give a shit about a man if he didn't trust the person he was with. Myra had insisted they stay friends. He was friends with all his exes. The friendship had always been the best part of the relationships anyway. As was proven by the fact that he was godfather to Ryka's baby girl, a commitment he took very seriously and an honor he was grateful for.

There was only one ex he hadn't stayed friends with.

Myra's response buzzed in immediately. *Several times. Aren't you in America? Isn't it three in the morning there?*

Zee's bachelor party's just getting started.

She sent him a smiley face followed by a few dancing-lady emojis, beer mugs, and, inexplicably enough, monkeys.

Are you happy? he wanted to ask her. *With this new guy?*

Because he wanted happiness for her.

We set a date, she texted, before he embarrassed himself by asking that question. *September 30th in Tuscany. You have to be there.*

Of course. I'm happy for you.

I know.

Dots danced on the screen as Myra typed more, then erased what she'd typed. For a long time he stared at the phone as dots appeared and disappeared but no new text came in.

Zee shouted Rico's name from the dance floor and the guys raised their glasses to Rico across the room.

The room in Nevada.

Right next to California. Where Rico had been the unhappiest he'd ever been in his life. But also where he had still known how to be happy.

His best mate gyrated around the dance floor. Zee's Punjabi Indian half always showed up in his dancing. He turned everything into a bhangra, shoulders popping, feet thumping. The wild beat of the dance captured Zee's joy perfectly. He knew how to be himself without shutting any part of himself down. He knew how to be with someone he loved without holding himself back. He hadn't lost that ability.

The skin under Rico's brace itched. They couldn't get the darned thing off him soon enough.

He imagined the freedom of having his body back. Of being able to run and bend and move. For all the pain and discomfort, the surgery was going to give him that.

He raised his glass to his wildly dancing teammates. Maybe it was time to stop wishing for things to happen magically and do the work to fix what was keeping him from what he wanted. A family, love, the ability to *feel*. Maybe it was time to finally leave Ashna Raje behind.

Chapter Four

Ashi hated the idea of being left behind. There was this thing that happened in her chest when Mamma was about to leave, like giant hands were crushing her ribs. The need to stretch her neck and gulp air pushed at her, but she couldn't move because she was hiding.

Hiding behind curtains was never the smartest idea, but Ashi had found that you could hide anywhere without the fear of being found when no one cared about looking for you.

Still, she shrank into herself in her little alcove in the bay window of Baba's den.

"I will never let you use a child to tie me down." Mamma's voice had a way of getting deeper when she was angry. How many times had Ashi heard her mother say that the stereotype of the shrill woman had to be broken? That it was something the patriarchy used to prove us too emotional to care for ourselves? "Not that this marriage needs more deadweight to suffocate me."

Ashi's hand tightened around the curtain that hid her from her screaming parents. Actually, they weren't screaming, at least not yet, just hissing at each other in those muted whispers that adults used when they wanted to scream but couldn't.

"How can you say such a thing? How can you look at Ashi's face and think such a thing?" Baba sounded how he always sounded around Mamma—nothing like himself but like a spoiled child who was trying to sound grown-up.

Ashi loosened her grip on the fabric. Having the curtain collapse on her head would certainly give her away. If Mamma and Baba knew she had heard them, she'd never be able to face them again. The shame of knowing that her mother had never wanted her was bearable only so long as no one knew that Ashi knew. Shame had a way of multiplying when other people saw it. It made you naked and gross.

"This isn't about Ashi. Stop trying to use her. You put us in this situation. And now I get to make all the sacrifices. I get to be the mother who disrupts her life yet again, and you get your excuse to go off the rails and do what you do," Mamma said in her deepened voice. The slit between the thick velvet curtains exposed her in slivers, making her look as though she were being reflected in a broken mirror.

"In the end, that's all you want," Mamma continued. "To be His Highness Bram Raje, free to do whatever the hell your rotten heart desires. Don't pretend you care about Ashi. Anyone with half a brain can see that you only want her here so you can make me look bad. Everyone knows that the child babysits you more than the other way around. She's twelve, Bram. Have some shame!"

"You're abandoning your twelve-year-old again and you want me to have shame? At least I've never left her."

"Is getting drunk and passing out not abandoning her? Your brother and his wife had to take her in and you want me to have shame? This is the problem. You should have married a stupid woman, or at least one who lapped up your overentitled crap."

"If I'm such a bad father, you should stay here and protect her from me."

Mamma's hand went to her forehead, her gold bangles crashing together on her wrist. Even in America Mamma never bothered to remove her bangles or the big red bindi she wore in the center of her forehead. She always dressed like she was in the Sripore palace, no matter where she was. Always in her starched white saris, with her waist-length hair in a bun at her nape. She didn't care about fitting in or about not looking foreign, the way Ashna did when she dressed for school every day.

"How low can you fall, Bram? When will you stop using people this way? I don't leave her here with you, God knows I'm not that heartless. I leave her with Shree and Mina. Your brother and his wife are better parents to her than either one of us anyway. I'm the one who has to make the choice between my child and my work. You don't. You get to have both. You don't lose anything. Men never do. Your hands always stay clean."

"I lose you. I want you. And I don't get to keep you. I love you." Baba's slurring always got more pronounced as these arguments escalated and their voices got louder. The glass of scotch on the table between them wobbled as Ashi's vision blurred with tears.

"You bastard, I'm not a thing you get to keep. I begged you not to force me into this marriage. But you let them pack me up like a piece of meat and hand me to you. How is that love? If you knew what love meant you'd have cared what I wanted. You'd have seen that this could never work. Not just because I had already chosen my life partner, but because you and I have nothing in common, even without Omar."

Baba stood, swaying on his feet so much that Ashna almost left her spot to keep him from falling over the coffee table and crashing through the glass. But he sat back down, unable to bear his own weight. His voice boomed. "Do not say that man's name in my house. You hear me?"

Mom looked over her shoulder. "Keep your voice down! All that child needs now is to hear you bellowing at me. Already she hates me, blames me for this mess."

Ashi didn't. She didn't blame Mamma. Mamma was not the one who had tied her parents up in this mess. Ashi had done that. She was the one who couldn't be the kind of daughter who made her mother want to stay. She was the daughter who wasn't enough for her father to give up whatever it was he got from his scotch.

"What is wrong with the two of you?" Her aunt walked into the room and Ashi had the immediate sense that everything was going to be okay. "I could hear you shouting from the driveway. Where's Ashi?" She threw a glance at the window seat Ashi was hiding in and Ashi pulled herself back. "Seriously, Shobi, come on! Give a thought to what you're doing." She took Mamma's hand and patted it comfortingly.

"She's leaving again," Baba said, barely making the words.

"That was the deal," Mamma said. "We had a deal that I'd do three months here and three months there. But if he's going to make such a *tamasha* every time, how can I do this? How can I?"

Mina Kaki tucked a lock of Mamma's hair behind her ear. "You can't argue with him when he's like this. We'll figure it out in the morning. But you two can't do this with Ashna in the house. If you were going to have this conversation, you should have called me and I would have picked her up early. Where is she? Go look for her."

"I didn't mean to have the conversation. He started it." With that, Mamma left to look for Ashi.

"Bram, come on. Let's get you into bed." Mina Kaki called out to Aseem, Baba's valet, and he rushed into the room. "I've told you to call me when they start arguing. The next time you don't call, your employment here will be terminated." Her aunt was the sweetest person Ashi knew, but she could bring down a hammer like no one else.

Aseem made apologetic sounds and dragged Baba off the couch and into his study, where there was a daybed he used when no one could help him up the stairs to his room.

"I can't find Ashi anywhere," Mamma said, coming back into the room.

Mina Kaki stroked her arm. "I know where she is. Go up and calm down. I'll take care of it. She doesn't need to see you like this. Not just before you leave." She tried to whisper so Ashi wouldn't hear. She failed.

Mamma, who went to battle with everyone about everything, never argued with her sister-in-law. Especially not about Ashi. She left and Ashi quickly wiped her cheeks on the flannel sleeves of her pajamas. It was her first grown-up pair, pink plaid instead of the soccer ball and lollipop prints she used to wear. Mina Kaki had taken her shopping for them. Mina Kaki shopped for all her clothes, and Ashi had wanted pajamas just like her aunt's.

"Is it okay for me to come in?" Mina Kaki asked from the other side of the curtain.

Ashi let a sniff escape.

"I'm going to take that as a yes." Even so, Mina Kaki parted the curtain slowly, careful to allow Ashi a chance to pull it back if she wanted. But Ashi wanted nothing more than to crawl into her aunt's arms right now. She was cold. The cold was trembling inside her chest.

Mina sat down on the window seat next to her and ran a hand over Ashi's head. "I'm sorry."

Ashi wanted to tell her it wasn't her fault, but if she said anything she would never stop crying and she couldn't do that to her aunt. So when Mina Kaki pulled Ashna's head into her lap, she went easily.

Then, despite her best effort, she proceeded to wet her aunt's linen pants with her tears as her aunt stroked her hair.

For a long while they sat there without words, just the solidity of her aunt's lap beneath her cheek and the comforting rhythm of her hand on her hair.

When the tears slowed and Ashna sat up, Mina Kaki met her eyes, her warm, clear brown gaze fierce. "The only thing I want you to remember from anything that you heard today is this: It is not your fault. None of this is your fault, beta."

SOMETIMES ASHNA WONDERED how time hadn't touched her aunt at all. The Mina Kaki of her childhood had seamlessly transformed into the Mina Kaki of the present day. If anything, she'd become more energetic, thanks to her obsession with running marathons. Even her hair was the exact same color— rich, perfectly highlighted auburn—and the same length, a sharp-edged bob that skimmed her jaw, and no one ever saw her until she was impeccably dressed in perfectly fitted linen pants and tailored blouses. Their mother's seeming perfection was a point of amused frustration for her daughters, Trisha and Nisha, but to Ashna it was such a comforting cornerstone that the world fell back in place anytime she saw her aunt.

It wasn't like Mina Kaki to open the front door herself, but Ashna had called ahead instead of texting, which meant her aunt had heard something in her voice, which in turn meant that despite the placid calm on her face, Mina Kaki was freaking out on Ashna's behalf. Her overprotectiveness toward her children was legendary. Ashna wasn't certain of much, but the fact that Mina Kaki considered Ashna and her cousin Esha her own was an undisputable fact.

"I'm fine." Those were the first words she said when her aunt dropped a kiss on her cheek.

"I can see that." Mina Kaki would never do something as inelegant as rolling her eyes. She didn't need to because she could achieve the exact same effect with her tone. She had been a Bollywood actress before she married Ashna's uncle and moved to America more than thirty years ago, and her voice inflections were impressive things. "I've had tea sent to the upper floor. Let's head up there?"

The Anchorage, her aunt and uncle's estate, nestled in five acres of redwood forest in Woodside, was much more the home of Ashna's childhood than the bungalow she lived in. Ashna dropped off the bitter melon in the kitchen and followed her aunt up the stairs.

When Ashna had moved here from the Sripore palace at ten, a room decorated to match her room in Sripore had been waiting for her on the second floor. Ashna had lived here during the week and gone to school in Woodside. She'd spent the weekends with her father in Palo Alto. She'd only moved permanently into the bungalow after she returned from culinary school in Paris two years after Baba's death.

Her room in the Anchorage remained untouched to this day, same as her cousins' rooms. Although they all had their own places now, her aunt refused to entertain the fact that the Anchorage was not their primary home.

Yash, her aunt and uncle's oldest child, had been the first to move out. Or rather, he hadn't moved back home after college, as the traditionally Indian part of Mina Kaki's heart had wished. Yash was currently running for governor of California. So, the hope was that he'd be moving into the governor's mansion soon. That certainly made up for some of Mina Kaki's heartbreak over not having her children live at home.

Nisha, their older daughter, had been married for ten years

and lived in Los Altos Hills, and Trisha and DJ lived in a Palo Alto condo down the street from Ashna. Vansh, their youngest child, was always off traipsing across the world trying to search for things that made him feel useful. He was currently in Zimbabwe working on water filtration systems.

The only one of "the children" who still lived at home was Esha, Shree and Bram's oldest brother's daughter. Esha and their grandmother occupied a suite in the uppermost floor of the mansion. Esha hadn't left the estate in close to thirty years because of a condition where she couldn't handle any stimulation outside of what was familiar.

Every time Mina Kaki worried about Ashna, she tried to convince her to sell the Palo Alto bungalow. But the bungalow and Curried Dreams were all Ashna had left of Baba. Without them she had no idea who she'd even be. It was like asking her to cast off her body and rely on the promise that her soul would still be here. Or maybe it was like losing her soul and being left with only a body. Well, she'd never have to find out.

"Mom called," she said to her aunt as she followed her up the sweeping marble stairs. "To tell me about the Padma Shri."

Her aunt stopped midstep and studied Ashna as though she were an event spreadsheet from one of her fund-raisers.

"I'm happy for her," Ashna said, hoping like crazy that her voice sounded happy. "I really am."

"I know you are. It's huge." Pride flashed in Mina Kaki's eyes. She and Shobi were inexplicably close. Ashna had always wondered what someone who treated motherhood as sacredly as Mina Kaki did had in common with Shobi, who treated it like nothing more than bondage.

Mina Kaki sank down on the spotless marble staircase and Ashna sat down next to her.

"She wants me to come to India and speak at the ceremony."

"That's nice, right?" Mina Kaki took Ashna's hand.

"She wants me to shut down the restaurant, move there, and get involved in her work."

The pressure of Mina Kaki's grip on Ashna's hand tightened. "Shobi said that to you?" Irritation slipped into her voice.

"I said no."

That got Ashna a tilt of the head. An impressed and slightly disbelieving tilt. "And Shobi agreed?"

"Well," Ashna chewed her lower lip. "I told her I'm working on a Food Network show."

"No!" Mina Kaki threw her head back and laughed. "I can't believe Trisha and China pulled that off."

"They came to you first to try to convince me?" Of course Trisha would try that first. Trisha knew Ashna would do it if Mina Kaki asked her. But Mina Kaki must have refused, and that made Ashna want to hug her aunt.

Her aunt smiled. "Trisha really wants DJ to do that hosting gig. But she also believes it's the perfect solution for Curried Dreams."

"I know. I don't think I can do it, though," Ashna said.

Her aunt pulled her hand to her lips and dropped a kiss on her knuckles. "Are you joking? You're going to be spectacular. You've done far harder things."

Ashna's only response was a twist of the mouth.

Her aunt cupped her cheek. "The real question is, do you *want* to do it?" She paused, weighing her next words carefully.

"You have to start giving a little more thought to what you want, Ashi."

Ashna pulled her hand away. She didn't want her aunt to feel her hands go clammy.

"You don't have to figure that out right now. Just think about it, that's all."

Ashna wondered if she would bring up selling Curried Dreams, or offer to bail her out again. Like everyone else in her life, Mina Kaki believed that Ashna's obsession with Baba's restaurant was unhealthy. Ashna knew they meant well, but they didn't understand. Her family was everything to her, but Curried Dreams was hers and hers alone. She had to be the one to save it.

"Trisha is right," Ashna said. "It could help pay off the debt on Curried Dreams once and for all. Give me a clean slate if I win."

Mina Kaki blinked as though Ashna had spoken a foreign language.

She stood and pulled Ashna up to standing. "Well then, you're doing this."

They ran up the remaining stairs—Mina Kaki, probably because she was excited, Ashi, because moving helped curb her anxiety.

"Ashi is going to be a TV star!" Mina announced as they emerged into the suite of rooms Ashna's grandmother and her cousin Esha shared.

Aji, Esha, and Nisha were lounging on the white leather sectional and turned to Mina and Ashna as though that announcement were a simple hello.

The first thing Ashna did was lean over and squeeze her grandmother in a hug.

"It's been a full week!" Aji said indignantly, returning her hug. It was her way; she always counted off how many days it had been since she saw her grandchildren. She also always exaggerated the time. It had been five days since Ashna had been by to see her. But of course it was futile to point that out, because Aji would only tell her that five days was a working week, or that it felt like seven days, or something else no one in their right mind would argue with.

Instead, she said, "Sorry, I thought about coming to see you every day"—the truth—"but a lot's been going on at the restaurant."

Sadness flickered in Aji's eyes. She was the only one in the family who saw the value in holding on to Curried Dreams. It was a link to her youngest child. "A lot should always be going on at one's workplace," she said with a smile that crinkled her nose.

Ashna hugged Nisha, who stood to display her adorable baby bump, which seemed to have doubled since Ashna had seen her last, then turned to Esha to see if she was up for a hug. She wasn't, but she squeezed Ashna's hand and made one of her declarations. "Being in public needs armor."

Wasn't that the truth. Esha wasn't just incredibly wise; she was also clairvoyant. There was no armor from her sight, and what she saw always came true. Ashna had a sense that Esha not only saw but also felt her pain, no matter how hard Ashna tried to hide it. She sat down next to Esha, careful not to touch her except for the firm grip Esha's soft hand still had on hers.

Esha had suffered seizures ever since the plane crash she'd been in when she was eight. The accident had killed the other thirty passengers on the family's private jet, including Esha's parents. Esha had been the miraculous sole survivor. No one could explain how that had happened, or why the seizures and visions had started after.

HRH and Mina Kaki had brought Esha to California before word of her clairvoyance leaked out of the Sripore palace. Just the rumors had caused lines to form outside the palace gates for one look at the "Little Goddess" even as the poor *little goddess* went into seizure after seizure at the least stimulation.

Staying within the Anchorage estate and restricting contact to only the family had finally minimized the seizures.

"So, what is this about being a TV star?" Esha said with mischief in her smile.

Nisha poured tea from Aji's china service, a blend Ashna mixed specially for her grandmother that she called "Aji's Hug," and Ashna found herself smiling as she filled them in on China and Trisha's midnight visit and offer.

"I'm so glad you've decided to do it." Nisha rubbed her belly. She'd had to slow down her work. With her history of miscarriages, she was being cautious. It had to be hard given that she ran Yash's campaign and the election was less than a year away, with the California primary nipping at their heels.

"Have you found someone to help you with the campaign yet?" Ashna asked, only partially deflecting. She wished she could help, but strategy and politics were alien to her. Asking people why they wouldn't vote for the best man they would ever meet in their pathetic lives was not a workable approach.

Nisha let out a long-suffering sigh and popped one of their grandmother's ladoos into her mouth. "The last guy who seemed promising tried to 'handle' Yash. He also tried to tell him that his policies were too complex for the simpleminded voter. You can imagine how that went."

Yash's theory was that people rose to the levels you expected of them. Ashna wasn't sure that was true; she was certain it wasn't how recent political campaigns had worked. But Yash knew what he was doing, and he would only do things the way he believed they should be done, not in ways that would get him elected.

That was why she had the urge to shake anyone who didn't get him. Definitely a terrible strategy.

"We'll know when the right person comes along. Yash knows what he's looking for," Mina Kaki said with the kind of certainty that dissipated every iota of doubt in Ashna's mind about the existence of such a paragon who combined strategic wizardry, ideological integrity, and the family's nonnegotiable requirement: trustworthiness.

"Until then, I can totally handle it," Nisha said, part bravado, part desperation. "So long as I don't have to travel."

"Only, you can't run a gubernatorial campaign without running from district to district at the drop of a hat." This from Esha. Such an uncharacteristic thing for their ethereal cousin to say that they all burst into laughter.

"What?" Esha said, her always peaceful face quirking with

humor. "It's time for Nisha to loosen the reins." She patted Nisha's hand when Nisha pouted. "Don't worry. The person you're waiting for is almost here."

There, that was much more like Esha. All would have been well with the universe had Esha not reached over and patted Ashna's hand too, as though the words were also meant for Ashna.

Chapter Five

As a child, Rico had always had a hard time with waiting. Patience had not been his best virtue. As an adult, he prided himself on his composure. He'd worked hard to harness his restlessness, focus it, and set an example of decency and grace on and off the pitch—a tribute to his father, whose sportsmanship was just as legendary as his football moves. Right now, however, waiting to get his cast off was making Rico so restless that he had visualized himself ripping it off with his bare hands more than a few times.

It had been just a couple of days since he'd been back in London, but waiting another day for it to come off felt like pure torture. If he didn't stop pacing (okay, hobbling) around his flat, he was going to cut a trail in the floor. Kneading the knot at the nape of his neck, he made his way onto the balcony. Usually, the perfectly synchronous white facades of Kensington calmed him. Today, the sun was too bright, a complaint another Londoner might smack him upside the head for. He went back inside and held down the button that pulled the shades. They descended far too slowly.

My impatient baby. He heard his mother's voice in his head.

His mãe had loved to tell stories of how Rico gobbled down all the brigadeiro before she could get the condensed milk truffles molded into balls.

Then a time had come when his impatience had dissipated in the blink of an eye. Everything had dissipated when his mãe and pai left home one evening to go to the movies and never came back. Well, they had come back, but in closed coffins because the car crash hadn't left much of them. Everything had stopped that day and never quite started up again.

Rico had entered a fog that felt like glue, viscous and sticky around him. One moment he'd been in a hurry to rush from thing to thing—football, friends, school—then the next moment it had all vanished. There had been nowhere to go, nothing he needed to get to. That's how it had stayed as he moved, seemingly in slow motion, from Rio de Janeiro to his mãe's sister's house in California. She had been his only living relative. At least the only living relative who acknowledged him. His father's family had never acknowledged his mãe and him.

His pai had met his mãe in England while playing for Man U. He had asked her to go to Rio with him after he retired, and she had. He had asked her to keep their relationship quiet, and she had. If the fact that he never left his wife bothered her, she never showed it. She had once told Rico that she would do anything his pai asked of her. Because that's what love meant.

At fifteen Rico had still needed a legal guardian, and that meant leaving his home and moving to California. Not that he cared where he moved. His ability to care about anything at all had also vanished.

That's how it had stayed until he'd stopped a ball from hitting a girl on the head. Then everything had changed again. Almost everything. His impatience, his burning need to get to the next thing, hadn't come back. Not until he made his way to England and found football again.

Being dumped by someone you believed to be the love of your life because her family thought you were worthless had a way of shaking you out of the thickest stupor. Over the past decade, Rico had left that heartbroken boy so far behind that he barely recognized him in his own memories. At least, that's what he had believed until Zee's bachelor party. Apparently his young self was more tenacious than Rico gave him credit for.

Dropping onto the couch, he turned on his laptop. Out of habit he scanned the tabloids to make sure there were no fires to put out. Things had gotten batshit crazy with the guys at the bachelor party. Journalists had caught wind of it, and some employees from the venue had leaked information. Rico had spent all day yesterday negotiating with media outlets, releasing curated pictures of the party and throwing in videos and sound bites from Zee and Tanya about their wedding to keep the illegally taken pictures out. Information was power, and controlling how you disseminated it was the difference between disaster and adulation.

Being the public face of his team for years meant Rico could divert scandal in his sleep. He reminded himself that it wasn't his job anymore. That meant the team was going to have to find another face. But hell if he was going to let the tabloids make a mockery out of his best mate's wedding.

After making sure that the paps had kept their end of the bargain, Rico skimmed the news. In America, the California primary race was gathering steam. Yash Raje's name caught his eye. The candidate's speech at the last Democratic convention was possibly the most exciting thing Rico had heard in politics in decades. He inhaled the piece about how the candidate had used a wheelchair for a few years as a teen.

Rico had to laugh. Now that he had let the portal to his younger self open, everything seemed to lead right back there. Ashna had rarely talked about her family, but her cousin's accident had still been fresh back then and Rico remembered her telling him about how the doctors had declared that Yash would never walk again and how he had refused to believe them.

Yash's quote should have sounded like the usual politician drivel about being able to overcome anything, about the human spirit and its power, yada yada. Only, the man had a way of making you believe it. *The one thing my parents taught me was that only you can fix what you know to be wrong.*

"It's what my parents taught me too, mate," Rico said to his laptop.

In all these years he hadn't googled her, or kept track of her. He'd put all his attention into his game. Into proving her words about him wrong.

Don't you see? When you look at it from my father's point of view, you have no future.

Well, he'd ended up proving her father wrong, hadn't he? Even a washed-up prince too full of himself to see that they didn't live in the eighteenth century anymore would have to admit that Rico's future had turned out rather spectacularly.

He had returned to California only once, to bury his aunt. If the guys hadn't wanted to throw Zee the mother of all clichés, Rico would never have gone back to the US at all. And his head would never have turned inside out. The day after the party, he thought he had set it straight again. He'd come home. He'd tried to stop thinking about her and everything she had taken from him.

Moving his laptop to his lap, he propped his leg on the coffee table. On the surface, what he was contemplating seemed like a terrible idea; he was fully aware of that. This wasn't him googling an ex. What he was doing was actively working on bringing closure to something he had ignored for too long.

Look at where it had landed him. Thirty years old with a string of lovely women who hadn't stayed with him because he didn't know how to give them what they needed. Every one of his exes was happily married to someone else. Actually, strike that, not *every* one of them. He had no idea what the girl who had set him on the path of "emotional unavailability" was up to.

He could imagine her as a society wife. Married to some doctor, or corporate bigwig, or lawyer, someone her father considered appropriate.

How had he gotten her so wrong? It was a question he hadn't asked himself in a very long time. His fingers hesitated only another second before typing her name into the magic box that was Google.

The first thing that came up was her father's restaurant, Curried Dreams. Apparently she ran it now. Had the old bastard retired? Executive chef, indeed! Who would have thought Green Brook High's star goalkeeper would be off making tandoori chicken? He certainly had not seen that coming. She'd wanted nothing to do with cooking. The picture of her was fuzzy, something someone had taken from a distance without her permission, but the bearing was unmistakable.

Next, Rico's eyes landed on an *Entertainment Weekly* link about a new show on Food Network. Ashna on TV? He supposed she'd grown out of her obsession with privacy and her shyness off the pitch. Getting her to take a picture for the yearbook with the girls' soccer team had been hard enough. She was going to be on TV? Really?

The calm that spread through him as he scrolled through the piece was impressive. Time was a healer after all, because he felt nothing.

The article said she was going to be one of the professional chefs who was going to team up with a celebrity and compete with five other pairs to win one hundred thousand dollars. It was all a bit crass for the Rajes.

"All I've ever wanted was to be a chef, so this is a dream come true!" Something about the quote made him want to toss his laptop across the room. He slammed it shut and pushed himself off the couch. Anger rolled in his chest. He was pacing again. Hobbling like a bloody idiot.

The last thing she had ever wanted to be was a chef.

Rico never let himself get angry. At least not angry enough to raise his heart rate and heat his earlobes.

Before he could talk himself out of it, he picked up his phone and dialed Rod.

Yes, having an agent with a name like that was a bit of a ridiculous cliché as well, but Rod was the best Hollywood sports agent and Rico happened to be in a position where he had access to the best. Rod was responsible for the fact that Rico had been one of Calvin Klein's longest-serving under-wear models. At first he'd done it on a dare, but he didn't mind the money it brought in.

"Hey, Rico, my man, how's the knee?" Rod boomed, be-cause his name wasn't the only cliché about him.

"You know anything about Food Network shows?"

"Okay, let's skip the small talk, then. Food Network is be-coming bigger than it's ever been. But no, I've never worked with them. Anything in particular you want to know about?"

"Yes, they have a new show, *Cooking with the Stars*. I want to be on it. As one of the celebrities."

There was a full minute of silence. Which was a good thing, because, holy bloody hell on toast, what was he doing?

This was probably the first time in his life that anyone had made Rod Singh speechless.

"Why?" Rod managed finally.

A brilliant question.

Rico dropped back on the couch. "I'm tired of modeling underwear. I think it's time to learn some cooking." And be-cause anger was still hammering in his heart and heating his ears from that quote and that picture, and the shit ton of memo-ries exploding inside his head.

"No, seriously. Is this a dare, like the Calvin Klein thing?"

"Something like that."

"I don't think they can afford you. Let me ask around, but I'm guessing it's more for failed boy band stars, retired soap opera actors, struggling comedians, authors who are looking for sales. That sort of thing. Too far beneath your pay grade." You had to love agents. Rico said a grateful prayer for his.

"I don't need to be paid. If we win I'll donate my part to that animal rescue your little girl couldn't stop talking about the last time you brought her to London. How does that sound?"

"The second half sounds great. Ami will be thrilled. But not the first part. We're not doing unpaid gigs."

"Fine. Work it out any way you want. You can get your commission and we'll give the rest to the charity. I don't give a shit, Rod. Just make it happen."

"Are you feeling all right, Rico? I know the surgeries and retirement suck. But listen, we're flush with offers. If you're open to reality TV, we have a hundred options. I can get you on *Big Brother.*"

Rico would rather stab himself with an ice pick, in the knee even. "I know I just threw you, so I'm going to let the *Big Brother* comment slide. But if you bring me any reality shows other than this, you're fired."

"Right. I'm terrified. But okay, no reality shows except something on"—he cleared his throat—"Food Network."

"Nope, not *something* on Food Network. *Cooking with the Stars.*"

"Got it. Anything else?"

"Yup. I need to be partnered with a particular chef."

Chapter Six

Ashna rummaged through her jewelry drawer. The only way she could get through meeting the celebrity she would be partnered with was to wear the ruby earrings her grandmother had given her when she moved to America. Aji had worn them when she met Ashna's grandfather for the first time. They were supposed to help with new beginnings. And, well, today was the day for them. It had been three weeks since she had called China and said yes. A wasted call, because China had assumed that's what Ashna would do and sent out the press release already.

The earrings were sitting next to a mother-of-pearl box in the far corner of the drawer. With a shaking finger, Ashna traced the gold inlaid roses on the box. Inside it, Shobi's engagement ring sat ensconced in folds of white satin. Ashna had dug the ring out of the garbage after Baba had dropped it there after the last fight Ashna had witnessed between her parents.

"Everything okay up there?" Trisha and Nisha bellowed

from downstairs in one voice. The Raje girls bellowing, a historical day indeed.

"Almost done," Ashna bellowed back, because why not? She hooked the rubies into her earlobes.

Nisha was the keeper of the family's fashion profile. Which meant none of them had developed the ability to go out into the world on important days without Nisha picking out their clothes, whether it be for weddings or job interviews. Except the ruby-red prom dress that hung at the very back of Ashna's closet. Nisha had no hand in buying that one. Her family didn't even know she had gone to prom, or that her date had bought her that dress.

If Ashna had a penny for every time she had thought about burning the dress, she could have paid off Curried Dreams's debts. Now that she had come unhinged and was doing things that were drastically out of character for her, maybe she'd finally get around to it. Burn the dress, burn the betrayal that went with it.

Goose bumps prickled across her skin, and she rubbed her arms. When would this stop? This sudden jolt of memory at the most unexpected times. The worst possible thing for her to do right now, just before the filming crew arrived at Curried Dreams to shoot her first meeting with her celebrity, was think about any of that.

Shutting the drawer, she gave herself one last inspection in the mirror.

Nisha had picked out heather-gray trousers for her to go with the red chef's jacket that all the chefs were going to wear on the show. A stroke of luck, because red was Ashna's favorite color and it always made her feel just a bit stronger. Nisha had tried to convince her not to pull her waist-length hair back into a bun. But they were shooting in the kitchen, and Ashna would never leave her hair down in a kitchen. Her bun was, as usual, as wide as her neck and so heavy that her head felt weighed down with it. Given that she had never had hair shorter than this, her head should be used to the weight by now. Not unlike the mind, the body could get used to living with things without becoming entirely comfortable with them.

Ashna had often considered cutting her hair. Freeing herself from this thing that everyone who had ever loved her seemed to define her by. Maybe when she burned the prom dress she'd also cut her hair and sell Shobi's ring and donate the money to her mother's beloved foundation and then tell her what she'd done.

Yup, she had definitely come unhinged. Although, amazingly, she felt entirely calm. So calm, in fact, that it was almost disconcerting. She shook out her hands, then patted down her hair and smudged the black kohl she had lined around her eyes. Kohl made her already freakishly large eyes expand to nocturnal-animal proportions. She touched up her favorite red lipstick. The show was about how she cooked, not how she looked, she knew that, but she needed every piece of armor. Not that it would help her get around the little problem of passing out when faced with a cooking challenge.

She lifted up her chef's jacket and reapplied deodorant, then touched a dot of rosewater behind her ears. There wasn't actually going to be any kind of real cooking happening today as far as she knew, so a hint of perfume wouldn't hurt. Plus, the special rosewater that was extracted at the Sripore palace was designed specifically to not interfere with your normal olfactory functioning like the oil-based perfumes they sold in stores.

Finally done, she found Nisha and Trisha standing at the bottom of the stairs, obviously contemplating having to go up and drag her down.

"We should be at Curried Dreams by now," Nisha said in her big-sister voice. She was Mina Kaki's mini-me. Poised to a fault but somehow also incredibly warm.

Both sisters tucked strands of Ashna's hair that had come loose from her bun behind her ear, a favorite Raje gesture for showing affection.

"Stop it! Stop acting like it's my wedding day. You're making me nervous."

"You're wearing trousers and chef's robes. I think Aji and Ma might have a coronary if you even thought about getting married in that," Trisha said.

Since Ashna was never, ever planning to marry—given her genetic predisposition for failure—she'd never have to think about what kind of wedding dress would not give her aunt and grandmother joint coronaries.

"You look lovely," Nisha said.

"You have nothing to be nervous about," Trisha added with the confidence of someone who wasn't about to make a complete ass of herself on camera.

"I let you talk me into going on television and competing with some of the best chefs in the country with an unknown and possibly crazy celebrity. Why on earth would I be nervous?" Ashna said.

Trisha looked not the least bit guilty. "Stop it. You're going to rock this, and DJ will be on the set with you."

Ashna laughed. "In that case how can it be anything but amazing? I mean, who would not embrace public humiliation just to spend time with your DJ?" Never in a million years would Ashna have imagined that her impatient, entirely too self-sufficient cousin would be so moony over someone. Honestly, though, Trisha was right; having DJ on set was the only comforting thing in this entire nerve-racking mess.

"I'm dying to know who your celebrity is," Nisha said, heading to the back door. "Do you think it will be one of those NFL players? They're my favorites on *Dancing with the Stars.*"

"Yes! There's nothing quite like a big man being dainty," Trisha said as all three Raje girls picked their shoes off the shelf and slid them on.

"Ugh, no athletes, please. This isn't a contest of endurance or strength. Or, um, daintiness?" Ashna adjusted the strap on her kitten-heeled sandals. She had considered wearing sneakers, as she usually did in the kitchen, but it was just introduction day, so why not?

"Maybe one of those ex–boy band types. A Jonas brother? Who was the cute one?" Nisha conjured a brow brush out of thin air and gave Ashna's eyebrows a sweep as Trisha held the door open.

Sunshine flooded into the house. Early spring in Palo Alto used to be Ashna's favorite time of year. Before it became the season of bad memories and she forgot how to love it. Yearning for the simplicity of a love like that—for the way light filtered through trees, for the smell of air saturated with possibility—unfolded inside her.

"Nick?" Trisha tucked her arm into Ashna's and pulled the door shut behind them.

They followed Nisha, who was pregnant-waddling purposefully down the path that led to the gate in the fence.

"Nope. Nick's out. He just married Priyanka Chopra so he's too big for this now," Nisha threw over her shoulder. "The other cute Jonas, the one with the great hair."

"I'm pretty certain it's not going to be any of the Jonas brothers." Could it be, though? She hated not knowing. She had begged China to tell her, but of course China's favorite line at the moment was "I'll lose my job."

Trisha made a face. "I've been badgering DJ about it. Either he doesn't know or he won't tell me. You know what's annoying? I can't figure out which it is, and he loves that. Do you think there's something wrong with British men?"

Nisha and Ashna rolled their eyes.

"You just want us to tell you again how perfect we think DJ is," Ashna said.

Trisha's response was a dreamy grin.

As they cleared the thicket of jacarandas and got to the deliveries parking lot, Nisha's phone beeped. "It's China. They're on their way. We have to be inside before she gets here with your star. Hurry up."

"Eeek! Is the star with her now? Ask her, ask her!" Trisha grabbed Nisha's phone "WHO IS IT??? TELL US!" Trisha read off as she typed in all caps. Nisha jumped up and down, baby bump and all.

They stared at the screen, waiting for a response.

Can't tell you. But . . . S C O R E!!!

Yes, China had put a space between each letter. Given China's legendary texting laziness, that made the butterflies in Ashna's belly turn into bats.

"What on earth is that supposed to mean?" How had Ashna thought herself calm? Now she couldn't even think the word *calm* without getting light-headed.

Trisha linked arms with Ashna. "Let's get in there and find out."

Nisha took her other arm and the three of them marched across the parking lot. They had walked down this path thousands of times, but Ashna had never before been this conscious of each step.

A Food Network van was parked by the ramp. The crew was already in her kitchen, and the door was propped open.

The bats in her belly grew rabid. Her heart had never beat quite this hard.

"It's going to be a sweet southern grandma," she muttered. "God, please."

"What?" both sisters said together without pausing in their march.

"I've had my fingers crossed for a sweet southern grandma–type celebrity. It's my best shot." She had been chanting it to the universe. *Please, please, all I need is a sweet southern grandma.* Not to deal in stereotypes, but maybe a southern grandma would know what she was doing enough that Ashna might not need to cook in front of the cameras at all. "I told China that I wanted a sweet southern grandma as my celebrity. So, 'S C O R E' has to mean she found me one, right?"

Nisha and Trisha shook their heads at her and disappeared into the kitchen. Ashna followed them, mentally chanting the shlokas Aji had taught her for when she needed to calm down.

There was equipment everywhere, lights and cameras on giant stands. Trisha and Nisha were already introducing themselves to the crew.

Only today's meeting with her star would be shot in the Curried Dreams kitchen. The actual show was going to be filmed on a set in San Francisco over five weeks. Two episodes a week—a cooking episode shot over two days and an elimination episode, and then a grand finale with the two teams that made it that far. A young man in a hat that said FOOD NETWORK and a very Secret Service–looking earpiece jogged up to Ashna. "I'm Jonah," he said with an excited smile. "They have your star circling the block. We want to get some anticipation footage of you waiting to see who it is."

He snapped his fingers and everything lit up like a movie set. Suddenly Ashna's kitchen felt nothing like her kitchen. She took it in, mouth slightly agape, and tried to contain her nervousness.

"Perfect!" Jonah grinned at her as though she'd somehow given him the exact expression he'd been hoping for. "Can you go in and pretend it's just another day? How about chopping something. Maybe vegetables?"

"You want her to chop vegetables and *pretend* it's just another day?" Trisha said with all the drollness of someone who was not being asked to act normal. Whatever the hell that even meant. "I think she has the acting chops for that."

"Great!" this Jonah person said with disturbing alacrity, and zero awareness of Trisha's sarcasm. "That's what I thought. Let's find you some vegetables!" He headed off to the pantry.

At this point Ashna's ears started ringing so loudly that she had to focus hard on what people were saying because she could barely hear them.

"This was a terrible idea. What the hell was I thinking?" she whispered as she walked across her kitchen to where Jonah had found her stash of bitter melons. *Please don't touch those*, she was about to say, but he bounced away and managed to find a chopping board and placed it on the prep counter.

Nisha stroked Ashna's back. "You're going to do great. This celebrity person is lucky to have you." She tucked the lock of hair that always came loose from Ashna's bun behind her ear again.

Jonah opened and shut a few drawers, then pulled out the biggest meat cleaver from Ashna's knife drawer. That thing could sever a lamb shoulder as though it were butter and he was handling it like it was a toy.

"This should work for your . . ." He threw a baffled look at the vegetable. "Odd-looking cucumbers."

If Ashna weren't fighting off rampaging panic, she would have smiled. "They're bitter melons." She had no idea where that very-uppity-chef-like tone had come from, because that was not her at all. "You want me to chop vegetables with a meat cleaver? Are you sure you work for the Food Network?" Ashna took the cleaver from him with the care it deserved.

To his credit, Jonah looked sheepish. "I just started last week. I was with National Geographic before that."

Ashna didn't know what to do with that information so she walked to the knife drawer and switched the cleaver out for her biggest santoku.

"That one's impressive too. It'll work!" Jonah said.

Glad you approve, Ashna wanted to say, but panic and snark weren't mixing inside her today. "It's a Misono santoku," she said instead.

These knives were Baba's prized possessions.

The smooth wood of the handle filled her hand and brought her back to this moment. She was doing something different this time. Not repeating the same thing and expecting different results. Given how much people loved tossing out that advice, it had to work. The blade caught the gleam of the camera lights.

"Go ahead and get started on the chopping here, and he will walk in through there." Jonah waved his hands and positioned Ashna where he wanted her. Then he started to arrange things on the countertop so the camera picked them up.

Okay, so the celebrity was a he. That meant no grandma. Ugh.

"She will be fine," Trisha said, pushing Jonah away from Ashna so he wasn't crowding her.

Ashna pulled a breath all the way to the center of her, the way India, her yoga instructor and Northern California's foremost stress management therapist, had taught her. India was China's big sister and Ashna needed to go see her right now.

Jonah herded Trisha and Nisha to the other side of the

room. Then he pressed his finger into his earpiece in a gesture so theatrical that, of all things, that's what made Ashna smile.

For the first time that day she relaxed. Shifting her focus to the familiar motion of the knife, she started slicing the bitter melon into slivers.

"Okay, and we're rolling," Jonah said. "Just remember to be yourself. Don't worry about the cameras." Which was not something you ever said when you didn't want someone to worry about cameras.

He turned to the door, and with no more warning than that it flew open.

Time did a backflip.

For the longest breath the world around Ashna disappeared. Then it slammed back into her chest and all the oxygen left the room.

A vise clamped around Ashna's lungs. Cold sweat broke across her forehead. She raised her elbow to wipe it. The knife's blade gleamed at the edge of her vision, and the heavy wooden handle started to slide from her hand. She tightened her grip.

Breathe.

The man, at once broad and limber, strolled toward her, his stride lazy. As lazy and graceful as it had ever been. Reflective sunglasses covered his eyes, completely obscuring them. Dark hair was pulled back from his face in a bun. Thick, perfectly trimmed stubble highlighted the sharp lines of his jaw. How she even recognized him she had no idea. He looked entirely different, yet so familiar that the vise tightened around her lungs.

Her elbow was still pressed into her forehead. Frozen there.

He stuck out his hand, that too-wide, too-finely-etched mouth pressed tightly together, his tell that things weren't as boring as his body language suggested.

The knife slipped from Ashna's grip.

Screams erupted around them. The blade flashed in the lights as it fell, pointed tip down, toward Ashna's sandal-clad feet.

A ball spun across the air, slicing through years in an instant. A hand reached out to catch it. The hand closed around the handle, missing the blade by a breath just as the tip scratched the leather of her sandal. Without touching her skin.

He was on his knees at her feet, knife held in one hand like a ninja. His sunglasses had gone flying as he leaped. Breath panted from his mouth—the only sound Ashna could hear—as golden eyes met hers, the green flecks on fire. They were still edged in thick spiky lashes, still one slightly smaller than the other, still stunning enough to steal her breath.

"You okay?" The voice floated up across the years. A thunderclap of emotions spun those years into a tornado around them. Ashna fell to her knees in front of him, almost grabbed his face the way she had done the first time she kissed him.

Pain flooded his eyes, yanking her back to her kitchen, to the clang of the knife on the floor next to them. To the pandemonium of voices asking—demanding—to know how he was . . . how she was . . . what the hell had just happened? But the pain in his eyes—

"You're in pain," she said, springing to her feet and grabbing his arm. "Someone help him up. He's hurt himself." His eyes squeezed shut as Jonah grabbed his other arm, and together they helped him up, but he couldn't straighten his leg. Obviously couldn't put weight on it.

"Someone call 911," she shouted, then remembered that Trisha was a doctor. "Trisha! Where's Trisha? Someone get Trisha—"

"Relax," he said, steadying her with those kaleidoscope eyes. "Breathe."

"I'm here." Trisha squatted down in front of him and reached for his leg. "I'm a doctor. Hi. Dr. Trisha Raje. May I?"

He nodded at Trisha, then threw a quick look at Ashna again, which didn't help her breathe at all. "I'm fine. I just landed on my stitches."

Ashna's heart spasmed.

From across the kitchen Nisha mouthed, *What the hell was that?*

"I'm going to have to cut that. The pant, not the leg." How could Trisha joke right now? But he smiled.

Ashna handed her a pair of shears. Trisha cut the fabric, exposing one massively muscled calf. He'd always had the most beautiful legs. The most beautiful body. The most beautiful—

His knee was swelling so fast it looked like it might burst. A fleshy pink scar edged in angry red staple marks stretched at its seams. In his eyes was pure agony.

Trisha pushed the denim out of the way and examined the knee. "We need to get you to the ER. There's internal bleeding. They'll have to drain it," she said as though talking about scooping seeds out of bitter melon. "That was spectacular, by the way. I think you saved Ashna's toes."

"Pleasure?" he said in that way he'd always had of turning everything into a question.

I love you?

Who made words like that sound like a question?

"I am so sorry," she said, her voice shaking despite her best effort, everything inside her shaking.

"No apology necessary," he said. Then his voice tipped suddenly low and cold. "Not for this."

Just like that he was a stranger again, a stranger who had just slid across her kitchen floor on his hurt knee.

The way his gaze touched hers was the opposite of his voice. In his eyes was every bit of the knowing they had shared.

Ashna stepped away from him. Suddenly she was shaking for a whole different reason. He was wrong; this was the only thing he deserved an apology for. Every other apology was his to give. Not that all the apologies in the world would change anything.

"The ambulance is here," Jonah shouted across the kitchen.

Paramedics wheeled a gurney into the kitchen and helped him onto it. They threw out a string of questions about what had happened, his pain level, the kind of surgery. He answered patiently, his lips barely moving because his jaw was clenched in pain.

Trisha supplied medical-sounding words that turned distorted at the edges in Ashna's ears. The room floated as though she were underwater watching it undulate.

"It's a good thing we're barely a mile from Stanford Hospital. They should have you fixed and good to go before it gets worse," Trisha said.

At this point his knee resembled a small melon, a very angry melon with a scar that looked ready to rip open. But the initial blast of agony was gone from his eyes. It had to have taken an insane effort, but he had himself well under control.

Ashna's hand tightened on the stainless-steel countertop. She wanted to step closer to the gurney and ease the pain he thought he was hiding. The thought made her livid at herself.

His eyes searched for something. Her gaze followed his to the floor and found his sunglasses wedged under a cabinet. Picking up the aviators, she handed them to him, careful not to let their fingers touch, even as he avoided touching hers.

In one quick motion he covered his eyes, and the mix of steady green and volatile gold disappeared behind the reflective blue.

When they started to roll him away, Ashna tried to follow, but the front of her sandal slid off her foot and hung from it like a dog's tongue. The strap had been sliced almost right through, and the last bit of leather holding it together came apart. If his reflexes hadn't been what they were, she might have had a few toes missing right now.

Then again, if his reflexes hadn't been what they were, her life would not have taken the turn it had all those years ago.

Ashna watched them wheel the gurney out. The rest of the crew, and her cousins, followed. Only Jonah stayed back, fluttering around the kitchen looking strangely excited. Then he followed too.

He was almost out the door when he stopped, slapped a

hand to his forehead, and turned to Ashna. "Shit, he never got a chance to introduce himself. That was Frederico Silva, the legendary striker for Manchester United."

Car engines fired in the parking lot. A single siren blast rang through the air, then dropped into silence. Jonah ran out the door.

Ashna sank to the floor, shrinking back into the cabinets and under the countertops. "I know," she whispered into her suddenly empty kitchen. "I know exactly who he is."

Chapter Seven

W hat are you hiding from?" It was a strange question
coming from someone you didn't know. Too intimate
for a first conversation, especially if you were huddled under bleachers. So intimate, in fact, that a person couldn't be
blamed for losing her heart to it.

Then again, maybe it wasn't those words that stole Ashna's
heart. Maybe it was the strangely shaped eyes, one slightly
smaller than the other, and the utter lack of feeling in them as
he said those words. A question so personal with not a flicker
of anything.

Nothing.

Ashna watched eyes. Studied them. As Green Brook High's
star goalkeeper, scanning eyes and body language across the
pitch was what she did. A goal took seed long before the ball
hit the net, stretching it back against its knots. Or in her case,
before her gloved hands slapped around the ball before it got
near that sacred net. This season alone she had prevented
forty goals.

His eyes held nothing.

Whose eyes held nothing?

Whose clear—what color were his eyes? She couldn't tell in the shadows—held nothing? At first she thought they looked almost black, like her own. Then she scooted out from her crouch under the bleachers and he straightened up, and the beam of stadium lights fell across his face. Emeralds glinted in the shadows.

There was this stained-glass window in the Sagar Mahal, the Sripore palace that had been Ashna's home until she was ten, all in shades of green. Glass chips from the palest jade to the deepest moss and everything in between. Gold filigree edged each piece. At night the glass pieces seemed lifeless. In the day, the sun infused them with light, turning them into gemstones so luminous Ashna could stare at them for hours, mesmerized.

"Hello?" He waved his hand in front of her face. "Did you have a seizure or something? Are you OD-ing?"

"OD-ing?" Yes, that was the first word she ever said to him. In the two and a half years that followed—the best years of her life—he would insist it's what swept him off his feet. That absurd word, said with enough incredulousness to cover all the questions she'd had at the sight of the first person who had found her in a hiding place she'd counted on for a year and a half without being found.

The real miracle was that she had never doubted that she really had done that. Swept the most beautiful boy she'd ever seen off his feet. How could she have doubted it, when the air became saturated with sensation every time they got near each other? The earth softened beneath her feet when he laughed. Eyes that had seemed lifeless until that laugh filled them with light, Fourth of July fireworks over the bay.

"I'm not hiding," she said with all the indignation of a liar. Then, just to prove it, she stepped out from under the bleachers, dusting off her soccer shorts and jersey.

It was safe now anyway. Her teammates were gone. She usually hid until they left, so she didn't have to go through the entire song and dance of why she couldn't go out with them on a Friday night after practice.

She had to get back to Baba. Fridays were hard on him. Curried Dreams stayed open until midnight on Fridays and Saturdays, so she went to Palo Alto to help.

It's not like she couldn't tell her teammates this, but she didn't want to. No one needed to know anything about her family. She liked having her life divided neatly into airtight compartments, nice and tidy. No one in her family knew that she had gone back to playing soccer either. It wasn't a small thing to hide, playing a varsity sport, but Trisha had graduated early, and Vansh was at boarding school, so Ashna was the only Raje at the high school, which had worked out perfectly when, as a freshman, she had rediscovered the sport by accident.

When she'd lived in Sripore, it hadn't been a choice. Mamma's life revolved around getting girls to play sports, so naturally her daughter had to play. Ashna didn't let the pop of sadness drag her down. The days of her mother caring about what Ashna did were long gone. When Baba moved her here, he and everyone else in the family seemed to forget that she'd had a life before that. It was as though that twenty-hour flight erased her life in Sripore.

In freshman year, Ashna had found herself at the tryouts. She had no idea why she'd gone, because she hadn't allowed herself to miss it. When she made the team, the idea of telling anyone didn't even enter her mind. Baba wouldn't have come to her games anyway. He'd gotten so big in the past few years that he was having a harder and harder time getting in the car. Driving out to the Anchorage once every few months to see his mother was the only time he left home and the restaurant. She didn't want Mina Kaki and HRH coming to games and making a big deal out of it. As for Shobi, it was out of the question. Ashna did not need to give her parents another reason to fight.

Exactly when the secret started to feel good, Ashna had no idea, but having something all her own had felt great. One less thing in which her success or failure was naked in front of everyone. Her cousins were her best friends, but she couldn't even tell them. The lie had become comforting in a way she couldn't explain.

"Are you sure?" the beautiful boy said, meeting Ashna's eyes more directly than anyone at school ever looked at one another. There was something adult, unafraid, something deeply confident about the way he met her eyes, as though he didn't know how not to see her.

"Yes, I'm sure I'm not OD-ing on anything, but thanks for asking."

His mouth twisted. He had a mouth like the models in the perfume ads from Nisha's glossy magazines. A wide, lush mouth made for hinting at a smile by the slightest pulling up at the edges. He said nothing more, just waited for her to answer the question he'd really been asking, the one she had deflected so clumsily.

"I'm hiding from the girls on my team." Hearing the words pop out of her mouth surprised her so much she blinked up at him.

A frown folded between brows that were thick and arched. "Your teammates are not nice to you?" He had an accent of some sort. Something South American or European, she couldn't decipher what kind exactly, but it explained how he looked. Boys in Woodside didn't look like this, sun-kissed in the way of glossy magazine models.

"No, they're very nice to me."

"You hide from people who are nice to you, then?" He even cocked his head with an accent. Something about that made her want to laugh out loud.

"Every single thing you've said to me has been a question," she said needlessly.

She wasn't sure if he meant to answer, but before he could, his gaze flew to the right of her head and before she could respond to the warning shout he gave, his hand shot out and caught the ball before it smashed her in the head.

One-handed, his palm splatted against the leather, fully in control.

Shouts rose behind her. With the kind of skill she'd only seen pros display, he spun the ball up in the air, bounced it with his knee, and then letting it drop to his feet he juggled it a few times before bending it in a perfect arc to the exact spot on the pitch where some boys from the soccer team were waiting for it.

At first there was complete stunned silence, then cheers rose from the pitch.

His face shuttered. His entire body went into lockdown. Ashna had never seen anyone pull on armor, but this had to be how it looked. He turned, eager to make an escape, but then he threw a glance at her and paused. Possibly because her mouth was hanging open.

"Hi . . . Excuse me. Do you go to Green Brook High?" the soccer coach called, jogging up to them.

The boy gave the barest nod and Coach Clarence stuck out his hand. "Do you play for a club?"

The boy shoved his hands into the pockets of his jeans and shook his head. "I'll see you around," he threw at Ashna, and started to walk away.

The coach ran after him. "Hold up a minute. I'm Coach Clarence. And you are?"

He looked over the coach's shoulder and saw Ashna still watching him. How could anyone look away from him?

"Frederico." He did not add a last name, and he looked straight at her when he said it.

Ashna's insides did a skipping thing she had never experienced before. His name melted on his tongue and seemed to flow through her blood. A ripple of something too sensitive for comfort ran across her skin. She blushed, and his brows did that curious folding-together thing again.

"I want you to try out for the team tomorrow," Coach Clarence said.

The tryouts had closed months ago. Coach had never taken on a player midseason. The man barely spared a glance for anyone, and Ashna had never heard him use that tone. Not even with his star players.

"Four P.M. tomorrow. My office, Mr. Frederico." He held out his hand again and kept it there until the boy took it.

Coach Clarence shook his hand with both of his, the way fans shook the hands of celebrities, and went back to the pitch beaming.

"You're not going to go to his office tomorrow, are you?" she said.

"Did you want me to go?" Another question.

Why would I care? That was the logical thing to say. *I always want you to do what makes you happy.* That was what she really wanted to say, but it made no sense to have that thought about a stranger.

In the end she said, "Why don't you want to play?"

This speaking-in-questions affliction had to be contagious.

Ashna counted her breaths as he looked at her for what felt like the longest moment ever. How had she thought his eyes held nothing? She couldn't even remember the person who'd had that thought. In the space of ten minutes she had forgotten who she was before he had found her. Before he said his name that way, all those consonants tilting up at the ends, as though the language she had spoken forever had suddenly become poetic, potent, *beautiful*.

For the first time in Ashna's life she was aware of the air around her. There was a glow to it, all the particles shimmery glitter. She looked down at her feet to make sure they were still on the ground and wiggled her toes inside her shoes. It felt so much like floating that finding her feet not dangling in the air was bit of a shock.

It wasn't until he answered her question that she knew her life would never again be the same.

"Maybe I don't want to play for the same reason that you were hiding beneath those bleachers?"

Chapter Eight

Ashna had once hidden in the trunk of a car when the chauffeur drove her home from school through a crowd of rabid journalists, just before she left Sripore forever. And now she was on *Good Morning America*. How on earth had this happened?

Well, she wasn't exactly *on* it, she was in her room folding and refolding her laundry as *Good Morning America* played on the TV, with the hosts discussing her. The jolly bunch couldn't stop cracking up about her expression when Rico walked into her kitchen. As if that weren't mortifying enough, they zoomed in on her face and froze the frame. Her pupils were dilated, her mouth agape.

To Ashna, that face said: *What the hell is this jerk doing here?*

To everyone else, that face seemed to say: *I've never laid eyes on a being this hot!*

No, seriously that's what the very chirpy blond person was saying. Those exact words. Ashna threw a bra at the TV.

They zoomed in on Rico on his knees in front of her, looking up at her with those damn eyes as though his heart were in his mouth, his hand gripping the knife like someone showing off some ancient dagger-wielding martial art moves.

Rubbing her knee, she avoided looking down at her toes. The digits were all firmly attached to her foot. Thanks to him. Also thanks to him, that foot was in her mouth for all of America to see.

"I'd drop a knife on my foot too if I saw *that* walk into my kitchen, if you know what I mean!" the dark-haired one said, winks flying.

Well, Ashna would be glad to lend her the knife.

The Misono people had sent her a new set of their best. The nerve! Apparently their sales had seen a sharp uptick. What was wrong with the world they lived in? They had asked her to model for an ad for them. She'd rather chop off her toes than feed into the madness.

It had been a week since that stupid clip had gone viral. Why was it still everywhere? Wasn't this the age of overnight sensations and flashes in the pan?

She looked at her underwear drawer. Everything was rolled up and arranged in a warm-to-cool rainbow of colored silk, just like her closet. She adjusted one of the rolls so it lined up perfectly with the one next to it. When she had left for Paris after Baba's death, Mina Kaki had insisted on her seeing a therapist there. He had diagnosed her with PTSD resulting in acute clinical depression and anxiety, triggered by losing a parent so violently. He had encouraged her to use her need for order to help ground herself. Usually organizing things did help her calm herself when the fear of panic loomed. Right now? No such luck.

Although what she was feeling right now wasn't exactly panic. It was rage. How dare he? How dare he show up at her restaurant?

Now, after all these years. Now, when she no longer thought about him. Ever.

For all the things he'd been, he'd always been proud. Yet he had never given her a hard time about keeping him secret from her family. They had both been comfortable with secrets. She'd believed that they had both wanted to—needed to— keep what was between them private, because the intensity of it had felt so overwhelming, so intimate.

How wrong she had been about him. In the end, the intensity of their connection had meant nothing. Having his pride hurt was all it had taken for him to betray her. One thing she knew for certain was that she would never depend on anyone that much again, or let anyone abandoning her cripple her that way.

She pulled her trembling hand away from her knee. She couldn't let that time in her life emerge again. She turned off the TV and called China.

"Hello, superstar!"

"I can't do it." Ashna hugged her phone to her ear with both hands as though it were a puppy in pain.

When China didn't respond, Ashna started to pace the length of her room. Outside her window the town was waking up; newborn sunlight caught the copper finial on the roof of Curried Dreams. Would she ever be able to look at her own restaurant again without seeing Rico slam down on his hurt knee?

"You have to find someone else. Please."

"Ashna! What are you talking about?" China said finally.

"You have to understand. It's . . . it's . . ." How on earth had this happened? Gold and green eyes flooded her thoughts.

"You can't back out. Not now," China said, her tone unshakable.

It didn't matter how unshakable China was, Ashna couldn't do this.

"My . . . my mother needs me." Dear God, she was going to be reborn as a frog in her next birth for this—the Hindu version of hell. "It's . . . it's . . . it's *Shobi*! You know how things are with her." As a matter of fact, China had no idea how things were with Shobi. Like everyone else in Ashna's life, China simply avoided the subject of Ashna's mostly missing mother as though it were an unfortunately located wart.

China responded with silence.

Ashna soldiered on. "Well, she just won this crazy prestigious award, it's the Indian version of the Presidential Medal of Freedom. She wants me to be there when she receives it. I have to go to India. She needs me there. Shobi never needs anyone!" God, she wasn't just going to be a frog, but her frog self was going to get struck down by lightning and burned to a crisp.

Why hadn't she just told China the truth? Rico's grown-up bearded jaw and man bun did a slow spin around her head, and a groan rose deep inside her. Then she thought about having to call Shobi and backtrack and the groan threatened to turn into a wail. This entire thing about being stuck between the devil and the deep blue sea was every bit as impossible as it sounded on paper. Only, the devil was green-and-golden-eyed and the sea was an ocean of maternal disappointment.

Shobi had been persistent since their lovely last call. Just today she'd called five times with her usual Shoban Gaikwad Raje disregard for little things, like what others wanted. The fact that Ashna was not answering her calls was just making her push harder. Or maybe Shobi had seen the footage of Ashna maiming one of the world's most popular athletes. If she hadn't watched the video yet, that would make her the only human with an internet connection who hadn't.

The video had been viewed over five million times. That was five million people who'd seen her, a professional chef, drop a surgical-grade knife at the sight of a man every major magazine had declared the sexiest man alive.

And she had landed him in the hospital.

Or he had landed himself there while trying to keep her toes from being severed.

He was a hero.

She was a wreck.

Again.

"Plus, I don't have a celebrity anymore. I broke mine, remember?"

China laughed. "You did not break him. He's fine. The doctors drained his knee and he's as good as new."

Ashna ignored the relief that loosened the tightness in her chest at hearing he was fine and tried again. "China, I'm not—"

"*Oh!*" China cut her off as though she'd just had the greatest epiphany. "Now everything makes perfect sense!"

No, nothing made sense. Or at least none of this should make sense to China.

China lived in the apartment above the yoga studio next door to Curried Dreams. The yoga studio had been in China's family for over a hundred years. *Before anyone in America had any idea what yoga or yoga pants were*, as her sister India, who now ran the studio, loved to say.

After Ashna had moved to California, China, India, and their brother Siddhartha were the only children she had been friends with aside from her cousins. But of course, like her family, they hadn't known about her and Rico.

She had never breathed a word about him to anyone.

Her two secrets in high school. Soccer and Rico.

"What makes perfect sense?" Ashna asked, working hard to sound nonchalant.

"Well, I was wondering how you agreed to do the show. Now I get why." China sounded positively impressed with herself for solving that most challenging of puzzles. "Your mom wanted you to go to India for her award thing, and you used this as an excuse to get out of that."

Having friends was incredibly annoying. Good thing Ashna had so few. There was no point denying it. Plus, when it came to Shobi, the less she said the better. Every time Ashna opened her mouth about her, people drew all sorts of conclusions.

China chuckled. "Here I was thinking you were doing it to help a friend—namely me." More chuckling, because of course

China wasn't actually upset. Who could be upset with a friend who always did as you asked? "And I was so thrilled when you got the luck of the draw." China made an appreciative sound. "Although none of us at the channel can figure out how the powers that be were able to get someone like him on the show. Unless of course it has to do with what happened in your kitchen."

There it went again, Ashna's heartbeat, speeding up all the way to bursting. "I have no idea what you're going on about," she mumbled with more of that blasted nonchalance.

China wasn't listening, she was having one of her conversations with herself. China vs. China, her siblings called it. "Or maybe it's the surgery. Of course! His injury has caused him to retire earlier than he expected, and he's looking to do something different with his life."

And a Food Network show was what he had settled on? Ashna wasn't a betting woman, but she'd bet her restaurant on the fact that Rico wasn't looking to be a cooking channel star.

China stayed on the runaway train of her thoughts. "I can't even imagine what they're paying him. Do you think he needs the money? He sure doesn't look like someone who does. I mean, just having someone line up that beard probably costs my month's salary. See, that's it, these celebrities can blow through money on all sorts of things. Celebrity does that, it makes your tastes all kinds of perverse and over the top." The sound she made was anything but disgusted. "Did you see him, though? I mean, I'd love to see him do perverse things."

Ashna cleared her throat. "Isn't that wrong, given that he isn't a woman?"

"Well, he's beautiful. I'm a lesbian, not blind."

Okay, time to turn China's train around and bring her back on track. "If he can't do the show will they still pay him?" Could it really be that Rico needed the money?

"He's doing the show. And he'll be fine so long as he doesn't go slamming and sliding on his knee trying to heroically keep women from slicing off their toes at the sight of him."

Ashna groaned. Inside she was wailing. She fell back on her bed.

Her ex–best friend let out a full-throated guffaw. "I get that he's hot and all, but girl, keep your panties on!"

"Shut up. The knife slipped. It was an accident."

"That's not what the camera saw."

Ashna jumped up again and started pacing again. "Listen, China. Please please please please, do not make me do this. Please. I cannot get on a set with him after that. Please. *Please!*" If it sounded like spineless, pathetic begging, that's exactly what it was.

"Ashna, love," China said with not a whit of humor left in her voice, "these are literally the best viewership ratings the channel has ever had. I mean *ever*. Like ten times over, ever. The CEO had me in her office yesterday. They're doubling what they're paying you. She just gave me a huge bonus. They will do anything to make sure you don't try to get out of your contract. After that video going viral"—she made an excited squeaking sound—"the chance of you getting voted off any-time soon has become almost zero. You can actually win this! I'm sure the rest of the chefs aren't thrilled, but they'd be stupid to not understand that everyone is going to be tuning in to watch. So, win-win for everyone!"

Ashna didn't care. As China rhapsodized the impending success of her show at the expense of The Video—and Ashna's self-respect—Ashna made her way down to the kitchen and pulled out her tea jars. She spooned a little tulsi, the slightest pinch of ginger powder, and Darjeeling loose leaf into a strainer cup, drawing strength from the alchemy of those flavors mingling. She'd find another way to save Curried Dreams. Just a few weeks ago the show hadn't been an option. She would pretend those weeks hadn't happened. God, how she needed those weeks to not have happened.

"You don't understand," Ashna said. If everyone was going to accuse her of trying the same thing over and over and expecting different results, she might as well go with it. "The award is a really big deal to Shobi. She doesn't want it to look like she has no family to share it with. It's important to her to show everyone how she has it all." A blatant lie. Shobi was, in fact, a vocal advocate of women not pressuring themselves to "have it all."

It was yet another pet lecture: Men don't have to choose between family and achievement, so why should women? Every time we talk about women having it all, we focus the conversation on whether or not women should choose one over the other, which reinforces the problem it's trying to solve.

"You're the one who doesn't understand," China said, suddenly dead serious. "When the head honchos called me into a meeting this morning, giving me a bonus and you a raise wasn't the only thing they wanted to talk about. I was the one who brought you in last minute; they know we know each other. I promised them you weren't going anywhere. I know I've been saying this, but I'm not kidding around. If you leave the show, I will lose my job."

ASHNA IS HOLDING *Trisha's hand. Her terrified grip is too tight.*

Trisha tugs Ashna closer to the cliff that drops straight and sharp into the ocean. The idea of throwing herself off it makes Ashna's stomach bounce up to her chest.

Nisha sits cross-legged on the blanket, playing Three Two Five with Mina Kaki and Mamma. Nisha is uninterested in getting her new swimsuit wet; it's a pretty purple with yellow swirls. Trisha and Ashna wear sporty navy Speedos.

Every one of Mina Kaki's features is strained with worry. "Girls, you don't have to do it," she calls. "Come back here and we'll play Bluff instead." Mina Kaki uses her high-pitched protective voice.

Next to her, Mamma widens her eyes in reproach. "Stop transferring your phobias to the children, Mina."

"You let Vansh and Yash do it," Trisha says in her defiant voice as she tugs harder at Ashna's hand. "Let's go before she stops us from doing this too," she whispers to Ashna.

"I don't want to."

Shobi stands and Ashna's heart sinks at the determined look on her face. "Go, girls. Do it. There's nothing to fear but fear itself."

Trisha squeals. "I love you, Shobi Kaki!"

Shobi grins. "I love you back, Shasha bear. You're my brave tigress!"

Mina stands. "Come over here, Ashi. You don't have to jump if you're scared."

"Why would she not want to?" Mamma says, a frown twisting her mouth. "You want to, right, Ashna?"

Ashna freezes. She can't answer her mother, but she tugs her shaking hand out of Trisha's.

Trisha runs screaming to the edge by herself ready to throw herself off . . .

ASHNA SPRANG AWAKE on the couch, her heart skittering in her chest. Her phone was vibrating in her hand. She touched her jeans. No swimsuit, thank God. The pitch darkness of the living room made the flashing of her cell phone dance like a strobe light against her black T-shirt.

"Shut up!" she hissed at it before hitting talk and pressing the blameless thing to her ear.

"Hello, beta."

Shit, being woken from sleep meant she hadn't checked caller ID. Ashna pulled the phone away from her ear and checked the time. Three A.M. Had Shobi really ambushed her in the middle of the night, knowing she might answer the phone without checking?

"What's up, Mom?" She got off the couch and stretched her stiff back, half expecting to feel the sandy cliff from her dream beneath her bare feet.

After her call with China, Ashna had obsessively mixed

and sampled tea blends, labeling them things like Apocalypse Averted and Nowhere to Run. Then she'd settled into the couch to think with a cup that she'd finally gotten right (Hidden Strength). Her social media and text messages were filled with The Video and her brain had shuttled wildly between knowing that China was being her dramatic self and believing that her best friend's job hung in the balance. With so much spinning in her head, it was a miracle she had fallen asleep.

On the phone Shobi sounded almost surprised that her ambush had worked. "I'm just checking in to see if you'd given any thought to our conversation?"

Okay, so at least Shobi hadn't watched the clip. Thank heavens for tiny mercies.

Was it still called a conversation if only one person speaks? "Our last *conversation* ended with you telling me what I do is worthless. What exactly did you want me to give thought to at three A.M.?" Ashna made her way up the stairs to her room.

"Ashna, please let's not argue," Shobi said in her deliberately cool negotiator's tone, which made Ashna dread the thought of backtracking.

Please let's not argue was Shobi code for *Let's do this my way.*

Thanks to her grotesque luck, right now doing it Shobi's way was the only way to not end up in front of a camera with Rico again.

"I've been thinking a lot about us," Shobi said in that same determinedly calm tone. "I understand that you aren't excited about my Padma Shri. I even understand why coming here and being part of the awards ceremony would make you uncomfortable, but having you resort to lying about a new job, that just broke my heart."

Ashna stopped at the top of the stairs and squeezed the banister. Shobi didn't believe that Food Network would employ her daughter. That shouldn't have surprised her, and Ashna was livid at herself for letting it.

Shobi let out a long-suffering breath when Ashna didn't respond. "I know you're angry with me, but do you have any idea what the Padma Shri is? Can't you see, I want you—and all women—to believe that you can achieve whatever you want."

"Except saving my restaurant, or being on television?"

"Come on, Ashna. I'm your mother, I know how much you hate the spotlight. You won't even cook with your grandmother watching. You want me to believe you're going to cook on television?"

Ashna's mouth went dry. How on earth did Shobi know this? No one knew this about her.

She swiped the stupid tear that slipped from her eye. Letting the woman make her cry was not something she did anymore.

Stay upbeat.

"Food Network believes I can do it." She didn't care that she sounded like a petulant child.

How was it fair that Shobi got to be right in this? Ashna was cutting off her nose to spite her face. Twice over.

Something trembled in Shobi's voice. "Listen, beta, the way I said it last time was wrong, but what I said wasn't. At least consider getting away for a while. Come see the work we do at the foundation." She sounded so sincere Ashna almost believed it, then she went on. "You've given so much time to your father's dream, don't I deserve the same consideration?"

No. Baba's dream meant something because he'd used Curried Dreams to give Ashna a life. Shobi had used her work to take herself out of Ashna's life.

"You have to let that lost cause go." That sounded an awful lot like an order. The thing Shobi hated most.

Baba had loved poking at her about it. *FYI, that was not an order. Before you go off saying no just because you're too important to be ordered about.* Growing up around parents who fought constantly was not something any child should ever experience, because it was impossible not to carry it with you for the rest of your life.

"Get to know the foundation. It might be something that speaks to you, and it's not in shambles."

Laughter spurted up Ashna's throat. She tamped it down. "You were doing so well and then you had to go ruin it. You may not believe this, but I am going to win this show and then I'm going to pull my restaurant out of *shambles*."

Guess she was breaking those chains after all, and if she had to deal with the boy—man, now—who had ruined her once, then so be it. She'd free herself by breaking both those chains in one fell swoop.

Chapter Nine

Why had Rico thought that freeing himself from his cast would free him from pain? The thing Rico hated most about being a man was this dumbass notion of never being allowed to show pain. Except on the pitch of course. There you got to milk the heck out of it. His knee hurt like a . . . like a witch. A witch with a broom stuck through her knee. A broom with spikes that had been dipped in acid and set on fire.

Nonetheless, he smiled at the journalist from *Sports Illustrated* sitting next to him in the back of his limousine as though he had never in his life suffered an iota of pain.

She was furiously taking notes, so he focused on the Quality Street–style San Francisco homes slipping past them like the reels of the old films his mãe had been obsessed with.

"It's okay to admit you're in pain," Zee had said to him that morning on the phone. "Even if it's just taking a moment to whimper like a puppy in the privacy of your bathroom."

Rico needed a moment in a bathroom.

He also needed to channel Zee's disregard for preconceived notions, radical in their world. Zee was the kind of pretty boy who made Rico look like a lumberjack. But he was so comfortable with it he matched up the earrings he wore, in both ears, with Tanya. They even had a hashtag. #TeeZeeTwinning. The fans loved it.

We're not here for the macho stereotypes, we're here for the game. Zee had the best lines. Zee also still had the game. Rico didn't. Not that he would ever be jealous of Zee.

Rico wondered what the journalist was scrawling away on that pad. All her questions had been about endorsements and what he did for leisure. Other than good old CK, he endorsed brands if they backed the causes he believed in. One of the best things that had happened to advertising in this past decade was that social conscience had become part of it. Sure, brands exploited causes for profit, but they brought focus to things that needed attention. The world was nothing if not symbiotic, and one of the things Rico was proudest of in his life was that Manchester United had partnered with UNICEF to raise funds to build schools across Asia and Africa.

As for leisure, well, there hadn't been much of that in the past decade. In his future there seemed to be nothing but leisure stretched out like endless desert sands.

Not that he could say that when asked about his plans—another favorite question. He'd mouthed the same drivel he'd been handing out since he signed on for the show. He was excited about turning to his causes and hobbies. Learning how to cook was step one. Then he'd plugged the show some.

The journalist put down her pen and started the recorder up again. "So, you'd only recently had surgery and you still dived to catch that knife?"

Truly, he wished they'd stop with the knife. It wasn't like he'd meant to do it. It was a damn reflex.

A reflex that came from muscle memory. When it came to Ashna Raje, even though his brain felt nothing, clearly his body begged to differ—proving that it was time for him to deal with whatever issues his subconscious had held on to for so long.

There were only so many ex's children he could be god-father to. He'd just found out that Myra was expecting a baby. She'd hinted at how she wanted no one but Rico to hold the title, because he was going to make a fabulous father someday. He would certainly like to give it a shot. With someone dependable and loyal. Not someone whose opinion swayed with the tide of those around her.

"Of course I dived to catch the knife. You can't just let someone get hurt when you can do something to stop it."

Rico shifted his leg and a good hard jolt of pain shot through him, a perfect reminder that he was only here to let go of the delusions his grieving teen self was still holding on to.

She's just a girl I dated in high school.

He was ready to move on, to get on the pitch and win. You always started the game not knowing how you were going to win. All you knew was that you had to. The only workable strategy was one you developed as you went along.

"A true hero," the journalist said with a level of worshipfulness that was always a bit disconcerting in close quarters.

"It's not heroic to help people when you can," he said calmly, even though he had the urge to snap: *It was a bloody reflex!* He smiled and sent up a prayer of gratitude when the car turned into the studio parking lot. The need to get out and straighten his leg gnawed ruthlessly at him. "It was lovely meeting you. If you have more questions, reach out to Rod. Let George know where you need to be dropped off and he'll take care of it." He patted his chauffeur on the shoulder and thanked him.

The journalist smiled. "This has been fantastic. Thank you and good luck with the show." Then she threw him one of those knowing winks that people had suddenly taken to tossing his way. "Just make sure there are no knives around when you see Ms. Raje, eh?"

He tried to smile, he really did, but the limo pulled under the portico of the studio and he got out with the speed of someone who hadn't just had his knee run through a shredder. He had never been so relieved to be done with an interview.

Taking Zee's advice, he stopped in the washroom to stretch his leg and whimper like a baby. He pulled his toes toward himself the way the physical therapist had taught him, and whimpered away as several spasms cramped up and down his leg. He stuck with the pain as his calf and hamstring loosened. Then he let out another whimper just because it felt so bloody good.

The pain had to be influencing how he was feeling about everything: retirement, the show, the reason why he was on the show. Had he really thought about fatherhood back in the limousine? What on earth was going on with him? He hardly ever gave thought to family. There was no reason to. He hadn't had any for a very long time and been just fine.

By the time he entered the studio staging area, arranged

from end to end with state-of-the-art cooking stations, he had his urge to whimper well under control. It was like walking into an oversize display case of model kitchens.

There was something ridiculous about hearing clashing cymbals when his eyes met Ashna's, because that rom-com bullshit was not real life. So, when he heard the loud crash as Ashna looked up at him with eyes that took up most of her face, he knew it was either his mind playing tricks on him or someone's awful sense of humor.

It was option two. Thank God.

Usually, Rico would have laughed. But terror flashed in Ashna's eyes when the bang of the cymbals went off. He thought she'd sink to the floor; instead she wiped a hand across her face and the bright horror was gone from her eyes. The set was filled with cast and crew, all of them in hysterics. With a determined swallow, Ashna pushed out a laugh through lips gone white because she'd bitten them too hard.

Rico followed suit and made the obligatory motions, an embarrassed but sportsmanlike laugh, a sufficiently self-deprecating shake of the head. The moment he reached her the entire set burst into applause.

One thing he'd say about her—she blushed like no one else he'd ever met. Her gorgeous skin went from warm brown to an almost fiery pink. It didn't help that Rico knew she was blushing with her entire body right now. He had loved to chase that blush across her skin.

From beneath her spiked fan of lashes she met his gaze.

He was about to ask if she was okay, but she caught the

question before he spoke the words and it made humiliation tighten her jaw and fade the flush from her cheeks. The Raje pride was alive and well.

How embarrassed she must be about the video. The girl who loved her secrets, viral on the internet. How was she even here right now?

"You two never got a chance to be introduced the other day," Jonah, one of the assistant producers, said, and threw a painfully obvious glance at the knife block on the red quartz countertop of their kitchen station. Everything on the set was accented in red, including the jackets all the chefs were wearing. A cruel joke, given how the color made Ashna look. But he was immune now.

He stuck out a hand. "Frederico Silva."

She raised her chin, which made her jawbones stand out sharply against her skin. He had spent an absurd amount of time thinking about that jaw once. Now he looked past the poetically sharp curve, unaffected, and offered her a stranger's smile.

"This is Chef Ashna Raje," Jonah said when she didn't introduce herself. Ashna had never been tongue-tied around him.

Her gaze traced the many cameras around the sprawling set, some hanging from the ceiling, some mounted on cranes, then found its way back to the hand Rico was holding out.

Another thing he'd never seen before was Ashna frozen. The speed with which she could block a goal had gobsmacked him every single time. The video going viral had to have shaken her, or maybe she simply hadn't expected someone she'd tossed out like garbage to return. His best guess was a little of both.

"It's nice to meet you," he said, and finally, she shook his hand.

Quickly. Pulling away so fast he couldn't be sure they had touched at all; maybe that's why his own hand hung there in her wake, his palm strangely alive when he pulled back and shoved his hand into his pocket.

With another suggestive smile—which was getting a little annoying—Jonah told them that they had the next fifteen minutes to familiarize themselves with each other before the mics went on. Then off he went with the self-congratulatory gait of someone who had just won the lottery.

The network couldn't have asked for a better accident than Rico's idiotic knife dive. Since it had happened on Jonah's watch, he had to be the hero of the hour.

Thinking about the knife sent a fresh jolt of pain through his knee. Maybe the decision to tweak his meds right now hadn't been his smartest idea. His old meds made him sluggish and the new ones did nothing.

Ashna's eyelids fluttered down as she glanced at his knee. "How is it?" she asked.

She hadn't bothered to come to the hospital that day. She hadn't bothered to reach out in the weeks after to ask how he was. Given that she was the reason his almost-healed wound had ripped open, it was the least anyone with even a modicum of decency would have done. Her warm bearing and impeccable manners had always felt so soothing, so familiar to him.

They had reminded him of his mother. But his mãe wasn't just polite, she was kind. There was a difference. It was another thing he had gotten wrong about Ashna.

"It's been two weeks. It would be fine now, wouldn't it?" he said, proud of how bored he sounded. *Fine* was a broad term, after all. He'd had to have another surgery, albeit a small one this time, to sew up the opened rip. Having fluid drained from your knee was never a party for anyone.

She blinked again. Had she always used her eyes quite so much instead of words? The only times he remembered her clamming up was when it came to her parents. In contrast, he'd talked about his mãe and pai to her constantly. She'd been the only person he'd ever been able to talk to about them. That ease, that openness, it's what had gotten him in trouble in the first place. So, this new her was going to make life so much easier for him.

Come to think of it, everything about her seemed different now. She was so altered, in fact, he barely recognized her.

"I'm glad," she said, deep tiredness dragging at her lids.

He should ignore it, but the exhausted disinterest annoyed him more than it should.

"That's all you have to say about me saving your toes from being severed?" It came out an angry hiss.

She threw a glance around the room to make sure no one was listening. Everyone seemed too preoccupied to pay them any attention. The crew was pretending to give the chef-celebrity pairs space to get acquainted, but of course any camera-worthy moment would be fair game for the screen.

From the way Ashna was looking at him it was clear that getting acquainted with him was akin to diving into a pit of snakes.

"You took me by surprise," she finally answered his question. "I should have been more careful. I'm sorry about your knee."

It wasn't like there was no remorse in her voice. It was more like there was a determined effort to keep her apology contained. She wanted him to know that she was apologizing for his knee and nothing else.

I'm sorry. But only for this.

A direct response to what he had said to her the other day.

As though recognizing the burden of its role in this mess, his knee let loose another shot of pain. The knee that had cost him his sport. The sport that had saved him after being dumped by her.

This apology that she gave only for the ripping of stitches, only for that second tearing of skin and muscle, meant nothing.

Just like that, Rico knew why he was really here.

For years now he had burned with wanting that one word from her. *Sorry.*

When she'd first walked away from him he had felt nothing but panic. After that, for months, all he'd wanted was for her to change her mind. Then finally, when he'd lost hope, all he'd wanted was for her to at least be sorry. To give him some remorse, something that proved that he hadn't been such a colossal fool in judging her.

When he didn't acknowledge the apology, her chin lifted

again. "I do appreciate you saving my toes from being severed." Instead of remorse an icy coolness dripped from her tone, a mockery of what he'd done.

The throbbing in his knee spread all through him like rage. He stepped into her space, the memory of betrayal vibrating through him, and leaned close to her ear. "They were the first toes I sucked." His tone was cruel, but he didn't care. "Letting them get severed under my watch would be callous, wouldn't it?"

She stepped away from him, face flaming, her scent flooding his brain. Her hair still smelled like it always had. As though her essence was wrapped up in it, clean and fiery like freshly bloomed roses. He hated how it reached inside him and dug up memories. But like everything else about her, even her scent had become colder. The fire almost snuffed out, even the vibrancy of roses too restrained to be real.

The full blast of her jet-black glare met his. "Since when is being callous a problem for you?"

It was Rico's turn to stiffen, but he had spent too much time in the spotlight to let it show.

What about chasing her around like a puppy had been callous? Or about begging her not to leave him?

Please, Ash. I'll do whatever you want to make myself worthy of you. Don't leave me.

How had he had so little self-respect?

"Why are you here, Frederico?" she finally said, throwing another wary look around the room, and while there was something comforting about the fact that she had changed beyond recognition, how much she seemed to care about what everyone thought rubbed his nerves raw. Even at sixteen she had been more self-possessed than most adults he knew; none of the fads and waves of what their school thought was cool had ever seemed to register with her. She had been so brutally focused on what mattered to her that Rico had let being one of the things that did matter become his life.

Of course she'd like to know why he was here. Laying out his hand in front of her without any thought of self-preservation once had taught him well. He never left a play open anymore. "Didn't you watch the interviews? I'm here to learn how to cook. My career just ended and I need a hobby." He kept his voice cool, his smile cooler.

Her eyes narrowed. She scoffed without scoffing.

"Why are *you* here, Ashna?"

Her gaze fell to the wooden chopping board at their station. She adjusted it so it was perfectly aligned with the countertop. "I'm here for the only reason *anyone* should be here. Not to play games, but to win this competition." She made another adjustment to the already perfectly aligned board. "But that's not going to happen if we're on a team. We can't be together."

He had to laugh at that. "Not like I've ever heard *that* from you before."

Her face flamed again and something other than tired flatness glittered in her eyes for the first time, a small spark of the fire that had defined her, breaking through this new frigid exterior.

He crossed his arms and relaxed his hip into the countertop. "If what you say is what you mean"—another cool smile—"and you do want to win, then I think we've got a pretty good start. A record number of viewers are expected to tune in for today's show and they will be voting. And they already love us together." What had the journalist from *Sports Illustrated* said? Ah yes, "You can't fake this kind of magic." If only they knew the truth. Ashna Raje could fake pretty much anything.

Was she faking being calm right now, or was this coldness real? "Yes, but I'm not here to win a popularity contest based on some sort of rom-com the public is waiting to see unfold. This is a cooking show. It's my career, not a hobby, and I want to win based on my talent."

He was totally calling bullshit on that. Still, he had to be impressed that she had fallen into her father's legacy so easily and wholeheartedly. He had never imagined her running the restaurant. At least not until the very end, when he'd finally met her father.

"If this were about talent alone, half the scores wouldn't be based on audience votes. At this point the only way you're winning is if we're on the same team." So he sounded arrogant, so shoot him.

She swallowed. "We're going to have to lay some ground rules." Which wasn't exactly an admission that he was right, but he was taking it as such.

"Again, like I've never gotten that from you before." He sent a lazy smile at a camera. "What ground rules would you like to lay down this time?"

Her jaw clenched. "We can't talk about our past. None of that 'this time, last time' stuff. This show has nothing to do with that." The new cold flatness was firmly back in her eyes.

"What past?" He could do cold and flat too.

"Thanks."

Pushing off the station, he turned to face her. She was still fiddling with the chopping board. With one finger he pushed it out of alignment. Her hands stilled on the wood. She didn't look up at him.

"Don't mention it." He kept his finger on the board and held it in place as she tried to straighten it again. "I've had enough practice with you hiding me like a dirty secret."

She had pushed him into the bathroom once, when her cousin had walked into the In-N-Out they were at. Years of women using him as arm candy hadn't wiped away that memory.

She squeezed her eyes shut. Which was just as well, because there wasn't anything in her eyes he wanted to see. Bringing up their past wasn't going to benefit him either. It was certainly not the right strategy for closure.

Before either of them could say more, Jonah came back. "Sorry to interrupt." He grinned in his extra-smarmy way.

Ashna smiled at him kindly, obviously ready to hug him for the interruption.

"It's time to get to know the other contestants," Jonah said, the thick tension between Ashna and Rico sliding right past his powers of deduction. "They're going to do introductions. And guess what? You two are first."

Ashna stiffened. But he was Rico Silva; and it was showtime.

"Us being first sounds like a prediction, mate," he said, and held his arm out to Ashna.

Given the tight set of her mouth, he wasn't sure if she

would take it, but she slipped her hand into the crook of his elbow. The smile she attempted for the camera was a valiant effort.

Together they walked under the spotlight to applause and hoots. For better or worse, they were doing this.

Chapter Ten

Three steps with her hand on Rico's arm and Ashna knew he was in pain. His forearm was warm and ripped under the dark gray button-down he was wearing. No forearm on earth had any business being so . . . so . . . solid despite the pain his body was communicating. Thinking of him as solid made Ashna want to throw up.

Or burst into nervous laughter again.

The ironic consequence was that she involuntarily squeezed his arm. She felt him half turn toward her—the familiarity of his movements next to her only made the queasiness worse—and he put his hand on hers and squeezed back.

Really? Yeah, no!

She pulled her hand away, stepped under the too-bright spotlight, and smiled at China, focusing her attention on her friend to keep from having to process the combined attention of the cast, crew, and studio audience.

Next to her, Rico was having the exact opposite reaction. All the attention coming his way seemed to pump through him, inflating him into someone she didn't recognize. He gave the cameras what everyone seemed to think was his most dazzling smile. Every single woman in the room let out a sigh, several hands pressed against heaving bosoms. Ashna scanned the crowd to make sure no outright swooning had taken place.

Ashna threw him a look. Was he seeing this? Did he not find it ridiculous?

Nope, he was soaking it up, reflecting it back. It wasn't his usual loose-limbed confidence, but something more languidly in control, studiedly transparent. He was working the room and the cameras, and everyone stood there lapping it up in huge thirsty gulps.

The boy who hadn't given two shits (his words, not hers) about what the world thought of him was now this . . . this slick charmer. If China hadn't grinned at her like someone who had glimpsed heaven, Ashna wouldn't have been able to keep herself from walking off the set.

The network had announced this week that China was the lead producer on the show. This was it, China's dream. She cleared her throat into the mic and laughed.

"So, hey, hi!" China said, and applause and cheering erupted around her. Everyone was caught up in her excitement, softened as they were by Rico's winks and grins. "Welcome!" China was in her element with a mic in her hand telling people what to do. No wonder she had endured the disappointment of her family by not working at the yoga studio. This is what she'd been born to do, and she'd always known it.

Her usual producer's uniform, a jacket over a T-shirt and jeans, and sneakers, was new and extra spiffy today. She dropped a curtsy in response to the crowd's appreciation and explained their agenda for the day. First, she would introduce everyone informally, and then DJ, their host, would do it for the cameras. Ashna looked around, but DJ wasn't here yet.

"First up is owner and executive chef of Palo Alto's legendary Indian fine dining restaurant, Curried Dreams, Ashna Raje." A polite spattering of applause. "And her partner, the striker for Manchester United—the man you're all wondering how we managed to nab—Frederico Silva!" An explosion of cheers. "But here at the Food Network we give away recipes, not trade secrets." They loved that, and cheers ebbed and turned into laughter.

Standing next to her, Rico vibrated with good humor. Whether it was real or part of this New Rico, Ashna couldn't tell, but something about it was so joyful that a parched part of her soaked it up.

"We're tremendously excited about the show," China went on. "We fully expect it to be the next big thing." She threw a grateful smile at Rico and Ashna. "Already we're a household name thanks to a very generous and heroic act." Ashna worked hard to suppress her groan. Yes, she knew it made her a terrible person, but thinking about Rico slamming down on his hurt knee made her want to shake him. It also made her want to find him a chair.

Crazed applause.

Rico took a bow. Ashna practiced every breathing technique India had ever taught her, but then China touched her heart as she looked at Ashna, which was so sweet that Ashna found it impossible not to smile.

When the next wave of fawning and hooting died down,

China held out the mic to Rico and Ashna. Rico's hand pressed into the small of her back, it seemed to take him a second to realize what he was doing and he withdrew it. Which didn't remove the warm imprint from her skin. Rico waited for her to speak into the microphone, but she couldn't, her arms wouldn't move.

With all the smoothness of who he now was, he took the mic from China and gave her a hug. Really? The Boy No One Was Allowed to Touch (except her, of course) was all cuddly now?

The cameras were on them, but when China looked at her, Ashna could still see the *holy shit, he's good* on her face. Ashna made the effort to hold in her scoff.

"What an honor to be here," Rico said. It was unfair what the mic did to his voice. The bass, the silk, it all magnified manifold. Those rounded consonants of his accent, a mix of his Brazilian and English heritage, melted into one another as though they knew the impact they had on ovaries everywhere. Ashna counted at least five women pressing a hand into their bellies.

Ashna wanted to flip him the bird.

"What a stroke of luck to get partnered with the most talented of all the chefs here."

Applause broke out around them again, along with some friendly boos. He smiled at her—a smile that looked benign enough, but she knew he saw the virtual bird she was flipping him, and she was certain he drew immense satisfaction from it.

"These introductions aren't going to be on the show," she whispered when he had charmed the pants off the crowd sufficiently and they returned to make way for the next chef-celebrity pair.

"The cameras are on," he whispered back, his warm spearmint breath stroking her earlobe, "so everything is fair game. It's reality TV, Chef Raje. Welcome to show business."

Anger pulsed through her, displacing all the nervousness. She hated to admit it, but having someone who knew how to navigate this craziness was a plus. So long as he kept his word and left their past behind, and she didn't let herself forget it even for a moment, she could handle this.

China started to introduce the other contestants. Competitive spirit buzzed through the air and something long forgotten stirred inside Ashna, something that made her palms itch for the feel of a ball. She rubbed the feeling off on her pants.

First up was Tatiana Rain, a TV dog whisperer who was wearing a pink rhinestone collar around her neck. She was just as charming as Rico had been.

This was a pattern. Every star who followed was amply armed with the charm offensive. They did all the talking. The chefs—none of whom Ashna knew and all of whom had impressive credentials—followed Ashna's lead and merely stood by in support. There had to be a special camp where celebrities trained, because as they took the stage one after another, Ashna realized that they were all adept at owning the room while showing nothing real.

The fact that Rico did this better than everyone else here made her strangely restless. Only the audience seemed to exist for him. In this moment, Ashna could have been anyone—a thought that she chose to find comforting.

Next up was Lilly Cromwell, an older soap opera star from Tennessee with a stark southern drawl—the grandma Ashna had prayed for. Danny El followed, a child star who had aged out of the Disney Channel and was trying to make a name for himself in the adult acting world.

"Who's the child's agent?" Rico whispered to her. He was right, this was probably not the best platform if he wanted to be taken seriously.

Then came Song Ji Woo, an actor from a K-drama, which, the young woman was kind enough to explain in the most endearingly modest move, was what Korean TV shows were called. As if there was anyone alive who didn't know this.

Song was possibly the most gorgeous person Ashna had ever seen. She had one of those faces where exquisite individual features were arranged, well, exquisitely. Her unabashed excitement about being on the show added sincerity to all that perfection. Apparently she was a fan of Rico's (of course she was, insert eye roll here). Bouncing on her heels, she announced that she was only here to meet him. This resulted in more hooting and applause. The man executed another self-deprecating head bow that rivaled Song's sincerity (insert another truckload of eye rolls).

The last one to introduce herself was P. T. Cruiser (a pen name, one hoped), an author of cozy mysteries.

"There's an oxymoron, if I've ever heard one," Rico whispered to Ashna. After their turn, she had excused herself to go find Jonah and request that he get Rico a chair. Between the pain he was trying to hide and his stance, it was obvious putting weight on his leg was killing him. The high director's chair they'd given him meant he was perfectly positioned to commentate into her ear. Well, no good deed ever went unpunished, did it?

At least Ashna's annoyance at his quips kept her nice and distracted. Thinking about competing with these ambitious, talented people would have been exciting if not for her special affliction of only being able to cook Baba's recipes. With that gift there was no possible way for this to end in anything but staggeringly disastrous public humiliation.

The author made a joke about the show being the perfect setting for one of her novels—which were filled with murder and mayhem.

Just you wait, Ashna wanted to tell her. *Just you wait.*

THAT FIRST DAY on set had gone off like an especially heinous nightmare. And that was without actually having to cook. It had been just introductions and trying to get everyone comfortable with the set. An abject failure when it came to Ashna. She couldn't remember a time when she'd felt more uncomfortable.

For all the harsh and sudden ways in which things between them had ended, the years Ashna had spent with Rico were the only time when she had felt sheltered from the storm of her life. Now, a few hours in his presence, and the storm she'd believed she had harnessed ravaged her again.

And tomorrow the cooking challenges would start.

The producers, including her traitorous friend, were being unsurprisingly tight-lipped about everything. China had officially crossed over to the evil side. As for DJ, he had swept in, shot the introductions, and taken off. All Ashna had gotten out of him was a quick hug and a promise to catch up soon. There was some sort of emergency with one of Yash's fund-raising events in LA that Nisha couldn't get to, and DJ had jumped in. All hands on deck, that was the Rajes. DJ had slipped effortlessly into the golden circle just the way Ashna had expected him to.

Ashna wished she'd been the one to help with Yash's fundraiser, coward that she was. But running away never solved problems. Having tried that strategy, she knew its success rate was zero.

It was past midnight and she was still at the restaurant taking inventory and getting things set up for the week. Mina Kaki was going to help her manage Curried Dreams when she had to shoot. Wilfrieda and Khalid were going to share sous chef duties. She had taken care of the things she had control over. The rest she couldn't think about until she got there.

Just as she was ready to leave, her phone rang.

She answered because there were only so many problems she could push away for later.

"That knife didn't touch you, did it?" Shobi said with uncharacteristic maternal worry.

She'd seen the clip. Fabulous!

"I thought you stayed off social media." Shobi wasn't a fan even though her foundation had a following of hundreds of thousands, which of course she would bring up soon enough.

"Hate the thing. For the most part I leave it to my social media director. But Flora chanced upon the video and sent it to me."

Ashna loved Flora, her mother's personal assistant, but she wanted to shake her for this. "It wasn't how it looks. You know how TV is." How Media Jumbles Reality was another one of Shobi's favorite themes.

"It's that restaurant. Look at what it's done to you. By now you should have been in a committed relationship and not swooning like a teenager." Ashna made her way to the holding area and started wrapping silverware in napkins. God forbid if Shoban Gaikwad Raje might say anything as conformist as *by now you should be married* the way any other Indian mother would. But no, the keeper of women's rights had to say "committed relationship" instead. It would have been all fine and dandy had Shobi herself been capable of being in a committed relationship.

Ashna rolled a napkin with far more force than necessary. "Wow, I never thought I'd hear the 'you're thirty and not married off' thing from you."

Shobi made a horrified sound. "Oh please. I would never be quite so regressive. I just meant that I never saw you as the swooning sort."

Ashna had a good mind to let her think she was, indeed, the swooning sort. "I didn't swoon. The camera just makes it look that way. I was caught by surprise."

"Right. Surprise at how stunning a man can be, by all reports." Her mother chuckled, as though she had finally found her absconding sense of humor. So what if it had taken her daughter's public humiliation for her to find it.

Ashna lined the perfectly folded rolls neatly on the counter, ready for tomorrow's fifty tables, because at least the video seemed to be bringing in customers. "It had more to do with the fact that the man did not look like someone who could help me win. It's about winning. Isn't that what you've always taught me?"

Her mother made a scoffing sound, so much more within the Shobi lexicon than her previous good-natured chuckle. "Well, see, it's always about the damn restaurant. But you're right; that video clip is going to make sure that you don't get voted off. So it might help you win after all."

"I can win because of my cooking. It is possible, you know." It was actually not possible at all. How impossible it was reared its monstrous head inside Ashna.

Shobi's response was to twist this in the most infuriating way possible. "I'm not saying you can't. All I'm saying is that you should take a moment to explore why you're doing this." A pause that harkened the coming of another swift and brutal kick to the gut. "Why do you repeatedly let the restaurant be a punitive place for you?"

Sometimes Ashna just hated Shobi. But she hated herself more for answering the phone.

Awkward silence stretched between them. Not that they could have a conversation without those. Ashna shoved the perfectly folded rolls out of alignment, then adjusted them.

Finally, Shobi cleared her throat. "Why do we always end up here, Ashna?"

Ashna laughed.

Shobi cleared her throat, another ominous sign for what was coming. "Why don't we try something different. What are you doing with the restaurant when you shoot? Do you trust the people you've hired?"

A double punch this time. Baba's employees had robbed him clean after his death and it had been Ashna's fault for leaving them to do it.

"I was going to ask if you maybe needed help with it? You won't come to India, and it's been so long since we've seen each other . . ."

Ashna started pacing. Had Shobi just asked her if she needed help?

Once when Ashna had been ill and hadn't been able to get out of bed or eat without her aunt forcing spoonfuls into her mouth, her mother had apologized over the phone about being in the middle of a project it would be unthinkably irresponsible for her to *abandon*. Thousands of women and children were counting on her. She was raising money so underprivileged women could have toilets inside their homes instead of having to walk outside their villages every time they needed to use the restroom. Wasn't that more important? Couldn't Ashna understand how Shobi couldn't leave that, no matter how badly she wanted to be there?

Who could argue that those things weren't more important than a daughter who had inconvenient timing when it came to falling ill?

Even after Baba died, Shobi had flown down for a few days and then simply gone back to India for some project or other.

The last person Ashna had wanted to face then was Shobi anyway, given that after spending all those years blaming

Shobi for destroying Baba, Ashna had been the person to finally push him over the edge.

"What about the foundation? And the Padma Shri? There's
got to be so many events around that."

"I've built a strong enough team that they're taking care of
everything." Another swipe that wasn't lost on Ashna. "I won't
be able to get away for too long, I'd have to be here before the
awards ceremony in two months, but I do want to help. How
long do you shoot?"

"Not sure yet," Ashna said.

Whatever this was—this thing where her mother seemed
to have added "bond with daughter" to her monthly goals—
Ashna did not have the time for it.

"Mina Kaki is helping me. We've got it all worked out, so
don't worry about it." That should work because Shobi was
usually happy to hand her mothering responsibilities off to
her sister-in-law.

It worked. Thank God. After a few frustrated sounds, Shobi
let Ashna go.

Ashna packed up and made her way home. It was late, but
Mina Kaki was a night owl, so Ashna called her.

All she had to say was "Hello," and her aunt knew what she
was going to say.

"Don't worry about the restaurant. It will be well loved. I
have it all under control. Nisha's going to help me."

"But Nisha's swamped with the campaign."

"Actually, not being able to travel is giving her cabin fever,
so this will be good. She'll help when she can and I will be

fully focused on this." As always, the soothing timbre of her aunt's voice calmed Ashna.

By the time she let herself into the house, her breathing was even. "Has Yash found anyone to help?"

"He's considering a few people. I think he wants someone with strategy experience but no political history. Fresh blood, he keeps saying. In this climate we need someone who can manage crisis—media attacks and blowups." Her aunt chattered on as Ashna dressed for bed.

"Anyway, hanging out at Curried Dreams will be fun. It will also give me an opportunity to have lunch with Shree." Ashna's uncle worked right down the street at Stanford. "I haven't done lunch dates with him in a while. And here I am always going on about how you can't let your marriage sag like old breasts. This is going to be fabulous!"

"I love you, Mina Kaki." Ashna was smiling when she crawled into bed.

That. That was how you did motherhood.

Chapter Eleven

Shobi stepped aside to avoid the passing camel on Juhu Beach on her morning walk. She couldn't let her contemplation of how one got motherhood right cause her to get trampled by an animal. Although at this point, death by camel seemed like her best chance at getting Ashi's attention.

The sun was barely peeking out from over the ocean's edge, but the sky was already pink and orange, heralding its arrival. Shobi loved her morning walks. Getting here before five A.M. was the only way to avoid the crowds. Good thing sleeping past five A.M. wasn't for a mind like hers.

Not that Shobi had a problem with crowds. Being able to withdraw into yourself amid the hordes was something that became coded into your DNA early when you took birth on this soil. It was the essence of being Indian. Even living in a palace didn't afford you solitude. Not that physical isolation had anything to do with peace.

After her conversation with Ashi there was no peace to be had, even though there were only a few stray walkers on the beach.

A mother-daughter pair waved at Shobi as they walked by, both in running shorts and T-shirts. A pang of envy mixed with yearning tugged at her as she waved back and took in their easy camaraderie.

They did the usual perusal of Shobi's cotton sari as they passed. She didn't feel judged. Choosing to live in saris was a decision she had made a long time ago. She had fought the blameless six yards of fabric so hard during her initial years in Sripore, and then wearing them had felt like claiming herself during her time in America with Bram. Why did women do this, use clothing as a tool in their battle against society?

Because you took whatever tools you were given, that's why.

America. Where she had used her clothing to embrace her identity but lost her child.

Mina Kaki is helping me. No matter how many times Shobi heard those words, they sliced through her heart. As though a knife had dropped from Ashi's hands onto her chest.

Of course Shobi had watched the video. Flora hadn't stopped talking about it since she'd seen it. Shobi had watched it a few times. All right, more than a few times. An embarrassing number of times. She had watched it on a loop for hours.

It had been far too long since she'd seen her baby. Missing Ashi was part of her life, a chronic pain she had learned to breathe through and manage. But seeing her like that, exposed to the world exactly the way she was, vulnerable, guileless, beautiful—it had shaken years of suppressed pain loose inside Shobi.

Turning to the ocean, she took in the orange arc of the sun as it emerged over waves fallen gray in its shadow. A moment that remained magnificent no matter how many times you witnessed it. A moment that was never the same unless it reflected off a human retina and not a lens, no matter how skilled the photographer. Much like life.

The moment when Ashi had let the knife go at the sight of Frederico Silva played in Shobi's mind again. This was what the world had come to, recording everything in the constant search of an unscripted moment. A mass hysterical hunger for serendipity.

Now her child was a victim of it. The idea of Ashi in Bram's restaurant had always made Shobi want to burn the damn place down. Ashi had avoided cooking at all costs growing up. The way Bram had shoved their daughter into that role, doing something she hated, made rage burn through Shobi. She picked up her pace, breaking into a jog.

Could there be a greater irony than the fact that Ashi had landed a football player as a partner? As a child, the thing Ashi had loved as much as she had hated cooking was football. When she'd moved to America she had lost her sport just the way she had lost her home. Or maybe she had willfully cast it off as a symbol of rebellion against Shobi. It had been Shobi's dream that Ashi follow her footsteps to the cricket pitch, but Ashi had gravitated toward football. So Shobi had adjusted her dream to her daughter leading India into the international scene in that sport. Then Bram had ruined everything, as always.

Maybe Ashi still followed the sport. Was that why she had agreed to do the show? Because of Frederico Silva?

Something about her baby's face as she dropped the knife

had reminded Shobi of herself at sixteen. The first time she'd seen Omar home from college she had fallen off her horse and dislocated her shoulder. She'd known Omar her entire life. His father had managed her family estate since before Shobi was born. His family had lived in the staff quarters on the premises of her home, but that day had been a first meeting, if there had ever been one.

The strength of her agitation disoriented Shobi. It wasn't like her to not know what she was feeling; complete clarity was her gift. It was what had gotten her where she was today. Squatting down in her sari, she dug her hand into the wet sand and scooped some up. She shaped it into a ball, but it wouldn't hold for more than an instant, no matter how hard she tried.

A wave rolled to a stop inches from her sneaker-clad toes, then ebbed away. Why was this discomfort something she couldn't move past? She was used to Ashna's stubbornness when it came to blocking her out. But there was something about Ashna's being on the show that Shobi just couldn't wrap her head around. Or her heart.

She tossed the handful of wet sand at the ocean. The force of her swing dislodged a lock of hair from her bun. How did one soothe the discomfort of being a mother who didn't know her daughter at all? She knew who Ashi's friends were, what she liked to eat, things she had gleaned from conversations, found out from Mina. But had Ashi ever fallen in love? Had she ever had her heart broken?

Shobi herself didn't remember ever not being in love, with Omar, with her sport, with her work. How had she given birth to someone who at thirty was so uninterested in love, or in anything for that matter? So insular and controlled about everything.

Because you weren't around to teach her passion, the waves whispered to her. She threw another handful of sand at them.

Until Shobi watched her drop that knife she had wondered if Ashi preferred women. Would she have been able to come out to the Rajes if she did? Yes, she would. Ashi would be able to tell Mina and Shree anything. It was the reason Shobi had been able to leave her daughter in their care, to let her go for so long. She'd known she was in good hands.

Oh, who was she trying to fool. She had let Ashi go because she hadn't known how to be a mother, she hadn't known how to compromise with something she was forced into. Because losing herself entirely to motherhood was the price Bram— and the world—had demanded of her.

How she hated that man. Thinking about him still stung like oil burns across her skin. To think he had been her friend once. Then he'd betrayed her. So large had her anger at him been that she'd let go of something precious. Something she wanted back.

Why should Mina be the one who got to help Ashi? To be her mother? When Shobi wanted it so badly.

It's because you're here and not there with her, the waves whispered.

Shobi dusted the sand off her hands. Their last conversation had made it obvious that Ashi didn't want her. There had been sheer panic in her voice at the thought of having to see Shobi. "You don't know anything, so just shut up," she said to the waves.

They went back to their rhythmic churning.

Sitting down on the beach, Shobi removed her sneakers and socks and neatly folded and tucked them together. Her toes were their usual coppery red. Having her toenails painted was a habit she had picked up from her own mother, who'd insisted that it was a sign of gentility. Even in her cricket-playing days Shobi had kept her feet pedicured, the deeply embedded need to please her mother lingering on past all the work she had done to become the person she was under the conditioning.

"You must be so proud of what you've achieved," a journalist had said to her last week.

She was.

Wasn't she?

Shobi had no experience with questioning herself. If she had stopped for doubts, life would have stomped her into the earth.

She rested her chin on her knees and watched the waves.

"Tell me what I'm missing?" she asked them as they rolled and rolled without pause. They never got a break to question their actions. They had to keep going to sustain the life they contained.

That wasn't true. Even the ocean receded into low tide so the beaches might breathe.

Ashi had a way of breathing that told Shobi she was upset. It was her withdrawing-into-herself breathing, which she had used to lock Shobi out her whole life. The first time Shobi had noticed it was when she'd returned from the World Cup tournament when Ashi was eight.

"Mamma missed you," Shobi had said, and Ashi's eyes had

gone flat. She'd breathed in slowly and deliberately but had not responded.

Your daughter told you she's never learned to be happy.

Her child, who hadn't told her anything important in a very long time, had told her a truth that people spoke only when they were desperate to be heard. Or when they had given up.

Don't you see she's asking you for help? the ocean said.

"I offered to help her, and she panicked."

Maybe she just doesn't know how to ask.

The last time Ashi had asked for something, Shobi hadn't been able to give it to her. Another situation her daughter's father had put them in. A last devastating act.

"I want my daughter back."

Then go and get her.

I don't know where to start, Shobi wanted to say. There were just so many lies, so much Ashi didn't know. Shobi had always kept things from her, afraid of not knowing which straw of truth would break her. Or maybe she'd kept things to herself because she hadn't known how to share them with someone who had always borne the greatest brunt of her decisions.

It was time to fix this mess once and for all. It was time to stop tiptoeing around all the lies. Ashi deserved to be happy. Maybe it wasn't too late for her to learn how. Maybe there was still time for Shobi to show her that it was possible. No matter how hard the world tried to take happiness away from you, it was possible to fight back.

Who knew this better than Shobi? Because, good Lord, how hard they had tried.

Chapter Twelve

Shoban had spent the entire day sitting on the cliffs of the Sripore palace, staring at the ocean and daydreaming about Omar. Usually it was her favorite pastime. But since he had left for Oxford, even daydreaming about him hurt. It didn't help that it was her eighteenth birthday and not a soul here was aware of the fact, or cared.

For the hundredth time that day, Shoban opened Omar's birthday letter.

On your eighteenth birthday, eighteen reasons why you own my heart . . .

Pressing the letter to her own heart, she stood. If she didn't find some way to distract herself, she was going to explode.

She ran all the way to the stables looking for Bram, but he seemed to have disappeared off the face of the earth.

"Where's Prince Bram?" she asked the liveried chauffeur standing by Bram's family's Bentley.

The man straightened, saluted her, and informed her that he had no idea.

Bram never told anyone where he was going. It was the

most infuriating thing about him, these princely airs of his. He also only ate foods cooked a certain way, with annoyingly fancy colonial names like "braised this" and "sautéed that." Needlessly complicating something as natural as food with snobbery was an abomination, if you asked Shoban.

His older brothers were nothing like that. But Bram was always trying to play at being this person who was too important to be answerable to anyone.

"I like it when you worry about me," he had said to her yesterday.

"But what about Ma-saheb?" His mother worried about him. Everyone worried about him. "Why does having people worry about you prove that you're special?" she had demanded.

Bram, being Bram, just yanked her braid anytime she questioned him.

It annoyed her, but she let it go for the sake of their friendship. They'd been friends for a year, ever since their families had spent the summer together in his family's chalet in Switzerland.

So when her father had asked her to join him on his visit to Sripore she had agreed. Omar had gone back to England last week. She tried not to be one of those filmy melodramatic girls who acted all heartbroken when they were separated from their love. But truthfully, it's how she felt on the inside. Like someone had smacked a ball into her chest with a bat, and it had become lodged there.

In a stroke of bad timing, her cricket coach was on vacation, so their team got two weeks off. Being plagued with boredom was Shoban's worst nightmare. Her exams were finished and her applications were complete. This waiting to know if she'd get into Oxford or Cambridge so she could be near Omar was killing her.

She made her way to the cricket pitch. Taking a run down the wicket, she swung the ball into the net, flicking her wrist just as she let go. The ball shot a straight line for half the length of the pitch and then spun out and into a curve. If a batsman could have made contact with it, she would have been thoroughly impressed.

Her spin was getting better, but if her team was to have any hope of remaining undefeated until the state finals, she had to practice until it was flawless. She'd shattered the record for the most wickets at the state level, and if she weren't off to university she had a real chance at making the national team. Bram had promised to help her practice and now he was nowhere to be found.

"Tai-saheb?" Flora, one of the maids, cleared her throat. She had waited until Shoban had released the ball before speaking.

Shoban smiled at her. "Hello."

The girl returned her smile politely. The staff at the Sripore palace were impeccably trained. Her braid was pulled tightly back much like Shoban's, and her kurta was white like Shoban's. But where Shoban's was intricately embroidered with white thread and she wore it over blue jeans, the girl's was severely simple and she wore it over a traditional churidar.

Shoban wanted to ask if she'd mind playing cricket with her, but she wasn't sure if the girl would consider her too spoiled for assuming she had nothing better to do with her time. So Shoban simply asked what she wanted.

"Your father would like to see you, Tai-saheb," the girl said in polished Marathi.

The formality of the address made Shoban want to laugh. The Rajes were royalty and still lived somewhat in the style of their ancestors. Shoban's own family was only second cousins to the royal Gaikwads, and while Shoban was used to the pompousness at her uncle's palace, her own mother had run a fairly laid-back household before she had died of cancer two years ago. Bram's mother and Shoban's mother had gone to boarding school together and been very fond of each other in that way adults claimed to be fond of one another based on childhood friendships.

They had rekindled their friendship only after Ma's diagnosis. Until then Shoban hadn't known the Rajes, only known of them. Throughout Ma's illness Bram's mother, who was one of the dearest people Shoban knew, visited her regularly, and after Ma passed away, the maharani had taken Shoban under her wing. Then last year she had coaxed Shoban to go with them to Switzerland because she'd believed it would help Shoban make her way out of her grief.

Maya Devi had been right. Switzerland was beautiful in exactly the kind of way that soothed grief, and Bram had kept Shoban entertained with his shenanigans.

"Did you want me to show you the way to the library?" Flora asked.

"I do know where the library is. Thank you very much, Flora." Shoban took the wet wipes Flora handed her from a silver tray and cleaned her hands. She was about to run to the house but she didn't want to appear ill-mannered, so she forced herself to walk.

"You're sweaty, young lady." Shoban was used to every conversation with her father starting with a criticism, and then pretty much staying in that general realm.

"I was playing cricket."

As always, he acted as though she hadn't said those words. If he had his way, Shoban would saunter around the house arranging flowers or painting watercolors or practicing the piano or doing something "ladylike."

"With Bram?" he asked, proving that he had heard her.

"No, Bram is nowhere to be found."

Her father outright smiled at that, and Shoban wondered if he'd been drinking in the daytime. When Ma was alive, his drinking had been restricted to one scotch before dinner. After her mother died, she had no idea what his routine was. She barely saw him a few times a month at the dinner table, where they tended to eat in silence.

"You'd better get used to keeping track of the young prince. I hear he's not an easy one to rein in," he said, still smiling in that way people did when a pet or a child made them proud. Shoban hadn't seen him smile much since her mother's death.

"Why would I—"

"Sit down." He cut her off.

She sat. It was just the two of them in the library. The somberness of the place highlighted their usual awkwardness.

"How do you like the palace?"

"The Sagar Mahal? It's beautiful. But I've seen it before."

She'd been here a few times. It was the very symbol of the Indian royal palace, and photographs of it were all over magazines and television. What was not to like?

"Is something wrong, Daddy?" she asked, because despite all her mother's training to be seen and not heard in his presence, she had only so much patience for mysterious behavior.

He didn't look angry, so it couldn't be something she'd done. If Shoban recognized anything in the world, she recognized her father's disapproval.

She was a great believer in knowing his moods, because information was power. If she knew what to expect she could work it to her advantage. Another thing her soft-spoken yet whip-sharp mother had taught her.

"I would say it's the opposite of something being wrong." A smile tugged at his mouth, making discomfort nudge at Shoban.

"Stop looking so worried. I have a feeling this is going to make you very happy."

"Did you hear from Oxford?" she said excitedly.

He laughed. "Well, now even if you did hear from Oxford, I won't be the one deciding if you go."

What on earth could he possibly mean? She dabbed her sweating upper lip with the back of her hand.

"The Rajes have asked for your hand for Bram. This is—"

Her father was still speaking, but Shobi's ears were ringing and she could only see his lips move.

"Asked for my hand?" she said. "What for?"

"Why, your hand in marriage, of course," he snapped. "Are you feeling all right?"

Shoban jumped out of her chair. She was laughing. She had no idea why, but there was a maniacal panic in her chest and laughter was the only way to breathe around it.

Her father looked confused. She tried to tamp down her laughter. "Bram doesn't want to marry me."

Bram liked models and actresses, and wasn't he going out with that tennis player from France? She was Shoban, plain old Shoban, with thick brows and oily skin and hips too wide. What interest would someone like Bram have in her?

"As a matter of fact, he does. This is his idea."

The walls closed in on her. "I'm eighteen years old, I haven't even thought about marriage." What a liar she was. If Omar came to her door today, she would run out barefoot and marry him right then and there in the cotton kurta she was wearing. And he'd write a beautiful sonnet about the heartbreaking simplicity of it all, of her! Which explained why she would rather die than have this conversation. "I'm going to university this year."

"I don't think Bram will stop you from doing that. It's just a betrothal."

She was going to kill Bram. He'd always had a strange sense of humor, but this was going too far. This had to be a prank.

"I think there's been a mistake." She paced the room and tugged at her braid. It was too tight. There was a strand of hair pulling at her scalp and she needed to untie the whole thing so it would stop pinching like that.

Her father seemed to register that things were not going the way he expected them to. He studied her face with more than his usual disgust. She had to get her features under control or she was going to make a hash of everything.

What to do?

Shoban wanted to wring Omar's neck too. She had told him that they should talk to Daddy before he left for England this time. He'd wanted to wait until he made something of himself. A stupid law degree was not going to help them now. What was she to do? "But I don't want to get married!"

Her father's only reaction was to lean forward in his wing chair and glare at her as she paced the library.

He had no idea about Omar. He probably didn't even know that his estate manager had a brilliant son who was his daughter's best friend, her everything. He barely even knew that his daughter existed.

She was a stranger to him. Between chess, golf, and polo she barely even knew what he did for a living. He'd never had a job, never gone to work. He managed money for their wealthy relatives, Ma had once told her. He had always been this remote person who lived in the same home, and Shoban had never given him much thought. He'd returned the favor.

The first time he'd shown any interest in her at all was when Maya Devi asked her to go to Switzerland last summer. Now it all made sense. Well, not sense exactly. But it all seemed to fall into place in this rusty-slots-and-gears sort of way.

"What if you fall in love with that prince?" Omar had asked when she'd left for Switzerland, excited despite the fact that she would miss him terribly. They'd always sworn to be each other's kite lines, strings with enough give that they could fly. Never ropes and chains. "I don't think that prince is single," she'd teased him, then added, "I think my heart might be too full with someone else." Because no matter how secure you were, you needed to hear it.

She'd been right. Bram had spent most of their vacation talking about his many girlfriends. "What a waste," she'd said to him. "To spend all this time on so many women you don't care about. Imagine if you could spend all that emotion on someone you really did care about."

She'd been a good friend to him. Tried to get him to stop whiling away his life when he could do so much with it. This was how he repaid her? By playing an ugly prank on her?

"Shoban?" Her father snapped his fingers in her face. "I hope this is all just shock and excitement. I'm having a hard time understanding you."

"There's nothing to understand. I don't want to marry Bram."

Her father threw a look around the room, then marched to the door and locked it.

"Have you lost your mind?" he said in a voice so soft it rumbled in his chest. "Do you realize who the Rajes are?"

"I don't care. I can't do it."

"What is that supposed to mean? You put on a damn bridal sari and you walk around a fire and say vows. It isn't rocket science."

"I'm in love with someone else. And I will only marry him."

The slap landed across her cheek, fire exploded across her skin, numbing one half of her face, replacing every thought in her head with disbelief.

"If you were in love with someone else, you shouldn't have cavorted with Bram for the past year. I did not raise a whore."

That stung harder than the slap. "Bram and I are . . . we're . . . friends. I never gave him cause to believe anything more. I swear. I've only ever been in love with Omar."

Her father grabbed her arm and dragged her closer until his face was inches from hers. She wouldn't have believed the force of his grip, but the slap was still stinging her cheek.

Something in his eyes told her that he knew exactly who Omar was after all.

"Omar? Is that Aijaz's son?" He shook her by the arm. "You let that . . . that son of a servant touch you?"

I let him touch my soul, she wanted to tell her father, but the inside of her ear was in agony; it felt wet. She wondered if it was bleeding.

He pushed her into a chair and stood over her. His always neatly slicked-down silver hair had come askew, giving his rage a wildness.

"Since when has this been going on?"

Since forever, she wanted to say. *Since the world was a twinkle in God's eye.* That's what Omar always said: *I've loved you since the universe was a twinkle in Allah's eye.*

"That shameless, ungrateful son of a bitch."

She tried to stand up, but her father pushed her back down. "After everything I've done for him," her father mumbled almost to himself. "I will make sure he lives to regret the day he dared to step out of his measly gutter and look at my daughter." He started pacing. Shoban's heartbeat sped up with each step he took. "I paid for his daughter's wedding, for his wife's treatment and wake, his son's education, and he does this to me? Is the bastard stupid? He owes me millions of rupees."

Omar's father was in debt to her father?

Her father reached for the phone on the sideboard.

"Who are you calling? Daddy, wait. Please."

"I'm firing that son of a bitch. He will get out of my house and return every penny he owes me. I will make sure he ends up naked on the streets."

"Aijaz Uncle has worked for you for thirty years. How can you talk about him like that?"

"He's worked for me. Now he wants to use his son to make his way into my family?"

"It wasn't like that. He doesn't even know. Please don't call him." She needed to think. "Just give me a little time. I can fix this. I swear."

"Fix it?" he spat. "If you so much as step out of your room I'll make sure your precious Aijaz Uncle lands up in jail."

"What? You can't do that." She stood.

They were face-to-face. For a moment she thought he'd hit her again, but he just leaned closer to her. "Try me, then. The man owes me more money than he can ever repay. He has access to my estate. You can't even imagine the things I can accuse him of. I can have him locked up until his dying day. If you don't believe me, try me."

"Please, Daddy. Don't do this. Be fair."

He laughed at that. "Fair? You think I want to destroy a man I've taken care of all my life? You're the one who holds the power to destroy him and you want *me* to be fair?"

She sucked in a breath. Tears burned in her throat, but crying would help no one. She had to think. *Think.* "What are you going to do?"

"The bigger question, beta, is what are you going to do? What will you do to make sure a man doesn't have his life destroyed?" He walked to the door.

She followed him. "How can you do this?"

"Do what? Be a father and make sure you don't throw your life away on a servant's son from a religion that seeks to annihilate ours? When you can have the life of a princess and not shame our ancestors?"

"You know Aijaz Uncle doesn't believe anything of that sort. Omar doesn't even believe in organized religion."

"Oh, he doesn't, does he? Then why does he want to marry a Hindu girl to bear him Muslim babies? Go ask Aijaz if he would ever let his own daughter marry into a Hindu family. I'll give you the answer to that. He wouldn't. His wife, Shakeela—that boy's mother—was Hindu. Did you know that? She was born Sneha. If your Aijaz Uncle doesn't believe in religion, why did he make the woman he married convert?"

Omar had never told her that. He never talked about his mother. She had died when he was just a boy, so the story of how or why she converted was hardly relevant.

"I would never let you forsake your religion and heritage."

"I'm not going to." Omar would never expect her to.

Her father pushed open the door and beckoned to the servant waiting outside. "Good. Then we're on the same page. Now Ramesh will take you to your room." He turned to Ramesh, who had been his shadow for as long as Shoban could remember. "Take Baby to her room. She is not to leave there until I let her out myself."

Chapter Thirteen

Rico watched as Ashna left the room. Or, more accurately, she tore out of there the moment they announced that they were twenty minutes from shooting their first cooking segment. It was as though she were making a break for it after someone had locked her up for years. Granted, the set was a bit chaotic, but everyone other than Ashna seemed to enjoy it. This was just their second time on set, yet laughter rippled around them. Ashna swung wildly between being warm and fuzzy with the cast and crew (with obvious exceptions) and toppling headfirst into misery.

What had possessed him to start down this insane path? There was a reason you weren't supposed to make decisions at emotionally overwrought events like bachelor parties. If that wasn't a thing, it needed to be. Someone needed to warn sods everywhere to keep their heads when their friends were getting hitched.

How hadn't Rico anticipated quite how miserable his presence would make her? Or had he? It's not like he meant her any harm. All he needed was to move on. To convince his stubborn subconscious that there was nothing to hold on to. Meanwhile the darned thing was holding its poker face and giving Rico nothing.

When he followed Ashna into the lobby outside the staging area, he was at least eighty percent certain that it was to make sure she hadn't passed out or something. He was being a good Samaritan, that's all. Before he could catch up with her, DJ Caine, their host, stepped into the lobby. Rico had never heard of DJ Caine—not that he was up on the chef stardom business—but evidently Ashna had more than just heard of him.

The moment their eyes met, they flew at each other like lovers at the climax of one of those rom-coms Rico suddenly found himself inside. DJ wrapped Ashna in a hug. Ashna, who had been icy enough to give Rico frostbite, melted into this giant. Apparently being a fancy chef left you with enough time to be a gym rat. Who knew? Not that Rico wasn't fitter than everyone in the building. Who cared that he wasn't as tall as this guy. The best thing about football was that you didn't have to be tall or big, you just had to know what to do with the damn ball. That's why it was the most played sport on earth.

The chef might be big, but Rico could totally take him.

Whoa, time out! No one was *taking* anyone. What the hell was wrong with him? If any of his friends had said something so ridiculous, Rico would have smacked them upside the head. Reaching back, he squeezed his rolled-up ponytail.

"You holding up okay?" DJ asked Ashna, pulling away and making some sort of nauseatingly understanding eye contact.

She nodded, soulful eyes shying away from DJ's gaze, and gave him another hug. "I'm so glad you're here."

Ah! So this was why she was doing the show. To be close to her boyfriend.

Well, good. That made everything easier. Rico stepped away, giving them space as they chattered away, a little too intimately for public, if you asked him. But what did he know?

"You really lucked out with your star, love!" DJ said suddenly, and turned to Rico before Rico could make his escape.

Walking up to Rico, DJ held out his hand. "Huge fan, sir, huge fan! That run you had in the ninetieth in the final when you went top corner, bloody hell! The keeper had no chance! Wait till I tell my sister I met you, she's going to clean pee her pants."

Rico let him pump his hand. So the man knew his sport, so what?

"DJ Caine."

"I know." Rico shoved his hands into his pockets, his tone somewhere between stiff and downright sulky. "I was there for the introductions."

Ashna glared at him and he felt like a piece of shit. He hated when someone was a prick to fans.

"I'm sorry," he said into the awkward pause, because what was he doing? He could not let her take away his decency. He'd lost enough of himself to her. "I meant you're our host, so I know who you are." He reached out and squeezed the man's bicep. Holy shit! He'd been going for his shoulder. DJ looked alarmed. Rico had never felt like a bigger ass. "Very impressive credentials. Excellent. Excited to work with you. Fabulous," he gushed like an overcompensating moron.

DJ and Ashna exchanged confused looks and Rico excused himself before he embarrassed himself even more.

He headed back into the competition area, hating how idiotic he felt. Suddenly the atmosphere in here resembled a high school dance. Everyone seemed to be immersed in the business of impressing one another. Song, the Korean drama star, caught his eye and gave him a self-conscious wave from across the room. She was the only person in the crowded studio standing by herself. Her partner, an impressively tattooed Mexican American chef, was off talking to the mystery writer.

Rico turned around to see if his own chef had followed him. Not that he needed to check. Rico had always somehow known if she was in a room.

That was more than ten years ago, you knob.

He made his way toward Song.

She gave him a grateful smile when he stopped next to her and it felt like reclaiming his dignity.

"Pretty wild setup, huh?" He threw a glance at the six fully functional kitchens under one roof.

"My mother used to give me a hard time about never entering one kitchen—now I'm inside six at once!" she said brightly, eyes shining with humor.

For a moment, they absorbed their surroundings in companionable silence.

"So this is for her then, for your mother, you being on the show?" He leaned back into the counter, trying to take the weight off his leg.

Her smile dimmed. "My sister lives in San Jose, I wanted to spend some time with her. Haven't seen her in years. We . . . well, I've been working nonstop for the past ten years and she's got a family, children, a dog, you know, a *real* life." She blinked at him and waited for him to respond, but he knew she wasn't done. "That sounded a little regressive, didn't it? Sorry, I guess I've heard my mother repeat it too many times. She must have gotten inside my head."

This time the smile she gave Rico was so stoic, he patted her shoulder, not her bicep, thank God. "Isn't that how it's supposed to be, that all women eventually turn into their mothers?"

She looked mock-horrified, "Please tell me that isn't true." Her voice had a happy lilt to it that made everything she said sound enthusiastic.

"Well, based on what I'm seeing, if you have turned into your mother, she must be quite lovely."

The research Rico had done on each contestant indicated that after him Song was the biggest star here in terms of fan following. How entirely unaffected she seemed by it was even more impressive than her stardom itself.

"Thanks!" she said with that enthusiasm she couldn't seem to contain. "Actually, my mom is spectacular. Raised my sister and me by herself. So, I guess it's not such a bad thing to make her happy by finally learning how to cook, ha?" She threw a look at her chef, and Rico wondered why she had picked him. Sure, the network wanted everyone to believe that the pairings were surprises, but one of the biggest television stars in the world wasn't going to leave who she got as a partner to chance.

"Mexican food is my favorite," she said finally. "My sister's too, and of course our mother's. My sister already makes the most amazing tacos." Then she grinned her first real grin, not the one perfected for the cameras. "We're a teeny bit, um . . ."

"Competitive?" he supplied. "My guess is everyone here is."

"—or we wouldn't be here," they both said together and burst into laughter.

Her flashbulb smile dimmed again. "But my sister makes me look easygoing. She's a human rights lawyer. Works for the ACLU. She's at the border right now, trying to make sure the children separated from their parents are reunited."

"That's amazing work to be doing." Rico hated what was happening in America right now. The inhumanity of it was baffling. He'd been taken in by this country when he'd had nowhere else to go. For that he would always be grateful and loyal. He hadn't even been a refugee, just an orphan in need of a home. "People who have no empathy for refugees are soulless. No one who's forced out of their home has any interest in anything but embracing the land that gives them another chance. It's been proven over and over again, that refugees— and their children—go on to do great things for the countries that become their new homes."

"I just heard one of the guys who's running for governor of California say exactly that on the radio this morning. I think he's the guy my sister is working with on the border crisis."

"No way! She works with Yash Raje? I've been following his campaign and the man is amazing. I can't believe the bigoted nonsense that piece of shit Cruz has been saying against him."

"You're interested in politics," she said with exaggerated disappointment. "That means you too are going to like my sister more than me."

"Do you make all your friends choose? Between your sister and you?"

That made her laugh. Unexpectedly, she threw her hands around him and gave him a hug. "Honestly, I'm crazy proud of her," she said sincerely. "I'm so glad you're here. This is going to be so much fun!"

Her buoyancy was contagious, and for the first time since he had come back to California, the deep restlessness inside Rico relaxed. The room was filled with talented, interesting people. Song was right, this could be fun.

When he pulled away from the hug, he noticed that his lovely partner was back in the room. Yes, he felt it, shoot him.

A bitter little smile danced around her red, bee-stung lips—a combination of smugness and annoyance. Rico had no patience for it. And no, the fact that her chef boyfriend was right behind her, his body language all protective of her, had nothing to do with Rico's lack of patience.

Rico turned back to the sweet person he was talking to.

Song was watching him with awe, which made him extremely grateful right about now. "You guys are guaranteed to get through the first few rounds. Given the, you know . . ."

"The video." His eyes found Ashna again as she made her way across the studio toward him—not by choice but because DJ was heading this way and she had her hand hooked into his arm as though he were an overinflated life raft and she were swimming against a current gone wild.

Song gave him another hundred-watt smile, and he chose to mirror Ashna and cling on to it. "That was such an amazingly brave thing to do. You're a hero!" Song said.

And yet, he had barely received a grudging thanks for his heroism. "It's the curse of being a football player; you see a flying object and you automatically leap toward it."

She loved that, laughed heartily at it. Rico loved that he didn't have to work for her laughter, she gave it easily and he was as grateful as a starved puppy. As if he didn't like her enough already, she turned the conversation to his last World Cup final, one of his favorite topics. They had come so close to losing that one. If not for that goal in the ninetieth minute, they would have gone to penalties. Song wasn't kidding when she said she was a fan. She knew every detail of all the major games he'd ever played.

By the time Ashna and DJ made their way over, Song was in full-blown superfan splendor. The first thing she did when she saw Ashna was tell her how very lucky she was to have Rico as her partner. "Could you believe it when you found out?"

"No," Ashna said, voice dripping sweetness even as she threw all sorts of eye-daggers at Rico. "I still can't believe how"—*or why*, her eyes added just for him—"it happened." Then she ruined things by adding kindly that Song's chef was lucky to have her too.

Song beamed. "I'm so happy to be here!" she said delightedly before going off to join her chef.

"How is that knee?" DJ—yes, he was still stuck to Ashna's side—said, sounding annoyingly concerned. "Ashna just asked Jonah to bring you a chair until we start shooting."

Ashna studied her toes. They were covered by sneakers today, but the need to know if they were still painted bright pink stirred inside him.

"My knee is perfectly fine now, thanks. I don't need a chair."

"That's great news," DJ said with more of that sincere concern. "My girlfriend saw it the day you hurt yourself. She said it was a good thing you were so close to a hospital. Believe me, she never thinks anything is serious."

"Doesn't she?" Rico looked pointedly at Ashna, who looked back at him as though she'd like to kick him in his knee. "I guess she wouldn't have dropped the knife if she thought it was serious."

This seemed to throw DJ. "Trisha dropped the knife?" He looked to Ashna for confirmation. "I'm pretty sure Ashna dropped the knife."

You know those realizations where you're faced with your own stupidity? One of those zinged inside Rico's medicine-addled brain, for the second time that day. But the damage was done. He'd kicked the ball right at Ashna.

She slapped her hands around it with panache. "You're right, DJ. I was the one who dropped the knife. *Your girlfriend, my cousin Trisha*"—yes, she stretched out that last part like well-chewed gum—"*she* was just kind enough to look at Frederico's knee when he hurt it." All of this she said while looking at DJ, but of course, every overenunciated word was meant only for Rico.

"Ah." All sorts of understanding dawned on DJ's face, and on Rico's own face too, no doubt.

Before this painful conversation could drag on any longer,

China Dashwood, bless her, called them to order and requested that DJ join her at the front of the room.

"Go," Ashna said to DJ, with all the warmth of a dear friend.

As soon as DJ left, Ashna turned to Rico, anger brightening her too-large, too-dark eyes. "There's still time. The first episode hasn't aired yet. You can ask for any other chef and they'll give you what you want. I don't think I can do this."

"The habit of walking away from things must be a hard one to break," he said, when the last thing he wanted to think about right now was that particular moment from their past.

She's just a girl I dated in high school.

Her long, incredibly delicate fingers squeezed her temples, her jaw clenched, every inch of her screamed how badly she did not want to be doing this with him.

If she wanted to walk away, she was going to have to be the one to do it. Again. "As for how I behaved with DJ," he said when the silence had stretched out long enough that he knew she wasn't going to respond, "it was an honest mistake." None of this was about DJ.

"Dropping a knife from shock, that's an honest mistake," she said, the new shell she'd grown melting like ice around pine needles after a winter storm. "Being rude to someone because you're angry with someone else? That's just being spoiled and self-centered."

Fire burned in her eyes as their gazes locked. Just like that she was the girl who had gone to war for him, kept the coach from pushing him into playing when he couldn't. The girl who had blazed at a world he couldn't deal with and held him close until he'd learned how to again.

Eyes locked with hers, he was that boy again, the one who could handle waking up in the morning only because she was out there waiting for him.

China's voice rang out through the speakers. "All right then, people, it's time for the first cooking challenge."

Rico was about to join in the cheering that exploded around them when the girl who had been his shield, and then a sword through his heart, crumbled before his eyes. The fire inside her dissolved into panic. She imploded even as she stood there tall and proud for all to see.

Chapter Fourteen

After all these years of trying to put into words what an impending panic attack felt like, today of all days, Ashna finally had crystal clarity. A simultaneous unraveling and tightening swirled inside and around her. Ten tons of pressure compressed her into solid rock even as she dissolved into amorphous, weightless air.

The words *self-centered* and *spoiled* lingered in her mouth like the taste of particularly strong bitter melon doused in too much truffle, acrid and overpowering. The need to spit it out before she exploded with it gathered inside her. Then his hand was on her back, pressing into the curve where sensitive divots dipped into her skin on both sides of her spine. Like filings to a magnet, her scattering parts pulled toward his touch.

Walking through the kitchens felt like wading underwater, with the last of her breath running out fast. His hand stayed there, a too-heavy oxygen tank.

The unfairness of that, the anger at it, was the only thing that made it possible for Ashna to break the surface as they emerged at the front of the room and lined up next to the other competitors. DJ's lips moved. With a lag of just seconds, his voice followed.

"Our challenge today is . . ." Ashna squeezed her eyes shut. ". . . Omelets."

Until that moment Ashna hadn't noticed that Rico's thumb was stroking her. The second she came back into herself he dropped his hand. She stepped away, too furious at him for glimpsing her panic, too relieved at this incredible stroke of luck.

When a laugh escaped her, that relentless frown—probing at her innermost thoughts—folded between his brows, taking her back in time, grounding her deep in this moment.

"It's omelets!" she said with the kind of exuberant delight one might display when saying "I feel a pulse!" or "Yes, that's my glass slipper!"

He backed away from her, quickly putting distance between them. A good thing, because his hand still burned on her skin and because, well, they had omelets (*omelets!*) to make.

Ashna shook her arms out. Eggs were a brilliant, brilliant choice for a first challenge. They were seemingly easy to work with, but also an accurate test of culinary skill. More importantly, Ashna served spicy, curried omelets at the restaurant. Which meant she could make them exactly the way she did at Curried Dreams. It was one of Baba's most popular recipes.

"Oh, one more thing," DJ said, and the runaway truck in her brain teetered again. "You each have to cook your omelets separately. The chefs on one side of your station and the stars on the other. No helping each other. Everyone comes up with a dish that showcases who they are on their own."

Ashna's shoulders were shaking, relief again, laughter again. She had to work hard to not skip on her way back to their station. By the end of this day she was going to need a massage, from the bipolar locking and releasing of muscles.

"You'll be fine," she said to Rico when they got back, because he was still studying her and trying to make sense of her bizarre swings. "Cooking eggs is a standard test of basic cooking skill."

"I know *I'll* be fine," he said, the full blast of his focus mapping her relief. The emeralds in his eyes were too bright. The way they had been that first time they'd met under the bleachers. The need to see what no one else cared to see inside her, intense and naked. It had disarmed her then.

Today, it infuriated her. Made her brain forget the camera. Made her hands fly. She broke the eggs in a clean one-handed crack, whipped them ruthlessly into a thick froth, chopped the onions, cilantro, and green chilies in an unrelentingly brutal rhythm. All without breaking a sweat or sparing him a glance.

With minutes to spare from the mere twenty they were given, she turned out a fluffy and perfectly moist omelet with garlic-infused oil rolled into a crisp, flaky paratha.

Until they stood in front of the judges, she had forgotten where she was, who she was with.

The only place the livid energy inside her seemed to have manifested itself was in what the judges declared "abject underseasoning."

This made Ashna smile. When she looked at Rico, he was having the same reaction. For one quick meeting of their eyes, the ridiculously overdramatic statement joined them together with shared humor. His lips tilted up on one side. For the first time since they'd lined up to hear the challenge, she took a full breath.

Even though Ashna felt like she'd made the perfect cliff-dive into the ocean as the tide ebbed, the judges' focus wasn't on the chefs today. It was on the celebrities. They were the ones being tested for skill level without the assistance of their chefs. Rico had made an omelet stuffed with Portuguese sausage and peppers and served it with baked beans. Or attempted to.

As for his skill level, well, there wasn't any in evidence. His omelet (a generous label) was at once burnt—giving it a rusty color not commonly observed in nature—and uncooked—making it spring a watery leak when a judge pierced it with a fork.

Turned out eggs, much like memories, were unforgiving.

Naturally, the man was entirely unruffled by the judges' candor as they described every detail of his failures with flourish. He laughed, from a deep, unshakable place inside him. "May I suggest cleansing your palates with the masterpiece my chef just presented you with."

His chef didn't mean to blush, really she didn't, but she stuck up her chin and acted as though warmth weren't suffusing her face as the audience went crazy.

Thankfully, all the stars were in the same cooking boat—

more invested in the audience than the food—and the neglect meant that their omelets fell roughly into three categories: burnt, raw, and in Rico's case, partially burnt and partially raw. It made for a quick and lighthearted judging round that didn't require Ashna to say another word to Rico before she made her escape.

By the time Ashna was headed home her brain was so snarled up, there was no untangling it. The rideshare driver maneuvered the car onto High Street. India and China's building was a few minutes away. If India hadn't been off at her yearly yoga retreat, Ashna would have stopped by. She couldn't remember the last time she had needed one of India's yoga and meditation sessions so badly.

The idea of seeing Rico again tomorrow made the bats flap in her stomach with renewed fervor. They had taken up permanent residence in her rib cage, hanging by her lungs, ready to start flapping at the slightest excuse. There was no chance of her and Rico being voted off tomorrow. As if Rico's heroic dive at the knife weren't enough, his self-effacing charm in front of the judges today had made sure they had undisputed audience support.

Rico's face when she had called him self-centered and spoiled ran through her mind again. He'd hated that. His pride in being humble and fair had been one of the things she'd loved most about him. It was a lesson his soccer-legend father had taught him well. Then again, not well enough, because she couldn't believe how badly he had behaved with DJ. That entire painfully awkward exchange had dredged up a deep sense of loss inside her.

Who was she kidding, that sense of loss had been her constant companion for twelve years now.

This would be so much easier if she full-out hated him.

That cause was not helped at all by the fact that the first thing he'd done after the shoot was apologize to DJ, with humility and fairness.

But only to DJ, making sure Ashna understood that it had nothing to do with her. *You deserve my rudeness, only you, not DJ*, that apology had said to her. That's what she needed to remember, not his gentle touch in the depths of her panic.

The two men had practically fist-bumped, chest-bumped, and gone on their merry way as though being a prized ass were totally acceptable.

The car pulled into her driveway. Thankfully, her driver had picked up on her mood and left her alone. She still gave him a five-star rating on "fun conversation." Whoever had put that on the driver survey deserved a special spot in hell.

Across the jacarandas behind the house, Curried Dreams stood silent and stately. As a girl, Ashna had imagined the thicket of trees that separated the house from the restaurant as an enchanted wood from the fantasy books she loved. One weekend she had come home from the Anchorage and found that Baba had gotten someone to hang a hammock between two trees for her to read in.

Baba had always been weird about the fact that their house wasn't as grand as the Anchorage or Sagar Mahal. But Ashna loved the bungalow. She felt a kinship with it. Just like Ashna herself, it had been something Baba had tried to love, but it had fallen short of his expectations.

As Ashna stepped onto the porch, she noticed that the light was off. Ashna always left it on when she went out. Had the bulb blown out again? She'd just replaced it last month. Someone moved inside the door. Heart racing, Ashna dug in her handbag for her phone. She was about to dial 911 when the front door flew open.

Chapter Fifteen

Ashna screamed and dropped her phone.

"Good evening, beta!" Shobi said with all the calm of someone who hadn't just had the living daylights scared out of her. "Or should I say good morning?"

"Shob— *Mom?*" Ashna said, frozen in place, as Shobi squatted and fished the phone out from beneath the white wicker chair without dislodging a strand of hair or disturbing her neatly draped starched cotton sari.

"The very one." Shobi handed Ashna her phone and walked into Ashna's house as though it were her own. Which technically it was, if you defined ownership strictly in legal terms.

"What are you doing here?" Ashna looked around her usually fastidiously tidy living room, a sense of dread growing inside her.

Cups—at least four of them—were scattered across the coffee table along with file folders and papers, and a plate of cookies (or biscuits, as Shobi called them). An unfolded *kantha* quilt draped the antique Queen Anne couch. The pillows that usually lined the straight back in a perfect diamond pattern were strewn everywhere.

A sour feeling bubbled in Ashna's stomach. The house had always been in this kind of disarray when Shobi visited. It used to feel warm and cozy, until Ashna started to associate the mess with the constant fear of Shobi leaving. Ashna lined the cushions up, one mustard and one olive in order.

"Sorry. I'll clean up. I got caught up in some work. I . . . I wasn't expecting you not to be here. I . . . I have the garage code. I . . . um . . . I wanted to surprise you." Shobi smiled as though they were just any mother-daughter pair who routinely did things like surprise each other with visits. "I didn't realize you wouldn't be home." Shobi never rambled. Was she nervous? Shobi was never nervous.

"I told you I'm doing the show. We shoot in San Francisco. Traffic coming home was bad." Ashna picked up the empty and half-empty cups. Anger at the fact that Shobi hadn't believed her about the show rose fast, which led to the realization that it was Shobi's fault that she was stuck with Rico, and that did nothing to help the anger.

"It's not like I didn't believe you." Shobi picked up the plate of biscuits and followed Ashna into the kitchen. "It's just that I really wanted to see you and you refused to come to India. So I thought . . ."

Ashna started rinsing the cups out.

"We have to talk, Ashna. It's about time."

A horrid laugh spurted from Ashna. She pressed a fist into her mouth and swallowed it back.

She checked the Swiss cuckoo clock next to the fridge. In five hours she had to be up and at the farmer's market.

The need to turn Baba's restaurant around flared inside her afresh. Her mother's presence always made her grief, her protectiveness, her guilt over Baba a hundred times worse.

Suddenly, all she wanted was to get back to the studio and shoot the next episode, Rico's presence there be damned. Even if they received more votes than all the other teams put together she wouldn't feel guilty about it. Suddenly, any advantage that helped them win felt too small, even if that advantage came from the darned viral video.

"I really don't have the time for this right now." She turned to Shobi. Her waist-length silver-streaked black hair hung over one shoulder. Ashna patted her own tight bun. The huge red bindi in the center of her mother's forehead was perfectly placed just above the spot where her eyebrows would intersect if they met.

Unlike Mina Kaki's, Shobi's face was faintly lined. Light creases broke the flatness of her high forehead. Parenthetical lines bracketed her mouth, her passion for her work etched into her face.

"We have to make time, beta." She sounded so sad that Ashna wondered if something was wrong with her. Oh no, that's what this was about.

"Are you sick?"

"I deserved that," Shobi said, and reached out a hand, possibly to pat Ashna's, but Ashna couldn't be sure because she withdrew it. "I'm fine. Healthy as a horse. Getting a little thick around the middle, but that's about it." She was being charming, the way she was in her TV interviews.

"Then what do you want?" Now, after all these years.

"I want to help you." Shobi watched Ashna's face. "And myself. We deserve to at least try to have a relationship."

"Okay, I see what this is." Ashna rewashed one of the cups; tea stains weren't easy to get off. "I can imagine how overwhelming this is for you. Meeting your life's goal. I get it."

Shobi looked confused. The one thing Ashna knew her mother to be was a straight shooter, so why, now, was Shobi choosing to play games?

"The Padma Shri," Ashna said, scrubbing the cup. "Congratulations. That's huge. But now you need a new goal." She pressed a wet hand into her forehead. "That's what this is. A new goal. Wanting to fix things with your daughter." Shobi had finally decided to involve her in her Shobi-drama. Thank God, Ashna was too old to care.

Shobi pressed a hand to her forehead, mirroring Ashna's action. "Winning the Padma Shri was never my goal. Helping people was."

"Wow, so that's the part you decided to address in what I said?" Every single time her mother showed her where Ashna fell on her list of priorities it hurt as though it were the first time. How could she be so weak?

Her mother sighed. "Don't you at least want to try to understand what my life's been like?"

"I do understand. I was there, remember? Watching from eight thousand miles away." *Because you left me. Over and over again.*

"I was forced into a marriage with your father."

Not this again. "Thanks for sharing that. After overhearing your fights my entire childhood, you think I didn't figure that out myself?" She had heard those words innumerable times. "You didn't want Baba, you didn't want me. I know. You got stuck with us, and you did what you had to do to make sure you didn't lose yourself, to break the chains, to find your voice. All the things. Now look, Padma Shri! Boom! It all worked out. I'm proud of you and everything, but I'm not the 'Economic Status of Rural Women.' You can't fix me by putting the right systems in place." It was a little late for that.

Shobi just stared at her. Two women, strangers almost, separated by an expanse of black granite.

"You're right," Shobi said finally. "You're not a problem. And I am most certainly not trying to fix you. Really, beta, I am not. But—" Of course there was a *but*, and this would be over faster if Ashna just let Shobi get it out.

"But I see how sad you are and I see that it's my fault and I want to help. Is that so wrong?"

Ashna lined up the washed teacups. "First, I'm not sad. I have a good life. I like my work. It's not 'uplifting millions of lives,' but it is mine. If you're afraid that I'll say something to the media—someone from the *Times of India* already sent me an email asking if she could talk to me about you—don't worry. I know the drill. I won't say anything that makes you look bad."

Shobi rubbed her temples. Something like hurt flared in her eyes. "Thank you. But that's not what this is about. You have the right to not just *like* your work. You have the right to know what it feels like to—"

"No! You don't get to walk in here and stir shit up because you need some sort of closure or redemption or whatever one needs when all of one's dreams are fulfilled."

"Ashna, I'm trying to do the right thing here."

"No, you aren't. You're trying to ease your guilt. And you want me to fall in line the way I always have. And I'm refusing to do that."

Shobi turned away from her, temper flashing in her eyes even as she suppressed it, and grabbed another cup from a cabinet. She poured tea out of the kettle. Had she used one of Ashna's blends without asking her?

The amber liquid splashed into the cup, half of it spilling onto the granite.

Shobi grabbed a paper towel and patted the mess like someone who hadn't cleaned a thing in her life. "We're done with this foolishness."

Ashna tore another paper towel and wiped the tea clean. She couldn't agree more; whatever plan Shobi had come here with was foolishness and Ashna was done with it too.

Shobi took a sip. "You know that I'm the owner of Curried Dreams, right? I inherited it as his wife." Her parents had never gotten divorced. Ashna remembered how guilty she had felt every time she prayed that they would. "I think it's time to sell it."

Ashna dumped the paper towels in the garbage, hands shaking. The urge to press down, crush the garbage until it shrank to the bottom of the bin pushed inside her. "That's a new low, even for you." She gave in and jammed her hand into the garbage, pressing it down until it crushed and folded and smashed.

"You already hate me. I might as well do what's right for you and risk you hating me more."

"How is forcing me to give up my livelihood right for me?" She washed her hands to keep from shoving the garbage again.

"If it weren't for Curried Dreams you would actually be looking for and doing something you enjoyed. You'd get out from that dark place your father thrust you into."

Ashna was shaking now. All she wanted was to walk away. To crawl into bed. To get away from Shobi.

The habit of walking away from things must be a hard one to break.

Go to hell, Frederico Silva!

"Curried Dreams is not a dark place. I can turn it around. I'm close to doing it."

"You're not going to win that show. You don't even like being a chef! You can't win without passion."

"Thanks, Mom. And not all of us are selfish enough to put ourselves and our damn *passion* before everything else!"

Shobi gasped and Ashna sucked in her lips.

All the fight seemed to leak out of Shobi. She sank onto a barstool. But the hurt didn't last. Within moments Ashna could see the cogs in Shobi's brain turning again. This was probably how she looked when she was trying to sort through the mess of laws and corruption and centuries-old traditions to come up with a way for her foundation to solve problems.

Why hadn't Ashna inherited that ruthlessness, even just a little bit of it?

Shobi took a sip of tea. "This tea is great, by the way. I have to take some back with me. Where do you buy it?"

Ashna poured herself some and sat down across from her mother. "I'll get you some." This probably meant Shobi was getting ready to leave.

Try to show estranged daughter you care: check.

Leave when it doesn't work out: check.

For a while they drank in silence, both shaken after their outburst. But at least they'd be rid of each other soon.

"We don't have to end up here every time we try to talk," Shobi said quietly. It was her pretending-to-be-nonconfrontational voice.

Ashna rolled her eyes. "You just threatened to sell my work. How can we not end up here?"

"Okay, that was a . . . how do you young people say it? Something to do with acting like a penis?" Shobi didn't blush at the use of the word or show any awkwardness, but something told Ashna that it took effort. How had Ashna never seen how hard her mother worked to never come across as silly, to always be taken seriously?

"Dick move," she said. "We call it a dick move, and yes it was." All Shobi's moves were.

This was the first time ever that Shobi was owning up to one of them.

Ashna braced herself for the inevitable deeply impassioned lecture about a woman with agency being labeled with such a masculine insult.

Instead, another inscrutable silence followed. "I really want a chance, beta." Ashna had no idea what that meant. "Can we at least make a deal?"

Another wave of exhaustion swept through Ashna. The first part of what Shobi had said danced enticingly in front of her, but she knew Shobi well enough to know the second part was key. "What kind of deal would you like to make?"

Shobi got up and took her cup to the sink. She didn't wash it, but she did place it inside the sink. "How about this: If you win this show, I'll admit you were right. I'll sign over ownership of Curried Dreams. I'll even help you with money to renovate it. But if this show doesn't go the way you want it to, we sell the restaurant, and you find something you really . . . well, we sell it."

Ashna reached for anger, her trusty shield from Shobi. She ached to tell her she would never let her sell Curried Dreams—win or lose. But she didn't want to admit that there was a possibility that she wouldn't win. Perversely enough, something inside her wanted to see Shobi rejoice at her failure. To see Shobi destroy Curried Dreams, something Shobi hated and Ashna could never hate. A vicious part of her wanted to put Shobi in a position where she definitely demonstrated the selfishness and cruelty she was capable of.

As was their norm, the conversation was at a point where all Ashna wanted was for it to end.

"Okay," she said, not bothering to hide her exhaustion.

"There's one more thing I want," Shobi said.

Of course there was.

"I can't wait to hear what it is," Ashna said drily.

Shobi smiled; there was even a hint of pride in it. How messed up were they? "I want to stay here with you for the duration of our deal. Until the show is done."

Unbelievable! How did Shobi always, always find a way to defeat her?

"Why?" It was all Ashna could manage.

Shobi's face was a negotiator's mask—blank but not un-yielding. "Because I think it's time we got to know each other."

Laughter bubbled out of Ashna. Not anxious laughter, but mirth, because this was hilarious.

Shobi ignored her and barreled on, a bowler staring down the pitch at a batsman. "When you're free and at home, we have some of this amazing chai and talk. That's all I'm asking."

She was good.

Did she know this was Ashna's chai? Was her praise part of her strategy?

Ashna placed her hands on her father's countertop, cold and hard against her palms. "Are you sure you're not ill?"

Her mother shook her head. "I'm as healthy as a forty-nine-year-old who walks five kilometers on a polluted beach every day can be." Now they were both standing with their palms on the granite, mirrors of each other, gauging, opaque, ex-posed. "There's so much I need to tell you. It's the kind of stuff daughters go in search of after their mothers die. Maybe we can do it now while we're both still here?"

The lump in Ashna's throat was painful, but she swallowed it down. If she'd ever had any doubts about how Shobi had gotten her nickname of Dragon-Raje, they were gone now.

"Okay. But know that I'm only doing this for Curried Dreams. And for Baba."

Shobi bit her lip and nodded. Ashna had to be seeing things in her exhausted state, because for the first time in Ashna's life she saw tears shimmer in her mother's eyes.

Chapter Sixteen

Shoban had always found tears tiresome. The fact that she was crying in an ornate five-hundred-room palace made them mortifying. She was captive in a palace like some archaic fairy-tale princess—humiliating—and it was making her cry—beyond humiliating.

Her boarding school nickname was Heartless Shoban, because for some reason, the girls at her school equated having a heart with being a watering can. Her classmates cried when they watched movies; some even cried while watching ads. The last time Shoban remembered crying was when she said goodbye to her mother in the hospital, before her father had told them to take her off life support and then left the room before they did.

Shoban had cried incessantly then, the rivers flowing from her eyes obscuring her mother's body. Then at the cremation, she had realized that crying didn't ease the pain, it just displayed it for others to see, and she stopped, because it had felt wrong to do that to Ma's memory.

Now, alone in this room with enough carved teak furniture

to turn a forest barren, there was no one to display the pain to. So she let it out.

What she needed to do, instead of indulging herself with tears, was to contact Omar. But how?

She stopped pacing and jiggled the balcony door. It was open. She stepped onto the marble mosaic in her bare feet. The balcony made her feel like Rapunzel. She needed her hair to be long enough to make its way across the Arabian Sea, Western Asia, and Europe. Because across all that was Omar, entirely unaware of how much she needed him.

At home, every Sunday she made a trip to the long-distance calling booth across town in a neighborhood her father and his elitist posse of spies wouldn't be caught dead in for fear of muddying their fancy shoes. It was an hour-long trip one way, but for five minutes of hearing Omar's voice, Shoban would have done it a hundred times over.

The man who ran the booth was creepier than anyone Shoban had ever encountered. The entire time that Shoban talked to Omar, the man sat behind his rickety desk in his gauzy polyester kurta and undressed her with his eyes, his bony jaw rhythmically juicing the tobacco lumped in his cheek.

Shoban always took care to wear a loose-fitting salwar kameez that buttoned close around her neck, and wrapped her dupatta scarf all the way around herself. She tried to turn away when she spoke into the heavy black handpiece of the phone as she soaked up the gently melodic tones of Omar's voice. But turning her back on the telephone man's lecherous gaze only made the violation worse.

More than anything, she wanted to yell at him to stop, but

that was the only place in town where she could go to make that call without letting her father find out. If the man threw her out, she wouldn't get to hear Omar's voice at all.

Another sniffle escaped her. Swiping her face with her sleeve, she went back into her sandalwood-scented jail. What she wouldn't give to be in that creepy phone booth right now.

Omar knew she was visiting Sripore, so he would not be sitting by the phone in his landlady's house waiting for her call this Sunday.

It is dark without your voice, jaan. But I've gathered the sparks of your laughter in my heart for centuries, and like constellations in the night they will be my light.

He had whispered the words into the hollow behind her ear, into the dip between her breasts, into the wetness of her lips. She missed his gentleness. It had always eased the cynicism from her heart, kept her from choking on her own anger.

"Oh, Omar," she whispered into the empty room. "They want to steal our light. They want to use it to burn us away."

Daddy's lackey, Ramesh, was standing sentry outside the room. If Shoban found a way to escape, or to go the Rajes, she had no idea what her father would do. Without a doubt he was fully prepared to destroy Omar's family to get his way.

She went to the locked door and pressed her ear to it. Someone was talking outside, but she couldn't make out the words.

This was all so positively medieval—they didn't live in some village in a feudal area. They were educated people. Her mother had a master's degree in history. Shoban planned to get a PhD in women's studies. How could she get a degree in women's studies and be locked in a room so her father could force her into marriage? How was this happening?

The only solution she could think of was speaking to Bram. Yes, that was it. Bram would understand. He'd always been perfectly nice to her. When he'd visited her last month, he'd made her laugh and laugh with the stories of all the ways his parents and older brothers had tried to get him to toe the line.

Oh Lord, was that why he had visited? Because he had somehow decided that she was interested in him?

Her ear was still pressed to the door. The voices faded. Pulling away, she searched the room. There had to be a way. There was always a way. Her eyes fell on the ornate phone sitting on a console table. It had to have long-distance calling on it. This was a palace, after all. When she picked up the phone it made a strange long beeping sound. Pressing zero connected her to an operator.

"Hello, what number please?" the operator said, throwing Shoban.

"I wanted to make a call," she said, and the woman on the other end took a second to process that. Evidently not many people were stupid enough to say that to her.

"Yes, what number, please?" she repeated, her tone even more deliberately flat than the first time she'd said it.

"It's . . . it's an international call. To . . . umm . . . the UK."

"Yes, ma'am, what is the number?"

Omar's number hovered on Shoban's lips. The menace in her father's eyes when he threatened Omar's family flashed before her. What would happen if Daddy found out she had called Omar?

She touched her cheek. Her father had never hit her before. The flat-palmed slap stung afresh at the memory, making rage rise inside her. This was not like any of her previous rebellions. She had to keep her head for this one. This was war.

"Sorry, I can't find the number. I'll call back," she said, and replaced the handset.

Just in time, because the door swung open and Flora entered with a trolley. "I was just bringing you tea, Tai-saheb," she said, and looked discreetly away while Shoban wiped her eyes.

"Thanks. I do need some tea." She settled herself in the wing chair, legs neatly crossed, and smiled at Flora as she poured. "Listen, do you know where Prince Bram is?"

Flora set the silver teapot down and handed Shoban her cup. "I believe he's in his room. He just got home from riding, and I saw him head that way."

Shoban accepted the cup. "Thanks." She took a sip. "This is perfect."

Flora bowed her head in thanks but said nothing.

"Could you do me a favor and take a message to him for me?" Shoban said with all the casualness she could muster.

Flora waited, face passive, hands folded behind her back.

"Please tell him I was wanting to speak with him urgently. Actually, don't say urgently. Just tell him that I want to speak with him."

Flora nodded but stayed where she was.

Shoban forced the tea down and put her cup on the tray.

Instead of taking the trolley away, Flora nudged the silver plate with an assortment of biscuits toward Shoban.

When Shoban didn't take one, Flora met her gaze with a strange sort of fierceness. "Tai-saheb should eat. You're going to need your strength."

"Thank you." Shoban took the plate. She hadn't eaten all day. Suddenly she was ravenous.

Only after Shoban had made her way through half the biscuits did Flora wheel the trolley away.

Shoban cleared her throat, stopping her. "Can you go to Prince Bram now, please? Before you do anything else?"

"As is Tai-saheb's wish." With that, Flora left.

EXACTLY FORTY MINUTES later, a knock sounded on Shoban's door. It was too firm to be one of the servants, and Shoban braced herself, not knowing if it was her father or Bram.

"I believe I was summoned." Bram swaggered into the room in a linen button-down and khakis, freshly washed shoulder-length hair blow-dried into waves.

Shoban sat up on the love seat and Bram flopped down next to her. She ignored her reflex to scoot back. He was a big man, over six feet tall and with a wide barrel chest, and it was a small couch. But she wasn't about to shrink into herself like some sort of helpless waif.

"Come on in, Bram. Take a seat," she said, and Bram grinned.

Flipping his hair off his face, he gave her the boyish smile the magazines loved so much. A lock of hair fell over one eye as he studied her with more than his usual amusement. The teasing in his smile was overly intimate and an ugly feeling skittered down Shoban's spine.

Had he ever looked at her that way before? Why did she never pay attention to things like that?

Omar said she missed details. That she was too big-picture oriented. He was all about the details. She'd joked about never needing to develop that skill. He would be the one to take care of details for both of them and she would take care of the big picture.

"Should I call for some tea?" she asked, trying to keep her voice light.

"You're already acting like you own the house, ha?" Bram said, infusing his words with all sorts of meaning as he leaned closer to her.

"No!" She jumped up. "I was just being polite. This is your house." *All yours.* God, she wanted nothing to do with it.

There was an awkward beat of silence.

Bram sat up and Shoban tried to smile. Awkwardness could ruin everything. She had to remind him of their friendship. Friends helped each other.

She sat back down next to him. "You're not going to believe what my father said today."

Yes, this approach would work. If she turned it into a joke, he'd have no choice but to laugh it off too. The trick was to not hurt his ego. Bram was proud. He would never want to marry someone who wasn't interested in him.

He grinned again and pressed a hand into his bulky chest where it pushed at his shirt buttons.

"Daddy said . . . well . . . he said you had said . . ."

He burst into laughter. "Who would have thought a fire-cracker like Shoban Gaikwad would be reduced to stuttering." He reached out and took her hand. "Yes, darling, you can say it, we're getting married."

She snatched her hand away and stood. Her knees wobbled, but she locked them in place. "What are you talking about, Bram? What about Selma . . . your girlfriend? I thought you were with her."

He stood too, and despite herself Shoban stepped back, because he really was so much larger than her.

"Don't be absurd, Shobz. Why would I marry a woman who sleeps around?"

"But you're the one she was sleeping with!" She spun around and went to the balcony. The sun was on its way to the horizon, ready to be swallowed up by the waves. The oncoming darkness made her desperate to cling to the leftover light.

This was good. Shoban hadn't slept with Omar, but she was in love with him. If Bram didn't want to marry a woman who had slept with other men, surely he wouldn't want to marry a woman whose heart belonged to another man.

"Are you jealous?" he asked too close behind her, far too much glee in his voice.

Shoban felt like someone had thrown a bag over her head.

She tried to move, but her back hit his body and she froze. Maniacal laughter rose up her throat and she slammed it down.

"I don't mind you being jealous, though. Your fieriness is what I love most about you."

Somehow she maneuvered herself sideways and stepped away from him. "I'm not jealous at all, I promise you. And you don't mean that. You don't love me. I have nothing at all that someone like you would have any interest in. Truly. I can't do one single thing that you enjoy doing. Remember how much I hated going hunting in Switzerland? I hated it."

Her words seemed to shock him, and Shoban took advantage of his surprise to move across the balcony and tuck herself behind a rattan chair.

"So you don't have to go hunting with me," he said with a shrug. "Truth be told, I don't really enjoy it that much anymore either. Too many rules for what's endangered and what's not. We'll find other things to do together." The suggestive smile started to bloom across his face again.

"No, no we won't. Bram, God, I . . . You've been a good friend. I . . . really had no idea that—"

With a laugh he rested a knee into the chair she was hiding behind. "Oh, look at you, you're actually blushing. I didn't realize you were this bashful. It's me, Shobz. You don't have to pretend around me."

There was a wall behind her. His overpowering cologne clawed at her. Sliding out from behind the chair, she went back inside. "Good. Because I don't want to pretend around you. I knew you'd understand. I tried to tell Daddy that you would understand." God, please let him understand.

He followed her into the room, his lazy stride not quite so lazy anymore. "Of course I understand that you have to appear bashful. It's okay to do all that drama for the photographers and for my family. I know you girls love the blushing *bahu* shit. But I like you spunky, direct, unafraid to ask for things. We're going to be perfect together."

That might qualify as the world's most tasteless proposal.

He walked up to her again, not stopping until he was too close, and she realized that he might be the world's most tasteless man. Why had she laughed at his inappropriate jokes? Why had she put up with his obnoxious opinions?

This time, instead of backing down she put out her hand and held him back and out of her space. "You aren't listening to what I'm saying."

He looked down at her hand on his chest as though no one had ever stopped him from doing anything before, but he stayed put.

She pulled her hand back, wanting to wipe away the unpleasant sensation burning her palm. "We aren't going to be together, Bram. That's what I'm trying to tell you."

"What are you talking about?"

"I'm eighteen. I want to go to college. I haven't heard from Oxford yet, but I am really hoping they accept me."

He fell heavily into the sofa, but his gaze stayed on her. "I have no idea why you want to do something as deadly dull as studying when there are a million more fun things to do. But hey, if that's what you want, we can totally talk about you going to college after we're married. I can even have my mother speak with someone about your application." He winked. "A call from the maharani of Sripore should move things along."

This was who he was. All this while she'd told herself that he was being ironic when he said things like this. But he wasn't.

"Please don't speak to anyone. I want to get in on my own merit." The way Omar had, fair and square.

Bram laughed again, in that patronizing way that hadn't annoyed her before because she'd believed he wasn't her problem. "Have it your way, my fiery darling. Ma-saheb is correct. You are so right for me."

"You told Ma-saheb?" Shoban had the urge to start pacing again, but she was frozen in place.

"Of course. Naturally my mother was the one who spoke to your father. I'm not ill-bred, just ill-mannered sometimes." He winked at her again, and she wished he would stop.

She loved Bram's mother. If not for Maya Devi, Shoban would not have survived losing her own mother. She was the one who had helped Shoban see that life went on after the dark clouds of grief parted. Mortification burned inside her. How dare Bram have done this without giving her a clue. What was Maya Devi going to think of her?

"I can't do this, Bram." Clearly, there was no way to approach this other than honestly.

His patronizing smile didn't budge. It didn't even occur to him that her refusal might be real.

She folded her arms and for the first time since he'd walked into the room, she met his gaze squarely. "Listen to me." She said each word slowly. "I can't marry you."

He laughed again. "Come on. Do we have to do this? I didn't figure you for a woman who would exercise her privilege to say no just to get me to grovel." He rose. "I'm sorry, I should have gone down on my knee, done the ring thing. But I figured you'd appreciate the traditional approach better with the parents speaking to each other. I was such an arse. Sorry.

Wait here, I can set this straight. I'll be back in a minute." He made his way across the room.

"Bram, stop," she said before he reached the door. "Where are you going?"

"To get your ring—my grandmother bequeathed her engagement ring to my wife. Ma-saheb gave it to me when I told her about us. I'll get it and we can fix this."

Shoban walked up to him. "I'm in love with someone else."

If he laughed at that too, she was going to shake him. But he didn't laugh. He grabbed her arm. Hard. Hard enough that his fingers squeezed pain out of her flesh. "That's not funny."

She looked down at her arm where his hand was threatening to tear skin, then back up into eyes that had gone harder than she'd ever seen them. "I know it's not. None of this is funny. I'm in love with someone else. And I'd rather die than marry you."

Chapter Seventeen

Ashna was clutching Rico's arm so hard she was cutting off his circulation. The strange thing was that she seemed to have no idea she was doing it. Her eyes were glazed over and a blank smile was frozen across her face.

Rico overcompensated by grinning at the studio audience—visible only when the spotlight panned the auditorium seats—too afraid to move for fear of startling her out of her trance. Again.

It had been a week since their omelet challenge. There had been no elimination that first week, so today all the teams were competing to avoid being the first ones cut. Not that there was any chance that Ashna and he might be eliminated. Audience votes from last week and this week were going to be combined with the judges' scores and they had more audience votes than the rest of the teams combined.

"Before we get to the part you're all waiting for—the cooking challenge," DJ said, making Ashna's grip on Rico's arm tighten, "let's introduce our competitors one more time."

A wave of applause went through the crowd and Ashna's

lips stretched wider across her frozen face. Rico placed a hand on hers, not sure what else to do.

She blinked, her gaze falling on her fingers gripping his arm, and some color returned to her face. One delicate finger at a time, she released her hold. For a few seconds her hand stayed there, sandwiched between his arm and his hand. The fact that she did not immediately pull away and rub off his touch was telling. Whatever had just locked her up inside herself, it was taking everything from her. Again.

With a swallow, she got a hold of herself.

He tried to catch her eye, but all he got was the slightest nod before she looked away. He had no idea how he knew there was gratitude in that nod, but he did. The loose lock of hair that always seemed to escape the confines of her bun fell across her cheek.

I want to be your hair.

How many times had he said that to her? Not once had she needed to ask him what he meant. Her hair—midnight spun into strands—was always kissing her cheeks, playing with her collarbones, caressing her skin.

Her gaze slid to him again and then away, shaken by what she saw in his face. He stepped back, giving her space, hating how hard it was to do.

Her eyes were more exhausted than he'd ever seen them, and so filled with sadness they made it impossible to reach for the comfort of his anger. But he needed that anger. To wipe away the feel of her hand. To remind him that the sadness in her eyes wasn't his problem. She had walked away from the kind of happiness he had made glow in her eyes. He could have that happiness again, with someone who wanted it, needed it, as much as he did.

If he let the anger slip away, if he forgot why he was here, he would have no one but himself to blame for ending up alone. Again. Someone who betrayed you once would betray you again. Always.

Rubbing her hands up and down her arms, Ashna looked at DJ with the kind of affection that made Rico forget what he was trying to forget. The red chef's jacket made it hard not to follow along as her skin paled and blushed in turn as she found her way from fragility to strength then back again, over and over, giving him whiplash.

The cameras panned toward them and DJ threw the warmest smile her way. "Next up is Chef Ashna Raje and her partner, the greatest striker in the history of football, Frederico Silva."

The audience went wild, their share of applause noticeably louder than everyone else's. DJ made a production out of waiting for the applause to die down without seeming like a hack. The network had done well with their choice of host. The man had a deep, sophisticated voice and a London accent that moved comfortably between posh and working class. He grinned at Rico with the friendliness of someone Rico had not been an arse to just recently.

The person who had provoked him enough to make an arse out of himself turned to him and seemed to read exactly how guilty he was feeling. That of all things seemed to loosen out the knots she'd been tied up in since they had arrived at the studio today.

"Bonus points for calling it football, mate," Rico said, and the crowd booed playfully.

"And by football they both mean soccer," Ashna added. "This is America, guys!"

The crowd went nuts.

In high school she had sounded almost American, with only a little bit of a colonial lilt accenting some of her words.

Now she sounded completely American.

Rico had never been able to drop his accent, as they said here. With an English mother who had completely assimilated into Brazilian culture, he had grown up perfectly bilingual. Living in Northern California and then London might have altered how he spoke, but you didn't so much drop accents as pick them up. The belief that the way you spoke was how language was supposed to be spoken and that everyone else had an accent was much like all belief systems: it was a way to benchmark yourself as normal and categorize everyone else as strange, coveted or inferior. Accents were your native garb, and the only way to get one that wasn't yours was to pick up someone else's, either by association or because you wanted to sound more like them.

"Soccer, then," DJ said finally—in the accent that had obviously gotten him the job.

When DJ moved on to the next pair, for all her bravado earlier, Ashna's body sagged with relief.

She had never been the most social person. Rico hadn't either. They'd been two self-contained teenagers who had somehow cracked each other's shells and further destroyed each other's ability to need other people. This version of her, the one who was so acutely aware of people's reaction to her, made him want to break her loose.

Once the last of the competitors were introduced, DJ recapped last week's audience votes, starting with Ashna and Rico's position at the top. Ashna pushed the loose lock of hair off her face and smiled diffidently. Rico braced himself for the look that told him exactly how much she hated the advantage their viral video had given them. It never came.

If anything, she looked grateful for the advantage. He hadn't really believed her when she said she was here to win. Now suddenly he did.

DJ moved down the scoreboard and Rico studied the competition. The chefs all looked ready to do battle, keen on winning. The celebrities kept their focus on appearing affable and entertaining and upping their fan base. This was a marketing exercise for everyone. As for Rico, he didn't have anything left to market, nothing left to prove. He tried that word out in his mind, the one he'd been avoiding: *retired*.

The only celebrity who seemed somewhat unsure of how to navigate this particular landscape was Song. She beamed at him and he smiled back. Being an outsider was something Rico was intimately familiar with. When he'd moved to California, the first person who had not treated him like he was nothing more than his accent and his looks was Ashna. She had never told him why her family had moved, but he knew it had been devastating to her. Recognizing devastation in each other had been the magic that tied them together.

Finally, DJ was done and it was time for their second challenge, and Rico realized that twelve years of being separated from Ashna had done nothing to take away his ability to feel her devastation.

"Let's take a brief break before we move on to the challenge," DJ announced but she didn't seem to hear him.

Her shaking hands gripped the countertop. Then she seemed to realize that her hands were visible and hid them behind the countertop. Rico picked up a rolling pin and handed it to her.

She grabbed it and squeezed it so hard that it was a miracle it didn't splinter.

"Hey," he said, but again, it didn't reach her.

Over the years Rico had seen a lot of rookie nerves. That wasn't what this was. But it was definitely something. Something he had to figure out.

"It's just throwing ingredients together," Rico said, repeating her words from long ago.

His words seemed to strike her like a physical blow. Her gaze on the rolling pin in her hands sharpened, came back into focus.

"That's just something people who can't cook say." She was right. She had said it when she'd avoided the kitchen at all costs. He'd told himself it was her quiet rebellion against her father, the natural need for a teenager to seek an identity outside of their parents. Asking her about her parents had been off the table.

"But now you *can* cook, right? You made that journey, no matter what it cost." She stiffened. Maybe he shouldn't have said that last part, but it snapped her out of whatever this was. "You said you were here to win. To win you have to play the game." He jumped into pep talk mode. "Just stay inside the game and shut everything else out and you'll be fine."

The pep talk fell like a spark on her temper. "Must be nice," she snapped, her tone so cold a shiver ran through him, "to care only about what you want. To be able to shut everything else out. To have nothing to lose."

She thought he'd lost nothing?

When he'd first arrived here, all he'd wanted was for her to believe that. That she had taken nothing from him. But to see her actually believe it . . .

He knew his eyes had gone as cold as hers. "It's the orphan's advantage. No one to please. Nothing to lose."

She paled. His first offering of guilt from her. Fuck that. She could keep her pity.

"It's the only way to win," he said before she let out the apology hovering on her lips. He didn't want it. "It's the only way to stand back up when someone knocks you down. Or throws you out because you don't live up to some bullshit benchmark." Rico never let his heart rate rise. It was his greatest strength, being able to stay in the moment. "If I hadn't learned to shut everything out, where would I be?"

Instead of turning the pity in her eyes to anger again, all he managed was to make her go completely blank. Nothing, that's what she gave him. Nothing but soul-deep exhaustion. Not being able to read her drove him only a little crazier than seeing everything inside her.

Coming here was without a doubt the most asinine idea he'd ever had in his life.

"So your next challenge is . . ." DJ was back at the mic.

Ashna squeezed her eyes shut. Again. Like someone saying a prayer while stuck in the path of a speeding train.

Music crescendoed from the speakers and DJ went on: "To make a favorite comfort food from your celebrity's childhood."

The audience applauded, and a wave of half-relieved, half-enthusiastic reactions swept through the competitors. Ashna's grip on the rolling pin tightened.

"But first the fun part," DJ said. "Chefs, you get to guess your partner's favorite comfort food growing up. Bonus points for getting it right." Groans rose around them. "Stars, please write it down on the flashcard in front of you without letting your chef see."

It was a rather obvious icebreaker activity to bring out the celebrity and chef personalities, but at least it distracted Ashna enough that she was breathing again.

DJ started with Song and Miguel. Poor Miguel went through everything from shrimp chips to Korean barbecue and finally gave up.

Rico laughed and Ashna raised a brow at him.

"Come on," he said under his breath. "Think, numbskull."

"You know a lot about Ms. Woo and her favorite foods?" A hot spark of something replaced the tortured look in her eyes, and for a breath all was right with the world.

Rico shrugged. "It's got to be tacos."

Ashna was halfway through an eye roll when Song turned her flashcard over to reveal the word *taco* written in cursive so perfect it looked like a printed font.

It could have been any Mexican food, and Rico thanked his stars that the theory of probabilities had worked in his favor.

The surprised tightening around Ashna's mouth shouldn't have been quite so satisfying, but it totally was.

Next, it was their turn. Naturally, Ashna knew exactly what Rico's favorite comfort food was. One look at her told him that she hadn't forgotten. Was this cheating? It wasn't guessing if she already knew.

There used to be this Brazilian restaurant in San Francisco that was very creatively called Rio. Rico's birthplace, his hometown. It was the only place in the entire Bay Area back then where you got churros filled with doce de leite. They didn't begin to compare to the churros he had bought from the hand cart vendor down the street from his Leblon home, but still it had been something. Naturally he'd taken Ashna there too often.

"Mr. Silva?" DJ asked. "Any clues?"

"It's not mac and cheese?" he said, making the audience laugh.

Ashna let a smile slip too—the first bloom of it was even real, then all her other feelings turned it into a lip-stretch again. Would she pretend not to know? She bit her lip, and he knew she was wondering if he had mentioned mac and cheese on purpose, if he still felt the same way about it. Her obsidian gaze bored to the center of him. Everything was different about them, and yet nothing was.

"Definitely not mac and cheese," she said, her eyes revealing a flash of something they had both lost.

Her red-painted mouth twisted in mock confusion. "He grew up in Rio de Janeiro. So, it could be so many things. Such a rich tradition of comfort foods. Maybe not something entirely traditional. Umm . . . churros?" She said it exactly the way he had taught her to say it, many moons ago, while feeding the crisp-on-the-outside, pillowy-on-the-inside confection into her mouth and then tasting the sticky sweetness on her lips.

Her huge irises turned smoky.

Far too much knowing sparkled in the air between them.

She's just a girl I dated in high school.

DJ turned to him. "Is she correct?"

With the barest shrug Rico flipped over the flashcard.

CHURROS, the card said in careless all caps.

The audience lost it, screaming and clapping.

From their competitors, several pairs of envious, even suspicious, eyes turned on them.

"Wow! That easy?" DJ said, studying Ashna like someone who thought he knew her and suddenly found he might not after all.

Welcome to my life, mate!

"What can I say, I'm predictable," Rico said for the cameras. "Maybe I should've lied and gone with mac and cheese?"

That got him a half-fake, half-real smile from Ashna.

He disliked mac and cheese. She did too. *It feels like an incomplete dish*, they had loved to say. *Like it's missing an ingredient or seasoning or something.* How they had loved agreeing on things, finding common threads, even though every thread of the fabric he was made of had already been tied to her.

"You better be careful if she can read you that easily," DJ said.

Too late. But he smiled for the cameras. "Hey, having team-mates who can read you wins you games."

Another gleeful cheer swept the studio. DJ went through all the chef-celebrity pairs but Ashna and Rico remained the only ones who got it right. This seemed to fuel the audience's anticipation for whatever they had seen in that video. The competition had barely begun, and Ashna and he were already the undisputed favorites by miles.

As an athlete, Rico knew the value of having an edge. Ashna looked like she had just stolen candy from a toddler. Her guilt, her terror, feeling it all in his gut was doing nothing to ease his restlessness. This was not why he was here.

"You have half an hour."

As soon as the words left DJ's mouth, Ashna's skin turned ashen again. She looked seconds from hyperventilating.

He stepped close to her. "What on earth is going on, Ashna?"

She turned to him, hands shaking, eyes wide and blank.

He slipped an apron over his head. "Can you tie this for me, please?"

As though he'd thrown her a life vest, she stepped behind him and started tying, his body shielding her from the cameras.

"I can't do this." Her breath fell in nervous puffs against his spine.

"Do what?" he said without turning around.

"Cooking . . . c-c-cooking in front of the cameras . . . I—I—" Her hands were having a hard time making knots.

Before she could say more, DJ spoke again. "Oh, there's something I forgot to mention."

The competitors groaned. Rico could feel Ashna's grip tighten on his apron strings.

"The chefs don't cook today. Just the celebrities. Chefs, you get to give instructions, but hands off or your team will be instantly disqualified."

Commotion broke out across the workstations. Some teams had already started prepping and they stopped with loud exclamations of "Come on!" and "You've got to be kidding me!"

Tatiana, the dog whisperer, flung the handmixer she was holding across her station, knocking over a set of glass mixing bowls. Glass shattered all over the floor.

Crew rushed toward Tatiana's station amid gasps. Jonah called a break, telling everyone not to move until the mess was cleaned.

Behind Rico Ashna's trembling exhale warmed his skin. Her head fell forward, resting between his shoulder blades. He could feel her shaking. The fact that his body was shielding hers from the cameras, from the eyes in the room, turned all the confusion inside him to relief.

It took her a few moments—he counted them off with his breaths—to finish tying his apron and step away. The commotion from Tatiana still took up everyone's attention.

He turned to her. "Ashna?"

A vacuum cleaner started up.

Jaw clenched, she wiped a hand across her face and pressed it into her mouth. Then the most incredulous laugh escaped her. She thought this was funny?

The vacuum turned off and the cleaning crew inspected the floor to make sure all the glass was gone. Tatiana looked remorseful enough as she apologized, but some firm legal-sounding instructions were recited to her.

"Okay, everyone, back to your challenges. We've reset the clock. You get thirty minutes from now," Jonah announced, and the digital timer on the monitor started up. "Make it count."

Every sign of anything but stubborn purpose vanished from Ashna's face. "Let's go," she said, as though none of what had just happened had happened. As though this weren't the second time she had flipped that switch like someone who was two entirely different people. Neither of whom Rico recognized.

She snapped her fingers in front of his face. "You have thirty . . . twenty-nine minutes to make churros." She ran to the overstocked pantry and started pointing at things as she rattled off ingredients.

Whiplash, she was giving him whiplash. He filled his arms. Flour, eggs, cinnamon, brown sugar, confectioners' sugar, condensed milk.

"I haven't made churros since culinary school. We're going to have to wing it."

He followed her back to their workstation, lost and winded from her mercurial shifts. "Your memory seems just fine." Obviously, they both remembered more than they wanted to. "I'm sure you'll remember the recipe."

For the barest second she stiffened. Then she pulled a napkin from a stack, dabbed the sweat off her forehead, and started to throw out instructions.

"Break four eggs into the mixing bowl and beat them."

Breaking eggs was exactly what Rico needed, and beating the heck out of something sounded great. "Yes, ma'am."

He turned the handmixer on and started beating the eggs, the sound was loud enough to keep their conversation private. "Want to tell me what that was about?" he hissed, even as his face stayed genial for the camera.

"Not now. You'll overbeat the eggs," she hissed back, refusing to meet his eyes.

He raised the speed, and the noise level. "Not turning it off until you tell me."

She twisted the napkin in her hand, but she knew him too well to argue. "It feels like an unfair advantage. I don't like it." She pointed at the eggs. "That's enough."

He turned off the beater.

"Now the water. Two cups. Bring them to a boil."

He measured water into a pan and put it on the stove without slamming it like he wanted to. They fumed silently as they waited, fake smiles plastered across their faces.

"Now add the sugar."

"Really? This . . ." He stirred the sugar, then spun the spoon around to encompass her swings from panic to self-possession and then back again, over and over. "This is you"—he clanged the spoon on the pan drowning the rest of his words—"feeling guilty?"

She nodded, indignant as a liar. "Flour. Two cups. Sift it in."

"Sifter, please," he shouted, and an intern ran over and found him one. He started sifting, then banged the metal on the pan pretending to get the last bits off. "Bullshit."

Fresh sweat broke out across her forehead, making the errant strands stick to her skin. "If you don't start stirring, it will lump up."

Too late. The whole darned thing was a lump. "Add a little more water and work it loose." The cameras zoomed in as he furiously worked the gunky mixture. "Who would have thought my training would come in so handy in a kitchen?" he said to the cameras, arm muscles cramping.

The moment they backed off, he looked at her again, slamming the spoon against the edge of the mixing bowl some more. Hopefully, there wasn't a foul for being too noisy. "Then you shouldn't have said churros. You should have lied like you're lying now." More slamming of the spoon.

"That looks good," she said, her color high, even as she kept her face calm. "Turn on the handblender, that should work."

As soon as he started the blender up again she stepped closer to it. "And you shouldn't have written churros down," she whispered. "Or broken your promise to keep our past out of this."

Technically, he hadn't promised. "Acquiescing to your demands is not the same as making a promise." He beat the mixture so hard that the clumping water and flour had no choice but to smooth into dough.

"Add the eggs. That should make it easier."

Right, if only. He added the eggs, glad to run the blender again. "What are you hiding this time, Ashna? You're not eighteen anymore. When does the hiding stop?"

He turned off the blender but the silence between them felt louder.

Hand shaking, she dabbed her upper lip with the napkin and spoke behind it. "Can we focus on the churros? *Please.*" There was so much pain in her eyes, and shame, and helplessness. It was the helplessness that was killing her.

And it killed him too. "What next?"

She seemed to swallow a sob and squared her shoulders. "That dough needs to go into a pastry bag and get piped into the fryer. We have ten minutes. You still have doce de leite to make."

He called for a pastry bag and popped open the can of condensed milk. The old instinct to backtrack with her kicked in, to give her what she wanted, to ease her. He couldn't bear to see her hurting like this, and that was the truth. *Damn it.*

"The fryer is hot. Can you fill the pastry bag?" There was relief in her tone, and blind trust that he would do exactly as she asked.

Fortunately, filling the pastry bag wasn't half as simple as it looked. Piping the churros in long straight lines took far more skill than one might imagine, and focus.

When the first golden brown pastry emerged from the fryer, disbelief, maybe even pride, shone in Ashna's eyes.

Rico placed the churro on a paper towel, gobsmacked that he'd actually made those.

"You did it," she said. Something about her smile struck terror in his heart. It was too many things: surprise, even a spark of victory, and God help him, joy. For all her secrets, there was too much he saw. It was this dance that had gotten him into this situation in the first place. Too much knowing. Too much needing to know. He had to find a way to stop it. Because she would always hide. It was what she needed to do. And he was no longer the man who didn't care what price he had to pay for her to let him in.

Chapter Eighteen

Barely two weeks into the show and there was a wait to get into Curried Dreams.

The overflowing parking lot at lunchtime, the unique buzz of conversation in a full restaurant, people crowding the waiting area, all of it made Ashna feel too close to another time. She almost made her way to Baba's office to check up on him, and that thought made the walk-in pantry spin around her. She leaned back and rested her head against the wall.

Are you seeing this, Baba? I didn't fail you. I am not just like my mother.

The knot in her throat that made it hard to breathe would go away in a second. She took long, stretchy breaths. *Why did you have to ruin everything, Rico?*

Because that's exactly what he had done. He'd ruined everything. By being here. By knowing exactly what to do. By turning out those stupid perfect churros.

He loves me, Baba.

Boys like that only want one thing. In his case two. And neither one of those has anything to do with loving you.

Wilfrieda walked into the pantry and stopped short when she saw Ashna. "Sorry, boss, didn't realize you were in here."

Ashna almost turned away and pretended to look for something.

You're not eighteen anymore. When does the hiding stop?
I'm not hiding!

She was totally hiding.

God, she hated Frederico Silva.

"I needed a moment," she said to Wilfrieda, who looked like she had no idea what to do with herself in the face of her always-in-control boss with tears streaking her cheeks.

Ashna leaned over and wiped her cheeks on her smock. All these years she'd channeled Shobi to keep the tears away. She couldn't let seeing her mother tear up put a crack in that dam. "You've been doing great with the rush. Thank you."

Wilfrieda and Khalid were handling things fabulously, and the four more line chefs and extra waitstaff from DJ's network were a godsend.

"Your aunt did an amazing job of preempting the staffing situation," Wilfrieda said with the kind of worshipfulness Ashna was totally used to when it came to Mina Kaki. Her assistant held out her hands to display a pink glittery manicure. "She gave Khalid and me gift cards to her friend's spa. I can't remember the last time I got a manicure or a massage. You've been working so hard, boss, you should totally get one too."

Ashna touched a shimmery nail. "That does sound great and I'm totally coveting that color."

Smiling, they went back into the bustling kitchen. The Curried Dreams kitchen hadn't bustled in a very long time.

Baba had hated the idea of making people wait for food, so he had built his restaurant to be large enough to avoid that. He had underestimated his own abilities, because under him there had always been a wait despite the hundred tables. Ashna had never experienced the thrill of customers waiting.

At this rate, she would have to open the patio seating again.

"Where have you been hiding?" Mina Kaki said as Ashna put down the bag of flour she was carrying.

Ashna knew her aunt didn't mean she was actually hiding, it was just a figure of speech, but still she cursed Rico again for filling her head with things she had no time for.

She started measuring out the flour for the naan dough and Mina Kaki stopped her. "Freddie, you can take over the dough. Ashna, I think you need to do the rounds and say hello to the guests. You're what they're here for. Well, you and that hot partner of yours. You should ask him to come by."

Ashna made a face.

"We might need to put in an extension if he came by," Wilfrieda said, cheerily fanning herself.

"I'm sure Khalid appreciates that sentiment," Ashna said, throwing a pointed look at Khalid, who was blooming spices in a huge kadhai of ghee for the dal fry, with one eye on Wilfrieda.

"Khalid has a bigger crush on Mr. Silva than even I do, right, Khalie?" Wilfrieda said, her round face shining with humor, and Ashna looked around her kitchen.

Mina Kaki's magic was everywhere. It was like one happy family working together.

"No kidding," Khalid said, pouring the hot ghee into the

pan of dal and making it hiss and give out the kind of aroma that caused them all to emit appreciative sounds. "The staff have been all over social media getting our friends to vote. In fact, our Facebook group just hit a hundred thousand followers. Bless Mandy for starting it!"

The smile on Ashna's face froze.

Wilfrieda glared at Khalid, who returned his attention to the dal.

Her aunt tucked a lock of hair behind Ashna's ear and patted her cheek. "Go out and greet your customers. You've got to give the people what they want. While you're out there, ask them to vote for Yash." That made Ashna smile, and Mina Kaki added more softly, "Freddie was telling me that Mandy was telling her how hurt she is that you let her go."

The smile died on Ashna's lips again. "Really, Mandy said that? I never let her go. She quit." Mandy had lined up a job and not even mentioned it to Ashna.

"Maybe you misunderstood? Sometimes we believe the thing that is easiest to believe." And by *we* she meant Ashna. "It's easy to push people away before they leave."

Before the full impact of that could sink in, her aunt patted her cheek. "Now, don't get all bent out of shape, beta. You have to look for what's behind what people say. What Mandy said simply means her door is open." She spun an elegant hand around the kitchen. "If this keeps up, you might need someone with Mandy's competence and experience. Much as I love this place, all this steam is terrible for my hair." She patted her perfect hair and took her bag from the hook by the door. "Go on. I think everything is under control here. I'm going to leave for a bit. If you need anything, Shobi has offered to come over."

Ashna tried not to stiffen. Shobi had not set foot in Curried Dreams since before Baba died. It was really annoying that everyone kept acting like she was here to help Ashna. You couldn't help someone with a restaurant without being physically present *inside* the restaurant.

Her aunt opened her mouth, but decided to hold her peace right now. Good, because what she'd said earlier about Ashna pushing people away was ridiculous. People pushed *her* away.

"Did you know Shobi was going to visit?" More like ambush her. "Why didn't you warn me?"

Mina sighed. "What you're really asking is why I didn't stop her. I can't stop Shobi from visiting. Are you really angry with me about that?"

"I don't know."

"If you can't say, 'No, I'm not angry,' then you are."

Truth was, Ashna didn't know how to be angry with her aunt. If she didn't have Mina Kaki and HRH, all she would have was anger.

Thanks, Shobi.

"No, I'm not angry." Ashna smiled. "How can I be angry with you? Look at this place. You breathed life into it."

Her aunt shook her head. "No, you were brave enough to go out and do something that wasn't easy. That's what breathed life into this place."

Ashna hugged her aunt. "Why aren't you my mom?"

Mina tucked another loose lock of hair behind Ashna's ear. "Who says you can have only one? You are as much my daughter as Nisha and Trisha, so that means I am your mom too." She paused, considering her next words carefully, with the kind of tentativeness that she only displayed when it came to Shobi. "Can I tell you something, as a mom?"

Ashna swallowed, which was enough answer for Mina Kaki.

"Talk to Shobi. It might be time to stop believing the thing that's easiest to believe."

Someone called to Mina Kaki, and Ashna blessed the gods of timing.

"Go on." She dropped a kiss on her aunt's cheek. "I'll be fine. See, I'm off to 'do the rounds.'" With that, off she went without acknowledging whatever her aunt was trying to tell her.

Doing the rounds basically involved people telling her how much they loved the show and what a lovely couple she and Rico made. She tried to tell them that they weren't a couple but gave up when no one had any interest in her take on the matter. Instead, she told them to tune in for Yash's upcoming rally in Oakland next month and went back to the kitchen.

How had she ended up here? Her restaurant crowded, Rico back in her life. The mother who had done everything to stay away from her suddenly all over her like a rash. It was some sort of somersaulting déjà vu.

Whoever had told Ashna she needed to change one thing to change everything wasn't kidding around. Could she kill the person who had suggested it, please?

She picked up the last order. Baba's stuffed bitter melons.

The one thing no amount of changing could change was that Baba would never be here to see this. She tried to visualize him—if anything could put a smile on his face, it would be this. But all she saw when she thought about him was blood dripping from her hands. The oil in her pan started to smoke and Khalid left his station and threw the chopped onions in for her. "I can take care of it, boss."

"I got it. Thanks." She gave the onions a stir. The memory of Rico going at the lumping dough as though it were a workout machine brought her back to this moment.

This divine intervention or whatever stroke of luck she was having with the cooking challenges was not going to last.

"Just did the last call for lunch, we're almost done!" Wilfrieda announced, and everyone cheered.

This wasn't going to last either, not once Ashna had to drop out of the competition because she passed out from a panic attack on television. Not once her mother got to say *I told you so* and sold Curried Dreams.

AFTER THE LUNCH rush, DJ drove Ashna to the studio. Trisha and he had stopped by because Trisha was excited for DJ to meet Shobi. No big surprise that Trisha loved her. Shobi was the cool, badass (albeit mostly absconding) aunt.

"Your mother is magnificent," DJ said as they turned into the studio lot. "Now I know where you get your beauty, and your ability to kick arse!"

"You're too kind." *But I'm nothing like my mother.*

When they got to the studio, DJ went off to a staff meeting

and Ashna headed for the contestants' lounge. For the first time in years she had to do that thing where she tightened her gut to brace for the impact of seeing someone.

There he was.

The punch landed dead center in her ribs, like a ball slamming her at full speed. She let it vibrate through her, the impact zinging electric sparks right down to her fingertips.

He sat in a wing chair, feet planted, bent over a newspaper, lips pursed, eyes narrowed. It was his frustrated-with-the-world face.

The passion playing across his features, across his whole body, was mesmerizing. Ashna took advantage of how absorbed he was in what he was reading to study him. He looked almost nothing like the boy she had been in love with. His thick sable-brown hair was pulled back into that man bun that had the internet aflutter. Her insides, this one time, agreed with the internet, even though it was still wholly incomprehensible to her that he had grown out his hair. The texture of his hair, cropped short in the back and long in the front, was something she still felt between her fingers in her dreams. Also new was his stubble, a shade darker than his hair, not quite full enough to be a beard but almost there, lined up to perfection.

He was chewing on those distinctively shaped lips. Whatever was in that paper, it had him in a rage. Sensing her study, he looked up. Would she ever get used to the physical impact of their eyes meeting? Fighting the warmth rising up her cheeks was a futile exercise, so she waited for it to pass. He responded with a shuttered look.

Shuttered was perfect.

They made their way silently to the staging area for their first elimination. There would be no cooking today, just the judges assigning scores that would be added to the votes from two weeks to determine the eliminated pair. Afterward, the producers had a surprise planned. Another sadistic idea to torture the contestants with, no doubt.

Ashna and Rico stepped up in front of the judges—a mix of two chefs, a food editor, and inexplicably, a director of romantic comedies.

"I'm going to put this right out there," one of the chef judges started. "Your churro was nowhere near as delicious as your chemistry."

The smile on Rico's face froze in place, or maybe Ashna was projecting. When Rico was on camera it was hard to tell what was real and what was not.

The monitor played the judging clip from their cooking episode yesterday when the food editor had held up the churro. The churro had been admittedly lame. Or rather, limp. On the screen, it curved down in an arc. In front of them the judge traced an arc with her finger with impressive drama.

That made Rico bless everyone with his full-throated, self-deprecating laugh. The judge fanned herself with her notepad. Ashna pasted a smile on her face as they watched the rest of the footage of the judge holding up the curving churro.

Her mortification had to have shown because Rico leaned close to her ear. "Lighten up. It might not have been a fabulous churro, but it is another fabulous television moment, so they're going to milk it."

She realized she was leaning into his whisper and pulled away. Her body retaliated, soaking up the caress of his breath on her earlobes, and sent another ungodly zing through every one of her traitorous internal organs.

DJ threw Ashna and Rico a smile. How had DJ developed this repertoire of smiles for the camera so fast? He held out his mic. "The judges think your churro didn't . . . ahem . . . quite stand up to the test. What's your reaction?"

Would they stop with calling that churro names?

Rico was about to open his mouth, but Ashna grabbed the mic from DJ. "I agree that it could have been . . . well, stiffer, but given that this was Frederico's first time making one, I for one was very impressed. I've eaten a few churros in my day, and I don't think I've ever tasted one quite that delicious. Looks aren't everything."

The studio audience, which was in complete darkness today, lost its collective mind all over again.

DJ let out a delighted—albeit surprised—laugh. "You'll be glad to know that you weren't the only one who thought so. I think you're going to enjoy this next part."

The large screen played footage of the judge holding up the curving churro one more time to audience boos and then played clips of social media reacting to it. An endless number of people had an opinion on the matter. Someone had even spelled out their names in churros for an Instagram post.

ASHNA + RICO.

(Inside a churro heart. Groan.)

From behind the cameras, China bounced on her heels and blew Ashna grateful kisses.

Unsurprisingly, the judges' scores were as lukewarm as their criticism.

As they walked away, Rico's smile was too arrogant by half. It was the other half of his smile that told Ashna she had made a mistake by taking the mic.

One by one the other pairs braved the recaps and the judges' comments—mostly lackluster, except for Danny El, who had made, wait for it . . . mac and cheese that the judges "wanted to lick off their dishes."

As DJ waited for the combined scores to be computed so he could announce them, Jonah ran up to Ashna and Rico at their station. "That was amazeballs." He gave Rico a fist bump and Ashna a worshipful glance. "You guys are trending everywhere!"

What was wrong with people? Ashna didn't understand this obsession with other people's lives. Jonah pulled up Twitter and Instagram on his tablet and waved it about, parroting all the hashtags she and Rico now were: #knifegate #churrosolimp, and the one that made Jonah the giddiest: #Ashico, which when said out loud sounded far too much like the Hindi word *ashiquo* which, disastrously enough, meant "lovers."

There were also betting pools for when Ashna and Rico would go public with their "relationship." There was definite consensus about the fact that they were together. #Lobsters.

Rico was a sea of calm in the face of this tidal swell of information. Ashna felt like she was drowning. His studying—and steadying, dang it—gaze kept coming back to her, so she had no choice but to keep her shit together.

"Relax," Rico said as Jonah went off to accost someone else with data. "It only means that we aren't getting voted off anytime soon."

"First, never tell someone to relax if you actually want them to relax," Ashna snapped, feeling entirely cornered. "All those girlfriends and not one of them ever told you this?"

His brows flew up and Ashna had the briefest moment of satisfaction before awareness brightened his eyes and she realized what she had admitted to. Yes, she had fallen down the Google rabbit hole that was Frederico Silva's media coverage. Girlfriends, winning moments, underwear ads. It was quite the cornucopia of a life well lived. She wanted to sink into the floor. Even so, his openmouthed wordlessness was so darned satisfying she spun around and walked to the stage again, where the contestants were lining up and DJ was ready with the results.

Rico took his place next to her, his body tight with tension.

A small voice in her heart chided her for snapping at him when he had only been trying to help. Why did he do this? Why him? What was it that made him see all the way inside her?

Yesterday, he'd navigated the roller coaster of her panic unflinchingly. It was difficult for him to not push, to not immediately understand. Patience didn't come naturally to him, and yet when she'd asked for what she needed, support with the cooking challenge, space, he'd given it without question.

Ashna couldn't remember the last time anyone had put what she wanted before everything else. Actually, she did remember. That was the problem. No, the real problem was how horribly she had missed it.

DJ announced that Tatiana would be leaving them this week—thanks to a corn dog where the batter hadn't stuck to the dog. Tatiana and her chef hugged everyone, expressed remorse but also relief at going back to focusing on her dogs and his restaurant, respectively, and walked away.

Then DJ was on the mic again, announcing the surprise. "You've all been working really hard here. Some of you have had to be away from your families. So, we've brought your families to you. Our studio audience today is all friends and family."

The studio broke into happy chaos. The lights over the audience went on and Ashna decided that she desperately needed a new best friend, because China had brought in Nisha; Nisha's daughter, Mishka; Mina Kaki; and Yash. Which meant her family would see her with Rico. Which meant he'd see her with her family. A bleeding together of parts of her life she would give anything to keep separate. At least Shobi was conspicuous by her absence, and Ashna's relief was an unholy blast, because if Rico saw her with Shobi . . . well, he wasn't going to.

DJ invited the families to join the contestants in the lounge for wine and cheese and the contestants made their way there.

The first person Ashna saw when she entered the lounge was Yash. She squealed and flew into his arms and he pulled her into a bear hug. Cameras went off around them. With anyone else it would feel staged, given that Yash was a gubernatorial candidate and positive, seemingly ordinary family-life coverage was gold. But Yash had a way of swimming in the sea of hoopla without ever getting wet.

"OMG, what is Yash Raje doing here?" Ashna said, holding Yash tight. She didn't get to see him nearly enough anymore. This running-for-governor business was time consuming. "I've missed you. It's almost worth doing the show to get to see you."

His gray eyes twinkled. How he appeared so energetic after months of being on the road she would never know. "Totally lucky that I was back home for a day. When Ma told me they're letting us visit today, I had to come by and make sure they were taking care of you."

Ashna laughed. Across the room, Rico was introducing a friend from his soccer team to Song and her family. "I needed my big brother to come rescue me. It's been torture."

"But it's worth it because of the view?" Yash caught her studying Rico. Song handed Rico a baby swathed in pink frills and he pressed her close to his chest. Something low in Ashna's belly went up in flames.

"How on earth did China manage to bag Frederico Silva anyway?" Yash said with entirely uncharacteristic gushiness. "And is that Zia Malik? No way!" Yash being a fan was hilarious.

Ashna refused to make anything of the huge relief that had washed over her when Rico's friend had walked into the studio. The fear that he might have no one visiting him today had been unwarranted and she felt silly for letting it worry her.

"How are things on the campaign trail? The polls are looking good."

He let her ungainly change of topic go. "I'm doing fairly well in Northern California. San Diego is going well too. I might crack Orange County, crazily enough, and Death Valley, but LA is kicking my butt. They love Cruz."

Yash's closest opponent, Davis Cruz, was a popular actor and was selling himself as the next Schwarzenegger, if not Reagan. Cruz had ramped up his Latino outreach on one hand while slamming away at Yash's being an "outsider" and West Coast elite.

Yash was still beating him in the polls, but the California primary was coming up in two months and the gap was too close for comfort and had to be widened.

"You've been there every week. You'll turn them around."

Nisha and Mina Kaki walked over with a photographer and they took some family pictures. Mishka, Nisha's nine-year-old, was too busy being starstruck by Danny El to come spend time with her family and it made Ashna smile. Speaking of being starstruck, Ashna's eyes wouldn't stop seeking out the baby-carrying Rico. She caught him watching Yash as Yash shook hands with the crew, and the strangest excitement brightened his face.

"Enjoying the view?" Nisha asked.

Seriously, Ashna was going to scream the next time some-one said that.

Chapter Nineteen

Of course, Rico knew that Yash and Ashna were cousins, but still, seeing them together was strange. Most people's body language was different when they were around people they were close to, but Ashna took that to a whole new level. She was one person when she was around strangers and an entirely different person when she was with those she let in. There was a naked vulnerability to her with those she was close to. Until this moment he hadn't realized quite how much he had missed that degree of connection.

When China announced that their families would be visiting the set today, Ashna had looked like she'd been shot. It had made Rico search the room for her father, the last person on earth he ever wanted to see. He forced himself not to relive his meeting with the man, or the fact that Ashna had sided with him. Fortunately, it seemed that he had decided not to visit his daughter today.

"You've literally not taken your eyes off your chef the entire time I've been here." Zee had taken a flight down in the middle of his honeymoon—a completely idiotic thing to do, but also not at all surprising given that Zee knew that Rico's pathetic ass had no one else.

Rico turned to him. "There, I'll only stare into your pretty face for the rest of the afternoon."

Zee laughed, but before Rico could respond Song walked over with her mother and sister. Song's sister had brought her baby and as soon as Zee waved to her and said hi in that high-pitched way people said hi to babies, she made a leap at Zee. Or rather she leaped at the huge solitaires in Zee's ears.

The moment she was perched on Zee, she noticed Rico's bun and decided that was more worth her time than Zee's bling. Rico took her from Zee. Almost immediately, she wanted to go back, unable to choose between Zee's rocks and Rico's beard and bun. Song's sister tried to take her back, needlessly embarrassed, because both Zee and Rico were just vain enough to love the attention. Not that it mattered what anyone wanted, because the determined little person refused outright to leave Rico and go to her mother.

This seemed to thrill Song and embarrass her sister some more.

"I'm so sorry," this almost identical but somehow more put-together version of Song said.

"Please don't apologize," Rico said as the baby made a tight fist in his hair and tugged.

Being wanted this way by someone so tiny with a personality so huge was alarmingly satisfying. Rico would gladly take this uncomplicated, entirely self-assured love for as long as she wanted to give it.

"No wonder people have babies," Zee said. "Is this one of those biological clock things for men no one told us about?"

Rico laughed, but he'd been wondering the same thing. Not that all that godfathering hadn't softened him up for this. "Go on, I'm happy to keep her," he told Song's mother and sister. "You go ahead and mingle."

The lovely little girl, who was named Rose but smelled milky instead of floral, squeezed his face with her chubby hands and slobbered all over his beard.

Song dropped a kiss on his cheek that did not escape her mother's eagle eye and the three women headed toward Song's chef, chatting away in Korean.

"You know they're planning your wedding, right?" Zee said with all the amusement of someone who'd be flying back to his honeymoon in a few hours.

"Song and I are just friends," Rico said.

Zee scratched the back of his neck. "Yeah, but does Song know that?" Before he could elaborate on that unnecessary observation, his phone rang, and he excused himself. From the way his face went all fuzzy it was obviously Tanya. Rico shook his head as his friend walked away looking for a quiet corner amid the pandemonium.

As was his curse these days, Rico's eyes sought out Ashna. As it seemed to be her curse these days, she sensed his study and met his gaze. There it was, the fire in her eyes that set off answering flames across his entire being.

Yash followed her gaze to Rico and excitedly hurried over. "Yash Raje. I hope you don't mind me introducing myself."

Ashna didn't move.

"Frederico Silva. It's a pleasure!"

"I'm such a fan!" they both said together, and a tiny smile lit Ashna's eyes across the ten feet that separated them, even as she kept her lips pursed.

When she noticed that Rico had caught her smile, she turned to Lilly Cromwell, the soap star, whose visiting family included four daughters who looked like younger replicas of her.

Baby Rose reached out to Yash, and Yash stepped back. What was this? The most affable candidate the political scene had seen in years was afraid of babies?

"She doesn't bite," Rico said, suddenly an expert.

Undaunted by Yash's skepticism, little Rose, determined thing that she was, stretched toward Yash.

Rico held her out. "Some pictures might help with the media's issues with your being unmarried."

Yash raised a brow, then grinned. "Did my mother and sister put you up to this?" He took the baby from Rico and cameras started clicking around them.

For someone who'd taken the baby reluctantly, the candidate looked completely comfortable with her for the cameras. He turned to Rico as Rose examined various parts of his face—which had the same fine-boned structure as Ashna's. "The last World Cup, man, when Zia Malik crossed it to you in the box and you took it off the volley and to the back of the net. Unbelievable. And that goal in the ninetieth? And the way you spun the controversy with your teammates trashing that bar, it was something. You're the GOAT, man, you're the GOAT. Actually, no, you're the *game*, man!"

Baby Rose reached out to Rico again and he took her back and let her crawl up his shoulder and pull at his bun. "Speaking of being the GOAT, your Calicare for All plan—it's pure genius, mate. By removing profit-seeking private insurance, you lower premiums and eliminate costly deductibles. And by having corporations paying in for employees who opt out, you help fund it. How has no one thought of that?"

Yash seemed taken aback by that. Rico hadn't figured the man for someone who let his feelings show easily, but up close there was an almost vulnerable honesty about him, also very much like his cousin. Why wasn't someone in his campaign making sure the voters saw that side of him? Because it didn't come through on the TV screen or in his interviews at all and it was pure media gold if leveraged right.

"What a charming little girl." A gorgeous older woman Ashna had been speaking with earlier walked up to them. "And look how smart! She seems to have you two wrapped around her finger."

She had to be Ashna's aunt, and the other woman who followed her had to be one of Ashna's cousins. There was an unmistakable resemblance between the cousins, something about the shape of the eyes and the delicacy of the jaw, and of course the graceful bearing. Although, none of the others had the intensity, the vibrancy that Ashna's beauty was painted in. Hers were vivid strokes of oil pastels to their watercolors. And he was a really bad poet.

"You've got some good taste in men, baby girl," this subtler version of Ashna said to the child in Rico's arms.

Ashna finally crossed the distance and joined them.

Rico felt his stomach muscles tighten. He braced himself for the pretense of being a recent acquaintance. His star to her chef. Not the man who had sought her out because for ten years he'd craved who he was when he was with her.

"Here is *our* star. You two were amazing today!" Ashna's aunt said, wrapping her arm around Ashna's shoulders.

The look Ashna gave Rico was stubborn as hell, every bit New Ashna. "Looks like you've met them already, but this is my aunt, Mina Raje, and my cousins, Nisha and Yash—Trisha's sister and brother. And this is Mishka, Nisha's daughter. Everyone, this is Frederico Silva, my partner on the show."

Rico shook everyone's hand, trying to ignore the feeling of being kicked in the solar plexus. What kind of idiot got so caught up in something as stupid as being acknowledged by an ex he was trying to get over?

They laughed various versions of the same laugh. "Yes, we're aware that he's your partner on the show, Ashi!"

Idiot that he was, Rico threw a glance at Ashna. *Thanks!*

She went all stiff and defensive. *You didn't actually expect me to tell them now, did you?* Her answering gaze said.

No, he didn't, because no one could possibly be that much of a delusional arse.

"He's also the best living soccer player on earth," Mishka said. She obviously shared Yash and Ashna's love of the sport.

"You retired recently, I hear," Ashna's aunt said, "so where is home?"

"I'm kind of homeless right now."

That softened the defensiveness in Ashna's eyes and it made Rico wish he hadn't said it.

He turned back to her aunt. "I grew up in Rio de Janeiro and I've lived in London for this past decade."

"I read something about you living in the Bay for a few years. Is that true?" Yash asked.

"Really?" Nisha asked. "I didn't know that. Ashi, did you know that? Where in the Bay?"

Rico knew there was a reason he'd grown so fond of this baby, because she chose that moment to grab his bearded jaw and let out a mighty grunt, which was followed by the most vile stench of all time.

The smell cut through the air before anyone noticed the expression on Ashna's face. Groans broke out across the group along with choking laughter.

"Wow, that's . . . um . . . potent." Mishka pinched her nose. "Mom, is this what babies do?"

Nisha, who was obviously pregnant, laughed and tried not to wrinkle her nose. "Yup, and big sisters get first dibs on diaper duty."

"Practice?" Rico held the stinky little thing out to Mishka and she made a gagging face. Everyone was flat-out laughing now. Nothing like basic potty humor to save the day.

Ashna still looked like she'd seen several ghosts.

As if the smell weren't bad enough, the baby let out a god-awful holler. Song and her sister ran over.

"I think she needs a change," Rico said.

"Yeah, no kidding." Song took the baby from him. Her sister apologized profusely as they left to tackle their honorable task, which Rico did not envy.

"Speaking of babies, we need to get Nisha to her doctor's appointment," Mina said, tucking an errant lock of hair behind Ashna's ear, and a memory too clear and stark twisted inside Rico.

Ashna tracked her aunt and cousin as they walked away, her gaze filled with something between wanting to follow them out and the relief of having dodged a car while crossing the street.

It's not because I'm ashamed, his pai had always said to his mãe about never publicly acknowledging Rico and her.

I don't care, his mãe had always said.

Rico had wanted to believe them both. Now he didn't know what he believed and he would never know for sure.

Yash turned to Rico. "What you said before about my health care plan, not many people get that. Not many people have even read the report on my website."

Rico moved his focus to things that weren't lost causes. "The first time I read it, I thought I was reading wrong. The way you address the disbursement of funds and removal of costs, I couldn't quite believe it. You're halving cost while doubling benefit by bringing in volumes to a single source and supplementing funding from corporations. It's genius."

"That's an amazing way to explain it. Why didn't I think of that? I get too focused on the details, and it gets too technical. Not effective for speeches."

"Your speeches are great. It's just this issue, it's already complicated, it's easy to miss the forest for the trees." Yash's plan was seventy pages long. "And you're passionate about it, mostly the public just wants to see the passion and know that there are viable details that are turning you on." Rico smiled because, honestly, the details totally turned him on too. "Even if you just showed them the passion and stayed on message about reducing cost and supplying funding, I think they'd trust you with the rest."

"You want to read through the rest of my policies and come up with bite-sized spins for those as well?"

Rico already had.

Ashna looked even more like she was going to hurl, so saying that was pretty much out of the question. "Come on, anyone can do that." Which didn't mean he didn't want to be the one to do it.

The idea of helping Yash made Rico's heart beat in that primal way it beat when he ran out to the pitch. Something he hadn't ever expected to feel again.

"You were the face of your team for a reason, I see."

He tried to avoid Ashna's perceptive gaze. She looked distraught at what she saw. "A sports team is a PR nightmare waiting to happen. Especially today with the direct spotlight of social media. All the shit blokes pull, believing they can get away with it because their success makes them invincible, it's all out in the open now."

"And no one's buying the Boys Will Be Boys Kool-Aid anymore," Ashna said.

"Right," Rico said, meeting her eyes. "About time."

"Exactly," Yash said. "But you kept them looking squeaky

clean for almost a decade, and their image was quite a horror when you came in."

"Thanks. It's all about understanding and respecting the public's interest in you. They want something from you all the time: either you feed them or they come after you for it."

Zee had joined them again. "My man Rico was a master at keeping the media fed and focused. The No Cover-Ups policy worked well too. Once our blokes knew the team wasn't in that business, they showed their arses less. Then it was all fiancées and wives and kids and fashion houses and charities. The man's PR is ruthless." Being Pablo Silva's son and growing up an open secret, meant Rico had navigating his way around public opinion in his blood. That's why disappearing in plain sight in high school had been so easy for him. A handful of people was all you needed to really see you. The rest was an illusion you managed. But that made the people you let see you everything.

As Rico introduced Zee to Ashna and Yash, Ashna pointed to the couch and they sat. He wished she'd stop doing that, but he'd been standing for hours and the stiff throbbing in his leg was back. She tried to pretend she didn't see the relief on his face and shook Zee's hand.

Naturally Yash was a fan and rattled off Zee's stats in all his big matches.

"I hope you also follow American football, mate, because this soccer thing isn't going to get you elected," Rico said.

Yash responded with "Niners forever, baby."

"Do you follow football, I mean soccer?" Zee asked Ashna.

"Don't have much time for it, unfortunately."

"My old woman doesn't watch either," Zee said dreamily. For the first time that day Ashna smiled, her flat-out smile, the one that crinkled her nose. "Tanya finds sports in general barbaric."

"But not sportsmen, thankfully?" Ashna said, a hint of playfulness escaping into her voice.

"Zee just got married. He's supposed to be on his honeymoon, but instead he's here," Rico said.

That seemed to shake her. "Everyone should have a friend like you."

"Well, this slug's not a bad mate either. Tanya and I wouldn't even be together after all these years if it weren't for him."

Ashna didn't look at Rico, but he knew she wanted to. "Sounds like you and your wife have been together a long time," she said with the kind of genuine interest that would set her apart in an ocean of people.

"Since we were eighteen. You know how we men are. If we imprint on you young, you've got us forever. To do with us as you please."

She smiled at Zee so sweetly that Rico braced himself for what was coming. "Or you men want us to believe that, so we can never let you go and you can use our dependence to do as you please."

Zee looked delighted. "Are you saying men are more manipulative in relationships than women? That would go against the popular opinion, now wouldn't it?"

Ashna mirrored his delight. "The popular opinion that men have floated through the years?"

"I know a lot of women who agree that women are more manipulative than men."

"Just like you've heard women say women gossip more, or pull each other down, or only feel loved when men shower them with material gifts. Patriarchal opinions that centuries of being called 'the weaker sex' and being given only the domestic space and our own bodies to claim our power with have had us internalize?" Her smile wasn't quite so sweet anymore. "Your Tanya, would you be with her all these years later if you truly believed she'd manipulated you into it? What would that say about you?"

"Fair point," Zee said with a laugh. "It would say I'm a bloody idiot, now wouldn't it? I've actually never heard it put quite that way."

"You should have spent a day in our house growing up," Yash said. "Our mothers pretty much fed us shredded up pieces of the patriarchy for lunch every day."

Ashna smiled, but she had that look again, as though something had soured her stomach. A look that got particularly pronounced every time her mother came up. Another thing that hadn't changed.

Rico looked at his watch. Since Zee had only taken a few hours off from his honeymoon in Hawaii, it was time for him to head back. "Well, time for me to save your marriage again. If you don't take off now, you'll miss that flight. I'm not taking you in if Tanya throws you out again."

Zee hugged Ashna. "I'm so glad I flew in. Meeting you was totally worth leaving my honeymoon for."

That brought Ashna's smile back as she returned his hug. Yes, her nose crinkled again and crushed up parts of his heart filled out with emotions he hadn't experienced in years.

As Rico walked him out, Zee had the most sanctimonious smirk on his face. "So she's the reason."

Rico didn't respond, hoping to nip Zee's filterless musings in the bud. It didn't work.

"She's the reason why you're here. Everything makes sense now."

They waited for Rico's driver to pull the car up. "Does it? Because nothing makes sense to me," Rico said.

"How long ago were you together?" Zee asked with uncharacteristic gravitas.

"High school. But I barely know her anymore. She doesn't even acknowledge that she knew me, mate."

"Why is that?"

"Hell if I know."

George pulled the car up. "I very much doubt that. I've never heard you say that about anything. You do realize that your need to be a know-it-all is the most annoying thing about you, right?"

"No!"

Zee grinned. "The Rico I know would try to find out why. Because from where I was standing, it looked like she would very much like to acknowledge knowing you."

With that half-assed wisdom, his best mate drove off to his own simple life.

Chapter Twenty

Rico didn't care that Ash was hiding him. At seventeen, the one thing he knew for sure was that there was no connection between being hidden and being loved. His father had hidden him and his mother his entire life. Even after the car crash that killed both his pai and mãe, the press had only reported that Pablo Silva had died and that a friend had been in the car with him. They were buried separately, his pai in his family's plots, where his wife had joined him a few years later, and his mãe by herself. Rico didn't care. Once you were dead you were dead.

"Hindus are cremated. Thank God," Ash had said when he'd told her that his parents were buried separately. "So no one can keep my ashes from being sprinkled over your grave."

It was a bit crazy for teenagers to talk this way, but it had made him laugh. It was the first time anything about his parents had made him laugh since the accident.

It didn't matter that Ash had never introduced him to her tangle of cousins—all of whom he knew she loved with the kind of intensity that made her *her*. Meeting her parents or her aunt and uncle was out of the question. The idea of meeting anyone's parents made the memory of his parents in caskets come alive. He could barely stand to be in the presence of his own aunt, and he lived in her house.

He had never been to either of Ash's homes—not the one she lived in during the week and not the one she went to over the weekend. He had never been to her father's restaurant either.

None of that mattered.

They had been together for a year. They had met in the middle of sophomore year, and junior year had gone by in a strangely alive haze. All Rico knew was that his need for Ash was constant. She was with him even when she wasn't with him. Sometimes it felt like everything he did was just so he could recount it for her and make her smile, or be outraged. Because her caring about things, about him, made him matter again, made him alive. Rico liked feeling alive again.

He hadn't joined the football team, but between Ashna and the coach, they had convinced him to help with training. He assisted the coach during soccer season, mostly because he liked coaching her. Ash had convinced Coach Clarence that if he stopped badgering Rico to play, he could at least get him to help the team this way. Rico had never had to tell her that he just couldn't play, not when his mãe and pai would never get to watch him.

His father had been a football legend, a god, they called him back in Brazil. Rico had no idea what he would have done with that legacy, after his pai's death, had their relationship been public. When Rico was very young, he had barely seen his father. His mãe had been a single parent for the most part. Back then Rico had hated football. His mãe loved to tell the story of how Rico had been afraid of the ball—how he'd run from it when someone kicked it to him. When she'd told his pai, he had taken that as a personal insult and started to make time to play with him, and Rico had fallen in love with the sport. Football had given him his father.

"The fruit doesn't fall too far from a tree, no?" His pai loved to say anytime Rico won his league games for his age group. It was true; everything he knew about the game he knew because of Pablo Silva.

Rico hung up his smock in the back room and left Smoothie King. His shift had been canceled because the smoothie machine was broken. His boss had given him the rest of the day off and paid for his shift. Finding reliable teenage employees in Woodside was apparently not the easiest thing. Tests, sports, musical instruments, volunteer hours, their own start-ups— all of that took priority over a job serving yogurt mixed with wheat germ and coconut milk to other teens.

Rico was possibly one of the only students at GB High who had no idea what he was going to do with his life. A sin in this part of the world if there ever was one. From the age of thirteen he'd known he was going to play league football. Now he couldn't even imagine it. Ash wanted to go to UCLA on a soccer scholarship. Her father wanted her to go to cooking school, a laughable idea, because: Ash in a kitchen? Ha! If she wasn't training and sweaty, she was always moving and restless, as though she were still playing in her head.

Rico was also possibly the only student at their school who needed to make his own money. Being the love child of a football legend meant his financial support had died when the legend did, and Rico hated asking his aunt for money. He hated that she had to support him on her housekeeper's salary and make space for him in the cramped back house of the estate she worked at. Auntie Lena tried hard to make him feel at home, but he'd lost the only home he'd ever wanted to live in when he left Rio. The fact that Ash's uncle's house was just half a mile from Lena's meant he'd gladly live there forever. Being near Ash was a matter of survival.

Another reason the Smoothie King job worked so well was that Ash lived with her father Friday through Sunday. Ash had never told him that in so many words, but the weekends were hers. Which meant Rico needed his work to drive away the restlessness of being without her.

When he'd asked her what she did at the restaurant, she'd shrugged and said, "Everything. Except working in the kitchen." Her mouth had twisted as though tasting something foul. "I hate how crazy everyone gets about cooking. It's just throwing ingredients together."

His mãe had been obsessed with cooking; their lives had orbited around mealtimes. Taking Ashna out to eat was like taking someone unmoved by art to a museum. Food fell under that untouchable part of her life locked up in the vault where everything about her family sat.

The last time Rico had expressed an interest in visiting her restaurant, she'd turned to him with the first flash of fear he'd ever seen in her eyes. "My father is very old-fashioned. He isn't even comfortable with me being friends with boys. He can't know that I have a boyfriend."

This had struck Rico as odd. His parents had teased him constantly about any girls he was friends with. He'd brought home all the girls he'd gone out with since his first girlfriend at thirteen. He barely even remembered any of them; mostly they'd been friends, pretty girls in his grade who liked to say they had a boyfriend, especially a boyfriend who played football. They had maybe held hands and gone out for ice cream. Mostly, he'd done it because it had been what everyone expected of him.

Truth be told, his mãe had been more excited about the fact that he had a girlfriend than he was.

Now there was Ash, whom she would never meet.

Just the thought of Ash made his heart race. The darkness inside him from losing his parents became bearable when she held him. The sense he'd had since he'd lost them—that nothing would ever feel right again—eased when he made her laugh. If he could have one wish, it would be that his parents had met her. They would have fallen instantly in love.

Before he knew what he was doing, he had jumped into the Honda Civic he was slowly paying Auntie Lena back for and found himself on 280 heading to Palo Alto. He'd done this a few times, driven by Ash's restaurant on the nights she worked. He'd never told her, because frankly it was embarrassing to be needy enough to drive half an hour for the chance of catching a glimpse of the girl he spent every possible moment with on schooldays.

He pulled the car into a spot across from Curried Dreams

just as someone left. The mansion-like restaurant building reminded him of the grand houses in Humaitá where his pai's
family lived. It was all festively lit up. They were a few weeks
from Thanksgiving and Ash had told him that they had put up
holiday lights for Diwali, the Indian festival of lights. Seeing
them now felt like one of their inside jokes.

The only thing they didn't share was this, her family. If
Rico pushed or asked too many questions a wall came down
around her usually wide-open demeanor. Truth was, he and
she, they were enough for each other. If there was a part of her
life she needed to keep away from him, he didn't care.

Then why are you standing outside her restaurant?

He had no answer. All he knew was that he *was* here, across
the street from where she was, and it felt essential to be here.

Don't cross the street, a voice inside him said. *Don't.*

He crossed the street and made his way down the curving
driveway, walking past the valet parking stand with two layers
of cars waiting to be parked or taken away. He held his breath,
half expecting someone to stop him and ask what he wanted.
He was wearing jeans and his Smoothie King T-shirt, not the
best attire to meet the parents in. God, this was such a bad
idea.

He got a few curious looks, but no one stopped him, and
so he kept going. As soon as he pushed through the door,
the delicious aroma from outside intensified. The waiting area
was larger than in most restaurants he'd been to. The biggest
crystal chandelier he'd ever seen hung from the high ceiling
scattering golden light everywhere. Clusters of intricate paint-

ings in carved frames covered the walls. It was like walking into a palace. When Ash had said her father ran a restaurant, he hadn't expected it to be this fancy.

He was still studying the decor when someone spoke behind him. "Do you have a reservation, sir?"

He turned away from the life-sized dancing Ganesha statue and looked right into the eyes of a girl in a sari. Eyes that made him forget his name, eyes that had become his home. Only today they were lined in thick dark kohl. Her lips were a deep maroon and she wore a string of pearls that made her look ten years older. Then again, maybe it was the bearing with which she carried herself that was different, as though her shoulders were holding up the ceiling. He blinked. Maybe this was her mother.

It wasn't. Because she looked like someone had kicked her in the ribs. On the surface, nothing changed in her demeanor, but in her eyes something imploded. Her bewildered gaze swept the waiting area behind him and then landed back on him.

His own gaze swept the packed restaurant behind her and then came back to her.

From the very first day that they had met, the one thing that had never touched them was awkwardness.

Now it thickened the air and brought the crowded restaurant into sharp and loud focus around them.

"Ashi!" someone called, and he watched as she snuffed out every last flicker of recognition from her eyes.

"Do you have a reservation, sir?" she asked again.

"Hi," he said, more lost than he'd ever been in his life.

Before she could respond, a woman dressed in a tunic and pants made from the same fabric as Ashna's sari hurried up to her and whispered something in her ear.

Ashna's already frozen face went utterly blank, a placid, deathlike mask falling over her beloved, alive features. If Rico didn't know her as well as he did, he wouldn't have noticed, but he knew what the woman had said had cut her off at her knees and that she was struggling to stay standing.

Even though she didn't sway or stumble, just stood there rooted, he wanted to reach out and steady her. He wanted to ask her what had happened, but he didn't know how to ask this stranger who looked exactly like his girl.

"Take care of this gentleman, please," she said to the woman with the kind of authority he had never heard in her voice, then without any more acknowledgment than that, she walked into the restaurant and disappeared through a door, leaving it swinging in her wake.

"Have you been helped, sir?" the woman said. "Are you all right?"

He shook his head. "I'm fine. Thanks." And he walked out of the restaurant, not knowing what had just happened but needing to get out of there.

Chapter Twenty-One

All Ashna wanted was to get out of here. But of course, there was no peace to be had even in her own home. Shobi was always waiting, breathing down Ashna's neck to have her "bonding conversations" and rehash all the reasons why she had chosen not to be a mother to her.

"You okay?" Rico let himself into the green room. The other last person she wanted to see right now.

After her family left, Ashna had needed a minute to herself, so she'd found her way to the green room. A few of the families were still in the lounge with the cast and crew making their way through the substantial amounts of wine and cheese.

"I'm absolutely fine." *And if you say anything about hiding, I'll punch you.*

His eyes studied her in the mirror. Something about him seemed different since he'd left to see his friend Zee off.

"It was nice meeting your family." She couldn't tell if he was being polite or jibing her. "I'm a fan of Yash's work." Polite, then.

Ashna was used to the spellbinding impact both Yash and

Rico had on people, but this instant bromance thing was hilarious.

"I'd say it seemed mutual." In all her life, Ashna had never seen Yash gush. Yash had gushed.

Getting a smile out of Rico was more gratifying than it should be.

"Listen, Ashna . . ." He stepped closer, and she almost turned to him.

Before he could say more, the door flew open and Song walked in, a wide smile brightening her dewy, fresh face. Rico turned to her and smiled.

Her skin was like porcelain—not one single blemish. No bags under her eyes from all-night headaches. Her hair danced in a swishy bob around her softly rounded jaw. She was flawless, and filled with joy. And Ashna could see Rico's joy-seeking heart lap it up.

Ashna's bun pulled at her scalp and she tugged at it. It was extra tight today and all she wanted was to untie and retie it, so it didn't make her feel like a cross between a school headmistress and a spinster governess from a period film. The only thing she needed to complete the look was a big hairy wart on her chin.

Then she met Rico's eyes in the mirror and suddenly she was looking at herself through them. It had been her downfall, the way he looked at her.

He turned away from her, his gaze clinging to hers before he shifted his focus to Song. She said something about her niece and laughed, and fell against him. There might have been a little too much wine flowing at the family meet-and-greet.

Ashna's vision blurred, and the mirror turned hazy, shrouding Rico and Song behind clouds. They were both laughing now. Together.

How she had loved making him laugh. His laughter had always filled her up like sunlight streaming through a crack in a dank, dark room.

Only, now she knew the cold emptiness it left behind when his sunlight was gone.

She forced herself out of her chair and excused herself.

The pounding in her head was bad enough that she should go home, Shobi or no Shobi.

The party was still in full swing in the lounge. Tatiana threw her arms around Ashna. She was wearing a white dog collar with rhinestones today, matched up with her puppy—of course her puppy was her visiting family. "Sorry 'bout the tantrum yesterday. Totally bad form," she said.

"I'm sorry about the elimination," Ashna said petting the gorgeous black dachshund.

"Yeah, it's a bitch. But we were all competing for something when we know who's going to win."

"We don't know for sure that Danny's going to win," Ashna said, and Tatiana laughed a big belly laugh.

"I like you. No wonder men are throwing themselves at knives for you."

Which wasn't at all what men were doing. Instead of arguing the facts, Ashna took Tatiana's puppy from her and let it lick her nose while Tatiana reached for some fabulous wine from Ashna's favorite Sonoma winery.

Ashna wasn't a drinker. Having an alcoholic father meant

even the occasional glass of wine came with all sorts of complicated memories. When she did drink she stuck to her one-glass rule. It kept people she didn't know from asking why she didn't drink, and it kept people she did know from dumping sympathy on her head.

Ashna's star made his way out of the green room, with Song hanging by his arm, and was immediately surrounded by a mob.

She tried to slip out of the lounge, but DJ found her.

"What's the matter, love?" he said, his gaze on her cousin. Trisha had finished her consults and decided to join them.

Trisha made her escape from someone who had accosted her about a sore throat. "Do they not teach human anatomy in schools anymore? How hard is it to know that the trachea and lungs aren't part of the central nervous system and the brain stem? How hard is it to understand that I'm a flippin' neurosurgeon!"

DJ and Ashna smiled.

"That is, indeed, a question everyone must ask themselves," DJ said with utmost seriousness.

Trisha narrowed her eyes at him, not missing the teasing, but her laugh was free and heartfelt.

"Are you sure you're in love with Trisha?" Ashna asked DJ.

"That depends. What are you offering?" DJ said, waggling his brows, and Trisha elbowed him in the ribs.

"I know many ways to kill a man without anyone ever knowing what happened."

"Got it. The answer to your question, lovely Ashna, is that

I am very much in love with your cousin. Hers forever, etc."
Then he mouthed *Help me!*

The effect was ruined when he dropped the tenderest kiss
on Trisha's head. For the past twelve years the idea of an intimate relationship had made Ashna physically sick. Now she
hated the grip of envy that tightened inside her.

Trisha tucked a lock of hair that had come loose from Ashna's bun behind her ear, and turned suddenly somber eyes
on her. If she said anything about how Ashna would find the
perfect person someday, Ashna was leaving right now.

She didn't. Instead, she said, "You're spectacular on the
show. Everyone loves you."

"Actually, everyone loves Frederico Silva." Ashna was just
basking in reflected glory.

"What's not to love? The man tore open his stitches for
you." Trisha made a swoony sound and looked at Rico, who
was fully absorbed in keeping Song upright. "I wonder if he
looks that good when he wakes up in the morning."

"That's what you wonder, is it?" DJ said.

"I am human." Trisha made another exaggeratedly swoony
sound.

"Nah, you're a goddess." He kissed her again. "But carry on
with your ponderings. There's someone China wants me to
meet." He gave Ashna a hug and left.

They watched him walk away smiling to himself. Well,
Ashna watched him. Trisha watched his butt.

"Classy," Ashna said.

"It's even better without the jeans."

"Whoa! TMI, Trisha! The man is like a brother to me!"

"And aren't we glad I don't share that problem." Trisha grinned and poured herself a glass of wine from the well-stocked table. "So about Rico. Why are you looking like someone just stabbed you in the chest?"

Maybe because the man had. Except he'd stabbed her in the back.

"I'm doing nothing of the sort. Just tired." Ashna took a sip of Trisha's wine.

"Come on, Ashi, there's an incredibly hot guy in your kitchen and you're acting like you're being tortured. How often does that happen?" She took the glass back. "Well, DJ is often in your kitchen, so it happens a lot. But still."

"I'm not interested in him."

"Okay. Although, why aren't you?" An annoying brow wiggle. "Kidding. Seriously, though, he's going to help you win. You do want to win, right?"

"Ugh, that's the problem. I do." She considered telling Trisha about the Shobi Deal, but she had never been able to talk to anyone about her plentiful parental issues. "But I want to win for my food."

Trisha looked at her like she had no idea who she was. Ashna knew exactly what she was thinking. Ashna wasn't like DJ, who was a food whisperer. He had once told Ashna food spoke to him and he just listened. Ashna had pretended to understand.

Her palms went clammy. Food spoke to her too, but it didn't whisper, it screamed. Shrieks that curdled her blood if she dared to deviate from Baba's recipes.

Trisha squeezed her arm. "Sweetheart, you're here because

of your food, but in life you have to use all the advantages you've been given. It's ungrateful to kick away good fortune. Isn't that what we've been taught?"

DJ came back and said something to Trisha, and she laughed and pulled out her phone. Until Trisha had met DJ, she'd basically treated the whole world as not worth her time; now she was pulling up an article on arthroscopic gallbladder removal because one of Lilly's daughters had told DJ that she needed the surgery.

How did people change so much? Across the room Song dropped a kiss on Rico's cheek and he grinned as though he had not a care in the world. Then again, maybe people didn't change, maybe you just hoped they did.

Rico caught her watching him being all cozy with Song. Song followed his gaze. Brightening even more, she dragged him over before Ashna could make her escape.

"You're so lucky to have Rico as your partner," Song repeated, hanging from Rico's arm and slurring just a little bit.

Ashna refused to look at Rico.

"And he's lucky to have Ashna as his partner." Trisha stepped closer to Ashna and gave Song her famous *I can maim you with a scalpel* look

Which Rico caught. He held out a hand to Trisha. "Rico Silva, sorry I wasn't quite myself the last time we met. Thanks so much for taking care of my knee."

Trisha shook his hand with both of hers, suddenly all warmth. "I'm so glad you're all right. Thanks so much for saving Ashi's toes. Not many people would do that for a perfect stranger."

Rico turned to Ashna and waited. For what? Did he really expect her to tell Trisha about them? Now?

What would she say? *He's the boy I was in love with, the reason I caused Baba to die?*

When she stood there frozen, a bitter grin curved his lips, as though her inability to claim him as hers was one of their inside jokes.

"It was a reflex." His flat voice hid every whit of hurt banked in his eyes. "But I'm glad your cousin's foot is in one piece."

That made Trisha so happy she gave him a hug, which he returned wholeheartedly.

It was strange to see Trisha be all effusive. As for Rico, obviously he had changed his stance on physical contact and turned into this touchy-feely charmer. Foolishly, she ached for the days when they had been the same, perfectly mirrored.

They might not be kindred spirits anymore, but she knew without a doubt that his mind was stuck on the fact that she had let Trisha call him a perfect stranger.

Why is that such an issue for you?

He caught her jaw tightening and looked away.

"What an honor to meet Zia Malik today," DJ said excitedly and they started to talk about football again.

Ashna swallowed her groan. She couldn't bear another gushing rendition of that miraculous goal in the ninetieth. Spectacular as it had been (thank you, YouTube).

Ashna watched Rico watch Song rattle off some stats and misery engulfed her. "You all carry on. I have to get home." She made her way to the door.

"Ashna." Dear lord, please, why did he have to follow her?

She didn't stop but he caught her in the passageway. For a few moments they just stood there, circling the mess of unsaid things between them.

"Your cousins are lovely."

"Yes, they are."

There was something determined in his face, like the all-consuming focus before he went in for a penalty kick. "You're surrounded by love, Ashna."

"I know."

"Then why are you so miserable?"

Excuse her? "I am not miserable." She turned away and started walking again.

He followed her. "Being here makes you miserable. So why are you here?"

She shouldn't have stopped. "I've already answered that." She shouldn't have turned around.

The real question he was asking was in his eyes. Clear as day. "When was the last time you did something because you wanted to?"

She tugged at her bun, that stupid strand of hair gouging at her scalp. "I do a lot of things I want to."

"Right. I mean when was the last time you did something that made you feel alive?"

She hoped her face showed him exactly how much she didn't want him to say what he was going to say next.

"When was the last time you played ball?"

Sweat broke out down her back, prickles of ice over hot skin. The dampening spread to her palms, the insides of her elbows, the backs of her knees.

She could have named the exact date and time. "I think your friend is looking for you." Song was heading their way. She stumbled and Rico went to her. Ashna made her escape.

Despite her soccer scholarship to UCLA, Ashna had never really thought of playing as something she would do after college. She hadn't meant to let it go entirely either. In all honestly, she'd never given it a thought, believing that there would be time to make those decisions. As about everything else, she'd been wrong.

The last time she had put on her gloves, touched a ball, was when her high school soccer team had taken pictures for the yearbook. It had been after the season was over. She'd had plans with Rico after. Plans that relied heavily on the fact that his aunt was traveling and her house was empty overnight. It was going to be their first time spending a night together.

Ashna had lied to Mina Kaki and told her that Baba needed her at the restaurant, even though it was midweek. Then she'd freaked out. She'd been sure that Mina Kaki would call Baba, that Rico and she would be found out. She hadn't been able to relax until Rico asked if she wanted him to drive her home, and he had, without a whit of disappointment. For years, she had wished they'd had at least that one night together.

She went to the green room and took her time grabbing her jacket. No, she was not hiding. When she opened up her ride-share app she remembered that there was a huge tech conference happening in the city. It was going to be a twenty-minute wait. Ashna groaned. This was what happened when you became too dependent on technology.

Waiting in the green room was making her too restless.

She kept seeing Rico's eyes watching her in the mirror. So she made her way to the restroom through the thankfully empty lobby, trying not to think about how a ball felt in her hands. The hard kick of yearning made her want to scream. What would she give right now to feel the worn leather of the inside of a glove, the tightly stretched surface of a ball? Not for long, but just for one instant to have that smell of leather and turf flood through her, what would that be like?

Exhaustion dragged at her arms and legs. All she wanted was to go home and sink into her bed, without facing Shobi, without thinking about Rico, or all the other shit he was dredging up.

She washed her hands, avoiding her own eyes in the mirror. Her phone buzzed . . . her car was here. Finally. She was about to let herself out of the restroom when she heard a retching sound. Someone was throwing up in one of the stalls.

She walked to the stall the sound had come from. "Are you okay?"

The response was another mighty heave.

"Do you need help?" Ashna asked again, and saw that the stall was unlocked.

"I think I'm dying." It was Song. Of course it was. She reached back and opened the door, then returned to her crouch over the commode and heaved some more.

Ashna squatted down next to her and stroked her back. "Do you want me to call someone?"

Song shook her head. The poor girl looked miserable. "I should never drink red wine. It always makes me throw up. I'm such an idiot."

Ashna didn't bother to argue with that assessment. "You need some water." She fished out a bottle from her bag and handed it to her. "Rinse your mouth out before swallowing. That'll help settle your stomach."

Song did as she was told while Ashna kept a hand on her back. That usually helped with the dizziness. The water seemed to settle Song's stomach and she leaned her head against the stall.

Ashna pulled the flush lever, trying not to let the smell of alcohol-tinged puke bring back every bad childhood memory. "Think you can walk outside and sit down?"

Song nodded and Ashna helped her up.

For a moment Ashna thought Song would sink back down, but she leaned on Ashna and found her balance.

Ashna gave her a moment before she led her out. Just as she turned the corner out of the restroom looking over her shoulder to make sure Song was all right, she ran right smack into the rock-solid chest of Frederico Silva.

He grabbed her arms, steadying her, his touch gentle, his heartbeat frantic beneath her hands. She wanted to pull away, truly she did. They stood there like that, hands clinging to painfully familiar skin, soaking up who they used to be. Heat rose from him, his musky soapy scent working awareness into every nook and cranny of her being.

"I'm so sorry," Song said next to them, and Ashna's frozen body released. She took her hands off his chest.

"You all right?" Still holding Ashna, Rico turned to Song. There was such tenderness in his voice, Ashna wished she could disappear.

Speaking of disappearing, her ride!

She pulled away, fished her phone out of her purse, and ran out to the lobby. *No! No. No.* One missed call and two texts, and a canceled ride. She texted frantically, but it was too late. Darn it, the rideshare app searched and searched, giving her nothing.

"Hey, Ashna, everything okay?" Song asked. She was holding on to Rico but she looked much less green.

Ashna forced a smile, not that she wasn't glad to see Song looking better. "My rideshare just canceled on me. Let's get you to the couch."

"I'm so sorry! I didn't realize you were on your way out. Thanks so much for staying to help me. But why are you leaving? It's still early." Song tried to sit but lost her balance and fell onto the couch, taking Rico with her.

They tumbled back together, laughing, completely comfortable with each other. Ashna's arms tingled where he had held her.

She looked at her wrist, even though she wasn't wearing a watch, and felt immeasurably stupid. "It's late for me. I have an early morning." She fought to keep the smile on her face.

"How long before your ride gets here?" Song asked kindly, leaning her head on Rico's shoulder.

Every single time Song touched him like that, as though he was hers to touch, pain sliced through Ashna. The feel of his chest wouldn't stop burning on her palms.

The app found a ride. It was another twenty minutes, but the relief almost knocked her off her feet. "Not too long. Did you want me to get you a drink? Some ginger ale?"

Song's smile was grateful, and it made her perfect face glow. "I'm feeling all better. The red wine's out." She rubbed her belly. "We'll wait with you."

We.

"Thank you. Really, you don't have to do that." *Please don't do that.* "The car will be here soon."

"No, it won't." Finally, Rico found his voice. "There's thirty thousand people here for the conference. Wait times are ridiculous right now."

She hated how she felt his voice everywhere.

When she looked up at him, there was a frown folded between his brows. The one that made him look like the past twelve years hadn't happened. The focused gaze that had changed her life.

He typed something on his phone.

Ashna looked down at her own phone and channeled all her mental energy to will the wait time to move. It did the exact opposite. Still twenty minutes.

There was no way on earth she could spend another minute here with them.

"George will take you home." Rico stood, pointing across the lobby to the black town car that pulled up outside the doors. The black town car he had made appear in under a minute. "Come on."

Ashna didn't want his driver taking her anywhere. "George can take Song home when she's ready. My ride is almost here."

His jaw was set. "Song has her own car. She can drop me off if George doesn't get back by the time we're ready to leave."

Song beamed at him from the couch and opened her arms to Ashna.

Ashna bent and gave her a hug.

Of course, he'd want to drop Song off at her hotel *when they were ready to leave.*

Rico pressed a hand into her back. "Let's go."

Song slumped back onto the couch, waving at Ashna, and Ashna couldn't bring herself to argue with Rico in front of her. Not that his hand on her back was making it easy to form words.

Why did bodies have minds of their own?

They walked out through the automatic glass doors into the cool night and she shivered. He opened the car door and she got in.

Shutting her door, he walked over to the other side and opened the passenger-side door. "Curried Dreams, 300 High Street in Palo Alto," he said to the driver as he reached in and fiddled with the temperature control on the center console. The car, and the seat she was sitting on, warmed instantly. Ashna's insides followed suit. "Ms. Raje can tell you where to go from there." With that he thanked George, barely met Ashna's eyes, and went back to Song.

When the town car pulled up to her home, Ashna thanked George and tried to tip him. He refused with a smile and a "Mr. Silva is more than generous, Ms. Raje."

Those words dug into her already aching heart like sharp spikes as she got out of the car. It was probably the chill in the air but her nose ran, and she sniffed and pressed her jacket

sleeve into her face as she stood in the middle of her driveway and stared at Curried Dreams behind her bungalow. She
had no idea how long she stood there like that. Finally, when
she could, she dragged herself up the driveway and the ramp,
which had been put in for Yash's wheelchair when he'd had his
accident. It had come in handy later for Baba's scooter when
mobility became an issue.

Every light in the house seemed to be on. Every time Ashna
came home, she expected Shobi to be gone. Nope. Still here.
And yet she hadn't come to the studio with the rest of their
family. Mina Kaki had to have called her.

Come on, Shobi, how will the child feel if you're not there?

How many times had her aunt said those words to Shobi?

Shobi not being there had been a huge relief. Now that she
knew how dishonest she felt being in the same room with Rico
and her family, how much like a fake, Ashna was sure that
adding Shobi to the mix was something she absolutely could
not handle. Some relationships were just so ugly you couldn't
share them with anyone.

Chapter Twenty-Two

I think you should tell Ashna that we're together." It was easy for Omar to say. But Shobi had no idea where she would even start with telling her daughter all the many things she had hidden from her. How had she ended up here? With a thirty-year-old daughter who didn't know her mother was with someone. That she had been with someone since long before Bram died.

The look Omar gave her was almost as powerful over Skype as it was in person, intense with understanding. His neatly trimmed silver goatee had grown out just a bit and his gentle eyes were dimmed with worry. Those eyes and the way they saw her might be the reason she had fallen in love with him. They were certainly what had made her determined to return to him when every force in the world had conspired to separate them.

"I don't know how," she said without bothering to hide her despair. "The secrets between us have grown too large to swallow."

"Then break them into smaller pieces. Isn't that what mothers do?" A breeze blew through Omar's thick silver hair. He was having tea on the terrace of their Juhu flat. Shobi heard the crashing of waves from the beach behind him. It was Mumbai's premium view. Omar had bought the flat fifteen years ago, fulfilling a promise. Albeit an unspoken one.

Shobi had never needed any of the things from Omar that her family had expected from a husband for her. When you decided on your future so young, pragmatism had no place in it. Even so, those words had been everything: *Our house has been waiting for you, jaan. Only you can make it a home.* Not once had he asked her to leave her marriage. Not once had he questioned her when she had decided to.

"She's your daughter, how can she not be strong?" Omar took a sip from his stoneware cup. He refused to drink his black chai with lemon and honey out of Shobi's hand-crafted Wedgwood china.

After getting his law degree, Omar had ended up making his fortune writing for Indian TV and film. But his heart was that of a poet, incapable of the violence of unkindness, forever searching for the truth. How had he lived with her, a liar, for so long?

"When has telling the truth ever helped me?" Shobi poured herself another glass of wine and took a slow sip. The rich, full-bodied liquid warmed her despite the chill of Bram's kitchen.

"All your life. It has helped you all your life. Don't you see, Shoban, you *are* truth. The pain in your life comes when you're separated from your truth."

"Why are you telling me this now?"

"Because now you have the time to hear it."

He put down his cup and leaned in toward the computer screen. "I miss breathing the scent of your hair." It was something he had done for as long as she could remember, press his face into her hair and fill his lungs as though she were air.

When he'd done it that first time after she found her way back to him, he hadn't hesitated even for a moment. No one other than Shobi had believed she would be with him again. Except him.

"You are my breath," he mumbled in Urdu. "Follow the truth, jaan. Don't be afraid of it."

Shobi ached to hold him, to press against the starched hand-spun cotton of his kurta draped around his spare, tall body. Like his poetry, there wasn't an inch of excess in his form.

He held up the computer, giving her a view of her beloved ocean before letting her go with his "*Khuda hafiz.*"

She watched the computer blink off.

"You are the ocean," Omar loved to say to her. She had never lived far from an ocean. Not in Jaigaon, her family's home just south of Goa; not in Sripore, the Rajes' royal seat just north of Goa; and not here in Palo Alto. Although she could never think of this as home.

Except that her daughter lived here. Her Ashna, who had never been hers at all; Bram had never let her be. Not that she was special; it was what the world did to all women. Decided what they could claim, and at what cost. If they wanted more, it made them fight for it. In that, Shobi had given the world what it wanted. She had fought.

Except for Ashna.

She sat up on the barstool. The sound of the ocean, still in her ears, picked up force. The ocean inside her was a tidal wave.

How had she allowed this?

All her life she had refused to rely on anyone else to save her. So how had she stood impotent in this?

He had taken her child from her. But she was the one who had let him. And she was the one who had no idea how to get her back.

Shobi hopped off the stool and started pacing Bram's kitchen. She had no idea when Ashna would be home. It was a bit embarrassing to suddenly find herself waiting up for her daughter. It was a good twenty years too late to play the overprotective mother. She stared at the rice and dal she had cooked for when Ashna did finally get home. It was also a little late to play the nurturing mother, but she didn't care. She was sitting right here for as long as it took.

After her disastrous trip to the restaurant, she'd needed a bottle of wine. It had been horrifying how run-down Curried Dreams looked. It had to be breaking Ashi's heart. How did people do this? How did they handle their children's pain? Especially when they saw how unnecessary it was, how easy to fix. Why couldn't Ashi see what she was doing?

Shobi had found herself unable to help Mina as she directed the staff and took care of the dinner crowd. The restaurant was full. The way it used to be when Bram ran it. Ashna might be right, she might actually have a chance to turn the place around. Then again, what happened when the popularity of the show passed? Ashna had no love for feeding people.

Even when she'd helped Bram, it was always in other parts of the restaurant, never the kitchen.

Not that Shobi blamed her. Bram was an exacting monster in the kitchen. Well, he was that in all things, but his obnoxiousness was considered talent when it came to food. Shobi had once seen Ashna trembling outside the kitchen when Bram was in one of his culinary rages. When Shobi tried to ask her about it, she'd been mortified and had withdrawn deep into herself. In the end Shobi had done the only thing she could think of. Told her that she didn't have to ever go into a kitchen if she didn't want to.

The restaurant had always made all of Shobi's rage at Bram surface. Even today she hadn't been able to stand being there. How did Ashna do it? How did she go in there day after day with that room in the back, Bram's lair, where he'd trapped himself those last few years, where Shobi had finally told him she was done with their farce of a marriage, and where he had taken his own life, with no regard for the child who had found him in a pool of his own blood?

In the end, Shobi had left without helping Mina and come back to the house. The bottle of red wine she had been nursing all evening was only half-depleted. She poured herself another glass. She'd had to walk to the Whole Foods down the street to pick up the wine, because the house was entirely and completely dry. Dry enough to make Mahatma Gandhi proud.

It was understandable that Ashna didn't drink. Shobi remembered packing all the bottles in the house—hundreds of them, Bram was not one for moderation—into boxes on one of her visits and sending Bram's man Friday off to the Anchorage with them. It had been a desperate attempt to get the man to see sense. Seeing sense was another thing her late husband had not been known for.

The front door opened, and Shobi jumped up. Patting her sari into place, she made her way out of the kitchen, and stopped short when she found Ashna tiptoeing to the stairs. Ashna had obviously seen the lights on and had been trying to avoid her. The poor child almost made it before Shobi cleared her throat. The guilt on her face at being intercepted tugged at Shobi's heart.

"Hi, beta. How was today's shoot?"

At first when Mina had asked Shobi to join them on their visit to Ashna's set, she had agreed to go. Then she'd realized that putting Ashna through that in public without warning would be too cruel, and she'd stayed back.

Ashna stepped backward and off the stairs. "It was fine. Just some pictures and sound bites. Yash got some good coverage, which was great." She bit her lip. "They didn't tell us. So I didn't know families were coming."

"I know. Mina asked me. But I had an interview."

Ashna took her withdrawing breath and pulled on her blank face. "Right. How did it go?"

Was Ashna saying she had wanted Shobi to be there? "It was fine. The usual questions. I might have permanently given up on getting a journalist to come up with a surprising question. Your interview on the morning show was great. You came across as sweet and poised as always."

Ashna colored and rubbed a nonexistent spot off her giant

handbag. "Thanks. I barely needed to say anything. They are mostly interested in Ri . . . Frederico anyway."

Not for the first time, Shobi wondered about the football player who made her always cool and collected daughter stutter.

Shobi was almost certain there was something going on there. It wasn't like the man was trying to conceal his interest—no, his *wonder*—when he looked at Ashna. Strangely enough, it seemed a bit like how Shobi felt when she looked at Ashna, as though the hurt at being shut out by her was a physical ache. Like Shobi had her nose pressed against glass, hungry to get into that most hallowed place that was Ashna's heart.

Now that Shobi thought about it, Ashna seemed more than aware of it—the football player's regard, not her mother's. Which gave Shobi the niggling feeling that this wasn't the first time the boy and Ashi were meeting.

She could just come out and ask. But putting Ashna on the defensive right now wasn't the smartest strategy. She wanted to talk to her girl, just for a few minutes. Maybe even try to explain how they had ended up here on two banks of this generational river.

"What are you doing up so late?" Ashna asked too awkwardly, and Shobi thought again of the ease with which she talked to Mina. "Work?"

"Honestly? I was waiting for you to come home."

Ashna blinked. "Um. Sorry, I didn't . . . I'm not . . ."

"Don't apologize. It's just that . . . Have you eaten dinner? I made some varan bhaat."

Now she felt stupid. Boiled rice and dal was the only thing

she knew how to cook. But like her, Ashna had loved the simple comfort food as a child.

Maybe it was Shobi's imagination, but a sparkle broke through the weariness in Ashna's eyes. "Varan bhaat?" But she got a hold of herself. "I didn't have ghee in the house."

Shobi went to the kitchen and Ashna followed her with her usual tentativeness.

"I made some." Shobi popped the two bowls she had mixed into the microwave. "Ghee, now *that* I know how to make. I used to love the smell when our cook made it when I was little. So she showed me how to. Of course, she used to churn the butter from the cream first; I just walked down to the store and bought butter." Shobi put the bowl of rice and lentils mixed in with ghee and fresh lemon juice in front of Ashi.

For the next few minutes—the first peaceful minutes she'd shared with her daughter since she'd arrived—the two of them ate, letting the sticky, wholesome goodness melt on their tongues and stick to their palates and fill their mouths with that internal hug of a cherished comfort food.

"This is good, Shobi, thank you— I mean, Mom. Thank you." Ashna blushed and bent her head over the bowl to hide her embarrassment at the slip.

Shobi smiled. In that way that one smiled when one was trying to hide hurt. She knew Ashna called her by her name behind her back. She'd overheard her speaking to her cousins. It didn't matter. Shobi liked being called Shobi. Truly, she did.

"I was wondering. Would you like me to help with the restaurant tomorrow? Mina was saying she has something to take care of." Sure, the restaurant had made her uncomfortable.

Memories of a hated ex-spouse would traumatize anyone, but she'd go back in there for Ashna.

"Oh, that's okay, I can call Nisha. She'll help, or she'll find someone to help. You don't have to worry about it."

"I'm trying to help you, beta." There was an edge to her voice but only because being locked out so definitively was exhausting.

Ashna flinched. She put her spoon down and stared at it, as though her anger at her mother would be more productive when directed at benign cutlery.

"Why don't you say what you're thinking?" Shobi said, unable to hold it in anymore.

Ashna looked at her, words dancing on her lips, in her eyes.

Just when Shobi gave up on a response, Ashna spoke. "The question is, why? Why is helping me something you've suddenly taken up as your latest cause?"

Her causes had always been Ashna's nemeses; Shobi had sensed this long ago. But after her run-in with Ashna the day she'd arrived, that sense had solidified into realization.

"You're my daughter, Ashna. You may not see it, but helping you is something that has factored into all my decisions."

Ashna laughed, and there was almost a mean-spiritedness to it. Of all the things Ashna had said, that angry laugh hurt the most. Then Ashna turned it into a cough as though even hurting Shobi wasn't worth the trouble. "I don't think we define 'help' the same way. But thanks for 'factoring me in' when you could."

This was the problem with motherhood, the part Shoban didn't understand—why did it have to be an all-or-nothing game? Weren't mothers human? "Okay, I deserved that. So maybe I wasn't any help at all as a mother when you were growing up, but I'm trying to help now. Why are you so adamant about not letting me?"

Ashi went to the sink, filled two glasses with water, put one in front of Shobi, and drank hers down with such desperate gulps that Shobi feared she'd choke. "You want to sell my livelihood, but you want me to believe you're trying to help. Tell me how this works?"

"Okay, I'll try to explain." She took a sip of water. "But are you sure you're ready to hear this?"

Anger tightened Ashna's mouth. "Go ahead. I'll channel your *strength*."

Shoban wanted more than anything else for Ashna to let that anger out, but she looked wiped. There were smudges of mascara under her eyes. Either she had cried, or she'd rubbed her eyes from sleep like she'd done as a little girl. Maybe this wasn't the right time.

"Say it, Mom."

"Of course I don't want you to sell your livelihood. I want you to find a livelihood that gives you pleasure. You deserve that."

"Not this again."

"Do you truly have any love for cooking? Not for Curried Dreams, but for running a restaurant. Now you're showing up in front of a camera every day and you're this person you've been trying to be for twelve years in front of the whole wide world. Have you ever taken the time to ask what it takes from you? Being who you're not takes too much energy, beta. Have you ever asked yourself why you're doing a thing that gives you no joy? Your father is gone, there's nothing to prove."

Ashna picked up the glass and tapped it against the countertop, the controlled knocking of fragile glass on unbreakable stone a perfect foil to her anger. "Is there anything you don't blame Baba for, Mom? How can you ask me to come work for your foundation while accusing him of 'tying me up' for doing the same thing? Aren't you trying to tie me up in what you love too?"

And no one had stopped to consider what Ashna loved. She didn't say it, but it was right there in her eyes.

Shobi was doing it now. She was asking Ashna what she loved and Ashna was deliberately skirting the question. "You don't have to have anything to do with the foundation. Let's talk about what you actually want to do with your life."

This time Ashna's laugh was louder, wilder. "I love this. Suddenly you have time for me. And suddenly I'm supposed to know how that works. Trust, love, being able to ask for things, having heart-to-hearts, these aren't things you schedule into your calendar one fine day. How much time have you set aside, by the way? When does your real life need you back?" She squeezed her forehead. "Never mind. It doesn't matter when you go back. You want to know why I don't want your help? It's because I don't know how. I've never had it."

"I know that. But I was put in a position where I had no choice." The horror of leaving her little girl in the care of an alcoholic never went away, no matter how hard she tried. No matter how much she told herself that she had left Ashna in the care of Mina and Shree and not Bram. "I tried to take you with me, Ashna. I asked you to come home with me. You're the one who refused to leave your father. How can you forget that part?"

Shobi had repeatedly asked Ashna to go with her to India. Until a time had come when putting Ashna in a position where she had to make that choice over and over again just felt cruel.

Then there was the brutal reality of her situation, the part where Shobi had to travel so much for work. Since the death of Esha's parents and Esha and Ma-saheb's move to California, the Sripore palace had sat mostly vacant except for servants. Ashna would have to go to boarding school if Shobi forced her to go to India with her. She'd have to leave her cousins, her friends, be uprooted again. The only other choice had been giving up everything Shobi herself wanted and letting Bram win again. In the end, she hadn't been able to let what she wanted be the thing sacrificed. Because who was going to break that cycle if they kept capitulating?

"Wow! Are you seriously blaming me for not running back to India with you? What kind of choice was that to give a child? Baba didn't make me choose. He never left me."

"He did make you choose. You just always chose him. And how did he not leave you? By being in his drunken stupor? When did he ever ask what you wanted?"

Ashna's grip on the glass tightened. "Fine. You're right. You both abandoned me. Yay me. There, are you happy now? Is this the heart-to-heart you were hoping for?"

With that she left the kitchen and ran up the stairs.

Shobi watched her go, unable to follow her. She poured herself another glass of wine and raised a toast to the man who had tried his best to ruin her life.

"I thought I had beaten you, Bram," she said to the kitchen that captured his spirit. Dark, seemingly modern yet stubbornly traditional, reeking of privilege. "But you won, didn't you? First you put her inside me without my permission. Then you used her as a dog collar around my neck. Then you wedged a wall of lies between us that I would have to break her spirit to break down." She took a sip of the wine. "Congratulations, you sick bastard, you won."

Chapter Twenty-Three

Had the sick bastard really won? Shoban was sure women experienced all sorts of emotions when they sat on their marital bed. She had never imagined abject hatred being one of them. Hot-burning hatred for Bram, for her father, for all the men in the world who believed deep in their souls that what they wanted took precedence over everything.

The feelings inside her made an ugly contrast with the curtain of marigolds hanging from the canopy over the bed. Rose petals covered the sheets beneath.

The maniacal laughter trapped inside her churned with the bile that pooled in her belly. Laughter was the only way she could let air in and out. If she held it in, it started to singe her lungs.

Someone had threaded together the endless flower garlands. Hours and hours spent decorating the bed on which they wanted her to die, quietly, leaving behind someone they could claim and control.

Mrs. Brahmanand Raje . . .

She ran to the bathroom and threw up.

I will not cry.

She had not cried, not since Bram decided he would have her whether or not she wanted him.

She had not cried, not since Aijaz Uncle had broken down in sobs and begged her not to ruin their lives. His, Mahira's, Omar's. Another man who cared nothing for her.

Shoban had fought her terror and called Omar, but she hadn't been able to reach him. So she'd called his father. A little too late, because her father had gotten to Aijaz before her, with a warrant for Omar's arrest. Omar had helped his father with managing their estates and Shoban's father had been able to frame a case for embezzlement of millions. With her father's political connections, Omar had no chance.

If Shoban breathed a word to Bram's family, her father had threatened to have Omar thrown in jail. Shoban didn't know how to call his bluff.

"I will have no choice but to kill myself if you shame our families this way." Aijaz Uncle was not a man given to drama, so his words had been a nail in her coffin.

Shobi had imagined it with relish. All these fathers hanging by nooses. Dead. She could build a life on that. She wasn't so sure about Omar.

Oh, Omar. She missed him so much she could barely breathe around it. Her absolute belief that she would see him again had kept her standing through that sham of a wedding ceremony. This wasn't a marriage. Who cared how many rituals they put her through, how many pieces of paper they made her sign. Once she figured out how to keep Omar safe, she was going to burn those pieces of paper.

She gripped the mangalsutra around her neck, a gold chain threaded with black beads, a pendant of diamonds hanging from it. In the part in her hair was red powder. On the finger they used to tether women to the men who owned them was a band of gold studded with diamonds so brilliant she blinked when she looked at it. On her toes were toe rings. Four symbols marking her body to make sure no one ever mistook her for not being taken, owned. *Four* signs. And Bram wore none. Not one.

Omar and she had talked about their wedding as something they would celebrate by themselves, just the two of them. They had always known they'd elope. They were going to sign a piece of paper for the law, he would write her the most beautiful vows (she'd made him promise this), and then they'd take a boat to Sindhudurg and he'd recite them to her as they sat on the historic fort wall in the middle of the ocean.

She came back into the flower-infested room. A shield crossed with swords from some war the Raje ancestors had fought hung on the wall in front of her. There was an entire armory in the north tower, but it was all useless. Most of the guns and weapons were behind glass cases and as antique as the patriarchy that was holding her inside these walls.

She could find one of those guns, or throw herself off the balcony. There were a million ways to humiliate them by presenting them with her corpse on her wedding day. What would that get her? It would be the same as accepting Bram, accepting this new life. It would be accepting defeat.

Her father had done this so he could forge a relationship

with the Rajes, to attach himself to the place in society they a forded. Bram had done this to prove that he could. The reason why Bram did everything. How had she thought him harmless? Men like him were never harmless. Men like him, those gods of apathy, were worse in some ways than men like her father, the keepers of control, the true believers, who knew their way of life would be lost if their daughters rose to stand beside their sons.

No.

Shoban was going to stay Shoban.

One by one she started to remove the metal chains, the gemstone balls. She unhooked the nose ring, a cluster of pearls formed into a paisley around a ruby that her mother had worn at her wedding. Uncut diamonds formed into layered *jhumkas* hung from her ears all the way to her shoulders—earrings Bram's mother had worn to her wedding. More chains wound around her ears and hooked into her hair to hold it all in place. Everything tied up and tangled and secured.

Bangles from her wrists halfway up to her elbow, cuffs of gold interspersed with green and red glass. The breakable and the unbreakable clinking against one another. Amulets and anklets that had rubbed her skin raw. She cast it all off. One heavy weight after another.

An ungodly calm settled into her bones.

Next came the flowers in her hair. Enough of them that an entire garden had to have been massacred. Tuberoses and roses and five varieties of jasmine. The only other time she would be this covered in flowers would be when she lay on her pyre.

... they covered women in flowers—their wed-
... and the day they died. Who could have imagined
... two would feel so remarkably alike?

Omar's favorite song had been filmed on the wedding bed.
One much like this with curtains of flowers turning it into a
cage . . .

Kabhie Kabhie mere dil mein khayal aata hai
ke jaise tujhko banaaya gaya hai mere liye.

Sometimes a thought whispers in my heart
that your very existence was formed for me and me alone.

During the scene, the groom—also undesired—undresses
his bride as she sings the poetry composed by the lover she
had hoped would be her husband.

When Shoban had watched the song on the screen, her skin
had crawled at the groom touching the bride. *He has no right
to her body*, something inside her had always screamed.

That voice inside her was screaming now. The idea of anyone but Omar touching her made her sick.

"Give this a chance," her father had said after the wedding
ceremony was over. "It's for your own good."

"No, it's for your good, actually," she had said to him with
the same self-congratulatory smirk he and Bram had pasted
on their faces through the ceremony. "You are not welcome in
this house anymore."

Like the rest of the guests—not too many, because the wedding had taken place fast once Bram and her father had real-

ized that giving her time might help her escape—her father had rushed to congratulate her. But she had stepped away. "You made sure this was my home, and I am asking you to leave it. Get out."

He had leaned in to her. "Don't do all this tamasha right now and humiliate your family."

"You are no longer my family. I asked you to get out of my house, and if you don't, there will be a tamasha like you've never seen. You will drop the charges against Omar and send me proof that he is safe. If I find out that you harmed Omar or his family in any way, I will make sure I use all the power the Rajes wield to do to you what you threatened to do to Omar."

She had made sure Flora had her father's bags packed and in his car. That man would never set foot in Sagar Mahal again.

Shoban locked the door. She had no idea where Bram was. Probably being lectured by his brother, who had hurriedly flown out for the wedding from California, or saying goodbye to the guests, or handing celebratory mithai to the loyal subjects of Sripore. She didn't care. She undid the safety pins and removed her sari. Blood-red hand-woven Paithani silk embellished with twenty-four-carat gold thread. Bram's mother had asked if she needed one of the maids to help her undress. She didn't. Not that it had been an unkind offer.

Maya Devi had tried to talk to her before the wedding, but Shoban's father hadn't left them alone and after her experience with Bram, she wasn't sure if she could trust anyone. The bruises he'd left on her arms still stung.

She rummaged through the trousseau her father had probably paid someone an obscene amount of money to put together at such short notice. All these bright colors and silks. Clothes chosen for her by someone who had no idea who she was.

She looked through the duffel bag she had brought with her when she'd thought she was coming for a visit. She picked out a white cotton kurta appliquéd with white thread.

Widow's white. It calmed some of her rage, focused it. Until she was in Omar's arms again, she would only wear white.

When she stepped out of the room, Flora jumped off her stool. "Tai-saheb, you need something?" She looked confused by Shoban's suddenly and starkly unbridal clothes.

Shoban shook her head. "Just need to get some air."

Flora started to follow her, but Shoban raised her hand. The action much more imperious than she was feeling. "I'll be back in a bit. I just need to be alone."

Flora looked up and down the long corridor. Was she supposed to be spying on Shoban? Guarding her? Finally, she sat back down on her stool. "If you go straight down and make a left, the door at the end leads to a terrace that's unlocked and private."

Shoban thanked her and followed her directions. If she didn't get some fresh air, she was going to suffocate.

The huge terrace overlooked the ocean. Shoban stumbled out and sucked in a lungful of air, then coughed it out. Because someone was smoking behind her.

"Shit," a female voice said, fanning her hand in front of her face.

Mala, or was it Mona? Shoban couldn't remember her name, but she was Bram's older brother Shree's wife. She used to be some sort of Bollywood film star, but now they lived in America.

"I'm sorry," Shoban said, heading back to the door, "I just needed some air. I didn't know there was anyone here. And please, it's okay." She pointed at the hand her sister-in-law— what on earth was her name?—was holding behind her back. "I won't tell anyone."

The woman, who was ridiculously beautiful and still in the bright blue-and-gold sari she had worn to the wedding, smiled, and moved her hand from behind her, exposing the slim cigarette between her fingers.

"I'm Mina," she said kindly, holding up the cigarette before taking a deep puff. "I do it only occasionally." She waved the cigarette with the elegance of a . . . well . . . a film star. "The palace stresses me out. It's a lot, isn't it?"

"I'd say," Shoban said, turning around. "How do you deal with it?"

Mina laughed and raised the cigarette again. "Reinforcements. You want a puff?"

"I . . . I don't know how."

"You put it in your mouth like this, like a whistle, and you breathe gently. You don't have to. I don't want to be a bad influence."

Shoban took the offering and placed it between her lips. It was slightly wet, and she felt completely surreal standing in the bright moonlight with a cigarette between her lips. But if anything was going to take the edge off how she was feeling, she was going for it. She inhaled, then, afraid of bursting into a coughing fit, exhaled quickly.

"Wow, you sure you've never done this before?"

"Should I have pretended to cough, to make sure you believed I was a good girl?"

Mina—the name suited her—laughed. "Pro tip: a 'good girl' would not have taken the ciggie in the first place. She'd have said, 'No, thank you.'" She said that last part in a high-pitched falsetto while blinking vapidly.

For the first time in days Shoban heard her own laugh. "And she would have stared down at her toes." Shoban stared at her toes coyly, making Mina laugh. She took the "ciggie" back and took another puff.

Mina lit another one.

"What if we get caught?" Shoban asked.

"Shree is standing guard downstairs. He won't let anyone up. This is the Secret Balcony of Sin. Apparently, our husbands used it to get into all sorts of mischief."

Our husbands. Shoban sucked the smoke all the way into her lungs this time and did break into a cough, but she also felt light-headed, which felt good right about now.

Mina thumped her back.

"Shree doesn't mind?" Shoban asked to avoid the curious gaze Mina was giving her.

"He does. He's a doctor. So he isn't a fan of the risk factors. But it's my body and I only do it a few times a year."

"He sounds like he's really nice." Suddenly she missed Omar so much she squeezed her arms around herself.

"He is. Listen, you and Bram. Everything okay with you?"

Shoban dropped the cigarette. She was about to bend down and pick it up, but Mina put a hand on her shoulder. "Leave it. The stories I've heard about what Shree and his brothers got up to here, I wouldn't pick anything up off the floor. You can share this one. It's my last one."

Shoban took the offering, and turned to stare at the ocean. The two moments of peace with this woman had distracted her from the prison she suddenly found herself in.

"You feel like telling me what the matter is?"

Shoban laughed. A perfect specimen like Mina would never understand. Then again, Shoban had seen something sparkle in her eyes when she talked about Shree, so maybe she would.

What would she even say, though? *I hate your brother-in-law. He just forced me into a marriage with the help of my father*? Rage burned in her throat and she turned away.

"Did you know I was a child star?" Mina took the cigarette from Shoban and leaned into the railing next to her.

Shoban studied her. "*Baby Minu*? That was you, of course." Shoban's ma had loved her films. "Didn't you win a Filmfare Award?"

Mina's face was a mask, her beautiful features frozen taut, a kind of deadness Shoban couldn't reconcile with the smiling woman from before.

"I don't remember. I don't remember any of my childhood roles. My therapist tells me it's PTSD memory loss." Another drag of the cigarette. "I was forced into them by my father."

Shoban wasn't sure if she should reach out and touch her, comfort her in some way.

"It's okay. I'm fine now." Mina took one last drag, although nothing was left of the cigarette. "But I do recognize someone in a situation that they don't want to be in."

For the next few minutes they stared out at the ocean, watching the fractured moonlight scatter on the waves.

Shoban was the first to break the silence. "You know how you just talked about Shree? I could tell that thinking about him makes your heart flutter."

Mina smiled, letting the demons go from her eyes. "It does. I'm so glad you get it. You were so quiet during the wedding, I almost thought—"

"I do know what that feels like. But it's not for Bram."

"Oh." Mina touched her forehead. "Dear God. Why didn't you stop it? Why didn't you say no? Don't answer that. You did. Bloody hell. What are we going to do?"

"I don't know. If I leave, my father has threatened to destroy Omar's family. I don't know what to do."

Mina pushed a lock of hair behind Shoban's ear. It was a careless gesture and absurdly comforting. "I knew the man was a weasel." She studied Shoban. "I hope it's okay to call your father that."

Shoban waved away her words. "Oh, please. Calling him a weasel is insulting weasels everywhere."

Both women smiled.

"You can come live with us in California."

"I don't want to live in California. I want to go to Oxford and study there with Omar and then come home and get married and start a life here with him, in India."

"Shree can talk to Bram. Maybe he'll agree to an annulment."

"An annulment?" Just the thought of that made Shoban feel human again. She took a deep breath. Silver waves broke on black rocks. In her heart Shoban knew it would not happen. "My father would make Omar pay too high a price."

"We'll come up with a solution," this virtual stranger said, pressing closer to Shoban as she stared out at the ocean. Their arms touched, the smell of tobacco and jasmine hung around them. Half an hour ago, Shoban had felt completely and utterly alone in the world. Now, hope nudged at her. Maybe she would find a way.

"Shree always says that everything has a solution so long as you keep your head. Maybe let's sleep on it. Tomorrow, without the exhaustion of a wedding, we'll come up with something. Maybe tomorrow we'll talk to Ma-saheb and Shree and—"

"No." Shoban turned to Mina. "I can't tell them. Not until I've thought about how that would impact Omar."

Mina squeezed her shoulder. "Okay, I won't tell anyone."

"I don't want to go back in there."

"I don't imagine that you do. But maybe just talk to Bram. Tell him the truth?"

Shoban laughed. "I did." The bastard was excited by the prospect of breaking her into submission.

Mina tucked another lock of hair behind Shoban's ear. "I'll make sure he doesn't come to your room." Her voice was suddenly steely. "At least for tonight, you don't have to worry about it."

Chapter Twenty-Four

Ashna pushed a stray lock of hair off her face and Rico dug his hands into his pockets. The longing to touch her hair, to be the one to push that lock behind her ear, was a force inside him. All damn night he'd dreamed of touching her, of her hands on his chest. Of the scent of roses lingering in his car.

This closure thing had well and truly blown up in his face.

As he walked into the holding area outside the room where promo videos were being shot, her eyes found him and came alive, and clung, and said a million things he knew she didn't know she was saying.

Blown. Up. In. His. Face.

They were one elimination down. If they lasted to the end, they had four more cooking segments, and a finale to shoot. That was another four weeks with her.

Four whole weeks.

Just four weeks.

His heart felt like a pebble in his chest.

Ashna and he were still head and shoulders above the rest of the teams in viewer votes. Social media would not stop buzzing about them. The early episodes had brought in a record number of viewers. Rod had been inundated with joint interview requests, but it was clear that Ashna wanted nothing to do with Rico outside the studio—or even inside it. Their popularity wrecked her.

Question was, why did knowing that wreck him?

Why are you here?

Why couldn't he stop asking that?

She caught the question in his eyes and stiffened. Turning away from him, she found China and gave her a hug. Was that it? Did her being on the show have something to do with China roping her in? The idea of her letting someone pressure her into doing something she didn't want to made something wild move inside Rico. Something an awful lot like his underperforming survival instinct.

Finally, she turned away from China, squared her shoulders, and made her way toward him. He couldn't believe China hadn't prepared her for what it was like to be in the public eye. Then again, if Rico hadn't had an existential crisis at Zee's bachelor party, Ashna's experience on the show might not have turned into an international media explosion.

An explosion that was working excellently for China Dashwood and her team. Yes, Rico was aware that they had been friends from before he and Ashna had met. Yes, China was yet another person Ashna had hidden him from.

This is Frederico Silva, my partner on the show.

A perfect stranger.

That's all he was. That. Was. All.

Never in the past ten years had he looked at wanting to win

as anything but a singular goal. Now he wanted to both return to the arena and walk away, in almost equal measure.

The fact that his knee felt like it was leaking pain up and down his body didn't help. Today was probably not the best day to try to wean himself off the narcotics completely. The new regimen his doctor had put him on hadn't worked. The road to freedom from pain wasn't going to be an easy one, but easy was overrated.

Lilly Cromwell stopped Ashna and the two women exchanged hugs. When had Ashna developed relationships with everyone on the show? Everyone wanted to chat with her, unthreatened by her and Rico's wild success with voters. Not that he didn't get it. That innate kindness she emanated was a tranquilizer, an intoxicant. Who alive could resist it? Today's social stops were also obviously her avoiding making her way to him.

Pulling out his phone, he pretended to stare at it so he wouldn't stare at her. She was impeccably put together, as always, dark kohl outlining her singularly shaped eyes, heavy lidded and slanting upward on a curve. Bronze dusted her lids. All the skillful makeup did nothing to hide the exhaustion weighing her down. Her hair was gathered into a bun at her nape. She had hated putting it up. In high school she had either left it down or braided it.

It's too heavy and I always have this one hair that tugs at my scalp and drives me crazy.

He wondered if it still fell all the way down to her waist, and if the thick blunt ends would still spill across his forearms when she tilted her head back to kiss him.

"Hi." Finally, she was standing in front of him. Instead of her usual red chef's jacket she was wearing a maroon silk blouse that put her collarbones on full display.

Her collarbones had a way of mirroring her moods. They stood out in sharp relief when she was screaming at someone at the goal line. The curve was smoother, gentler when she was being determined off the pitch. Two completely different ways in which she could be fierce. Of course, something entirely magical happened to those lines when she was aroused.

She caught him skimming the bones radiating from the perfectly shaped hollow at the base of her throat. Her gaze drank in whatever she saw in his eyes.

"Hi." He tucked his phone into his pocket. It had sucked as a cover anyway. Moreover, he was a grown man, a world-renowned athlete. *Try to remember that, will you?*

She gave him a searching look and it had to be the lack of meds because a hungry pit opened up inside him. The camera was watching, so he held out his arm as they were called to the interview area.

There was only a moment of hesitation before she slid a hand into the crook of his elbow. Her hand was ice cold even through the cotton of his shirt.

They walked down a corridor lined with Food Network legends. Cameras clicked, and her fingers tightened on his arm even as she kept a good six inches between their bodies. Which was commendable because the giant magnet between them had gone back into overdrive.

The effort of holding himself at the distance she'd stipulated intensified the pain in his body, and idiot that he was, he overcompensated by trying to appear excessively relaxed and in control.

Jonah led them to another waiting area with stiff-backed chairs and she let go of Rico's arm, leaving it even colder.

She asked Jonah about his two-month-old and he showed her pictures on his phone before running off to put out some fire with a smile on his face.

They were going to shoot extra footage before the competition segment. Usually it was DJ asking questions, and that put her at ease. Today it was a crew they hadn't seen before. Her nervousness was palpable.

"It's just an interview," he said, hating how seeing her like this made him feel. "Just pretend you're at a party and answer as though someone's chatting with you. It's not a performance. Just be yourself."

"Just be myself?" She looked down at her hands. "How is everything so easy for you?" She bit her lip, clearly regretting the words the moment they left her mouth.

Sure, *this* was easy for him: being in the public eye, knowing how to navigate the spotlight.

"Not everything," he said quietly. Obviously, some things were easier for her than for him, because twelve years later he was the one back here, still looking for closure, not her. "I could ask you the same question."

The universe shifted in her eyes. They softened with loss, then hardened with the effort to cover it.

"I thought you wanted to be here. To save your restaurant. You chose this." *Over me.* "Then why is it so hard?" It came out harsher than he'd intended, but he couldn't be stupid enough to give up control again.

Did she regret making that choice?

She regretted something. That was clear.

Is this also something Daddy dearest is demanding? Why is it still so hard for you to stand up to him? The words almost came to his tongue, but her father still made too much rage rise inside him. And letting her see his rage at him had cost him everything once.

You're a bastard. She's a princess.

How had an asshole like that made her?

Her hands shook in her lap and she gripped them together. "You would never understand."

How were they back here, where it mattered if they understood each other or not? But it did and here they were.

"You're right, I don't. I couldn't have imagined it, you following in your father's footsteps, you taking over the restaurant. You hated it, Ashna." That day when he'd shown up at Curried Dreams uninvited, he'd seen misery inside her. The kind that had shaken him all the way to his young soul. It struck him that the misery he'd seen that day had congealed inside her now, burrowed so deep he couldn't separate her from it.

"I don't hate it. Will you please stop saying that!"

He'd never said it before.

Embarrassment suffused her face.

"Well, you don't love it, that's for sure. Then why? Only because it's what your father wants you to do?"

Her eyes went flat. The flatness so stark it shone under the lights. "Why is that so wrong? Look at you, you ended up on the pitch eventually, didn't you? I guess our legacies aren't as easy for us to get away from as we want."

"Except I actually love football. I wasn't forced into it because it's my legacy."

She looked like he had hit her. He wanted to take his words back. He wanted to turn back time. He wanted to run for his life.

She's just a girl I dated in high school.

And he was a bloody liar.

A bloody liar who was in so much trouble.

"You didn't always love it," she said so quietly he almost imagined it coming from inside his own head. How hard she had fought to bring him back to it. In the end her betrayal had done what her love hadn't been able to.

"You're right. I did lose my love for it for a while."

"How did you find your way back to it?" she asked. It was a question with so many other questions rolled into it, he wasn't sure how to answer.

In the end honesty felt like the best path. "When I tried to play in high school here, everything felt like a legacy, like every single thing I did on the pitch said something about my pai, and I just couldn't do it. But when I found myself on the pitch after . . . after I went to England, I didn't give myself a chance to think. At first everything was automatic. Coded into me since I could barely walk. Then I realized that it had never been just me on the pitch until then. My pai had always been there with me. I had so much to learn, so much to unlearn, and when I embraced that, suddenly, for the first time the game was mine."

China walked in with her crew and Ashna blinked away the storm in her eyes at his words. They were led into the interview studio, where they proceeded to answer the usual barrage of questions. How special it was to be here. How special it was to form a bond with each other (a bond between strangers!). How food was nourishment not just for bodies but for souls, and so on and so forth. He filled the silence with sound bites. She did the monosyllables.

"When did you know cooking was your passion?" the interviewer asked her, and the layer of misery at her core rolled to the surface.

Her lips stretched, desperate for a smile. "I . . . I always . . ."

"I'm so glad she's passionate about it, because I've always been terrified of the damn thing," Rico drawled with a wink. "I mean, she literally had to walk me through the churro in baby steps. I still managed to mess it up."

The interviewer chuckled and picked up the perfect pass Rico threw him. "I don't think we're allowed to criticize that churro. I believe Ms. Raje said it was *the best churro she'd ever tasted.*"

For all her being flustered just now, fierceness shone through her smile. "You should have tasted it. It was."

For all his smoothness just now, Rico couldn't come up with a response to that.

Satisfied at canning another perfect on-camera moment, the interviewer moved on to rehash The Video, making Ashna shut down again. She really hated that video. Rico really hated that she did.

Thinking about his slide across the floor refreshed the pounding in his knee.

"So you ready for your next cooking challenge today?" the interviewer asked.

"Can't wait to get in there and cook up a storm," Rico said, overcompensating for her silence again.

When they were done, Ashna hurried out of the studio, racing right down the passage and out through one of the back exits into the open air. Rico had no idea why he followed her, dragging his damn leg with him.

She leaned her head back and sucked in a breath. The bun at her nape loosened and Rico's insides did a godawful leap.

"Can they talk about anything other than that stupid video for one damn second?"

He let the door slam behind him. "Right, the stupid video of me tearing open my wound because you couldn't keep a grip on a knife."

She squeezed her temples, hands shaking. "You know what I meant." Her fingers rubbed her skin so hard it reddened. "Did you really tear . . ." Her gaze dropped to his knee. The need to touch him, to comfort him, flared in her eyes.

He didn't want her looking at him this way. It was this look, this look that drank his pain up into herself, that had screwed him in the first place.

"It's nothing," he snapped. "And it isn't a secret that I tore open my stitches. If you had cared to ask you would have known."

She tugged at her hair, trembling fingers seeking that one

errant strand that pulled at her scalp. The realization that he would do anything to stop her from hurting like this was a soft tap inside him, right on the nerve that made him want to double over.

He was about to tell her it was okay, lie and soothe her, but she faced him, remorse dimming her eyes. "It's not nothing. You saved me from getting hurt and I'm so sorry that you hurt yourself." There was that look again. The one that said *I can't bear to see you in pain*. The one that said his pain was her pain. He knew what a lie that was. He knew.

"You've apologized already. It hardly matters now. One year ago, you might have cut my career short. But I'm already done with that. Timing is everything when someone inflicts pain, isn't it?"

Seconds ago he'd wanted to take it all away from her; now he was hurting her when she was down, when she was hurting for him. When the only thing that had distracted her from whatever she was struggling with was his pain.

Her look said she couldn't believe what had become of him.

He couldn't believe it either.

"True. Timing is everything." Those were the words that cracked her voice. A thin hairline fracture that she swallowed around. "And the timing of that video means we can win this, doesn't it?"

"Any advantage is an advantage," he said, because suddenly they were both masters of saying one thing and meaning another.

For a breath, her gaze clung to him so tight he almost reached for her.

"If it bothers you so much that the advantage is based on people loving us together, all we have to do is stop acting like it's a big deal and they'll stop."

Shock widened her eyes. Whether it was from what he had said, or the fact that he had said it at all, he didn't know.

His own heart thundered with realization.

Well, bugger him sideways, the public did have a way of identifying something real. It's why people loved watching sports. You couldn't lie on the pitch when the clock was breathing down your neck. There was no way to hide your heart when you locked in on your goal, when winning became the sum total of who you were.

"Why is winning this so important to you anyway?" He had to know. She'd been a madly competitive player, but that part of her seemed to have been entirely snuffed out.

She swallowed, the long column of her neck straining. "If I don't win, I'll have to shut my restaurant down."

Wow. Okay. That explained so much. But it made fresh rage rise inside him. "Then why aren't you competing harder? Why aren't you even in that kitchen when we cook?"

The trembling started again. Her lips, her hands. She wrapped her arms around herself, and sagged against the wall. Her mouth opened but nothing came out.

"What is it, Ash, what are you not telling me?"

The word hung in the air between them. A name he hadn't let slip from his lips for twelve years.

Pushing away from the wall, she started pacing. Her hands went to her hair, and with a frustrated grunt she unhooked her bun. Hair cascaded down her back. Electricity kicked in his gut like a damned bolt of lightning.

She shook it out, then gathered it back in a bun.

Leave it down. Just for another moment.

She let it go and pulled the sharp dagger-like hair clasp out of her mouth. "We can't win, Rico. We can't win because . . . because . . ." Her hands went to work on the bun again. She rolled it back up and poked it with the dagger to keep it in place. No points for guessing what else the dagger pierced.

"Because what?"

Her eyes were stripped bare when they met his. "Because I can't cook."

His brain had to still be stuck on her hair, because that made no sense. "You made that omelet perfectly."

"I can only cook certain things."

Excuse him?

"I've . . . I've never told this to anyone." Her hands twisted together. "I can only cook things on the menu at Curried Dreams. If . . . if I try to cook anything else, I . . . well, I can't."

Suddenly everything made sense.

Then, nothing did.

"Can you . . . can you please not ask questions. Please." She was breathing hard. Her hands were shaking like leaves in a storm, a storm she had swallowed whole and trapped inside her lungs, under her skin.

He reached out and took them. "You've never told anyone?" They were ice cold and he wrapped them in his. "No one?"

That made her laugh and she clamped her mouth shut. It made her eyes water as she choked it back.

He tamped down the rage that rose inside him. He was going to dismember whoever had done this to her. "I'll take care of it," he said.

He'd tell the network that he wanted to be the one doing the cooking. They'd accommodate him. He'd make them. He'd make this go away for her.

His thumb traced the backs of her hands. The rise of veins, the ridges of tendons, the sparklers bursting in his heart. Letting her hands go was going to be the hardest thing he'd ever done.

"Thanks." The word was the barest whisper on her lips.

He'd never known how not to give her what she asked for.

I need you to not ask me questions right now. I need to handle my father my way. Please.

Look where it had gotten him. "How do you hold in so many secrets, Ashna? Why?"

She snatched her hands out of his and pushed him away.

His hands fell like lead to his sides. "Why does he have such a hold on you?"

That made her step back. Without another word she went to the door. Yet again, done with the conversation, done with him.

But she stopped and Rico hated the relief of it. "You know what? I don't want you to take care of it. I will take care of it myself. I don't need your help."

"How? How will you take care of it? By walking away?" *Again.* "You're a chef, and you're telling me you can't cook! I could never have imagined you like this. What happened to you?"

"I should never have told you. I should have known you wouldn't understand."

"Understand what? Is this what happens when you push away what you want for too long? You forget who you are."

This wasn't her. This Ashna had suffocated the Ashna he knew—his Ash. She might have been just a girl he dated in high school, but that girl had breathed life back into him and he had to bring her back. Even if she wasn't his anymore.

She leaned her head into the door. "Is this what happens when you do exactly as you wish for too long? You stop understanding anyone? You end up selfish and alone?"

Damn right. And it was a condition she had thrust him into. "So, you're not alone, is that it? You're surrounded by people who love you. People who love you so much that you need to hide anything that's important to you from them?"

"Will you ever let that go?"

Never. "Sure, I'll let it go. But have you ever thought about what it means to hide what's important to you from those you love?"

"Have you ever considered that maybe I hide it because it's not worth sharing?"

That should have hurt, but it didn't. He knew she was lying, and she knew it too.

"Or maybe if you stopped hiding it, you'd have to admit its worth. You'd have to admit your own worth. You'd have to admit that you're deserving of happiness. And if you did that you'd have to fight for it, and maybe you've forgotten how to fight for anything."

Her hand squeezed the doorknob until her knuckles turned white. His heart felt like that doorknob, squeezed tight in her grip. Silence flooded them like a spotlight, leaving no place for their words to hide.

They stood there like that, time slipping and sliding around them. In the end, she was the first to leave. Instead of going back into the studio, she ran around the building and disappeared, exactly the way she had done twelve years ago.

Chapter Twenty-Five

Wanting to run away was never a conscious thought Ashna had. It was this constant, beating sense that was threaded into her being. So much a part of her that she never examined it. She had sure as hell never acted on it.

There was only an hour before they started shooting the competition segment. But she couldn't stand to be at the studio. She ran out onto the Embarcadero and slowed to a walk.

Her hand went to her phone. She had no idea what she was doing when she dialed Shobi's number. Hindi rap burst from the speaker instead of a ring and Ashna hung up, realizing that she couldn't remember the last time she had called Shobi.

Anger pulsed inside her. The constant, inexhaustible anger at Shobi, at Rico. Every single time she walked away from him, she felt like she had walked through fire, and the flames had burned off her clothes, leaving her naked, her flesh blistered.

The memory of his hands wrapped around hers lingered like a phantom touch. The solidity of his arm beneath her fingers every time they walked into the studio had become a phantom crutch. Why had she taken strength from it? How had she let it soften her?

Soften her enough that she'd exposed herself to him and he'd used it to strike at her.

How dare he talk to her about fighting for things? She'd fought so hard for him that she'd pushed her own father over the edge. In return he'd left her.

It didn't matter that he regretted it now, because obviously, he did. It didn't matter that he saw right to the center of her. That he remembered everything she'd been, everything she'd wanted so badly to be.

She'd shared so much with him. What it was like to grow up in Sagar Mahal, a child alone in a palace. Parts of her she'd never shared with anyone else. But it had felt essential for Rico to know about the home she'd grown up in. Especially because she had never been able to let him into her real home.

Have you ever thought about what it means to hide what's important to you from those you love?

The look on his face when he'd shown up at the restaurant one evening out of the blue had never stopped haunting her. The hurt in his eyes when she'd walked away from him without acknowledging him had burned inside her all weekend. The terror that she'd lost him, the certainty of it, had been worse than anything she'd ever experienced.

How could she have acknowledged him? It had been one of their busiest days, and Baba lay drunk in a room upstairs, unable to move.

As Rico had stood there, eyes expectant and probing, waiting for her to unfreeze, Baba had soiled himself. Tara, one of the hostesses, had whispered the news in Ashna's ear with Rico watching.

It had been the most humiliating moment of Ashna's life. Or at least the most humiliating moment that she cared about. When her parents screamed at each other in front of the whole family, in front of her cousins, she had learned not to care about the shame. This had been different. Rico saw her as strong. With Rico she got to be self-possessed, like her mother. Droll and humorous, like her father. She got to be a version of herself unstained by irreparable pathos, because he gave her the gift of not coloring his vision with sympathy like everyone else in her life.

It had meant everything. Especially when all the stories of his childhood had felt so wholesome, his parents' love for each other and him so undamaged.

That night, cleaning Baba up without having him create a scene had taken an hour. The crowd in the restaurant hadn't thinned until after the midnight closing time. Ashna had slept on the floor next to Baba in his room behind the kitchen, because she didn't want him alone, in case he threw up in his sleep. The EMT had performed CPR when that had happened the month before, and he had choked on his own vomit. She couldn't have him go through that again.

The next day had also raced by. Sunday-brunch prep started at five in the morning, and Baba hadn't risen until almost twelve hours after that.

Her finger had hovered over Rico's number several times on

Sunday evening after she was back at the Anchorage. But he hadn't called, and she hadn't been able to.

On Monday when she got to school, Rico was waiting for her at their usual spot near her locker. There had been a moment of terror when they studied each other, not knowing where to go from there. All Ashna wanted was to go back to how they had been, to erase those moments when he had stepped into a different part of her life. A part of her life that could take away what they had with each other. Because how would he even recognize her in that part of her life?

Rico had grabbed her bag from her, taken her hand, and asked her about calculus homework. Just like that he'd given her her wish, erased those moments that could have changed everything. And he never brought it up again.

Ashna found herself all the way at pier 24. She had walked from pier 33 without realizing it. She leaned into the railing, letting the cold metal dig into her belly, and stared at the Bay Bridge. Sure, the Golden Gate was beautiful, but this one, this one seemed to have all the magnificence but none of the glory. The female in the marriage between San Francisco's two beloved bridges, Shobi would say.

For some reason the thought made her laugh. It started as a soft whimper of a giggle. Then it broke through her. Laugher pumped out of her, hard and fast, until she doubled over the railing of the pier. Her feet left the ground. For a second she was suspended. She leaned farther, needing to turn herself over, inside out. Needing to empty the laughter out of her. Get rid of it once and for all.

She let it go. Spat it up. Let it convulse from the very depths of her like deeply settled morning phlegm. And expelled it. Shaking out every last drop, wave upon wave pumping out of her. On and on and on.

When she finally straightened up, unfolding from over the railing, the world whirled around her, a twister spinning her and forcing her to close her eyes.

Had she really forgotten how to fight?

She was fighting for Baba's restaurant.

No, she hadn't forgotten how to fight. She had never learned how to win.

Shobi had picked her war. Everything was female pitted against male to her. She saw nothing beyond that. It's why she had won.

It's how Rico had always been with the ball. Nothing else, only that one thing. The world distilled down to one point, one thought, his goal, the deepest meditation.

Ashna wanted that. The GB High girls' soccer team had been undefeated her senior year of high school. She had loved winning.

What makes you happy?

Go to hell, Shobi!

Maybe you've forgotten how to fight for anything.

Go to hell, Rico!

Her ebbing laughter swelled again, wrapping around those words. Tightening and loosening with the muscles of her belly, shredding them inside her and throwing them out, laughter and sobs mixing seamlessly inside her.

Shobi and Rico were the two people who had stolen from her the ability to fight. Now they dared to shame her for it. And she was letting them win.

Throwing her head back, she let the last of her laughter hiccup out of her. The calm gray-blue bay stared back at her, meeting the sky along the jagged lines of Oakland. She wiped her eyes and patted her bun in place. Everything inside her told her to turn around and run, but there was nowhere to go.

There had never been anywhere to go. From the moment she'd heard that shot, there had been nowhere to go.

The phone rang in her bag.

Shobi.

She touched talk on the screen and didn't wait for a hello. "You said you wanted to help me, right? Then tell me how you do it. Tell me how you keep from caring."

"Hello, beta," Shobi said. Then a breath. "I do care."

"You were married to someone, had a child with them, and then when they died you weren't even there to pick up the pieces."

"I tried. I tried to be there for you. You asked me to leave."

She had. She had told Shobi she hated her, that she wanted nothing to do with her.

I want you to leave. I don't ever want to see you again.

What Ashna hadn't been able to say was *I killed him. I left him too, like you did, and it killed him.*

Self-loathing twisted her insides.

You're just like your mother. Selfish. The last words Baba had said to her.

"What is it you really want to ask me, Ashi?" Shobi's voice

was gentle. The kind of gentle Ashna would have killed for growing up, when all she'd gotten from Shobi was a general's marching orders.

"Do you ever feel any guilt?"

"Yes. More than you can imagine. But for what you went through. Never for what Bram did. Why do you? He was an adult. He cheated you out of the life you should have had by not thinking about you."

"He was ill, Mom! His mind had become entirely sick. Don't you have any empathy?"

"Is it guilt, then? The reason you don't let yourself live? Is it that he had no life and you deserve the same thing because you couldn't save him?"

What was it with everyone suddenly coughing up these insights for her? "I thought you wanted to help me. When will you understand that shitting on Baba doesn't help me?"

"Why does every conversation we have end up being about him? My leaving you was never because you weren't precious to me. Every single time I left you it tore my heart out."

"You still did it."

"And that was my fault, the fault of my circumstances. Not your fault. I wish I could tell you how sorry I am. The fight exhausted me, beta. There were many times when I gave you up because I didn't want to put you through a battle you were too young to be caught in the middle of. My only hope then was that when you grew up and saw my side as an adult you'd give me a fair chance and I'd be able to explain myself. I'm sorry."

Ashna was so tired. So sick of the apologies.

But Shobi's words turned over inside her, filling the vacuum Rico's words had left behind.

"Can we talk when you get home?" Shobi said, voice unrecognizably soft.

"Maybe. I don't know. I have to go." Ashna ended the call and picked up her pace.

All her memories around Baba's death were fuzzy, like someone had gone over them with a marker and blacked parts out. The only clear part was the blood. It was a good thing Rico left her. His betrayal turned out to be a kindness. There was no way she could have faced him when she couldn't see past the blood on her hands. Too dirty for him, too damaged for anything beautiful.

I love you, Ash. I'll do whatever you want to make myself worthy of you. Please don't leave me. I'm going to start playing again. I'm leaving for the UK. Please, just call me back.

When she got that message it was too late. It had been the last time she heard his voice.

Don't ever contact me again. We can't be together.

After sending that last message, Ashna had pulled her hand back and thrown her phone into the bay. The last time she'd made a throw. The last time she'd expected to say anything to the boy she loved. She wished her last memory of him wasn't him calling her father a *sick asshole*.

Months before, Baba had sent in an application for her to Le Cordon Bleu. A week after the private cremation, she had left the ashes to her aunt and uncle to spread over the cliffs at the Sagar Mahal and flown to Paris and started at the culinary school. The family had used all its influence to hide Baba's suicide and keep it out of the papers. Baba had never had friends, but his patrons believed he'd gone back to India and left the restaurant to Aseem and Baba's executive chef.

In Paris, cooking hadn't given her solace per se, but it had connected her somehow to Baba and eased the boulder of guilt off her chest. Growing up, Ashna had hated being in the kitchen or having anything to do with food. At first it was because she'd wanted to be outside with a ball, but then Baba's insistence on everything to do with food being just so had felt stifling. *This is how biryani must be cooked. This is how a crab shell must be cracked. This is how trifle pudding must be eaten. Focus on the food, Ashna; how will you taste it if you're too busy talking?*

In Paris, his rules, which she had found suffocating growing up, had become comforting. The exact opposite of how Rico had gone back to soccer. He'd found freedom in it and she'd used it to lock herself up. Cooking had been Ashna's long-drawn-out apology. Every chop, stir, dice had felt like she was doing something to erase what she had caused.

Then Baba's executive chef and Aseem had absconded with money embezzled from the restaurant over the two years she was in Paris. Ashna had come home to find Curried Dreams stripped dry, its glory gone. Her uncle and aunt wanted to press charges, but the scandal would make the suicide public. No one wanted to open up those wounds, least of all Ashna.

Her first day back at Curried Dreams, she had been filled with resolve, if not hope, that she would turn things around. Everything she'd learned in Paris had been bursting from her fingers.

Then she had tried to make a curried coq au vin.

The panic attack was so severe, she passed out from it. A horrible black gunk had choked her lungs. Congealed blood had filled her nose. The boom of a bullet had deafened her. Over and over and over again, making her heartbeat race to exploding.

She had woken up surrounded by her staff looking down at her on Baba's kitchen floor.

Instinctively her hands had turned to Baba's recipes. Recipes she'd placed no value on when he lived. She remembered thinking them too rich, too heavy, too dated. Now it was all she could manage with her chef's hands. It was the only way to avoid the boom of the gunshot, the near explosion in her chest from the palpitations.

Staring down at her hands, she tried to bring her focus back to her phone, gripped too tightly in her hands.

Where are you? A text from China.

Rico had passed a rolling pin to her that first day, when panic had made her hands tremble.

I'm almost there. She texted back and broke into a jog. The beating of her heart felt somehow different in her chest.

SO excited for today's show, China texted back. Then, *You know how much I love you, right?*

Ashna texted a heart back, thanking the gods of technology for emojis.

My pai always said that you couldn't win unless you played like the game was a matter of life and death. That's how you keep the goal, Ash.

Sadness and anger overwhelmed her. She had missed Rico's

return to the game, missed something she had hoped and prayed for with all her heart.

So he hadn't fought for her, for them. But he'd fought for something and won. While here she was. Could it be that he was right? Until she'd met Rico, she had never really given happiness any thought. With her cousins she'd always felt gratitude for having them, more love sometimes than she could bear. It had come with a definitive sense that she wasn't like them. Never in her life had she expected to feel what she had felt with Rico, that bursting, full-bodied joy of being enough. When she'd tasted it briefly and lost it, she hadn't questioned the loss.

It had felt natural, inevitable.

How did you fight what was natural and inevitable?

The bubble of emptiness she'd been trying to breathe around for years pushed to the surface. She needed a win.

As she got back to the studio, for the first time in years she felt the adrenaline in her veins. Pushing away the kick of fear and anxiety, she reminded herself that she had cooked just fine in Paris. That she had only developed her phobia of cooking off-script after coming home to Curried Dreams, after letting someone run it into the ground.

Blood and guilt.

Keep your mind on Paris. Don't think about the panic, she told herself as she made her way through the isolated lobby and to the green room. Everyone else was done with their hair and makeup and was already in the staging area. Jenny, the HMU artist, made quick work of Ashna's face and touched up her bun.

"I wish you would leave it down," Jenny said. "It's so pretty."

"Never in the kitchen," Ashna told her. "My first boss would hunt me down." Andre had sent her a text wishing her luck that morning, so she knew he would be watching the show.

Keep your mind on Paris.

The pulse of panic beat faintly in the pit of her stomach as she made her way into the studio. If she had a panic attack they would just have to roll her out on a stretcher.

God, were they going to have to roll her out on a stretcher?

The image of Rico being carried out of her restaurant sprang to life in her mind just as her eyes found him across the room. His athletic form was slumped over his phone at their kitchen station. He looked up and relief flooded his eyes at the sight of her.

Less than an hour ago this had felt impossible: being here, facing a cooking challenge.

He stepped toward her and something moved beneath the relief in his eyes like dark shadows.

"What happened?" she asked. "You're in pain."

He swallowed instead of answering.

She looked at his knee, hands itching with the need to touch him.

"I'm fine." But the tightness around his eyes and mouth said he wasn't.

"Aren't your pain meds working?"

He didn't answer, but she knew that look. How tiresome being a hero must be.

"Please tell me you're taking them." She wanted to shake him. "What's wrong with you, Rico?" Pulling out her phone, she did what anyone in their family did when faced with pain and illness. She texted Trisha. "You have to speak to Trisha. She deals with a lot of people in pain, she can help."

"I'm all set with the meds. Thank you."

"There is no good reason to be suffering," she said incredulously. Of course she'd looked up the kind of surgery he'd had. One had to be crazy not to take pain meds so soon after. Especially when one had been crazy enough to slam down on that knee.

For her.

"You decided to stay," he said, changing the topic with no finesse at all whatsoever. The exhaustion from the pain made the usual sincerity in his eyes twice as potent. "And cook?"

"Yes, you didn't talk to anyone, did you?" Given his "I'll take care of it," she wouldn't be surprised if he had charmed China into changing the format of the show.

"You asked me not to," he said simply, and she had the oddest urge to cry.

For a few seconds they were back at her school locker, him taking her bag from her, willing to do as she wanted, no questions asked.

"It isn't easy to be here." A tiny piece of honesty felt right. "But it will be a waste if you're in so much pain, because we can't do anything when you're like this." She checked to see if Trisha had responded to her text.

"I'll be fine," he said, but it sounded like a whimper.

"Please tell me where your pain meds are." How did men make do without purses and bags? She would be lost without her bag.

He watched her search his surroundings with what amusement he could muster. "I can't take them. They make me loopy."

"Loopy how?"

"Loopy as in saying whatever the hell pops into my head." A speaking look. "But also, unable to sleep and terribly queasy and unable to think clearly."

It was tempting to discount everything he had said to her by blaming it on the meds, but she knew what he had meant and what he hadn't. Knowing his thoughts was her superpower. (Yay, her!)

"Well, then, you're on the wrong meds. Why haven't you told your doctor?" She typed in the symptoms he'd listed and sent them to Trisha.

It took Trisha precisely three minutes to send Ashna a few options for alternatives that she wanted Rico to ask his doctor about.

Ashna made him have his doctor call in a prescription. Then she had China send someone from the crew to pick it up. If the shoot had to be delayed, it had to be delayed.

The rest of the contestants were gracious. All except Danny, who had the gall to roll his eyes as though this were all part of some sort of drama. The idea of beating his conceited ass made the adrenaline return to her veins with added force.

The sheen of sweat on Rico's brow made her belly cramp. How could he torture himself this way?

Within half an hour after taking the new medication, that green pallor receded from Rico's face, and his sun-kissed glow started to reappear.

"Thanks," he said as everyone took their positions again. The look in his eyes made the word unnecessary.

It wasn't until Jonah started shouting instructions on his megaphone that the reality of the cooking challenge came back to her.

"If you need to stop, we stop," Rico said, and she almost choked. He'd said those words to her at a very different time in their lives.

He made the connection at the exact same moment that she did, and heat flooded his eyes.

Despite herself a smile broke across her face, which made one burst across his.

DJ started his introductions and they were both grinning like fools when the camera turned to them.

Today's challenge was to make a street food that celebrated the star's heritage.

"This is great." Rico smoldered at the camera, giving her a sidelong look that told her he knew he was smoldering. "Brazil is the land of street food." The way he said *Brazil*, the word ending with a *u* instead of an *l*, had always made her weak in the knees. "Let's ask the chef what she thinks."

"Are we guessing again?" Hearing the playfulness in her own voice shot a bolt of energy through her. "Because you know we could use the extra viewer votes."

Rico laughed, and the audience went crazy.

As the studio filled with laughter, Rico's eyes found her. "It hasn't changed," he whispered.

It was the strangest thing, but in that moment Ashna knew there would be no panic attack. She was going to do this. She was going to cook today. There would be no stretcher carrying her to the hospital. She was going to kick Danny's butt with this challenge.

They were going to make tapioca pancakes, another thing Rico had talked about in the stories from his childhood.

"Is there a particular recipe?" she asked, refusing to let the word *recipe* wobble on her tongue.

"My mãe never made them at home. But I know they have coconut and you can eat them with doce de leite."

She tried not to smile. If you cut him he might bleed doce de leite. How had he sustained his condensed milk addiction as a pro athlete?

"You made the doce de leite really well last time. You want to get started on that and I'll get started on the pancakes?"

Without a moment's hesitation, he grabbed a can of condensed milk. There wasn't a whisper of doubt in his actions that she could do this. Her heart gave one hard thump as she reached for a mixing bowl, but when she watched his hands, sure on the pot as he set the condensed milk to boil, it fell back into its normal rhythm.

She got to work soaking the tapioca in coconut milk. Usually tapioca needed to be soaked overnight, but the show had some presoaked stuff that should work well enough. She added in some fresh shredded coconut and mixed it with her hand until it clumped together when pressed. Her grandmother added peanuts when she made sabudanyachi khichdi, which was a savory tapioca hash. The nut protein kept the tapioca from becoming gloppy when cooked. Ashna powdered some cashew nuts and added those to her mixture.

By the time the pancakes were sizzling on the pan, Rico was done with his part and flipping them as she instructed. They had only twenty minutes to pull off the challenge.

"These are good." Rico popped an extra piece in his mouth.

"As good as the ones they sold at your fiera livre?" As soon as she said it, they both froze. This was all on camera. At least she wasn't holding a knife.

"No." Rico smiled at the camera. "Better."

The skip of joy in her heart brought with it a shadow of fear, but she ignored it and grabbed square black platters and started to plate the bright white pancakes in delicate quarter folds to form a clover. She handed spoons to Rico and he poured doce de leite into them and placed them next to the pancakes.

They were done a good two minutes before the rest of the contestants, but they would still have to act like they were rushing at the end because it made for better television.

"It looks a little plain," Rico said, taking in everyone else's workstations, where everything from empanadas to elephant ears and patajones (Danny, naturally) were being tossed up. "Should I cut up some strawberries? It could use some fruit, and maybe whipped cream?"

He was right. It needed something. Plain would definitely get them hammered by the judges. But not strawberries and whipped cream. Not anything so predictable.

Ashna raced to the pantry, picked up a mango, and tossed it at Rico. Then without waiting to see if he would catch it, she turned to grab some saffron and ran back to their station.

"Can you dice the mango?" Before the question was even out of her mouth, he was slicing.

DJ called out the one-minute warning.

Ashna pinched out a fat clump of saffron into a metal spoon, mixed in a few drops of milk, and held it over the fire. The saffron dissolved into the milk, turning it orange, and despite the smells from all the workstations, the aroma of saffron permeated the air.

DJ started to count down the last ten seconds.

Ashna drizzled the saffron milk onto the four spoons of doce de leite just as Rico arranged the mango at the center of each plate.

"And your time is up!" DJ shouted, the strain coming through in his usually calm voice.

The chefs and stars stepped away from their dishes, covered in sweat and breathing hard. Ashna's heart was trying to beat its way out of her chest. It took her a moment to realize that she had stepped back and into Rico. Her back pressed flat against his chest as she sagged into him.

His hands stroked up and down her arms.

He seemed to realize that he was holding her just as she realized it. It took him a moment to let her go and for her to step away. Every part of her buzzed with life.

When she finally gathered the courage to look at him, she found him watching her, the intensity in his eyes far too familiar. Dragging her gaze away from him, she took in their plates. Hope rose from the very depths of her. All she wanted was for the judges to not hate their dish.

"You did it," Rico said close to her ear, and goose bumps danced up the back of her neck where his breath fell against her skin.

She had. She'd done it.

When she meditated, there was this moment that her body fell away, when the weightless essence of her started to spin. Coming out of it was always disorienting, like pulling on clothes but being at a loss for what they were. This felt exactly like that.

For the first time, she wanted to be here doing this one more time, then one more until the end. She had cooked.

She

Had

Cooked.

A whoop escaped her, and she pressed a hand to her mouth, laughing.

"This is actually really good," the director judge said when Rico and Ashna stood before the judges for their comments. "It's hard to make tapioca pancakes that aren't chewy or tough, but these are soft and light. The coconut mixed with the cashew gives a lovely depth of flavor."

"This doce de leite is perfect." The food editor judge said. "That saffron you added at the last minute is exactly what we're looking for in this competition. You're the mentor and we want you to teach your mentee how to elevate their flavors. This saffron does that."

Ashna felt her smile all the way in her heart. "My grandmother makes a rice kheer with coconut milk and saffron and she garnishes it with mango. Tapioca has that same starchy blandness as rice, so I thought it would be perfect."

The judges all nodded, thrilled with her answer.

Then the chef judge, whose job it was to be the bad cop, poked at the pancake with a fork. "But this is the second time you've made doce de leite on this show. The saffron was a great twist, but I'd suggest showing us a little more range if you want to go all the way. Work together to figure each other's flavors out. That's what this is about. Don't rest on your laurels."

His meaning was clear. He was accusing them of trying to get by on the strength of their popularity. That made Ashna angry. Their dish was really good. Unlike the other contestants', it had no flaws. It was actually the best thing made that day. There were no words for how that felt.

"I'm proud of the food we put out today," she said. And being able to verbalize it was like wrapping the cloak of the accomplishment she was feeling tighter around herself.

"I am too," Rico said behind her. "We reached across a great distance in terms of style and culture and blended it perfectly to honor both. I think the world needs a lot more of that."

"Another perfect shot from Frederico Silva!" DJ said.

Everyone including the judges came to their feet clapping and the smile across Ashna's face stretched her cheeks so wide they hurt.

When she stole a glance at Rico, he was soaking up her smile, her joy, as though he'd been starved for it. If ever he'd made an effort to hide his feelings around her, she knew he'd given up that fight.

"You two have great chemistry and this dish speaks to that," a judge said worshipfully. "Just give us more."

"More. More. More," the audience chanted and Ashna felt Rico's hands squeeze her shoulders, warm and triumphant.

Chapter Twenty-Six

Watching other people hug Ashna had become a particularly painful experience. Not that Rico didn't understand their need to do it. He watched Jonah throw his arms around her with a sensation in his chest that fell somewhere between agony and hope.

It had been two weeks since Ashna had defeated, with a flaming vengeance, the demons that had been eclipsing her cooking. They had survived two more eliminations (if their staggering audience votes could be called surviving). Last week they had made a picnic basket of sandwiches, and yesterday Ashna had helped him turn out the perfect persimmon and mango tart that paired with Sonoma wines they had been assigned.

Ashna's French training meant pastries were Rico's new weakness. They still hadn't made it to the top of the scoreboard with the judges. Mostly because Disney Danny cooked like someone who had been covertly training to be a chef for years and was at least as good as his chef, but also because Rico had put too much mayo on the sandwiches and chopped the fruit like an amateur, which, hello, he was. Ashna's reaction had been to tell the judges that as far as she was concerned Rico had already proven his knife skills. Another viral moment.

P. T. Cruiser had been the second star to be eliminated. The street food challenge had felled her when the undercooked beans in her chili dog had almost taken out a judge's fillings. Lilly, who cooked like a southern grandma, had been eliminated last week. Inexplicably, Ashna had teared up.

Today, in an unexpected move, the judges had announced that they could not fairly eliminate one of the three remaining contestants, so Rico, Song, and Danny, and their chefs would be competing in a three-way final.

Jonah left Ashna to come to Rico and informed him that the internet was overwhelmingly delighted that #Ashico had made it to the finals.

"There you are!" Song jogged up to Rico, as soon as Jonah moved on, and threw her arms around him, hugging him a little too hard, and then holding on.

They were in the lounge and Ashna was talking to China.

Song threw a look at Ashna that lacked its usual warmth. "You were spectacular today. Can you two go a little easy on the rest of us?"

Rico caught a flash of something too close to hurt in Ashna's eyes when she saw Song hanging on to his arm.

Was Zee right? Did Song think Rico had feelings for her other than fondness and friendship?

Did Ashna?

China and Ashna walked up to them. Granted, she was Ashna's friend, but the look China threw Song was filled with all sorts of shade. It made Song cling harder to Rico.

"Good job today, all of you," China said with a stiffness he hadn't seen her display before.

"Thank you," Song said, mirroring China's stiffness before letting go of Rico and sauntering off.

"Well then," China said, turning to the two of them with her warmth reinstated. "You were both spectacular! To literally no one's surprise."

She waved them over into her office, possibly to avoid any perceived favoritism. Although, whatever had just happened did not help that cause. Usually the set had a cozy familial feel with many of the producers, chefs, and celebrities being old friends and longtime colleagues. Plus, the network was seeing the highest ratings in its history, so no one cared much about who showed Ashna and Rico favoritism.

China shut the door behind them. "You two are single-handedly—well, double-handedly? Does that sound dirty?—making my career take off! Have I said thank you?"

Ashna came the closest he'd seen her come to beaming and it killed him a little bit. After watching her in the kitchen these past few challenges, it was going to be impossible to accept anything but right-out fierce joy from her.

"Actually," Ashna said in that playful way you had to know her to recognize, "it's been . . . it's been . . ."

"Fun?" China said, even as Rico thought it.

"Yes, it has. It's been so much fun! Also, Curried Dreams

has a waiting list for reservations. So, I should be thanking you!" She threw Rico a sideways, albeit guarded, glance. "Both of you."

It was a scrap, but it made him want to run a lap around a stadium, especially now that his knee didn't feel like exposed nerves. Turns out, Trisha was the genius Ashna claimed she was.

Over the past two weeks they had fallen into a rhythm—a rhythm that resembled a tango and kept him up at night with yearning, but a rhythm nonetheless. They had somehow become a real team, building each other up, relearning each other, compensating for each other's flaws, spotlighting each other's strengths, and making some delicious food.

"I told you so!" China said. "There's one more thing I think I might need thanks for." She threw a speaking look between Ashna and Rico.

His nemesis, the famous Ashna blush, spread up the column of her neck, and across her cheeks in a slow ruthless burn.

Had he really thought he could put away feelings this precious? That they could be gone forever? For all the fragile peace they had managed to negotiate and all the feelings Rico could no longer deny, the hope that bubbled inside him was terrifying.

"I'll leave you two to catch up," he said and without waiting for a response, he let himself out.

"I can't believe you did that!" he heard Ashna hiss the moment he left. "What is wrong with you?"

China laughed. "What? I might have found someone to melt through the famous Ashna Raje ice."

The problem wasn't the melting. All it took was for them to be in the same room and there were puddles all over the place, not a sliver of ice in sight. The problem was the ghosts of their pasts, and how much those ghosts had altered them both. The problem was finding each other around the ghosts, melted or otherwise.

As he waited in the lobby for George, who was stuck in traffic, an alert he'd set up on his phone popped up. He'd been following something that had caught his eye about Yash Raje's campaign. A small piece tucked away on Bloomberg about Yash's long-term girlfriend had been nagging at Rico since he'd read it in the car this morning.

He knew he should stop being obsessed with the campaign, given that the man's cousin held the power to trample Rico's heart again, and the more connections there were between them, the more it was going to hurt. Problem was, Yash was fearless. His stand on immigration, on health care, on the environment, it was a blast of unvarnished truth and brilliant policy, and Rico couldn't help but get excited every single time he learned more.

Except, there was something deeply disturbing going on with this girlfriend thing. Obviously, a bunch of conservative journalists were digging away at the story and softening the soil of public opinion with these seemingly harmless pieces with suggestive undertones hinting at salaciousness. Rico had never been wrong about preempting an oncoming scandal. He had to find out what was going on.

Zee was right, being a know-it-all was definitely an affliction

Rico suffered from. He dialed his mate and checked his watch. Tanya and Zee had to be back in London by now.

"What's wrong?" Zee said the moment Rico said hello.

"Why does something have to be wrong? I'm just checking in to make sure Tanya didn't decide to give you back after the honeymoon."

"You miss me. You want me back. Admit it."

Rico laughed.

"How's your lady love?" Zee asked.

"She's not." That was the problem.

"Does she know that?"

"I don't know. I don't know anything about her anymore." Except he knew. He knew more than he needed to know. "That's not true. But there's no going back. I have no idea how to go back."

"You know that season when you put Sunderland back in the Premier League? You were such a bloody pain about reviewing game footage. You had to identify why we didn't make every single goal we missed. You were a beast about figuring out mistakes and making sure we avoided them in the next match. You were such a pain in the arse that we all wanted to kill you."

"And your point is?" Although he had a sense of where this was going.

"Be the arse you are and figure out what went wrong."

Shit.

"What? You just figured out your best mate's a bit of a genius, didn't you?"

Rico had to laugh at that. "I've been an idiot."

"Apparently we're all idiots. But my old woman tells me that when we see it we can fix it."

"She's the genius, then. And a saint for staying with your ugly ass." But they had to be right. Rico wasn't sure how to figure it out, but he knew exactly where he could start.

"Give my love to Tanya, okay?" With that he got off the phone.

Then he dialed another number and put everything in place. For all the things he couldn't figure out, there was one thing he had figured out, and he couldn't leave it be. He went looking for China Dashwood again.

"Rico!" China said when he let himself into her office. "Did you need something?"

"As a matter of fact, I did. I need a huge favor. You got a minute?"

She was instantly all ears. As the star of her show, he could demand anything, but something told him that she was going to be protective of Ashna and he had no idea how this was going to play out.

"Can you make up an excuse and let Ashna have your car again today? I know you had her take it home for you last week. I'll have my driver take you home, or wherever you want to go."

She pushed a hand against her hip, no longer the eager-to-please producer. "What are you up to, Mr. Silva?"

"I just need a ride somewhere and Ashna's the only person who can drive me there." He showed her his hands, palms up.

"I don't mean Ashna any harm. You have to see that. She needs this. I promise. She'll love it." At least he hoped she would. He just couldn't see her this way anymore.

China narrowed her eyes at him. "What makes you an expert on what Ashna needs? What is going on between you two?"

He shrugged. "We're paired up on your show."

Her whole stance was mama-bear now. No producer-pleasing-her-star in sight. "Thanks. That part I know." She studied him with unnerving focus and he stared right back.

Her hand slapped her forehead. "Holy shit. How did I miss this? This isn't the first time you two are meeting, is it?"

He didn't answer that. That wasn't his to tell. Ashna would tell her family and China in her own time, if at all. He just had to do this.

China dropped into a chair, then jumped up again. A whole new wave of understanding suffusing her face. "That's why you asked to be on the show. Oh God, you're Frederick Wentworthing her."

He shouldn't know what that meant but he totally did. "I'm half agony, half hope, Ms. Dashwood." He tried to shrug, but she looked in his eyes and her whole face turned into a giant *awwww*.

She pressed her hands into her face. "You can't do that to me. You can't quote *Persuasion* to me."

It was his mother's favorite book. It's where his name had come from. "Listen. I'm not going to force her to do anything. I'm just going to ask, and if she says no, I won't pressure her. I promise."

"Why do I get the feeling you're pretty sure she won't say no?"

"As I said, half agony, half hope. Now, can you please find her and tell her you need her to take your car?" It was the most childish thing, but he crossed his fingers as he dug them into his pockets.

Chapter Twenty-Seven

Ashna hadn't been suspicious of China asking her to take her car home again. At least not until she found Rico sitting on the couch in the lobby on her way out. She tried to look away quickly when he caught her ogling him, again, but didn't quite make it. Arousal so intense lit his eyes that for a moment her body forgot where it was and burned with it.

"What are you still doing here?" she asked, going to him.

He rose, shrinking the huge lobby around her. "Waiting for my ride. George is stuck in traffic."

"How far is he? I can give you a ride, I have China's car."

He looked far too surprised for such a simple offer, and suddenly she was embarrassed for offering.

"You probably need to get home and rest that knee." Her voice came out too soft, too invested.

"Why do you do that?" he said, not bothering to hide the wave of emotions in his eyes.

"Do what?" she asked, not bothering to hide her caginess.

"Care with your actions when you're trying so hard not to care with your heart."

Because I do care. Even though she wished she didn't. "Can't we just be decent to each other?" For the past two weeks, they'd managed just that, despite the giant unyielding force tugging them together. "Why does it have to be any more than that?"

Because it was. And they both knew it.

He shrugged, and dropped it, as always aware of exactly how much she could handle. "So the show. You're killing it," he said.

Her cheeks warmed . . . her heart warmed.

"Listen, Ashna, I was wrong about you and cooking. It's obvious how talented you are. I understand now why you took it on. Those mango pies . . . they were . . . I can still taste them." He'd eaten every last bite of the leftover tarts after the show.

She tried to say thank you, but a strangled sort of sound came out of her. It had been a long time since she'd thought about cooking in terms of loving it or hating it, or even as a choice, but the joy her food gave him seemed to unsnarl how she felt about it.

His hand came up, but it stopped before cupping her cheek. "What's wrong? What did I say?" he asked. Or his eyes asked, because she wasn't sure she heard his voice.

Everything inside her leaned into the impending touch. He pulled away as though realizing just how bad of an idea touching her right now was.

How badly she wanted him to touch her terrified her.

How could she explain what was wrong when nothing made sense anymore? She had worked hard to keep her life organized, her thoughts in order. Questioning how she felt about food; missing the feel of a ball in her hand, obsessing over her mother's intentions and words, these musings about what her life would have been like if this or that had happened were self-indulgences she had no time for.

When she didn't answer, he backed away again. Their new dance. "Were you serious about that ride?"

If she had even a whit of sense, she should refuse, but there was something in his eyes, a deep eagerness. She had to find out what it was.

It didn't help that Shobi was at home, waiting for her, suddenly inexplicably patient. Last week, Shobi had even started to come into the restaurant. She'd sensed Ashna's discomfort with having her in the kitchen and chosen to help at the register. Given how busy they both were, they had barely seen each other at home. But in the few moments they did get, they'd fallen into a pattern of eating varan bhaat and trying out one of Ashna's chai blends. Any time Shobi brought up the past, everything inside Ashna shut down. Shobi seemed to sense that and with her usual strategic determination avoided it.

Rico had the same strategic determination in his eyes as he waited for Ashna to answer. What was he up to?

"Of course, I'll give you a ride. Wait here, I'll bring the car to the front."

That made him laugh. "I'm not in pain, Ashna. Trisha's meds are working well."

"Fine." Hiking her bag up her shoulder, she started walking to the car without waiting for him to follow her.

They walked silently across the parking lot to the Employee

of the Month spot, exchanging glances when they saw the sign. She opened the passenger door for him, but held back from helping him in.

When she got in next to him, he gave her another one of those looks. The one that made her wonder what he was up to and made her want to bounce in her seat like a child.

"I'm not going to the hotel. You don't mind, do you?"

It was ridiculous to have to suppress a smile with all the things she was feeling. "Where are we going?"

"Washington Square."

That was just a couple of miles away, which was unnecessarily disappointing.

They rode in silence that would have been companionable if not for the electricity arcing between their bodies. Too soon they turned into a sports complex and pulled under a portico. A valet jogged up to them.

"I'm not staying," Ashna said to the eager young man, who did a double take when he saw Rico and ran to open his door.

Rico thanked Ashna and walked away as the boy chattered to him. There was almost no limp in his step, and something about that made her heart twist in her chest.

Circling the driveway, she went down the palm-lined road, and was almost out the gate when a phone rang in her passenger seat. It wasn't her phone.

Just like that, it was clear what that look on Rico's face had meant.

She pulled over and answered.

"Ashna?" Rico said with all the casualness of a bad actor.

"Sorry, I forgot my phone in your car. You don't mind bringing it back, do you? Oh, and could you bring it inside, please?"

Her heart skipped as she maneuvered the car back to the parking lot and went inside. What oh what was the man up to?

The receptionist led her through the lobby and in through a door. The smell was the first thing that hit her. Leathery sweat and turf. The too-bright lights of the indoor soccer pitch made her blink. The smell, the lights, all of it spun together, making her stumble.

A woman's soccer team seemed to be practicing. Or mobbing Rico. Suddenly they parted from around him and someone tossed him a ball. Rico spiked it up on his good knee, then made a header right into the goal. The cheer that went up was deafening.

His gaze sought her over the cheering heads, not a doubt in his eyes that she was watching. It would have been easy enough for her to hand the phone off to someone outside, but he'd asked her to come inside and known that she would do as he asked. He waved her over, but her feet wouldn't move. It had been too long since she had set foot on turf.

He waited. Everyone turned to her and she found her feet moving.

"Your phone."

He ignored the phone she held out. "Their keeper has the flu."

The air in her lungs contracted. What did he think he was doing?

He held up his hand and someone threw him a ball. He offered it to her.

Her hands trembled to reach for it. Her feet trembled to step back.

"It's this one time."

"Your phone." She picked up his hand—the one not holding the ball—and pushed the phone into it. The spark that shot up her arm as their fingers touched didn't surprise her. Being around him was being submerged in sensation, there was no point fighting it.

"They can't practice without a keeper. Can you help out? Please?" He didn't say it loudly, but she felt the weight of the team's focus.

She took the ball, hands fitting around it like second skin, lungs filling out. "I'm not dressed for it." She looked down at herself in the jeans and peasant top she'd changed into.

He looked over at a redheaded woman and she brought him a duffel bag. "A clean uniform. There's shoes in there too. Seven and a half."

He remembered her shoe size.

"I don't think I could even if I tried. I've forgotten how."

"It's like riding a bike," he said with a smile from long ago, and just like that she passed the ball to him, spinning it into the air.

And the bag was in her hands.

And she was in the changing room.

And then on the pitch at the goal line.

And the world outside her box ceased to exist.

At first everything was a blur. Every inch of her skin tingled, blood rushing into vessels after being choked out. Pins and needles, numbing her. The woman with the red hair was a good striker. The first time she kicked it in, the ball sailed to the top corner. An age-old fury rolled through Ashna. It almost knocked her off her feet. As she picked up the ball and threw it back, the fury spread through her.

Not past these hands.

Words that had been her soul.

The next time the ball flew into the box, her hands slapped around it. The striker snarled at her. Ashna laughed. The sound swallowed her whole.

"You're a one-trick pony, aren't you?" she mumbled to the striker.

And she was. Every goal she tried was the same. Top corner. Not a single one went through after that. Ashna robbed every single one. Punching it out.

Not past these hands.

The slam of the ball against her sternum, the slap of it against her gloved palms branded her, and danced across every inch of skin, so essential it blasted her out of herself and back into herself.

The game went on for a lifetime. It was done in a flash.

Back in the locker room, the scalding spray of the shower engulfed her, gathering all that she had found of herself—the straining muscles, the stretched sinew, the wild thrumming heart—into herself.

On her way out, the captain of the team invited Ashna to join them. They played in a local league twice a week—just a bunch of women who loved the game. The pull to say yes was a whirlpool that sucked her toward itself, but that wasn't her life anymore. She promised to think about it.

By the time they were walking back to the parking lot Ashna was exploding out of her skin. Exploding.

Rico watched her as she rubbed her hands together, gathering up the lingering sensations. "Everything is going to hurt tomorrow. How am I even going to work tomorrow?" she said, trying to remember where she had parked. Everything from before the game was a haze.

"You're not even feeling that. You run? Work out? This was nothing."

He was wrong. It was everything. When she ran, she was chasing something. Mostly chasing the thoughts out of her head. Pushing herself, punishing herself. When she'd played soccer in school, she had played the game, that was it. Keeping the ball out of the goal, that's all that had mattered. Her entire existence had focused on that one thing, and the exhilaration of it had been at once more intense than anything else and yet so elemental, it was the simplest part of her.

That's how she felt right now. Her cheeks burned, her heart floated, energy coursed through her.

"Were they even a keeper short?" Where on earth was the car? A red Mazda in a sea of sporty red cars. Thanks, China!

To his credit, he didn't try to hide his guile. "They were a player short. They usually rotate the keeper since theirs went on maternity leave."

One of the players had told Ashna in the locker room that Rico had met the team this week when he'd visited as a favor to his agent.

The team had made him think of her.

"You could have just asked me if I wanted to play."

"Would you have?"

"Now you'll never know, will you?" She pointed the keys down an aisle and pressed the emergency button.

He chuckled at that. How had she forgotten how much she loved his chuckle?

"You were fierce today." How had she forgotten how much she loved the way he looked at her?

"It's a sport. It's easy to forget who you are." She tried to be nonchalant, but her heart was pounding too hard for it.

"You're not just fierce on the pitch, Ashna."

She pointed the key down another aisle, and the car alarm went off. This conversation was setting off its own alarms. She pressed the unlock button and silence returned.

They walked to the car, their arms touching, their fingers flirting with what they really wanted to do, tangle with each other. When they got to the car Ashna gasped. Across the parking lot the Bay Bridge was lit up against a fading sky. Instead of getting into the car, Rico leaned against the hood. She joined him. The view was mesmerizing. Ashna loved San Francisco, but it had been a while since she'd taken the time to notice its wonders.

"I'm sorry I didn't just come out and ask you to play today. But there has been another thing I've been wondering, should I just ask you?"

"Sure," she said as they stared at the serendipitous view that she hadn't even noticed on her way in.

"Why did you give up football?"

Laughter swelled in her chest. Maybe a small laugh even escaped her. Every memory with him rose to the surface. He had attended every single one of her games. He'd worked cramps from her calves. Held her face when she cried because she'd let a crucial goal go. *You're fierce. You can do this.*

It was plain in his eyes how badly he wanted to understand. It made the mismatched size of his eyes more apparent. Even more important than how well he had understood her was how badly he'd wanted to. How much she had needed that. How many things it would have changed to have had it for longer.

For a few moments the emerald centers hypnotized her. But the golden flecks asked questions she had no answers to, questions that proved how little he knew her now.

"I grew up," she said finally before pushing off the hood and getting in the car.

Chapter Twenty-Eight

One moment they were standing close enough that Rico could drop a kiss on her head, and the next moment she was inside the car, leaving behind the scent of her wet hair. God, her hair smelled like magic.

He followed her into the car.

She turned the ignition and looked at him. "Can I ask you a question too?"

"Sure."

"How did you convince China to give me her car?"

"I don't know what you're talking about."

"Right. China told me she's going to some sort of corporate dinner and wanted me to take her car home, so she could, you know, imbibe."

He shrugged. They were both suppressing smiles and it felt even better than straight-out smiling. It wasn't fair how every cell in Rico's body lapped up just how good it felt.

Shifting gears, she pulled out of the parking spot.

They merged into traffic with cars packed back to back. She switched gears again. On the drive in he'd been in such a haze of anticipation, he hadn't noticed that the car had a manual transmission. He had no idea she could drive manual. There was something insanely hot about it.

She caught him looking at her hand on the gear box. "My uncle insisted we all learn how to drive stick shifts. Wanted to make sure we had essential life skills."

"Driving manual is a life skill? I must have missed that memo." He barely drove anymore. Hadn't in years.

She looked mock-horrified. "What will you do when you're stranded in . . . um . . . anywhere in the world where they still drive only stick?"

"Take George with me?" he said.

Her answering laugh was husky and teasing. She followed it up with a quick lesson on the gears and the clutch.

It was the first time they were talking. Not using words to transfer pain and regret, just talking. Suddenly he was terribly curious about her life.

"Is it hard to manage the restaurant with the show?" Talking about the restaurant felt tenuous, but they were crawling along. He'd never been so grateful for traffic.

"My aunt's helping. That's Trisha's m-mother." Her voice stuttered on the word *mother* and she pursed her lips, obviously mortified that it had.

"I know," he said gently, knowing their moment of casual conversation had passed. "Is your mother still in Sripore?"

Another word that made a muscle twitch in her jaw. At first he'd found it amazing that she had grown up in a palace, then he'd realized that to her it was just a home she missed.

When was the last time you visited? If he asked her, he'd

have to deal with the fact that he'd never gone back to the home of his childhood even when he went to Rio.

"She's here right now."

Okay. The one person she had never talked about was her mother. All Rico knew was that any mention of her mother turned Ashna into a ball of longing and anger. Having her here was obviously not a simple thing. "Does she live here permanently now?" He had no idea why he pushed, but it felt important to.

"She's been here a few weeks." A breath. "She just won a prestigious national award in India and she's having . . . never mind."

"Let me guess. She's having a Large Life Moment. She wants to go back and examine all the things that went wrong." If that didn't cut too close to home, Rico didn't know what did.

Is that why you're here? Maybe the question didn't actually shine in her eyes. Maybe he just imagined it. "Something like that," she said.

"So, you don't want her here then."

"She's my mother." She kept her voice dead flat. It was one of those lines that could mean entirely different things depending on which word you emphasized. Like one of those acting exercises. But she didn't let emphasis fall on any single word.

"And yet you don't want her here." That he would do anything for another day with his parents was plain in his voice.

Growing up, Rico could never have imagined being able to live in a world without his parents. They hadn't let him feel unloved a single day that he'd had them. For all the challenges a relationship like theirs had to have come with, his mãe and pai had always put his happiness before everything.

Even though Rico knew none of the details, he knew that Ashna's parents had inflicted the kind of hurt on her that had become woven into her fabric. Her father had willfully snatched the possibility of happiness from her hands. How Rico hated him. Not for the first time, Rico regretted how badly he had reacted to the man.

For years he had been too angry to admit it, but the things he had said to Ashna about her father had been thoughtless. It had ruined everything, pushed her into a corner where she'd had to choose between Rico and him. And she had made her choice.

At least her mother was a safe topic. "If your mother is here to fix things, why don't you want her to?"

They were at a standstill again and Ashna wiggled the gear stick impatiently. "Is it that easy? To fix things you broke?"

He stared out the window. Six lanes of traffic unable to move, the gridlock turning a small distance endless.

"I don't know." He stayed silent for a while before speaking again. "But does it matter?" He twisted in his seat and met her eyes, the glossy black clouded with painful memories. "Does it matter if it's easy or hard? If the person is essential to you, then fixing things with them is essential." The word felt magical in his mouth. The way his tongue wrapped around it, he could almost taste it. *Essential.*

That's how this felt. Being here. Figuring this out. Her.

"Your mother isn't someone you can just cut out of your life. If you could, you would have by now."

Her knuckles turned white around the steering wheel. He'd hit a nerve.

"Or you find a way to stop the person from being essential to you." She slipped a glance his way. "How do you do that?"

Was she suggesting that it was something he had greater expertise at than her?

All he could do was stare at her. The stalled traffic meant she could meet his stare.

"You think I know?" His hand rubbed his leg. How was he in love with a girl so willfully obtuse? She had literally dumped him because her father believed she was too good for him. She'd walked away from him without a backward glance and now all he could get from her was this sense of being wounded.

She didn't look away. Just watched him the way you watch liars, with curiosity and disbelief.

His hand kneaded the knots that seemed permanently lodged around his knee. "Sometimes when people leave you, you get so caught up in trying to convince yourself that you can cut them out of your life that you think you've actually figured it out. You keep moving. You ignore the feeling of being chased, even as you can't stop running and running to get away. But then you realize that you haven't moved at all. Those who are essential to you have always been an absence. Even when you refused to acknowledge it, their void was always there."

Their eyes were locked together, turning them into one being, indecipherable from each other. One gaping, stubborn void.

"All I know is that I would do anything to have another moment with my mãe." As that truth left his mouth, another truth solidified through him. He would do anything to have another chance with Ashna.

She reached out and touched his hand. He watched their hands as they came together. Before she could pull away he turned his hand and wrapped his fingers around hers, his hold ravenous with need. Everything outside of the intertwining of their fingers ceased to exist. For the first time in as long as he could remember, Rico fell into himself. Breathed.

"Maybe your energy is better served in understanding the wound rather than wishing it wasn't there," he said.

A car honked and Ashna started. The traffic was moving. Sliding her hand out of his, she joined it. They were a block from his hotel.

"You're very wise today," she said, forcing a smile into her voice.

The feel of her hand lingered in his. He pressed it into his chest, leaned back into the seat, and closed his eyes. "Maybe it's the meds. Better wise than loopy. Or are they the same thing?"

"What were you thinking, not taking pain medication after a surgery like that?" The intimate scolding in her voice was even more potent than her touch.

"I like to be present. It's become . . ." He opened his eyes. "Essential. It's part of the game."

"So, the game, what happens next?" she asked.

The road before them was lined with taillights, an endless frozen constellation impatient to move.

"Nothing." The word sounded as final as it was. "That's retirement, I'm told."

"What do other retired players do? Coaching? Broadcasting?"

His pai had coached after retirement. "I don't think that's my path. I was lucky with my career. I only ever had to worry about my game, about winning. That's what I miss, the singular goal, the high of achieving it." He felt winded by all they were sharing. He hadn't discussed retirement with anyone. For all his love for his team, it just wasn't the kind of thing they talked about. But letting her see the emptiness of it, right now that felt essential.

"Good thing you have the show, then," she said with the kind of look Rico hadn't thought he'd ever see her give him again. "You get to win another thing."

Another laugh escaped him. "You don't sound overconfident at all!"

Her answering laugh was only slightly embarrassed.

"I meant what I said earlier, Ash. You've been great on the show. It's been amazing."

"Thank you. It's been . . . It's . . . Rico, you have no idea. I . . . I still can't believe I did it," she said, as if in a trance.

All those memories of her guarding the goal that Rico had buried deep rose to the surface and wove into the sight of her on the pitch today, flying at the ball, tentative only for minutes before giving it everything.

"I can't believe I played either," she added quietly.

"You did it," he said. Words he had said to her more times than he could count.

No, they couldn't just be decent to each other. She wasn't just a girl he'd dated in high school. She was everything. He'd been an idiot to think otherwise. He wanted that Ashna back. The one who had screamed at the ball and played like her life depended on it. The Ashna who kicked butt in the kitchen, even when it wasn't easy for her. The Ashna who saw him exactly as who he wanted to be.

"Do you really think we can win?" she said more lightly.

"My father loved to say that winning was inevitable if the idea of losing was so painful you couldn't bear it."

"I know." She turned into his hotel's driveway. "You have to play like your life depends on it."

He touched her hand on the gear shaft, needing the contact. "Winning really is that simple: you have to want it enough to hold nothing back. Most people spend a lifetime trying to understand what it takes. But that's all it is. Single-minded love and tenacity."

She pulled under the columned porte cochere and turned to him. "That doesn't sound simple at all." She released the gear and turned her hand in his, as though her need to touch him was as strong as his.

A lock of hair freed itself from her bun and fell across her cheek.

At long last, gazes locked, he did it, he reached out with his other hand and slipped her hair behind her ear. "That's because there's another piece that complicates it." His thumb stroked the delicate shell of her ear and she trembled. The earth beneath them trembled. "Fear. The hardest part is to acknowledge how badly you want it and to stop being afraid of getting it. Because sometimes you lose because you can't bear the idea of winning something you think you don't deserve."

She closed her eyes and he watched her, both hands holding her.

"We're here," he said needlessly. She opened her eyes—intoxicated from their touching—and found him again, mirroring exactly how he felt.

Her gaze moved past him to the valet who rushed over to get Rico's door, then backed away when he saw them. Ashna untangled her hand from his. He dropped a kiss on her fingers before letting go.

"Thanks for the ride, Ash." He got out, attempting grace, but only managed it because she had cared enough to help him.

She might've been influenced by her father, but her feelings weren't fickle, and she wasn't a coward. Maybe that was the reason why she let those she loved have their way. To use that love to pull her in opposite directions was to tear her in half.

He turned around and leaned into the car window. The need to go back to her, to press his lips into her hair, her eyelids, any inch of her he could have was an inferno. But she had to want that enough to come to him herself, free of anyone's influence, even his.

Every piece of him might feel like a puppy ready to follow her to the ends of the earth, but their only hope was a love that felt balanced, that didn't need constant validation. That was only possible if they both believed in it and believed themselves worthy of it.

"Thanks for . . . for today, Rico." Her eyes, were limpid pools of longing, and yes, fear.

"Talk to your mother, Ash. Give her a chance. Maybe you've missed things. Maybe you can't see them because you've let someone else's thinking influence you."

Some of the softness left her eyes. "Thanks. Even if I were influenced, she's never done anything to disprove that opinion."

He pulled away and she drove off, leaving him with the sense that there was something they both hadn't said. Something that was essential.

Chapter Twenty-Nine

"Maybe you should come stay with us," Mina said in the way Mina had of saying things to influence you without sounding managing.

"What you're trying to say is that I should give Ashna some space." Shobi paced Bram's kitchen, while Mina sat primly on a barstool at the island.

It had been weeks since Ashna and she had argued. It had also been weeks since they had said a word of consequence to each other. Shobi had considered pushing her, but Ashi's shutdown mechanism was so hard and quick, she didn't have it in her to let it topple their fragile truce.

That truce had to mean something.

Ashna seemed to have come out from under that cloud she had been dragging around like the blanket she'd loved as a baby. It had to be the show, because Shobi had seen Ashna smile to herself the other day over her tea. Asking her about it had hovered on Shobi's lips, but she had been afraid of sucking the joy from her child again.

"She's under a tremendous amount of strain. Giving her a

little space would be a kind thing to do," Mina said, sipping delicately from Bram's bone china.

Maybe being afraid to topple the peace wasn't the best approach. But how to leverage it?

"Leaving her alone all these years was what caused the problem in the first place. I should never have let her go, Mina. I should never have let Bram take her away."

Mina watched Shobi pace the kitchen and didn't say the words Shobi knew she wanted to say. "You regret leaving," Mina said instead, something she had predicted Shobi would do years ago.

"Leaving her, always. Leaving Bram, never." Did it matter what she should have done, what any of them should have done? "For the first time in my life I feel like I have a chance to make amends. When I got here, I didn't. Her hatred of me was daunting. But something has changed and I can't let it slip away from me again."

That morning Omar had asked when she was coming home. *Do you think I should give up?* she'd asked in response, because when it came to Ashna, she had never made a good decision.

Has she ever asked you to leave? Omar had asked.

No, she hadn't.

Then I know you will stay until she does.

He was right. She couldn't leave this time. Not even if she tried. The Padma Shri ceremony was a month away. Whatever would be, would be.

Shobi met the probing in Mina's gaze. "Don't you think something about her is different? More responsive, more open than she's ever been?"

"Ashna has always had too vulnerable a heart, Shobi. That's been the problem. She feels everyone's pain and internalizes it, and wants to take it away. I think the reason she's had such a hard time with you is that she didn't know what to do with yours. She finds your rage at the world too daunting. She blames herself for it."

Shobi dropped onto the barstool next to Mina and rested her elbows on Bram's granite. "Do you really think I should have let it go? Forgiven Bram. For Ashna. Do you really think that would have made her a happier person? How long do we do it, Mina? Put our heads down and do what's expected. I couldn't. I couldn't make the compromises it would have taken to become what my father and Bram expected me to become. When do we stop this?"

Mina reached out and plucked a napkin from Bram's napkin holder. Her eyes were determinedly dry, but she had to blow her teary nose. A small part of Shobi wished she hadn't brought this up. Mina would always regret that night. Shobi had worked her way through it, but Mina had never truly forgiven herself for sending Shobi into that room where Bram had once and for all destroyed any chance their marriage had.

Shobi leaned over and tucked Mina's hair behind her ear. "How the hell is your hair still this thick and soft with all that coloring and styling?"

Mina laughed a watery laugh. "Save your reverse snobbery. Some of us choose to take care of ourselves. Not everyone is Shoban Gaikwad Raje, rocking the silver mane."

"And who could ever be Mina Raje?" Smiling, Shobi moved her hair from one shoulder to the other. "Through everything, you've been my anchor, Mina." She took Mina's hands. "You have to know that."

Despite whatever nonsense people liked to spew about women pulling each other down, Shobi would never have been able to come out of her marriage standing without Mina and their mother-in-law. Mina was right, though, Ashna had suffered most in all this and been the least responsible for it.

For a while both women sipped the tea blend Ashna had to have put magic in. "She's so beautiful," Shobi said, needing to use every ounce of her strength to keep her voice from cracking. "Being around her used to hurt. Now I don't know how I ever left her."

"Tell her that."

"I've tried." That was a lie. "Actually, I have no idea how to. Talking to me makes her so angry, so sad. I don't know what to do with that."

"She's never been the same after Bram's death. If anyone tries too hard to dig into that or to get her to talk about it, she withdraws so deep into herself, I used to fear she'd never come out. But I think the time for truth might have come." Mina had to pull out another napkin and blow her nose some more. "She was covered in his blood, Shobi. She sat there with him in her lap until the ambulance got there. She wasn't even eighteen."

"It's terrible to hate a dead person as much as I hate him, isn't it?" she said through a constricted throat. She started pacing again.

The kitchen was exactly as it had been twelve years ago. Bram's kitchen. Every detail made to his unbending standards.

Many years ago, before he had conspired with her father to break her, Shobi had appreciated his love of beautiful things. He'd had such an eye, known how to make spaces, clothes, food beautiful. Just the way Omar had always known how to make words and thoughts beautiful.

They were both men who saw beauty. But where one believed in nurturing it, the other had known only how to grab. He had crushed every beautiful thing he touched because he only valued his wanting of it, his grip on it, not the thing itself.

"I have to tell her." There was so much she hadn't told Ashna, but she didn't need to tell Mina which particular secret she was talking about. Mina knew them all.

Mina nodded. "Telling her might be the only way to get her to start to understand any of this."

Shobi had finally told Bram that she wanted a divorce. Ashna was finishing high school. She was almost an adult ready to leave home and go to college, away from Bram's influence. There was no longer the need to lie to her. Bram's threat to keep them apart no longer worked. Shobi and Omar had been together for years by then, and other than Bram's threats there was no reason to hide their relationship.

Never in Shobi's wildest dreams had she expected him to put a bullet through his head because of it.

"She'll hate me even more than she already does. She already blames me for his death; telling her it was me who pushed him over the edge will just confirm her belief. I'll lose her." Just the way Bram had wanted her to.

Mina was kind enough not to mention that Shobi had lost her a long time ago. "Or you'll get her back. You're right that something about Ashna is different now. Maybe it's the show. Maybe it's the fact that Curried Dreams has actually turned around. It's been years since I've seen her happy."

Shobi loved Mina for having been such a good mother to her daughter, but she hated it when Mina explained Ashna to her, especially because she was always right.

What if Mina was wrong this time?

Shobi bore no guilt about the fact that her leaving had caused Bram to end his life. That was on him. But Ashna would never understand.

Shobi was tired of the secrets. There were only two things to do. One, tell the truth, or two, stick with lies. The lies had kept them here for years, stuck in this quagmire but safely confined to the pain they were already used to. The truth was going to make things worse, inflict pain that might break them, but then there was a chance that it might start them down a path to healing.

"Truth is supposed to set us free, isn't it?" Shobi said.

A small laugh escaped Mina. "Is it just us or does everyone have past lives they struggle to share with their children?"

There was another long beat of silence. How far they had both come from two young royal *bahus* smoking on a secret balcony. Unlike Shobi, Mina had navigated everything with such grace. She'd held her family together without damage. Then again, she had been blessed with a life partner who loved and respected her. Shobi thought about Omar and the familiar pang of longing for Ashna to have been his squeezed inside her.

"We haven't had common lives, that's for sure," Shobi said, "but they haven't been unique either. Marital rape is hardly rare." All those years of managing it, but anger still bled into her voice when she said the words out loud. "There's just too much Ashna doesn't know. I have no idea where to start. It doesn't help that she romanticizes Bram so much.

"'Your father raped me and then I stayed with him for eighteen years because he threatened to take you away from me.' How do you say those words to your child?" How did you say the million other things that wove around that truth? Were there even words to explain all the things she would have lost if she'd walked away from what being married to him meant or for having made that bargain.

"Maybe she doesn't romanticize Bram quite as much as you think. She saw his fall far closer than the rest of us," Mina said sharply.

No one had realized quite how bad things had gotten with Bram. It was the most widely known fact about alcoholism, that it made you excellent at hiding things. They should have looked harder, but they'd missed the extent of it. Ashna was the only one who'd borne witness, who had shared responsibility in his secrets, because her mother had failed her.

"She might be stronger than you think," Mina said.

"I don't know." Why should the onus of strength fall on Ashna? Hadn't she seen enough? "She's not like Trisha or Nisha, she doesn't have their spirit." Which was Shobi's fault, of course. "She's too fragile, Mina. How can I do it when she's finally holding herself to—."

Mina held up a hand. She was the one who noticed the sound first.

Shobi spun around.

There she was, Ashna, looking like someone had crushed her ribs with their bare hands.

Mina was the first to speak. "Ashi, hi, beta. How long have you been standing here?"

Ashna was staring at Shobi, devastation in her eyes. "Long enough." Very slowly she turned to Mina. "Do you think I'm weak too? Does everyone just tiptoe around me?" Her voice was barely a whisper, but she might as well be screaming.

Mina stood and went to her, but Ashna scrambled back. "No!" she said more loudly, and turned back to Shobi.

She was shaking, every tendon in her neck stretched. For all her effort she couldn't make words.

"Beta . . ." Shobi said.

"No! Please." A long silence stretched before, finally, she spoke. "Remember that deal we made? You wanted us to talk. Let's start with this. How was I born, Mom?" Her voice broke on the word Shobi had cherished like a dream.

"I'm not sure what you're asking me." Shobi kept her voice strong, because old habits were hard to break, and because she had no idea how much Ashna had heard.

"You know exactly what I'm asking. If you hated Baba from the very beginning of your marriage, then how was I born?" So Ashna had heard the worst part, then.

Words stuck in Shobi's throat. This wasn't how she'd wanted Ashna to find out. Actually, that part, the cruelest piece, she'd never wanted Ashna to find out.

Ashna laughed. "My entire life I've tried to figure out your marriage, to piece together the ugliness from overheard fights where you tried to destroy each other with words. Now it all makes sense. That's why you never wanted to be around me. I . . . I was the ugliness in your marriage."

"That's not true. Ashi, listen to me. I—"

"No. You don't have to lie anymore. Why did you even have me? Is that why you had to marry him? Oh God." She gasped for air.

Shobi looked at Mina.

"*You* answer me. Why are you looking at Mina Kaki for help? Why does she have to do all your dirty work for you?"

Shobi went to Ashna, even as she scrambled back, until her back was pressed against the swirling railing of Bram's bloody staircase. "Mina's done the best part of my work. She got to raise you."

"No, Mom, not now. Don't. Manage. Me. Just be honest with me. No more lies."

"Okay," Shobi said. "Okay, so here's the only truth that matters. None of this is your fault."

"Stop it. Stop saying that. Will everyone please just stop saying that. It is my fault. How can it not be my fault? I'm the product of . . . of . . . God, Mom, if you stayed in a marriage like that for me, then it *is* my fault."

"No, it isn't. It's Bram's and my fault. Mine because I didn't know how else to do this, because I wavered when I should have been stronger. And his, because . . . well, because he was him. And society's fault for teaching him that it was his right because he was a man and a prince, and God knows what other unearned privilege."

Ashna pressed her hands to her ears, tears dripping from

her beautiful, tortured eyes. Shobi thought she knew what it meant to hurt, but she couldn't have imagined this pain.

"I don't give a shit about society. I don't care. How can you make this about your damn crusade against the patriarchy?" She turned and looked at the door, as though gauging her distance from it. "You're right. I don't have the strength for this, for more lies. You were both right after all. I am too weak."

With that she walked to the front door and out of the house.

"Ashi, beta, come back," Mina called after her, following her to the front porch.

Ashna spun around and faced Mina. "You wanted me to stop believing the easiest thing to believe. There, you got your wish."

Shobi stopped next to Mina. "I know this isn't easy. But hear me out, please. Just give me a chance to explain."

Ashna threw her head back and made a sound that broke Shobi's heart.

"It's okay," Shobi whispered, but Ashna heard her, because she wrapped her arms around herself. "I'm not leaving, Ashna. I'm sorry I did before. No matter what happens, I'm never leaving you again."

Ashna's arms tightened around herself.

"Come inside, Ashi," Mina said.

Mina's voice unfroze her where Shobi's had not. She turned her desperately helpless eyes on Mina. "I can't. Please. I can't be here right now."

Shobi and Mina watched, as Ashna made her way down the driveway and stood there staring at the house Bram had built.

"I'm sorry." At long last she looked directly at Shobi, horrid guilt in her eyes. "I'm so sorry. I just need some time. Please." With that she walked away, legs unsteady, a baby learning to stand, a toddler learning to walk, a teenager backing away from a parent.

Shobi sat down on the front step, wishing she could burn down this bloody house Bram had put more thought into than he'd ever put into the child who'd loved him. "How did I let everything go so terribly wrong?"

Mina sat down beside her and rubbed her shoulder. "It's going to be okay. She's stronger than we think. At least now you can put the lies behind you."

Chapter Thirty

Mina's arm was wrapped around Shoban and she was rubbing her shoulder. The touch made Shoban's stomach churn even as it made her feel grounded again.

Rage roiled in her chest, pressing out against her ribs, a continuous state for her now. It had been three months since Bram had shoved himself into his room, into his marital bed, and into his wife's body.

Thinking about it like that, from a distance, was the only way Shoban could bear to live in her skin, and to not put a bullet through Bram's brain.

I was drunk. I don't remember anything. She's lying.

His excuses had been endless.

But she's my wife.

Finally, that last one, his truth.

Shoban had screamed but he had slapped a hand across her mouth, the pads of his fingers pushing up against her nose, cutting off her breath, and torn through her underwear and her flesh.

Jumping off the couch, Shoban paced the clinic's waiting

room as Mina watched her, eyes filled with the wretched guilt that had become permanently lodged there.

Shoban would not have made it through these three months without Mina.

Mina had found her on the palace cliffs. She'd been sitting on the rocks and staring at the ocean the morning after, bruised everywhere, but with only the bruise that split her lip visible to the world.

Shoban had pushed herself out from under Bram after he passed out on top of her. She'd taken herself to the shower and washed off the blood but hadn't been able to wash off the violation, no matter how scalding the water. Pulling on a white kurta over jeans, she had walked out of the palace and to the cliffs as the sun started to break the horizon.

She had no idea how long she'd been sitting there when Mina found her on her morning run. On the night of the wedding, sometime after Shobi had left Mina outside the balcony, Mina and Shree had put a heavily drunk Bram in one of the rooms in their suite, where they had believed he had fallen into an inebriated stupor. How Bram had let himself out of there and made it into Shoban's room, no one seemed to know.

Mina had apologized and apologized, but it wasn't her fault.

When Mina and Ma-saheb asked Shobi what she wanted to do, all she could think was *I want to put a bullet in his head.*

She couldn't remember if she had said the words out loud, but the intense full-bodied numbness that she couldn't shake off had been both a blessing and a curse.

Pressing charges wasn't an option. Shoban had no witnesses, and no judge would hear a marital rape case. Bram had been sent off to a rehab facility in Switzerland. A banishment, a peace offering, a cover-up, Shoban wasn't sure which.

Mina had let Shree and Ma-saheb return to California, to her three children, without her. She refused to leave Shoban's side, sitting with her day and night as Shoban said nothing. All Shoban could get herself to do all day was practice cricket at the palace pitch. Run and toss. Run and toss. Over and over and over. With Mina sitting cross-legged on the grass watching her.

The numbness hadn't turned to rage until Shoban had fainted one afternoon while running down the wicket, the sun turning her skin clammy where her hairline edged her forehead. Just one day before she crossed over into the second trimester, the doctor had declared Shoban pregnant.

How an act that ugly, that violent, could result in such a thing, Shoban couldn't believe. But she and Mina had made their way to the family planning clinic in Goa where they took care of such matters with discretion. It was the very last day in the pregnancy that the doctor would perform the procedure.

Grotesque feelings so acrid she could taste them swirled inside Shoban, but she had no names for them. Her ability to decipher her own feelings seemed permanently lost. Unable to curb her restlessness, she sat down next to Mina again. Mina took her hand and resumed her stroking, which, God help her, was actually soothing.

The woman sitting across from them in the waiting room smiled at them. "A girl, ha?" she said, throwing a glance at Shoban's stomach, a camaraderie in her voice. A demented sort of commiseration shone in her bespectacled eyes.

She was dressed in designer jeans and a silk blouse, and her hair was blown out and highlighted. "How many do you have already?" she asked, not needing an answer or even acknowledgment from Shoban and Mina. "I have two." She widened her eyes, as though such horrors were entirely incomprehensible. "Now, until we know it's a boy . . ." She twirled her manicured hand around the clinic, indicating the fate of her unborn girl children.

The gesture made the white walls spin around Shoban. A typhoon churned up her guts. She sprinted to the bathroom and brought up everything she had ever consumed. At least, that's how it felt.

It was the first time she was throwing up and it would not stop. Cramps locked her belly, her lungs, her calves, her toes. Everything spasmed like bubbling hot lava, desperate to leave her body.

With a soft knock Mina came into the bathroom and bent over her, pulling her hair back as Shoban vomited again and again.

When the heaving died down, exhausting itself, they sat on the stall floor, face-to-face.

"What if it's a girl?" Shoban said, the words scraping her throat raw. "What if it's a girl?"

Shoban wasn't sure if her tears came first or Mina's. But they sat there and cried, two women who knew how unwanted they had been.

That's when Shoban first saw her, felt her. Her baby girl. Inside her. So very beautiful. With large too-forgiving eyes, and tiny too-loving hands, and a heart that had no vileness in it. None at all. And Shoban knew with the deepest certainty that she would bring only beauty with her. A beauty without which Shoban would never heal. Never feel whole again.

Without a word, Mina took Shoban's hand and they walked out of the clinic. Words didn't find them again. Not in the car, not as Mina pulled the Jeep onto the beach and they walked and walked until the day turned to night.

In the months that followed, Mina returned to Woodside and Ma-saheb came back to Sripore. Then Mina came back for the delivery. The two of them taking turns to stay by Shobi's side.

Baby Ashna came into the world exactly on her due date, screaming as though she wanted to wake the dead and just as beautiful as Shoban had imagined. A thick head of silky black hair, puffy baby eyes that stretched clean across her round face, and a mouth so pouty and determined that the sight of it made Shoban cry and cry as she pressed her to her breast.

"Let's take her to America," Mina said, pressing her close and unabashedly inhaling her baby smell. Her own Trisha was two. Unlike Shoban, Mina had craved and cherished being a mother. Unlike Shoban, Mina was born to be a mother.

Shoban wanted nothing to do with America. The idea of living anywhere but here in India was entirely incomprehensible to her.

"I want to go back to playing cricket," Shoban said that first day they went back to the palace from the hospital with baby Ashna. The thought had been bubbling beneath the numbness for a while. Shoban had put off committing to the national team because she had believed she was off to Oxford; now she could see no other path for herself.

"Will they let you play now?" Mina asked.

"Women athletes compete in the Olympics after childbirth," Shoban said.

"That's a great idea," their mother-in-law said. "You have to find something to keep yourself busy. The commissioner of the Board of Control for Cricket is a cousin. You focus on your recovery right now. I'll call on him."

"I still want a divorce." Shoban had no idea why she had waited so long to say it, but seeing her baby's face had made her resolve stronger. She never wanted to see Bram again. Oddly enough, she couldn't let herself think about Omar either. Missing him was a pain that sharpened all the things that hurt.

He hadn't made any contact with her. She had no idea how much he knew and what betrayal he believed her capable of. Shoban was just too exhausted to sort through any of it.

One thing she did know: the idea of not having Mina and Ma-saheb in her life made her want to roll up in a ball and never get up. Given that her hands were full of baby, that was not an option.

Her mother-in-law picked up Ashna, who immediately grabbed at her aji's pearls and spat up on her pristine white Chanderi sari. "We'll talk about all that later. When you're strong enough," Ma-saheb didn't bother to wipe the spit-up as she gurgled at her granddaughter with smitten eyes. "From now on only what you want will happen, beta." Ma-saheb always knew exactly what Shoban needed to hear.

It was easy to assign manipulation to her actions, but Shoban had to believe in something and she believed that these women understood, and that their love was her only chance.

Shoban settled back into the palace. She told herself it was temporary. But it was the best place for Ashna. There were nurses on staff, and a bright and sunny nursery with the most beautiful carved rosewood cradle. Not that Shoban could let her baby sleep anywhere but in her bed, where Shoban could roll over on her side and nurse her when she woke in the middle of the night.

"No matter what happens, you're never getting rid of me," Mina said as they both lay on Shoban's bed with Ashna between them and the quilted Kashida canopy bright above them.

Shoban had never gone back to Bram's room. A new suite of rooms had been made up for her in a different part of the palace after her wedding night. Oddly, Shoban felt more at home in her rooms here than she had felt anywhere else in her life.

Maybe because Ma-saheb had kept her safe and sent her son away without lobbing one single doubt or accusation in Shoban's direction.

Maybe because she and Mina had found each other here.

"If something happens to me, you'll take care of her, right?" Shoban asked Mina, voicing a worry that had been eating away at her.

"I'll take care of her even if nothing happens to you. Isn't that right, Ashi-pishi? You're your Kaki's baby girl, aren't you?" Mina blew into Ashna's belly and she gurgled around a smile. Her first smile. The two women sat up, awed beyond words, and tried to get her to do it again. She complied, proving definitively that she was ticklish and not gassy, and consequently the most perfect baby on earth.

When Ashna was three months old, Shoban started playing cricket again. Until Ashna was two, Bram stayed out of their lives. His mother made sure he went from rehab in Switzerland to Paris to work with a cousin who ran a chain of restaurants in Europe. He had made his mother promise that he could come home if he stayed clean for two years.

By the time he came home Shobi had already made her way onto the national team. Women's cricket was entirely ignored in a country obsessed with cricket, but that only made the flame that had always flickered inside Shobi grow into an inferno. The women on her team each came from struggle. They swallowed the neglect of their passion because it gave them power, even though no one bothered to acknowledge it.

Shoban learned their stories, the battles they fought to reject the expectations of their families. Expectations that they be demure and feminine in preassigned ways, that they might play their beloved sport only if they returned after to the kitchens and bedrooms, mothers and daughters-in-law and wives. The more Shoban encountered the stories of her teammates, the fiercer the monster inside her grew until a woman she barely recognized emerged from her.

Shining Shobi. It was the name her teammates gave her, because she never tired of pushing them to fight, to win, and to claim the power of their wins to fight on and off the field.

When the opening batsman (yes, that's what she was called even though she was a woman) showed up at Shobi's door one day, beaten by her father because she refused to comply with some directive of his, Shobi learned that the Raje name was the sharpest weapon she could wield. One phone call to the commissioner of police, and the dynamics of power shifted. Direct access to media, access to safe houses and charities the family ran, the ear of celebrities and influencers: it all rolled drop by drop into a wave of seismic force.

Suddenly, right at Shobi's fingertips was the power to change things, to not bend, and it took root inside her, fast and strong. Or it simply watered the seed that had always been within her. Before she knew it, she became Shining Shobi, every iota of fear inside her burned away as though it had never existed, and one too many people looked to her for strength.

When Bram returned, with the belief that his short banishment had been sufficient penance, all Shobi could do was laugh. He was full of apologies, as though remorse were all it took to erase evil. A great reset switch that she would be complicit in flipping over her dead body. But she would not give up her new life either. They would have separate lives. The only thing shared between them would be Ashna, because the simple acts of hugging her and spinning her in the air had been enough for Bram to win their daughter's love. Shobi had always sworn that Ashna would make her own choices no matter how young, that she would hone her own spirit as she wished.

Loving her father was Ashna's right, and Shobi couldn't snatch that from her even as Bram trapped them in a power struggle. As Shobi's popularity in the media grew, Bram found new and increasingly exasperating ways to humiliate himself publicly. The more the family tried to curb him, the more creative he became in his wildness. Until finally, on a hunting trip, he shot a blackbuck, an endangered antelope, one of earth's most majestic creatures. It was a repeat offense that came with a jail sentence, and not just a fine like the first time. A fine that would've crippled anyone not born with a diamond-encrusted spoon in his ungrateful mouth.

A weird sort of thing had happened in the two years when Bram was gone. Shobi had developed an internalized mechanism to shut him out. Maybe her subconscious knew that it was the only way to achieve everything she wanted to achieve without letting him take that away from her.

The more she shut him out, the less he was able to do the same. The numbness toward Bram, combined with the fire her work gave her, might have worked had it not caused the collateral damage that Shobi didn't quite acknowledge until it was too late. Her Ashna.

Whenever Shobi's work conflicted with something Ashna needed—unable to demand it because that wasn't her—Shobi told herself she would have time to fix it. But Bram sought out the gaps between Shoban's shrinking time and Ashna and stole her affection away. When other children had only the natural distance between generations to chart, to Ashna's lot fell navigating the grotesqueness between her parents.

By the time Bram laughed in Shobi's face, the perpetual tang of alcohol on his breath, and told her that the one thing she would never have was her daughter back, it was too late. The most precious thing in Shobi's life had become too tenuous and slippery for her to hold on to.

After the hunting incident, Ma-saheb couldn't get the authorities to bury the charges a second time. The only solution the family could come up with was to remove Bram from the country to avoid arrest. Shree was able to extract him to America amid a media circus. Ashna became the butt of teasing at school, and a target for hungry paparazzi. Once that happened, Shobi lost all avenues to win. She had to focus on damage control for Ashna, even as she struggled to hold her foundation together, because far too many people depended on it.

She tried to reason with Ashna, explain to her that Shobi couldn't leave with them, and she couldn't keep Ashna with her either. Shobi promised to make their time together make up for their separation. She didn't account for the fact that to Ashna the abandonment would become the sum total of their relationship, or that the only way Ashna would know how to handle it was by completely withdrawing and insulating herself from Shobi.

Before she knew it Ashna stopped holding her, stopped calling her mamma, stopped hearing anything that came out of Shobi's mouth. It was amid that tornado of Ashna's rejection and withdrawal that Omar returned after making his way out of the lies his father had told him to save his own skin. It wasn't much, but in some ways, it was everything.

Chapter Thirty-One

The last thing Ashna had expected was to return to him today. But it felt natural. Essential.

At first she had walked aimlessly, without knowing where she was going. Past the restaurants her aunt called "hip" that were the beating heart of Palo Alto, the giant Whole Foods that was perpetually crowded, the Philz Coffee that made her feel like she was soaking up the coffee aroma with her skin. Little things that had made this place her home for so long. A home that had terrified her and excited her in equal parts when she had first come here.

"It's going to be fun," Baba had said to her. "We've always had fun together, haven't we?" Baba had encouraged her to play soccer instead of cricket. He'd taken her hunting, something her mother hated. Shopping trips to Milan. Oysters in Catalonia. Macarons in Paris. Decadence had been his weapon.

Decadence that had filled Ashna with guilt when her mother railed against it as she draped on her white cotton saris and went to war in places so neglected no one had even heard of them. But at least it had made Shobi stop and take notice. Missing her mother had been a live thing inside Ashna for as long as she could remember.

"We'll make it a fresh start. Your mother wants us to be miserable. We'll be happy. That'll show her."

Even at ten Ashna had known these were not things one parent should say about another. A part of her had hoped that if Baba got them out of his system maybe he wouldn't be so pathetic around Mom. In her presence, all he could do was drink and whimper, and no one stood up for him.

Ashna circled the block and went into Curried Dreams. It was closed today. Which was why her aunt and her mother had been at home. Ashna went into the janitor's storeroom and retrieved her cleaning cart. Mina Kaki had hired a cleaning service. In just a few months, how much everything had changed from when Mandy and Ashna had soldiered on with nothing more than hope to fuel them. The restaurant was spotless, but Ashna washed and wiped everything. She remembered the expression on Mandy's face when Ashna had let her go. Before she had asked to be let go.

Her legs felt shaky as she made her way to Baba's office. She had never been inside the room after they had cleaned out his remains. She tried to push the door open but she couldn't do it.

The last day Baba had been alive played in her head. He'd found out about her and Rico and demanded that Rico come and meet him. The feeling of inescapable doom had pulled over Ashna like someone sliding a plastic bag over her face. She had begged Rico to stay away from Baba and gone to see him herself. At first she'd tried to explain how much Rico and she loved each other.

Boys like that only want one thing. In his case two. And neither one of those has anything to do with loving you . . . He is not like us. Life is hard enough with someone who's your social equal . . . I'd rather die than let you shame our heritage just because you're panting over a son of a whore who lives in a servant quarter.

Rage had exploded inside her, a nuclear blast wiping away a lifetime of placating him, determinedly seeing him as someone he was not.

You're sick. It's not just the drinking and vomiting, you're sick on the inside. How did I ever stand being near you?

She didn't care that he looked like Ashna had kicked him.

It's because your mother couldn't stand being near you. You had no choice. This boy is going to do it too. He's going to leave you like your mother did.

Ashna had run out of the room, but it had felt like dragging herself out because he'd cut off her legs.

You're just like your mother. Selfish.

She sank down by the door. Maybe she'd sleep here tonight. For one terribly long moment the thought was comforting. Then Ashna jumped up.

But she still saw herself on that floor, rolled up in a ball. A part of her had been lying there, outside his door, for twelve years.

It was time to get up and move on.

Breaking into a run, she made her way out of the restaurant

and started walking. She walked and she walked. The sun was long gone from the sky, leaving suburbia in a blanket of lights. She found herself on Caltrain headed to the city. By the time she got off at the Fourth and King station, memories had clogged up inside her like sludge, a backed-up drain that wouldn't move.

How could so much anger for your parents live inside you, even as you hurt for them? Wasn't hurting for someone a sign of love? How could she love someone capable of such hateful things?

Why had she blocked out Baba's cruelty until now? For the last few years of his life he had barely ever emerged from behind the haze of depression and alcohol. All Ashna had wanted was to help him, to save him. To show her mother that care was what people needed, and time.

How colossally stupid she was.

She'd completely ignored the fact that Shobi *had* shown nothing but care for all the world. She'd given all her time to it.

So much Ashna had blocked out. A year after moving to Palo Alto, when the high of the restaurant's success had made Baba seem the happiest Ashna had ever seen him, she had asked him if she could move back home to Sripore. He'd taken his rifle out of its case and looked Ashna straight in the eye.

"You've already lost your mother. She doesn't want us. If you leave me like she left us, I'll have no choice but to kill myself. Then you'll have no one left."

Ashna had been ten.

Mina Kaki had found her terrified and unable to get out of

bed the next day. Her aunt had tried everything to get Ashna to tell her what was wrong. But Ashna hadn't been able to. Mina had called Shobi to ask her to come out and take care of Ashna.

Ashna had picked up the extension and overheard their conversation. "Can you manage things with Ashi one more time, Minu? I have to be in Ratnagiri. We're inaugurating our biggest school yet. It's going to serve all of Konkan. Too many people are counting on me." At least Baba wanted her badly enough that losing her would kill him.

Finally, Mina Kaki had been the one to "manage things." She'd moved Ashna into school in Woodside. HRH and she had given Bram no choice, insisting Ashna needed her cousins and the feminine influence of her aunt and grandmother. Now Ashna wondered if he hadn't been relieved to be rid of her.

If her aunt and uncle hadn't moved her into their home, what would Ashna have done?

And yet instead of going to the Anchorage, tonight Ashna was headed to a hotel where a promise waited for her. A promise that she could be strong.

After walking God knows how many miles to the hotel where she had dropped him off hours . . . years . . . ago, she stopped outside the huge plate-glass doors. She had no idea what his room number was. She didn't have his phone number.

She was about to turn around, because collapsing outside a Ritz-Carlton was a little too over-the-top for her, even with the current drama in her life.

"Ms. Raje!"

When was the last time she'd been this relieved to see someone?

A question best left unanswered.

"George! Hi."

The older man gave her a kind smile. He was still in his uniform. "Are you here to see Mr. Silva?"

She nodded, hoping he couldn't tell she'd been crying.

He was wearing sunglasses, and it hid what was in his eyes, which felt like such a kindness. The idea of the world seeing her, anyone seeing her right now, felt violating.

Except one person, apparently, because she was willing to break into his hotel room.

"Can you tell me his room number, please?"

He didn't laugh at her or seem suspicious. His face remained entirely without judgment.

"Twenty-one hundred," he said quietly. If he was afraid he'd get in trouble, he didn't show it.

Ashna would fight tooth and nail to make sure he wouldn't get in trouble.

"Thanks, George. Can you please . . . um . . . not let him know I'm here? It's . . ."

"It's a surprise. Mr. Silva is a very lucky man." He held up a key card. "If you follow me, I'll get you all set with the elevator." He went into the hotel lobby and she followed him, trying to make up for her bedraggled state with poise. *Thank you, Mina Kaki, for teaching me that.*

They made their way to a bank of elevators under a row of what had to be the brightest chandeliers Ashna had ever seen. Her grandmother would be horrified at their brightness. The chandeliers at the Anchorage and at Sagar Mahal were always adjusted just so.

When the elevator opened, George followed her in, swiped the card, and then stepped out.

"George." Ashna stopped him and gave him a quick hug, then pulled awkwardly back into the elevator. "Thank you."

His smile was encouraging. "It's going to be all right, Ms. Raje."

It sure didn't feel like that, but she hoped he was right.

It was one of those elevators that deposited Ashna directly into a lobby with a single wide ornate door. The urge to turn around warred violently with the need to see him.

She got out of the elevator and walked to the door.

And knocked.

And waited and waited and waited.

Then turned around and went back to the elevator.

A door opened behind her.

"Ash."

God, his voice.

Turn around.

She felt him move closer. His heady smell enveloped her. Dear Lord, he'd been in the shower.

His breathing was right behind her. The heat of his body. Tears streamed down her face. Her eyes were probably swollen. Her hair was still wet inside her bun; she had meant to dry it at home.

All that walking had left her skin slick with sweat. She probably smelled like a skunk.

"Ash? Sweetheart?"

It was the stupidest thing, but the way he turned both words into questions sliced all the way through her. A sob made her shoulders jerk, and she pressed a hand to her mouth.

His hands were on her arms, so gentle it only made the tears worse. He turned her. Despite everything swirling inside her, the sight of him punched her in the center of her chest. A seventy-mile-per-hour kick she blocked with her whole body.

He leaned forward, his eyes meeting hers. The mossy green centers pushing out the gold all the way to the edges, the mismatch in size magnified. They drank her in before he spoke. "I thought opening the door in a towel might be a bit too obvious." His hair was down, and it fell in damp waves around his face down to his shoulders.

"So you pulled on middle-school-boy shorts?" Through her tears a smile escaped. He was wearing bright yellow basketball shorts that hit his knees and covered his scar.

Other than the shorts, his entire body was as bare as the day he was born. Every inch of him was tanned and ripped and gorgeous. Exactly the way all those YouTube videos of him working out promised. But all Ashna saw was a leaner, softer version. An eighteen-year-old body that had held her exactly right. So right that nothing had ever matched up.

She closed her eyes.

Hands cupped her face. His released breath at the touch sounded as ragged as her own.

She opened her eyes and took in the full blast of his relentlessly focused gaze.

"Do you mean it?" Her voice was a whisper.

He swallowed, his thickly stubbled jaw tightening. "Mean what?"

"Everything you say to me with your eyes?"

He groaned, the depth of his soul bared by the sound.

Then he was bending to her and she was stretching up to him.

The first touch was feather light, the barest skimming of lips against lips. Then a zing so powerful strength drained from her legs. She reached for him, clutching his arms, his shoulders like a lifeline. His hands angled her face, fitting her mouth exactly so. Invading and cajoling and opening. All at once. Everything at once.

Hunger rose inside Ashna like a tidal wave. She gnawed at his lips, pushing-pulling, met his tongue. Sweet relief, wet and thick in her mouth, filling her up all the way to the back of her lungs. No air, no breath, just the taste of him everywhere. Everywhere.

And his hair. God. His hair in her hands. Flowers she'd clutched at the temple had felt less like worship. She threaded her fingers through the strands, fisted them so hard they dug into her palms, tugged around the sensitive skin between her fingers.

All of her, she wanted all of her touching all of him that way. Tight and wrapped. No spaces. Her legs wrapped around his hips as he lifted her and carried her in.

"Rico." She pulled away, hands still in his hair as he kicked the door behind them. "Your knee." She slid off him, hands sliding to his cheeks, his beard at once rough and smooth and more erotic against her palms than she could ever have imagined. She stroked him even as she pulled away.

He tightened his hold on her, a full-body hug that said: *Don't leave me.* "My knee is fine, Ash. I swear. Forget about my knee. Please." Breathless. He was breathless and he touched her lips with his again. Then again. "Baby, how, tell me, how did we let this go?"

Her heart spasmed at that. She soaked up his taste. Sunshine would taste like this. A fresh summer stream with a hint of melting sugar. Crisp and sweet.

She wanted to bottle it up, blend it into a tea, drink from him until the day she died.

Her lower lip slipped from between his lips, clinging to the soft suction, his mouth resisting letting her go. He dropped a kiss on it, swollen and sensitive beyond words. All of her too aroused and tender to bear.

"Is this what you hear me say with my eyes? Is this what you don't believe?"

"I want to believe it." She couldn't stop kissing him. His mouth had been her undoing. His jaw. Everything intoxicating as she touched it with her mouth, stroked it with her tongue. "I want you to make me feel beautiful." Her lips were on his throat now, tracing the line where smooth skin turned to soft beard. Then up again to his mouth. "Please."

His answering kiss matched her fever. Then suddenly his forehead was pressed against hers, his chest pumping with breath, his hand stroking her hair. Tendrils had come loose from her bun to dance around her face, and he couldn't stop stroking whatever free locks he could touch. She was a skittish filly to be calmed.

"Ash, tell me what's going on? What's the matter?"

She pushed away from him, their bodies disengaging for the first time since they had touched. Turning away from him, she started for the door. "Great. So you don't want me either."

He was on her in a second, his hand on hers as she grabbed the doorknob. His body curved around hers, his breath in her hair. "Slow down. Please, meu amor, slow down."

"I don't want to slow down. I don't want excuses. I don't want to feel like this, Rico!" She didn't care that her shoulders were shaking, she didn't care.

"Okay. Okay. Will you let me do something? Promise not to stop me?"

She turned around, not in the mood to make any promises to anyone. There was only one thing she wanted right now.

"I'm going to pick you up and take you inside. My knee is fine. Will you let me do that without worrying about my knee? I really need to hold you."

"I can't. I can't let you carry me when your knee is hurting."

He threw his head back and groaned in frustration, and despite herself she smiled.

Taking her hand as though it was unspeakably precious, he tugged it. "But you will come inside with me? We can talk inside? Yes?"

"I don't want to talk." But she followed him into the enormous living room with a giant marble bar overlooking a clear view of the Bay Bridge, lit up. For the first time in her life she didn't care about the beauty of it, about the view, about anything but being in his arms again, being wanted. He slipped behind the bar and turned on the sculptural faucet that was almost as tall as he was. Almost as extravagantly beautiful.

"Water?"

She narrowed her eyes at him. Really? He wanted to play hostess right now?

He walked around the bar and handed her a glass.

Good, because if had been a plastic bottle she would have thrown it clean across the room.

She placed the glass down on the bar, refusing to be gentle, refusing to be managed. Glass clattered against stone.

She took his hand, gazes locked, grip firm. "Does this place have a bedroom?"

If anyone could fill a nod with erotic heat, this man could. She pulled him toward what had to be the bedroom (please let it be). He followed, eyes intense, hungry for her.

The sight of the bed was such a relief she almost cried. Turning around, she pushed him onto it, then climbed into his lap and straddled him. With a mighty moan that was pure need, he pulled her close. Body to body. Her legs tightened around his hips, all of her wrapped around him. He reached back and unclasped her bun as though he'd waited a million years to do it. Her hair cascaded around them as she shook it free, shook herself free. Then her tongue was in his mouth, and his hands were tugging at her clothes.

Their bodies recognized each other, coming together like

elemental atoms, their only purpose to fuse and re-form. Everything old turning into something new in an explosion of desire and trembling connection and unvarnished hope.

In the aftermath they lay panting, the screamed calls of each other's names echoing in the cavernous room, sweat and slick wetness still joining them where their skin touched, no words left on their lips, no breath in their lungs. Not for a long, long time.

There was just the tight grasp of their bodies. Hands clinging, inner muscles clutching, hair tangled, breaths mingling. She soaked up the oneness of them, too afraid to move, because how could this perfection last?

"If you tell me you don't feel beautiful after that—" Rico whispered, voice hoarse as she kissed his mouth, stealing the rest of his words.

Rolling onto their sides, they kissed lazily, their heartbeats surging up and down. They played each other like beloved instruments they'd lost to time and given up on. Taking notes with their touches. Relearning. Reclaiming.

Ashna had no idea when she drifted off, but when she woke up, the room was pitch dark. Inside her was a new brightness. Without even a moment of disorientation, she knew exactly where she was. Lying sprawled on top of Rico, skin on skin.

She knew from his breathing that he was awake.

"Morning," he said.

"What time is it? Can we have some light?"

"It's noon."

She sprang up and found him laughing. And gorgeous.

"It's barely seven." He hit a button on a remote and a complicated orchestra of blinds opened just enough to let in a gentle glow of morning light. The man was going to kill her.

Pulling her back to him, he kissed her soundly. A phrase that had to have been coined for this very moment.

Yes, she felt soundly kissed and it made her smile against his mouth. "You're a very loud man. That's certainly new," she said.

He talked during sex, a lot. The chant of her name with every term of endearment in the world, all of them. A lot of Portuguese. Every word lightning, striking straight at her womb.

It was probably the first time she'd seen him blush. "It's easier when you're not hiding."

She stiffened, but she knew he only meant how quiet they'd had to be in his aunt's house, even though his aunt had never been there when they were together.

He stroked her back, thumb tracing the keys of her spine. Soothing her again. "Growing up has to have some advantages."

It should, shouldn't it?

He sensed the shifting of her mood. "You want to talk about what happened?"

She pushed herself off him and lay down on her back. The restlessness inside her was nothing if not stubborn. "What I've always known about myself, turns out it's true."

He went up on an elbow and started stroking her hair again. Her restlessness quelled a bit, which in turn made her angry, because becoming dependent on him to keep her from feeling like this, like a stringless kite, had destroyed her once.

Breathe, his hand in her hair said to her.

Breathe, his kaleidoscopic eyes said to himself.

"Listen, Ash, we didn't get a chance to finish our conversation earlier. I . . . what you said . . . that your mother had never done anything to disprove your opinion of her, I couldn't stop thinking about that. She is doing something now, isn't she? She's here . . . just like—"

"Please don't." She couldn't talk about this right now, and still, somehow, she wanted to tell him everything she had overheard Shobi and Mina Kaki say. Everything about herself she now knew. Everything she had always known that she now had proof of. She wanted to burrow into him, scream it all into the solidity of his chest.

"You're right. She's here now." She stroked his face. "And you are too." They were both so brave, and how terrible she had been to them. "Everything you see in me, it's a lie." Her very existence was an ugliness.

"Everything I see in you is truth, and it's more beautiful than anything."

"No, it isn't." She sat up. "You don't understand. That's not true."

He pushed himself off the bed and stood, unabashedly naked and so very beautiful. "Can I show you something?" He held out his hand.

"I think I've seen everything you want to show me."

His eyes smiled and he made a beckoning gesture with his hand. "Come on."

She took it and stood, wrapping a sheet around herself, and followed him, dragging the sheet along as he led her to a huge mirror in the alcove. He positioned her to face her reflection.

Behind her he was a head taller. Wrapping his arms around her, he rested his chin on her head. Their bodies were made to fit together, perfect jigsaw pieces.

Their eyes met in the mirror and there she was. Seeing herself through his eyes, her downfall.

It had made her feel wanton, always. Not a word she'd known to use in high school, but one of the many intangible things she had ached for ever since losing him. He brought out this hot, pulsating spirit inside her, turned all of her into reckless desire. Hair down loose, arms akimbo, breath not held. Ready for anything. *Her.* The her who had thrown herself at the ball on the pitch. The one who had pushed Rico down on the bed and climbed on top.

In every part of her life, that was all she ever wanted to be, forcefully the same on the inside and the outside. Able to say what she wanted to say, able to do what she wanted to do, able to think of herself as she wanted to be thought of.

So many people loved her, and yet her love for them was tainted with fear. Her cousins, her friends, her aunt and uncle, her aji, they would always love her. Their love wasn't conditional, the logical part of her knew that. But she couldn't stop working for it, aching for it. She never felt worthy of it. Because they knew the truth about her.

Only with him had she never had to work for it.

Despite how that had ended, she wanted what they'd had again with a terrifying desperation.

He kissed the top of her head without looking away from her. She needed his gaze and he would not take that from her.

Look at you. Look at what I see. He didn't have to say the words.

Being with him was the only glimpse she'd had of being fearless, of not being in need of armor. All the rest of her life had been spent in fear of being unwanted.

And now she knew it definitively.

Marital rape is hardly rare.

Ashna's stomach turned and instinctively Rico's arms tightened around her.

He is not like us. Life is hard enough with someone who's your social equal.

That had been such a terrible lie. Life was hardest when you pushed away love. So many terrible lies her father had told her. It still felt like betrayal to think critically about Baba, even as her rage shifted inside her.

It doesn't help that she romanticizes Bram so much.

Mom had that wrong. Ashna had never romanticized her father. She'd just felt like he was all she had. Actually, that was a lie. Truth was, she had always felt like she was all he had. In the end, she'd been right, because when she left him, look what happened.

Finally, eyes still clinging to Rico's unwavering gaze, Ashna spoke the one truth she could tell. "I was never fierce, Rico. It was what you imagined me to be. No one else ever saw me that way. Just you." How much she had needed that. How many things it would have changed to have had it for longer.

"That's not true, meu amor. I've seen you with your family. Everyone sees you that way."

She's too fragile.

She pulled his arms from around her, but she kissed his hands before going back to the bed and retrieving her clothes. "My family sees that I'm broken."

He stood in the doorway watching her put her clothes on. Then he followed her lead and pulled on his shorts.

"I come from the kind of dysfunction you can't even imagine." She thought about her mother, powerful to a point that standing in her presence made you judge yourself against her. But so physically small. And her father had been a giant; even as a young man he'd been close to three hundred pounds and over six feet tall. For all her fierceness, Shobi would have no chance against him.

No wonder Mom had never wanted her. And all Ashna had ever done was judge her for it. She'd been a person who punished the victim, her own mother.

Dear God, if she threw up in this beautiful suite with Rico watching she would never forgive herself.

Rico came to her and cupped her cheek. "Tell me what happened."

Where could she even begin?

"My mother never wanted me."

"Did she say that to you? Did you have a fight?"

She had to laugh at that. How she envied him the innocence of thinking a parent could only say those words in anger, without meaning them. "I grew up hearing my parents fight about how they never wanted me." If he wanted to understand her, well, he was welcome to wade through the mess that she was. "It's not just that either. She was forced into a marriage to my father."

"That's sad. But not your fault."

If one more person said that to her she was going to poke their eyes out.

"It is my fault." She twisted her hair into a bun. "Because without me she would have moved on. She would have left him. But my father . . ." How did you say the words? "My father forced himself on her." She had no idea when her forehead ended up on his chest, pressed into his sternum, his skin warm and salty against those ugly words.

This is what she'd missed most. Someone she could hold when everything spun.

"You know why I hid you from my family? It was because I couldn't let them see the lie I was being with you. And I couldn't open that door and let you see me on the other side either. I didn't want you to see the real me. I wanted to be what you saw, wanted to know what being wanted without pity felt like."

He stroked up and down her arms. "What I see is the real you. That was you on the pitch. You in the kitchen."

"No." She shook her head so violently, her unpinned bun loosened and slid down her back.

The green of his eyes darkened. "You're not broken. You're hurting. You can hurt and be fierce at the same time." He said those words like someone who knew. Age-old pain was naked in his eyes and something deep inside her grew ravenous.

All she wanted was to rise up on her toes and touch her lips to his again and again. But now he knew. Suddenly she couldn't tell what it was that shone in his eyes, love or pity.

Then she remembered the loathing in his eyes after he'd met Baba. It came crashing down on her. All of it. He had seen who she was when it came to her father. And the first glimpse of it had made him run.

Who are you, Ash? How can you stand being around such a horrible person?

When she hadn't been that girl—the one on the pitch, the one in the kitchen—he hadn't wanted her.

"I have to go," she said, unable to breathe.

"What? Why?" His eyes grew wild at the idea of her leaving. She knew exactly how he felt.

Except he knew how to survive, to thrive when things went wrong. She didn't. She couldn't go through losing him again. "Because I'm not the person you think I am." Look at how she had run from her mother. "Because we're too different. We couldn't cross that distance once, how will we now?" With that she started walking to the door.

Chapter Thirty-Two

Rico was next to her in a minute, his arms around her, his lips in her hair. This entire morning had felt like trying to hold on to her as she slipped away. But he would hold on until his arms fell off. He no longer knew how not to.

"Distance? You call what's between us distance? This connection is distance? We're the same person, Ash. We're practically inside each other."

For a second her body went slack as she gave in to the urge to lean back into him. But then she groaned and held herself apart.

How could she not see? She was in his breath, his bones. Without even touching him she filled him up from the inside out. When they touched, there was no him left. From that first day when he had stopped that ball from hitting her. From that day he had never been the same, and he knew she hadn't either. There had been no him, no her, only them.

A tortured laugh hissed out of her. She turned around and something in her face made him let her go and step back. The entryway to the suite was too narrow. They couldn't go too far from each other. A bloody metaphor if there ever was one.

"Our connection didn't matter before, and it matters even less now." She pressed herself into the wall behind her. "It's the other things. Our lives, how the world has been to us. That's the distance that's too far for us to reach across. I mean, look at you. You're one of the greatest athletes of our time. You're on magazine covers, Rico! You're on calendars. Grown women drool over you. Grown men weep when you score a goal. And I've barely left my restaurant in ten years."

"This is about my work? About the way I look? You think I care about any of that? You see the way women look at me, but you don't see the way I look at you? I can't look away from you, Ash!" He leaned back into the front door, a desperate move.

The black of her irises was so wide and deep, so clear he could dive into it and disappear. "Your eyes . . . for twelve years your eyes have haunted me. The way they look at me, all the way into me, the way they make me feel like I'm home, finally. Sometimes when you look at me the way you do, I can't move, I can't breathe, I can't feel myself as separate from you. How can you do this? Those years we spent together, how can you call them false?"

"I'm not. They weren't. But you met me when you were grieving, when you weren't yourself." Her voice hitched as though she'd just figured out some big Eureka-moment truth. "Oh God, even now you're vulnerable, in pain, grieving the loss of work you love." She pressed a hand to her mouth. "That explains so much."

He pushed his hands through his hair. He'd grown the bloody thing out because he'd been so lost after losing her that he hadn't remembered to cut it. After his first big win for Sunderland the rubber band holding it back had broken and he'd shaken it out, and the action had become a post-win ritual, a talisman for the fans. "So what? So something in the universe knows to bring me to you when nothing else works. Isn't that something? Only you, Ash. Why isn't that enough?"

He hadn't felt this lost, this helpless in a very long time. He was seventeen again, fifteen, with no one. If she walked away from him again, he'd have no one. "You know my greatest fear? It's that I'm not . . . that I'm not separate from you. That this being half of myself is what I'm stuck with for the rest of my life, because I don't know how to be whole without you. It's why I found my way back here, to you, because I couldn't stand to be that way anymore. Why isn't that enough?"

She swallowed as though it hurt her throat to do it. Had she not just been in that room with him? In that bed? Wasn't she tired of this, of fighting to stay away from him? For so damn long.

"Because you know how to heal, and when you do, you'll walk away. You did once."

"What? You threw me out. You let someone convince you that I wasn't good enough for you. First it was my being the boy who lives in a housekeeper's quarters, now it's being the man on a calendar. Do your father's words really mean so much that nothing else matters?"

A ravaged sound tore from her throat. Their past would never leave them alone. A million storms passed in her eyes.

"Ash, please, please say what you're thinking. Don't shut me out." He reached for her. But she shook her head so violently he pulled back.

"That's what you think of me? That I bought into that nonsense my father believed? That's who you think I am? Or was it just easy to damn me like that so you could move on and leave me?"

"I'm not the one who left you! You walked away from me. You chose him."

Yes, he had ignored what she'd asked. Just that once.

I do not want you to meet my father, Rico. Please. Let me take care of it.

But her father had called and left a message with his aunt. *Tell him to come see me. Tell him if he tells Ashna, he'll regret it. She's underage, having him thrown in jail won't be hard.*

Wow, he's all grace and warmth, Rico remembered thinking with all the cockiness of an eighteen-year-old. He hadn't believed the jail thing. Ashna would kill someone before she let that happen. His aunt had been terrified, but Rico had been sure he'd charm the man once he met him. So he'd gone. At the appointed time, as though his girlfriend's father were a judge and Rico had a hearing.

You think Ashna will go against our wishes? Our daughter doesn't do anything we don't approve of. Why do you think she never brought you home? She's a princess, you're a bastard. Does she know that your mother was your father's whore?

Even now the words made Rico want to wrap his hands around the man's throat and squeeze the life out of him. He didn't care that he was Ashna's father.

Then your daughter's going to be with a bastard. Because try what you want, Ashna and I are going to be together.

The man had gone red in the face. Spittle had flown from his mouth. He'd issued his challenge with absolute faith: *Try bad-mouthing me to her. She'll drop you like the garbage you are.*

He had been rummaging in a drawer while shouting obscenities at Rico when the door flew open. *What are you bellowing about now, Bram?* A tiny woman in a sari had pushed her way into the room and Rico had pushed his way out, done with this bullshit.

Your daughter is a whore like you. That's what I'm bellowing about. Those were the last words Rico remembered hearing.

Ashna had found him underneath the bleachers. Angrier than he'd ever been in his life. *Your father's a sick asshole. How can you stand to be around him?*

He's my father, Rico.

And that explains so much. I don't think I can deal with him for the rest of my life.

What are you saying? Are you leaving me?

Without waiting for an answer, she had run out of there. Had she really believed that's what he'd been doing? Leaving her because he hated her father?

Rico had waited there all night. She hadn't come back. No matter how much he'd begged after that, she hadn't come back.

"What did your father say to you, Ash? What did he say that changed everything?"

She pushed her hair off her face with both hands and gaped

at him, so much horror in her face it was like these past hours hadn't happened.

"I had never fought with my father, Rico. Never. Not until that day when I told him I couldn't live without you, and I wasn't going to. But when I came to you, you had already met him and you didn't want me. Not after you'd seen the ugliness I came from. Just the way my father said you wouldn't."

"I sat under those bleachers all night, waiting for you to come back. You didn't answer my calls. Didn't respond to my texts. And then you told me you were done with me. You didn't even ask what he said to me. He called my mother a whore, Ash. He was terrible to your mother, too. A real charmer you've got there. How can you believe anything he says?"

She sank down on the bench next to her, breathing hard. Something was very wrong. She looked up at him and he knew her response would change everything. Like the silence in a piece of music before it hits a crescendo.

"He died."

The muted horror in her eyes said there was more.

"When?"

Her hand pressed into her belly. "Twelve years this month."

"Twelve years this month," his whisper echoed hers, knowing exactly where they'd been twelve years ago. Done with high school. Excited about their future together. She on her way to UCLA on a soccer scholarship. Him taking a year off. Maybe coaching for their high school until he had enough money to figure out what he wanted to do. His father's friend, his old coach from Rio, had taken a managerial position with

Sunderland and he'd been trying to get Rico to try out. But at that point playing had still felt impossible.

He sat down next to her, but she was staring straight ahead at the gold wallpaper.

"How did it happen?"

Her hands clasped together and pressed into her lips, memories flashing in her eyes, creasing her forehead.

"He shot himself in the head." She spoke the words loud and clear, as though practicing diction. "That day."

"Oh God." He lifted his hand to reach for hers, but she jerked back.

Silence wrapped around them, a silence so corrosive, it shoved miles and years between them.

"That's why you didn't come back."

She laughed again, or maybe it was a sob. There were no tears in her eyes. "The family kept the suicide out of the papers."

When he'd tried to reach her he'd imagined every scenario except this one. The only response he'd gotten from her was that she was done with him. Rico hadn't wanted to believe that her father had convinced her that he wasn't good enough for her. But he'd seen her horror at his anger at her father and he'd believed it. He had walked away and never let himself turn back. Now he wondered if the horror in her eyes had been about her thinking he was leaving her.

She was in a trance. Her body rocked back and forth, the barest motion. "I heard it. The gunshot. I found him. After I left you and went back to the restaurant to see him." Her voice was the thinnest, strongest thread. "If I had been there one minute sooner, he'd still be alive."

Rico slid closer to her. When she didn't draw away from him, he placed a hand on her back, and when she didn't shrink from that, he wrapped his arm around her, a horrible coldness engulfing him. "I'm so sorry."

She said nothing; he wasn't even sure she had heard him, but she let him hold her.

Losing her had felt like being on fire. His lungs blackened and useless, his skin singed off. Solid stabs of pain separating muscle from bone. Turned out his pain had been nothing. He had abandoned her when she had needed him most.

How would she ever forgive him? How would he ever forgive himself?

"I'm sorry," he said again, then again. "I should have tried harder to reach you." But he had believed that she had forsaken him and chosen to believe her father's lies. "I should not have left."

She touched his face, generosity that brought him to his knees. "You couldn't have reached me. No one could. Not for a long time. He wasn't the only person that bullet destroyed that day."

They sat there like that. The immensity of what they had just learned hanging in the air between them.

"Rico," she said suddenly, her voice oddly stronger. "When you went to see him. How did you know he was terrible to my mother? Is it because of what I told you earlier?"

"No. Because she walked in when he started yelling." Rico remembered her father rummaging in the drawer. Was that where he kept the gun he used to kill himself? The maniacal rage in his eyes was something Rico would carry to his grave.

There had been something unhinged about him, something about that moment that had always felt odd, but Rico had tried to bury the memory deep, like the rest of that meeting. Now he wondered if Ashna's mother had saved his life that day.

"That can't be right." There was an odd confusion in her eyes when Ashna focused on him. "My mother wasn't in America when it happened. She only arrived after his death."

"I'm one hundred percent sure it was your mother." Suddenly Rico remembered everything in stark detail. The ponderous gloominess of the room covered from floor to ceiling with books. The sharp scent of alcohol, sweat, and vomit in the overcooled air. The congested, raspy note in her father's voice.

"I even remember that she was wearing a sari . . . it was blue . . . and she had a huge red bindi on her forehead."

Ashna stood, her face leached of color. "I have to go." She opened the door and let herself into the elevator lobby.

He followed her. "What's going on, Ash?"

She came to him then and grabbed his face. "I'm sorry. For everything."

What the hell was that supposed to mean? "Tell me what I said. Tell me what to do. I know what I did was unforgivable, but please don't leave me again."

"It wasn't unforgivable." She bit her lip and looked at him in a way that made his heart burst with love and gratitude. "It wasn't your fault." The fierceness he'd missed shone in her eyes. "It wasn't mine either." She dropped a kiss on his lips. "I'm not leaving you. I promise. I just need to go right now, okay?"

"Let me take you home."

"No, I need to do this myself. It's something I should have done a long time ago."

He had no idea what she meant, but she had that look again, a look that reinforced her words. She wasn't leaving him, just leaving. *Please let that be the truth.* "At least let George take you home."

That of all things made her smile. "This is the birthplace of rideshares, Rico. You're not summoning George to drive me home, but will you please give him a raise?" She pressed a finger into the elevator button.

"Actually, you're wrong," he said. "Rideshares originated in Africa—Zimbabwe, it was crowdsourcing of carpools . . ." He trailed off, but it made her go up on her toes and kiss him again, hard and fierce.

He wrapped his arms around her and returned her kiss, gathered up her essence. But when she pulled away he let her go. Whatever helped her believe they'd make it, he would do.

"I love you, Ash," he whispered into her lips before stepping away.

"I love you too," she said simply, hands still on his face. "But that's never been our problem."

The elevator opened with a ding and she got in.

"I'm not leaving, Ashna. No matter what happens, I'm never leaving you again," he said before the mirrored doors cut them off, because that much he had to say.

Chapter Thirty-Three

All through the ride home, Ashna felt oddly strong.

The way Rico looked at her filled her heart. All the things they'd said to each other filled her heart. They'd held nothing back, and she was still standing. Hope flooded her like she'd sprung a backward leak.

Something precious lay within her reach, but she couldn't have it if she stayed the person she'd been. The only way to not be that person was to face the secrets she'd run from for so long. If Mom had been with Baba that day, what did that mean?

If unraveling her relationship with Mom meant unraveling with it, then so be it. She was already undone, and it wasn't as scary as anticipating it had been. All that mattered now was how she put herself back together.

Ashna opened her front door and let herself into her house, ready for whatever awaited her.

The living room was tidy. The mustard and green pillows arranged in an exact diamond pattern. The kitchen cleaned up. No dishes in the sink. No glasses or cups strewn about the place. No scarves or stoles draped around chairs.

Had Mom left without telling her? Again? Now, when Ashna needed her, needed the truth? Now, when she realized just how much she didn't know?

I'm not leaving. No matter what happens, I'm never leaving you again.

Words Shobi and Rico had both said to her. Her life had turned into a sonorous chamber with the same sounds coming at her from all directions. It couldn't be a lie.

An urge to scream swelled in her chest. On the way here, she had practiced what she would say to her mother. The questions she would ask. How patient she would be. She'd finally *listen*.

Now she wouldn't have the chance.

She stormed into the living room and disheveled the cushions. Her hands shook. Her skin felt too tight around her. The kitchen was empty too, and sparkling clean.

"Mom?" the word broke her voice as she called out.

She ran up the stairs and into her room and yanked open the dresser drawer. The mother-of-pearl inlay box winked up at her, concealing within it her mother's ring. The one Ashna had pulled out of the garbage at thirteen, another symbol of her parents' ugly marriage, which she'd believed made her ugly too. Pushing open her window, she pulled her arm back and tossed the box, ring and all, into the enchanted forest of her childhood, letting out the ungodly scream that was choking her.

"Ashna, sweetheart, what's wrong?" Shobi's voice hit her like something in a dream, piercing through her back like an arrow.

She spun around. "Mom?"

Worry creased Shobi's forehead. "What the matter, beta?"

"I thought you left."

"Mina and I were having tea on the patio. We didn't hear you come in until you . . . why did you scream?"

"If you screamed because you thought Shobi was gone, then that's good news, right?" Mina Kaki walked into the room behind Mom.

Then the funniest thing happened: both Ashna and Shobi rolled their eyes and smiled at the same time.

"Did you stay the night?" Ashna asked her aunt.

"I could hardly leave Shobi by herself when . . . well, you look better than you did last night." Mina Kaki raised a brow.

"I'm fine. I need to talk to Mom."

"I want to talk to you too," Shobi said, eyes exhausted and edged with bags that hadn't been there last night.

"The house . . . thanks for cleaning up." It felt like a stupid thing to say, but her mother smiled.

"Mina helped."

"In other words, I tidied up while Shoban Gaikwad Raje lectured me about being complacent in being judged for domesticity," Mina Kaki said.

"It's true. Who says our homes have to look like magazines? It's just another arena they use to make us compete and feel insufficient in," Mom said, and of all things, it made Ashna smile.

"That's all very good and dandy," Mina Kaki said. "But what if we don't all like to exist in chaos? Choice is a two-sided concept, Shobi-ji."

"Hello?" Ashna cleared her throat. Both women turned to her. This was not how Ashna had expected this day to go. Or yesterday. That thought was followed by the memory of her climbing Rico like a tree.

"Sorry," Mina Kaki said. "Why is your window open?"

Oh no, the ring! Ashna slapped a hand to her mouth.

"Umm . . . I just threw a three-carat diamond out the window."

The two women stared at her openmouthed. Possibly the only time in her life Ashna would get to see that.

Pushing her way past them, she ran down the stairs. "We have a lot to talk about, but I have to find the ring first. I think I know what I want to do with it." Suddenly she didn't want that ring lost.

The three of them went out into the yard below Ashna's window and started searching through the grass.

"That's the trajectory." Shobi used her finger to trace an arc from the second-floor window into the hedges.

"Behold someone who's turned analysis into an art form." Mina went to a giant rosebush where Shobi's arc had ended. "I think it's in there." She pointed without letting her finger touch the bush.

"Behold someone who's turned delegation into an art form," Shobi said.

"Really, you two pick today to turn into a comedy duo?" Ashna grabbed a fallen branch and pushed the thorny branches apart with it. Long-ago memories of her aunt and her mother laughing together sparkled at the edge of her consciousness. How many memories had she buried?

"There it is," all three of them said, and Ashna squatted down and used her leg to nudge it out like a ball.

It earned her impressed raised eyebrows. She slid the box into her pocket.

"I'll leave you two alone now," Mina said. "You have a lot to talk about. And yesterday was Monday and I didn't go home. So Shree's going to be extra grumpy today because Mondays are . . . you know . . . our day."

Oh God. Oh God. Oh God. Could she unhear this?

Shobi let out a full-throated laugh. Where had she been hiding that thing?

The same place you've been hiding yours, a voice inside Ashna said.

"The child looks horrified," Shobi said, making Mina shrug.

"They think we're celibate, don't they?"

"Mina Kaki!" Ashna said. "Thank you so much for . . . for . . . being here." That sounded terrible. "I mean . . ."

"I know what you mean." She patted Ashna's cheek. "You kids have to stop thinking of your moms as single-function devices. We have lives apart from you. We are people. We have orgasms." Before Ashna could die of mortification, Mina took her hand. "Can you walk me out?"

That was code for *I'm not done talking to you.*

"I'll see you inside," Shobi said, shaking her head at Mina.

Mina Kaki got in her car, rolled down her window, and turned to Ashna. "When Shobi and I were younger, we used to talk a lot about our girls growing up. We swore they would not face what we faced. We wanted to make sure you girls didn't have to fight our fights and the fights of our mothers. It's time to put that behind us, don't you think?"

Ashna nodded. She knew her aunt wasn't done.

"I like to believe we changed things at least a little, your mother more than me. But in this changed world, you girls can't seem to see how it was for us. You can't see our obstacles because we removed them for you. And now you get to judge us from a perspective that we weren't lucky enough to enjoy."

"I'm sorry," Ashna said around the lump in her throat.

Mina smiled the smile that had made Ashna's childhood bearable. "It's the last thing we want you to be, beta." With that she blew Ashna a kiss and was gone.

"You all right?" Shobi was just done putting the kettle on as Ashna walked into the kitchen.

Ashna flew into her arms.

Shobhi's arms went around her, tight, so tight they almost suffocated her. A memory burst through Ashna. Ages ago her mother had always held her like this, too tight for breath.

I'll die, Mamma.

I'll bring you back to life so I can squeeze the life out of you again.

Then those hugs had turned into goodbyes and Ashna hadn't been able to bear them anymore.

She couldn't breathe, but in that breathlessness the tears washed through her, taking with them so many things she'd let fester for years and years.

"I'm sorry." Those were the first words that came.

Shobi slowly let her go. "What are you sorry for?"

"I always blamed you for everything, but it was always my fault. And I thought you had left again."

Her mother wiped Ashna's tears with the end of her sari, a gesture so absurdly campy and Bollywoodish and so at odds with who Shobi was that a watery laugh burst from Ashna. She pulled away, some awkwardness returning.

"None of this was your fault." For the first time in her life those words didn't feel like thorns on her skin. "And I'm glad," Shobi added quickly, holding Ashna's hands, "that the thought of me having left didn't make you happy."

"I felt many things when you left, Mom. But happiness was never one of them." Of all the things Ashna had ever said to her mother, this was probably the most honest.

She pushed Shobi onto a stool. "Why don't you sit, I'll make us some tea. I know the exact brew that might make this easier." She brought ginger and lemongrass to a boil, then added a mix of Cunoor long leaf and Darjeeling as her mother watched. Then she wrote the words *Overdue Conversations* on the jar.

"You're very good at this." Shobi picked up the two steaming cups Ashna filled and took them to the living room.

Ashna followed her with a plate of biscuits. "Turns out I like flavors and how they make people feel."

Before sitting down next to her mother, she extracted the jewelry box from her pocket and put it on the coffee table.

Shobi looked at it. "You said there's a ring in there?"

Ashna opened the box and watched recognition dawn on her mother's face. "I dug it out of the garbage after Baba threw it away all those years ago. I used to dream of you thanking me for saving your marriage. I was so stupid."

Shoban blew into the steaming cup. "That's not stupid at all. It's incredibly sweet." She took a sip, and it seemed to loosen her shoulders. "I'm sorry I put you through that. I'm sorry for everything I put you through."

Ashna snapped the box shut. "Mom, I'm the one who's sorry. And please . . . please don't say it wasn't my fault. There's something else I have to ask you."

Her mother gave her a hard look. "No one forced me to have you. You were always wanted. I couldn't let you go because from the moment I knew you were inside me, I knew who you were going to be. Does that make sense?"

It was hard to drink tea with a constricted throat. Ashna put her cup down. "No. Not even a little bit." But it did warm her heart. "That wasn't what I was going to ask. But . . . thank you."

"What did you want to know, then?"

"Why didn't you ever tell me that you saw Baba the day he died?"

The surprise on Shobi's face was stark, but instead of getting flustered, she stayed calm and sure. "I didn't want you to hate me even more. I thought you'd blame me for his death."

Ashna picked up her cup again and took a sip. "I wouldn't have blamed you. Not because I was ever generous to you, but because it wasn't your fault. It was mine. I was the one to blame. I was the one who pushed him over the edge."

"No, you weren't."

They looked at each other over the cups of tea.

"There's so much you don't know," they both said together, as though this were a Shakespearean farce.

"Me first, please," Ashna said.

Shobi put her cup down and nodded, pulling her legs up on the couch and crossing them. "Fine."

"The reason I know you were there that day, it's . . . it's because, well, there was a boy there that day too. You met him when Baba was yelling at him."

Shobi's hand went to her mouth. "Oh. Now I know why Rico Silva looks so familiar. Oh, Ashi." She reached over and took Ashna's hand. "No wonder he looks at you that way."

Ashna felt the insistent warmth that always wrapped her up at the mention of Rico rise across her face. "I met him in high school. I was so in love with him, Mom." *"Was"? Please.*

"You didn't tell anyone? Not even Mina or your cousins?"

"No. I was terrified. I was such a coward. But Baba found Rico's messages on my phone and . . . and he told me that he'd rather die that let me be with Rico. I didn't believe him."

Her mother scooted closer and kissed Ashna's hand. She had warm, strong hands. Competent hands. "And you've spent the past twelve years blaming yourself for it and punishing yourself for it."

"I shut you out. I shut Rico out. I felt like a cheater when I was happy."

"Is that why Rico is here? For you."

"I don't know. I . . . Yes."

"He slid across your kitchen on his knees—after surgery—to keep you from getting hurt. Please tell me you see what that is?" She squeezed Ashna's hand against her chest. "That's love tinged with madness, love that takes you out of yourself. That's not love you take lightly, Ashi."

Ashna swallowed. She couldn't give up Rico if she tried.

"Did Bram tell you he wasn't good enough for you? That you'd be shaming the family? That you deserved someone at your 'social level'? Someone culturally and religiously similar to you?"

"Word for word. How did you know?"

"Because that's exactly what my father said to me." With a deep sigh Shobi squeezed her forehead.

"It's okay, Mom. Tell me."

"I love you more than anything, you have to know that. This, this having you look at me as though I am not the most painful thing in your life, I would sell my soul to never let this go. Just remember that, please, because there's more you don't know."

Ashna squeezed her mother's hands. "Tell me. I'm not leaving, Mom, and I won't push you away. I promise."

And so Shobi told her.

How she had ended up a Raje.

How she had become a mother and found her power.

How she had started her foundation.

How she had never looked at her own father again. Not even when he lay dying.

Finally, she told her why she'd been so angry with her father and Bram.

"Is his name Omar?" Ashna asked when Shobi told her she'd been in love with someone else. Shobi's shock was palpable. "I overheard your fights, remember?"

Her mother apologized again, but her eyes shone bright when she talked about the man. "Yes. The day I saw your

Rico in your father's office, I had come to California to bring Bram divorce papers. That's why I never told you I was coming, I had wanted to take care of that, then explain everything to you. It wasn't you who pushed him over the edge. It was me."

Or maybe it was both things happening on the same day. Or maybe it was just the fact that he could never reconcile with his life and find a way to treat his illness. A few weeks ago, her mother's revelation would have broken Ashna. Now it made her sad, but it also helped her understand so much.

"I wish I had tried to get him help," Ashna said.

"His family did try repeatedly to get him help. You can't fix something if you don't acknowledge it." Shobi pushed a lock of hair behind Ashna's ear. "I wish I had kept you away from all that, from him. I relied too heavily on Mina and Shree. I wish I had been a better mother. It was cruel what I let you go through. I want to tell you that it was because I didn't grasp the level of his irresponsibility as a father, but it wasn't on you to tell me how much his alcoholism has progressed. None of this is on you and I am so very sorry." For the first time in her life Ashna saw tears swell in her eyes and fall down her cheeks. "Funny thing is, I was so immersed in fighting cruelty that I didn't stop to think about my own. I wish I had done things differently."

Ashna wiped her tears. "No, you don't." Her tone had a hint of teasing, which stunned her. But she felt no anger right now and it was rebirth. "You would do the same thing again."

Her mother's smile was tenuous. "I want to say that I

would not. But it's not simple. I do wish you hadn't been hurt; that part I would change for anything. I would give up everything now, to keep that from happening. If you believe nothing else, believe that I've regretted not having you in my life every single day. But I didn't know how to put my head down and comply.

"Growing up, we were surrounded by stories of women being married off without their consent, and it was always about how they compromised, reconciled, and found love in the end. It was romanticized so much. What an abhorrent thing to tell someone—that your love isn't where your interests lie, or that your parents know what's best for you better than you do. You know what's best for you, beta, only you."

How could Ashna argue with that, or begrudge her mother not having put her head down and complied?

"So you just went back to him? Mrs. Shoban Gaikwad Raje who was in the papers all the time. Weren't you scared of the media, of scandal?" Even as she asked it, she couldn't imagine her mother being scared, and if she were scared, she couldn't imagine her bowing to fear.

Shoban gave Ashna a cheeky look that made her laugh. "Basically we snuck around. My choice, not his. I realize that it's not fair to him, but he's never asked for any more than I could give him. We don't hide our relationship, but we don't share it with the media either. I've kept the press's focus on my work and kept my life private. The world is filled with open secrets." She took Ashna's hands again and kissed them, gratitude shining in her jet black eyes. It was obvious how very much she wanted Ashna to like Omar. "When we first met, he was the only person I knew who wanted me to be me. By the time we found our way back to each other, I had become a person who could only be me, no matter what anyone else wanted. Maybe that's the big love story. Finding that."

Chapter Thirty-Four

It had been six hours since Ashna had seen Rico, but it felt like a lifetime. She missed him something fierce. The worry in his eyes when she'd left that morning, the determined hope, had been burning inside her. The fact that it hadn't occurred to him to push her to stay or to try to figure things out for her made her want to climb into his arms and never let go.

The final episode was being shot live today, an effort by the network to leverage the show's tremendous success. After spending all morning talking to her mother—about the past but mostly about the future, because Shobi was this tornado of forward movement—Ashna had left for the studio. Then she'd changed her mind and rerouted her ride to Rico's hotel.

Her heart raced as she went to the front desk and asked them to call him. The person who had stormed in here yesterday feeling irreparably ugly, that wasn't the person who smiled at the receptionist today.

Only, this new person was an idiot, because she hadn't considered that Rico might not be there waiting for her. He wasn't in his room.

It. Means. Nothing. She told herself as she said thank you and sped out of the hotel only to find that the rideshare time to destination was half an hour, because the street to the hotel was clogged up with traffic. If she called a car she would be late.

She started walking. It was a forty-minute walk to the studio. What had she been thinking coming here before the shoot? If she had remembered to ask Rico for his number, this wouldn't have happened.

When she got to the studio, Rico wasn't there either. Worry started to bubble inside her and she went to see if China knew where he was. She heard a scrambling behind the door when she knocked.

Inside, Song was sitting on China's couch looking preternaturally cool, except that her hair was disheveled.

"Do you know where Rico is?" she asked, because Song and China were both frozen in place.

Song jumped up and flew at Ashna. "Don't worry, he's almost here." There was an odd excitement in her eyes, even more than her usual enthusiasm. A weird sort of joy glowed from her.

"You know where he is?" Ashna asked, confused.

Song wiggled her brows and bounced on her heels. "Yes," she squeaked, "and I'm going to explode with excitement."

What on earth did that mean? Ashna looked at China—still uncharacteristically speechless—for an explanation.

"I have to go touch up my lipstick," Song said with a look at China that Ashna could only interpret as heat.

"She's not interested in Rico," China said the moment she left.

"Oh," Ashna said, recognizing China's tone. It was possessive. "*Oh!*"

China beamed at her. "Um, yeah. Lots to tell you."

Ashna beamed back. "Rico's not interested in her either. And um . . . I have lots to tell you too."

With matching squeals they hugged each other and Ashna rushed to the green room.

In another twenty minutes Ashna was waiting at their kitchen station by herself, red chef's jacket on, hair in a bun, red lipstick, bronze eye shadow, her usual. Only, today she felt resplendent and madly excited.

There were three stations left. The auditorium seating had been doubled, for "surprise guests," China told her cryptically.

Rico, Song, and Danny were the stars competing in the final today, but the eliminated stars and chefs were in the studio audience. Lilly, Tatiana, and P.T. stopped by to say hi. Danny was "centering himself" in the green room. The man had become obsessed with winning. Ashna was sure the network was going to pick him up as a regular.

Then, just like that, the temperature in the room changed. Something shifted inside Ashna. She heard his steps behind her and smelled his scent, and her entire nervous system spun into eddies like pinwheels exploding in the sky.

"Hi," he said next to her.

She braced herself and turned to him. "It's five minutes before we start shooting. Everything all right?"

"Not at all," he said, his heart in his eyes. "I'm ruined for life." He slipped his hand into hers behind the countertop and more fireworks went through her. "You look happy. Things go okay with your mom?"

"I'm so happy, Rico. She's . . . there's so much I didn't know." Hiding her hope was impossible, so she didn't even try.

He dropped a kiss on her cheek, forgetting all about the cameras.

"Now that our missing star is here," China announced, "let's get started. Today we have a secret audience. They'll be watching you, but you won't know who's there."

"Fabulous," Rico whispered. "More people we can't get rid of."

The producers had decided to get downright sadistic. They announced, with some glee, that the work surfaces were being shrunk down to one small two-foot countertop. The crew made a big show of coming in and rolling away two-thirds of each kitchen station.

"We're live today," DJ announced. "There will be no audience voting. The judges will rank the runners-up and announce the winner."

Danny El gave Rico a jubilant smile and Rico gave him a thumbs-up.

Their challenge was to make a holiday dinner in half an hour and in that restricted space. Display teamwork in those tight conditions. Ashna's heart spasmed wildly every time their bodies touched, the memories of their night together a fire inside her.

Then DJ threw them their curveball. They could choose only five kitchen tools total to work with.

"Bring it on," Ashna said to the camera, "because I'm nothing if not a minimalist."

The first utensil they chose was . . . wait for it . . . a knife (insert womb-melting smile here), a ten-inch santoku, the exact same style that had started them off on their second chance.

"What did your family make for holiday dinners?" she asked, turning to him.

"Lamb chops. It was my pai's favorite thing to make."

Amazingly, lamb chops were also Baba's favorite thing. He had a near-perfect recipe. He had considered his recipes his life's work. Ashna knew she should be angrier at Baba than she was, but the only emotion she felt when she thought about him was sadness.

She also knew she couldn't follow his recipe. Not today.

"What's the matter, meu amor?" Rico said.

"I'm fine." She put a cast-iron grill pan on the stove. "What do you remember most about what your pai put in his lamb chops?"

"I think it was basically salt, pepper, and garlic." He squeezed his eyes shut and focused so hard that not dropping a kiss on his earnestly pursed mouth was the hardest thing. His eyes opened, bright with memory. "Of course. Mint."

"That's perfect. Since we're allowed only five tools, simple is good."

"My mãe always made rice and potatoes with it. How about we make lamb chops and a biryani-style pilaf?"

Ashna blinked. Since when was Rico such a foodie?

He shrugged but his lips tugged to one side in his crooked

smile. "What? I live in London. Of course Indian is my favorite cuisine."

Tossing an onion at him, she asked him to start chopping, and put the rice to boil.

Then she turned to the lamb chops. The automatic reflex to follow Baba's recipe to within an inch of its life rolled through her. But when she ignored it, the need to hyperventilate didn't follow. Next to her Rico was fully tuned in to her body language, dividing his focus between following the instructions she threw out and the job at hand.

As he'd talked about his father's chops, she'd imagined exactly how she wanted them to taste. An overtone of garlic and lemon and an undertone of mint. The rice would be simple, in keeping with the Brazilian tradition, but she'd liven it up with fried onions, cashew nuts, whole black cardamom, cloves, bay leaves, and cinnamon stick. All she wanted was to create something that tasted like Rico's childhood, combined with their future together, and it felt like she was flying.

Just like with her teas, she knew exactly what she wanted to taste and she knew exactly how to layer ingredients to coax out those flavors, those *feelings*. It was her and that alchemy and Rico's hands flying to follow instructions and help her make it happen.

"There's another thing we have to make," she said. Rico raised a brow as he stirred rice into the spice-infused butter. "I want to make tea. A festive chai."

He smiled, heat intensifying his eyes.

Really? Talking about tea turned him on? Wasn't the universe just full of good news today.

Smiling from under her lashes, she looked around at their two used pans. "Focus, Rico. We don't have any more utensils to use."

"You get the ingredients. I'll wash the pan we used for the rice."

She squeezed his arm and got to work.

"That smells amazing," he said as the chai came to a boil.

When she gave him a taste his eyes did things they should not be doing here in public.

"How are we going to pour it without a strainer?"

"Is a paper napkin considered a utensil?" Rico pulled one from a roll.

Well, someone would stop them if it was. Ashna placed a napkin on each cup, gave it a poke to make an indentation, and poured.

DJ started to count down the last ten seconds. Ashna finished tearing some mint and sprinkled it on the rice. Just as he called out "Time's up," Ashna stepped back and tossed the knife high up in the air.

The entire studio went silent, holding one long combined breath. The knife spun in the air, the sharp silver edge catching the light, and landed neatly back in Ashna's hand.

The crowd went crazy.

Rico picked her up and spun her around.

As the food was being transferred onto trolleys to be taken to the judges, China announced that their families were in the audience again.

The one-way screens between the staging area and the audience were moved away and there they were: her family. Her uncle and aunt; Nisha and her husband Neel; Mishka; Trisha; Yash; and right there squeezed between Trisha and Nisha, Mom.

Her mother's eyes shone with pride. She winked at Ashna after a quick look at Rico.

Ashna searched the audience for Zee, but he wasn't there, and her heart twisted.

As soon as they went to break so the contestants could mingle with their families, China brought Rico an iPad with Zee on live video chat.

Zee and Tanya were squeezed tightly together in the frame. Tanya was even more stunning than Ashna had imagined, hair in braids and beautiful black eyes that swept up at the edges. They were supposed to fly out last night, but Tanya had felt sick and they had gone to the hospital and found out that Rico was going to be an uncle.

"Another godchild, Uncle Rico," Zee said.

"Bring it on, mate," Rico said, joy brightening his face.

Just as Ashna and he said bye, her niece flew at her. "Ashi Maushi! Can you introduce me to Danny? He was so amazing!"

"Why thank you, darling." Ashna squeezed her. "I'm so touched to have you rooting for me."

"Well, of course you're going to win. Because everyone loves you and your new boyfriend."

"Mishka!" Nisha said.

"Come on, Mom! You and Dad said it too. Don't you always say we don't have to pretend with family?"

Nisha let out a resigned sigh.

Yash and Rico pumped each other's hands like they were long-lost loves too, and it made Ashna giggle.

Mom and Mina Kaki both squeezed Rico's cheeks and kissed his forehead.

"That's how *desi* grannies show their affection," Mishka said, and this time her father ruffled her hair and asked her to behave.

"What? At least I didn't say anything about how excited everyone is that Ashi Maushi finally found a boyfriend."

Ashna squeezed Rico's hand. He looked entirely unfazed by the circus, which made her press into him. A move not a single one of them missed.

"So actually." Ashna cleared her throat. "He's not a new boyfriend." She looked up at Rico and his eyes were intensely focused on her, his breath held. "Rico and I knew each other in high school."

"Knew?" Trisha said.

"Biblically?" Mishka said, and this time Nisha gasped and slapped a hand across her daughter's mouth. "What?" Mishka said, undaunted. "Trisha Maushi said she and DJ Kaka knew each other biblically when you guys were talking."

Rico started shaking with silent laughter against Ashna.

Ashna ruffled her niece's hair. "We were in love. We still are." She went up on her toes and kissed his lips, quick and full and tender, right there in front of everyone.

Shobi was the first one to start laughing. "All right then."

Mina turned to her. "She told you?" She sounded somewhere between offended and delighted.

An avalanche of questions came at Ashna. "You didn't tell us!" "So this was your junior year? See, I knew something was up. You were never home." "Did you go to Paris with him?"

"We'll talk later," Ashna said. "But we broke up at the end of senior year."

The mention of her senior year silenced everyone for a moment.

"Did you get on the show because of her?" Yash asked.

Rico's arm was still tight around Ashna. "Never stopped missing her. Googled her. Saw the announcement for the show and bullied myself in."

"That explains a lot!" Ashna said and kissed him again.

One of the assistants made an announcement for everyone to start getting back to their seats. The judges had finished deliberating and had their results.

Yash threw Rico a look Ashna couldn't quite interpret. "Thanks for the email you sent me about the news pieces being the start of a smear campaign. You were right, we've been able to trace some pretty tenacious digging. I was wondering if you had any ideas about how to address it. And, well, if you had any interest in helping with the campaign."

Rico looked at Ashna like a child thrown into a ball-pit of candy.

Really? She widened her eyes at him.

He shrugged. *You okay with that?*

Was he kidding? This was perfect.

"You're bringing him to dinner tomorrow," Mina Kaki declared before everyone was ushered back into place.

"Welcome to the family," Shobi said, and gave Rico a hug.

When they were lined up in the staging area again, Ashna could barely bring herself to care about what the judges thought. Then their plates were in front of the judges and adrenaline started to pump through her. Reaching for Rico's hands, she pulled his arms around herself.

His heartbeat thudded against her back. They were up first.

"What on earth was that?" the food editor judge asked, mimicking (very exaggeratedly) Ashna's knife move.

The rom-com director stood up and clapped, setting off another round of hooting applause. "That, my friend, was fabulous television."

"Looks like we're witnessing the beginning of something here." The chef judge who had been most critical of their food threw a suggestive look between them.

"What gave us away?" Rico said lazily, and Ashna laughed.

"So, we're not wrong, then?" the other chef judge asked.

Ashna shrugged at the camera.

"As a matter of fact . . ." Rico said, his tone insanely reckless.

Ashna's heart started to hammer. Her entire family was in the audience. The entire world was watching.

His hands rubbed up and down her arms. "There is something I've been meaning to ask Chef Raje, and it makes sense that you're all here to witness it." His hand went to his pants pocket.

Every single person in the audience gasped.

Ashna thought she was going to faint.

"Ashna Raje, would you do me the honor of—" he said with far too much sincerity and anticipation as he reached into his pocket. He pulled out his phone. "—of giving me your number? Because it's about damn time."

Ashna pressed her face into her hands, her heart falling

back in her chest. Laughter exploded in the room. Nisha and Trisha were on their feet whooping.

Instead of dying of mortification, Ashna burst into laughter—clean untainted laughter. "I thought you'd never ask," she said, bringing the audience to their feet again. Then, taking Rico's phone from him, she entered her number.

Finally, the judges tasted their dish, and loved it, but no one seemed to care.

The other two dishes were just as spectacular. Danny El had managed to make some sort of turducken, which was creepy and amazing at the same time.

When he won, Ashna could hardly begrudge him.

"I came here to prove something," she said when they shot reactions to the results. She sought her mother out in the crowd. "And to get people to discover Curried Dreams. What I'm taking away from here is something I never thought I'd find again."

If that wasn't the understatement of her life, she didn't know what was.

After a long few hours of celebrations and interviews, Ashna and Rico made their way back to Rico's hotel.

They started kissing in the elevator and Ashna was convinced her life had turned into a movie. They stumbled into the suite, still kissing.

Ashna hadn't been this breathless, this excited ever, and it had been a breathless few weeks. They kissed like they hadn't seen each other in centuries. Like parched earth in a cloud-burst.

"You almost gave me a heart attack there, Rico!" she said when they came up for air. "What is wrong with you?"

"Other than the fact that not being able to check up on you this morning almost killed me?"

"I'm sorry. Things got to be a lot with my mom."

He stroked her cheek. "She's lovely. There's so much of her in you."

She nodded and kissed him again, because hearing that made beautiful feelings dance inside her.

With one tug at the clasp in her bun, he made her hair slide down her back. "Did you really think I'd propose to you on live television? It's like you think I don't know you at all."

"Thanks for knowing me." She stroked his lips with the pad of her thumb. "Also, I would have killed you if you had done it. There were knives there."

He kissed her fingers and unleashed his chuckle on her poor heart. "First, I know how you feel about proposals putting the power of a relationship's future in a man's hands." She had told him that back in high school. She hated the rabid romanticizing of proposals—as though the act of women waiting to be claimed were a good thing. "If I did want to express my feelings—in a non-proposal—I would do it in private. Just you and me. Maybe in a room where I finally had you back in my arms, where I had prayed so hard to have you back, I don't know how I didn't crack the walls."

He fell to his knees.

"Rico, your knee."

"Good as new."

She went down on her knees in front of him. "What are you doing?"

"Exactly what you think. You ready? It's going to be a long

speech." He extracted a box from his pocket and flipped it open. There, on white satin, sat the most exquisite blood red ruby circled in diamonds.

She wiped the tear that slid down his cheek. He was too choked up to speak. "I'm waiting for the speech."

He swallowed and squeezed her hand, his own shaking. "All those years ago when we were together, I used to wonder what might happen if you left me. I remember the terror of it. Finding you after I had lost everything—it felt like too much. I used to have nightmares about losing you too. I knew I wasn't strong enough to bear it. I imagined each day to be hell, I imagined having no way out. But I had no idea.

"I didn't know then that hell would be in the littlest things—in meeting a perfectly lovely person and having my heart yearn for you, in touching someone else and wanting to feel you. My heart held you up like a mirror, a line on a wall where the height of my feelings would never again be as tall. It might have been easier without the intermittent normalcy between the blasts of memory, where your voice, your taste was so vivid it undid everything. After all those years of forcing myself not to give in to the yearning to search for you, it was the best thing I ever did, because it led me back to you, back to the me I had lost. I don't know how to be me without you.

"Ash, meu amor, will you please put me out of my misery and let me spend the rest of my life with you?"

"That *was* long," Ashna said through a sniffle. "And beautiful."

"I wrote it when you left this morning. On the hotel notepad." He pointed at the desk. "I thought I'd bring it to you, an old-fashioned letter. Then I read it so many times I knew it by heart, and I heard my mãe's voice telling me I couldn't say those things without a ring. I knew rings make you uncomfortable, but I did want to honor my mãe and get you something. Good thing Song's sister knows a jeweler."

This time he wiped her cheek.

She took the ruby out of the box. It was a pendant on a chain. Rising to her feet, she helped him up. "It's not something, Rico. It's everything."

"Turn it around."

On the back was engraved #*Ashico*.

She was laugh-crying so hard she could barely speak. "Will you put it on me?"

They walked to the mirror in the alcove, where he had shown her what it meant to be beautiful. There again in his eyes was the only thing that made anyone truly beautiful. Love.

Slipping her hair onto one shoulder, he hooked it around her neck. A chain that didn't feel like a chain but a lifeline. Then he kissed her neck, eyes locked with hers in the mirror.

"Thank you for finding me again." She leaned into his kiss, took his hand and pressed it against her full heart. "Happiness seeps into me when you're around, Rico. Without invitation, without notice, joy finds me. Being around you is being alive, it's breathing, it's home."

Then she let him lift her up and place her on the table against the mirror, and she was reminded again exactly how loud the love of her life could be.

Chapter Thirty-Five

*S*mashing the patriarchy is complicated business. It's true that you can't throw a punch without hurting your knuckles, but it's time to stop telling women that it's all or nothing, that it's only valuable if it hurts.' That was my favorite line, Mom," Ashna said, telling her mother again how fabulous her award acceptance speech had been.

"When you and Rico have a baby girl, she can be whomever she wants to be," Shobi said.

"So long as she's badass. And plays soccer—okay, any sport. And doesn't cut her hair. And takes over the restaurant. And her grandmother's institute," Ashna said with a laugh.

"Goes without saying."

Mother and daughter sat on a Sagar Mahal terrace overlooking the cliff that dropped into the Arabian Sea, drinking tea and watching the waves crash into rocks. Ashna leaned her head on her mother's shoulder. "If you had fallen in line, I'd have had a happy childhood. And I'd have married who you and Baba picked for me. It wouldn't have been a bad life, but then we wouldn't know what it's like to love these two."

Omar came up the cliff, the breeze ruffling his silver hair and squeezed Shobi's shoulders and dropped a kiss on Ashna's head. Then he proceeded to pour the tea Shobi handed him from a bone china cup into a black stoneware cup.

He dropped into a wicker chair across from them. "*Kya guftagu chal rahi hai ma beti mein?*" Whatever he said sounded incredibly poetic and Mom's eyes went soft and hazy.

Every woman deserved that, Ashi was thinking when a wet face pressed into her cheek from behind. "Yuck, you're all sweaty," she said, and Rico shook his head and splattered some more sweat all over her.

Rico and Omar were supposed to have gone for a *walk*. "How much did you run? You'll hurt your knee again."

"I won't. It's good as new," he said stubbornly and poured himself tea.

"I think the man is fully capable of gauging his own pain levels," Mom said as Rico kissed her cheek and sank down on the marble floor between Ashna and Shobi.

"Thanks, Mom, I'm not doubting his capability."

"And yet, you won't let me swim because I get ear infections," Omar said sagely into his tea. There was a warm strength to him, and Mom's entire demeanor relaxed in his presence.

"That's because you're not thirty anymore. And you get cranky when you're in pain," Shobi said with the most ineffective frown, because her eyes were twinkling.

"But he's old enough to know how to put some earplugs in his ears." Ashna shook the hand Omar held out.

"Want to go for a swim later, beta?" Omar said to Ashna. They had spent last evening jumping the waves and he had explained the backwards process with which Bollywood lyrics were written to retrofit already composed music. The man seemed to approach life with a sardonic yet empathetic eye, and a calm passion that was the yin to her mother's fiery yang.

"Of course." The Sripore ocean was Ashna's favorite place to swim, and she had forgotten quite how much she loved it.

The four of them sat there sipping Ashna's newest blend. She called it *Family Ties*. Tomorrow Rico and she would go back to their lives in California—Rico to his new job as Yash's campaign strategist; Ashna to the renovations they were doing on Curried Dreams. Her mother had paid off the mortgage and freed Ashna up to gather more debt in rebuilding it to be a chai and pastries place.

Ashna hated the idea of leaving Mom, but distance no longer felt like separation. They already had Shobi and Omar's next trip scheduled for Curried Dreams' grand relaunch in three months.

It had been Aji's idea to totally gut the place and "bring it into this new era."

"If I changed Curried Dreams, would that be horrible?" Ashna had asked her grandmother the day after the show ended, when she took Mom's ring back to return to her. It was a memory of her son, after all, and a family heirloom.

"Nobody in their right mind would say you haven't done everything possible to save your father's restaurant," Aji had said with her limitless kindness. "Sometimes, no matter what you do things can't be saved. Or even people. I should have said this to you years ago. But I never wanted to admit it. For a mother to see a child self-destruct is the worst kind of pain.

I do believe I tried everything with Bram. I tried *saam, daam, dand, bhed*—the traditional four steps to fixing any problem: logic, bribery, punishment, and separation. I tried affection, tough love, everything, but he was who he was. Every time life presented him with two choices he chose the easier one, the selfish one, and it destroyed him. What I didn't realize until it was too late was that you paid the highest price for it."

"I had you, Aji," Ashna had told her grandmother. "You made everything softer."

Rico leaned his head back on her knee, and Ashna ran a hand through his newly cut-short hair, her heart bursting with gratefulness.

"You know," Mom said, looking at Ashna in a way Ashna still wasn't used to, and might never be. Then again, maybe her mother had always looked at her that way, she'd just never been able to see it. "The night you were born, I remember having a vision, a vision like this, of us with this feeling in our hearts. Like anything was possible because we were loved and free. That vision filled me with so much hope, I scratched out your name on the birth certificate and put down the only word that could describe how I felt. *Ashna*."

About the author

About the book

Insights,
Interviews
& More . . .

Meet Sonali Dev

Ishita Singh Photography; Zariin Jewelry zariin.com

Award-winning author SONALI DEV writes
Bollywood-style love stories that let her
explore issues faced by women around
the world while still indulging her faith
in a happily ever after. Sonali's novels
have been named best books of the year
by NPR, *Library Journal*, the *Washington
Post*, and *Kirkus Reviews*, and they
regularly garner multiple starred reviews.
She lives in the Chicago suburbs with
her very patient and often amused
husband, two teens who demand both
patience and humor, and the world's
most perfect dog.

Behind the Book Essay

Any Jane Austen fan worthy of that title can identify the exact moment when they first connected with her work. My connection, ironically enough, was through a retelling. I was in seventh grade, growing up in Mumbai, when a TV show based on *Pride and Prejudice* came out. It was called *Trishna*. This was way back in the eighties, when the dinosaurs roamed the earth, decades before television shows became the norm for consuming stories.

It was a faithful scene-by-scene, character-by-character retelling that transferred Austen's story to a contemporary Indian setting. Mr. Darcy was played by a popular male model, and all the girls in my school—years before Colin Firth stepped out of that pond in a wet shirt—were overcome by Darcymania. For me, however, the magic was Lizzie Bennet (named Rekha in the show), an opinionated, irreverent girl who didn't bother with pandering to men (or anyone else for that matter) so they might find her desirable. It was like finding myself, like having the blueprint of who I wanted to be validated. The fact that she was loved for those precise reasons just made everything better.

I ran to the library, checked out *Pride and Prejudice*, and was lost forever. I followed it up with *Emma*, *Sense and Sensibility*, and *Persuasion*. I found all of Austen's heroines to be delightfully fallible without a trace of self-loathing or self-recrimination, which seemed the ▶

3

norm for all the women in the literature I was reading. It was terribly freeing.

Austen's heroines dealt with their flaws as though they were simply part of being human, something they admitted to when their characters experienced growth. And their solution was to improve where needed and dig in their heels where not needed. They were also sharply observant—even unapologetically critical— of the ridiculousness of societal norms and rules, another thing that was abundant in the world I grew up in, and which definitely felt ridiculous to me. So my connection to her writing has always felt seminal to me as a person.

I've visited the UK several times, but the desire to visit Jane's homes was always at the back of my mind. A pilgrimage I knew I would go on when I was ready for it. Something I couldn't push into, but that would come to me when the time was right.

It wasn't until I had written *Pride, Prejudice, and Other Flavors* and *Recipe for Persuasion* that I fully understood how much of who I am and what I believe about relationships is built on the foundation of Austen's books. It wasn't until I grasped this connection that a trip to Hampshire magically and with no effort at all fell in my lap.

I visited her home in Chawton on a drizzly November day, dragging my husband along so he could meet the woman who was at least partially responsible for shaping the obstinate, headstrong girl he'd married. We strolled from her humble home to her brother's substantially less humble house down a cobbled, meadow-lined path that might as well have been a time machine, if you ignored the stray car. On the way, we stopped at the chapel she worshipped in.

Back at the house she lived and wrote in for eight years and finally died in, I ran my fingers across the walls she'd walked past; read the letters she'd written to her family; and touched the tiny, terribly uncomfortable–looking desk she wrote at (despite the sign that told me not to). I walked the halls and rooms where the stories I love churned and formed in Austen's head.

I stood too long in the room where she fell ill too young, tears streaming down my face for no apparent reason, except that I was awed. Awed by the connection I, and so many people, continue to feel with her words. Awed by the power of this thing she loved to do, as do I. Despite all the years, culture, and technology separating us, as I stood there in that room, in that moment, I knew at least one thing that she had experienced: the terror and joy of telling stories.

If I were to sit down with my laptop in that very room, there would be a certain something I'd have to reach for to string together the words I wanted to say, that nebulous process of making stories; that terror of getting them wrong, or right; that obsession over the telling of them. This was the connection that erased all that separated us. This was the connection I felt in her room as palpable as the cold draft coming through her window.

It struck me, standing where she had stood, that this connection is what we seek when we read. To merge into someone else, to become them and experience the world as they do, and to have their story entertain us, inform us, maybe even change us. Something about finding that with someone who lived so long before me and so differently than I do was exactly what I needed. So, I tucked it away in my heart for the times when I'll inevitably need help with the terror and joy of telling stories—the thing Jane and I will always share. ␥

Reading Group Guide

1. Food has a significant role in how the characters relate to one another. Are there certain foods that have special meaning to you? Did you enjoy how the characters use food to help deepen their understanding of one another?

2. Sports also play a big part in the lives of these characters. Discuss how playing sports (or in Rico's case, not playing) affects their relationships with themselves and one another.

3. So many characters in this book are hiding different aspects of their histories. What are the things that the characters hide behind? What does each one learn in the end?

4. Ashna and Shoban both feel they are very different from each other, though, in fact, they have many similarities. How does that add to the tension of the story? What are some of their biggest similarities and differences?

5. There are some very difficult scenes involving marital rape and alcoholism. How do these add to your understanding of how Shoban and Ashna come to be who they are?

6. Shoban believes that by staying away she is making a better choice for both Ashna and herself. Do you think she's right?

7. Family, both found family and family by blood, is incredibly important to each of these characters. Discuss how the nature of these bonds impacts their stories.

8. So much of this novel is about second chances. Discuss how that theme comes across in the story. Do you believe in second chances?

9. Would you watch a season of *Cooking with the Stars*? Who would you root for?

10. *Recipe for Persuasion* borrows some of its motifs from Jane Austen's *Persuasion*. If Jane Austen were reading this book, what do you think she'd say? ∽

Discover great authors, exclusive offers, and more at hc.com.